FULL MOON SLAUGHTER

EDITED BY TONEYE EYENOT

READ ORDER)

143	7	23	59	33
231	15	91	171	73
255	51	189	209	147
309 (4)	101	199	259 (12)	
183	109	221	285	
	127	245	313 (14)	
	135	275		
	235 (8)	299 (10)		

Edited by: J. Ellington Ashton Press Staff
Cover Art by: **Meister Arthur Dunkel/Michael Fisher**

http://jellingtonashton.com/
Copyright.

Kitty Kane, Jim Goforth, Mark Leney, Veronica Magenta Nero, Michael
Noe, Wendy Potocki, S.K. Gregory, Jack Bantry, Juan Julio Gutierrez,
Roma Gray, Kevin Candela, T.S. Woolard, Dona Fox, Matthew Wolf
Kane, Justin Hunter, Donald Armfield, Essel Pratt, Roy C. Booth, Kerry
EB Black, James H. Longmore, Matthew Cash, Urwin Bower, Rufus
Skeens, Brian Glossup, Sharon L. Higa, Thomas S. Flowers, Brian Barr,
John P. Collins Jr., R.E. Lyons, Urwin Bower, Sandy Rozanski, John
Quick, Ash Hartwell, Kat Gracey, Michelle Garza and Melissa Lason –
The Sisters of Slaughter

©2016, **Authors**

CONTENTS

FULL MOON SLAUGHTER: FOREWORD

KITTY KANE

To accurately portray to you what it is I wish to describe here in reference to wolves, werewolves, and the packs in which these awesome creatures travel, I first must borrow a well-known and well-loved quote. It is anonymous, but I thank and acknowledge its creator all the same. The quote goes thusly.

'It is my nature to be kind, gentle, and loving. But know this: When it comes to matters of protecting my friends, my family, and my heart, do not trifle with me. For I am also the most powerful and relentless creature you will ever know.'

Within these pages, you will find examples of this. Some will show you what exactly it means to be part of a pack. A unit so tightly bonded they would die for one another. The pack always takes care of the young, old, sick, or injured. None are left behind, the pace always set by the slowest member. How many groups of humans would show the patience that this type of unconditional love requires?

However, on the bulk of the pages within, you will meet true, bone chilling, neck prickling horror as our authors hereabouts introduce you to the mighty werewolf. The wolf man, the lycanthropic mystery that many have pondered for many a year. Mysterious and feared, when the moon shines full in the sky, somewhere in the world, there are deadly shifts happening.

Coarse hair sprouts at alarming rates from all the pores upon the lycanthrope's body, the nose and mouth elongate into a canine type muzzle, teeth stretch themselves into razor sharp, deadly fangs. Finger and toenails quadruple in length as mighty talon like claws appear, the blood lust pounds in the werewolf's head, unrelenting as it commands him to kill. His head snaps backwards, he sees the moon in the heavens, shining full and bright, and he unleashes an unholy sound, as he does as he must. He inhales long and hard, and he howls his lycanthropic refrain to the celestial goddess of the moon.

Some say a werewolf cannot die unless shot with a silver bullet. Some say lycanthropy is a curse; who is to say it's not a blessing? If the wolf man bites or wounds you, will you become a lycan too? Will you too then feel the magnetic and irresistible pull of the full moon? Will you bay your lament at Isis above? Will you want to kill? Will it feel good? Would you still feel? Would you love, hate, care? Or would the animalistic tendency be all consuming, blotting out all emotion? Will you be a tender loving pack animal, sharing the burden of the old and sick as the wolves do? Or will you be a creature of no mercy, of blood hunger and of homicide?

In these pages, dear reader, you will find a veritable banquet of lupine tales, some will amuse you, some will make you cry, but one thing I promise you will find herein, are blood curdling, horrific, and chilling tales of what occurs when that mighty lunar body shows herself in her full glory.

I am Kitty Kane, I am a member of THIS pack; they are my everything, and my pack of awesome authors among these pages are going to show you, terrify you, but maybe make you finally sure, of what goes down during a Full Moon Slaughter. Arrrrroooooo!!

HOUR OF THE WOLF

JIM GOFORTH

Something dark this way comes
Something dark this way runs
Howling at the midnight suns
Scared people take down your guns

Something dark this way stalks
Something dark this way walks
The hour you should be in bed
The hour you will be dead

In the forest of a million nights
Where there never shines the glow of daylight
Yellow eyes looking through midnight dark
Dripping fangs seeking your beating heart
This is a black curse on all mankind
In the hour of the wolf you will find
Your screaming goes on in your mind
On in your mind
On in your mind
On in your mind

Something dark this way prowls
Something dark this way howls
Heralding your utmost fear
Something dark is very near
Something dark this way heads
Something dark, you'll be dead
Heralding your utmost doom
Yellow eyes in the gloom

In the woods, you're all alone
In the dark, far from your home
Yellow eyes coming through the night
Beaming in on you like headlights
This is a black curse on all mankind
In the hour of the wolf you will find
Your screaming goes on in your mind
On in your mind
On in your mind
On in your mind
This is a black curse on all mankind
In the hour of the wolf you will find
Your screaming goes on in your mind
On in your mind
On in your mind

BIO: Jim Goforth is a horror author currently based in Holbrook, Australia. Happily married with two kids and a cat, he has been writing tales of horror since the early nineties.

After years of detouring into working with the worldwide extreme metal community and writing reviews for hundreds of bands across the globe with Black Belle Music he returned to his biggest writing love with first book Plebs published by J. Ellington Ashton Press. Along with Plebs, he is the author of a collection of short stories/novellas With Tooth and Claw, extreme metal undead opus Undead Fleshcrave: The Zombie Trigger, co-author of collaborative novel Feral Hearts and editor for the Rejected For Content anthology series (taking over the reins after volume one Splattergore. He also has stories in both Splattergore and Volume 2: Aberrant Menagerie).

He has also appeared in Tales From the Lake Vol. 2, Axes of Evil, Terror Train, Autumn Burning: Dreadtime Stories For the Wicked Soul, Floppy Shoes Apocalypse, Teeming Terrors, Ghosts: An Anthology of Horror From the Beyond, Suburban Secrets: A Neighborhood of Nightmares, Doorway To Death: An Anthology From the Other Side, Easter Eggs and Bunny Boilers, MvF: Death Personified, and edited volumes 2 and 3 of RFC (Aberrant Menagerie and Vicious Vengeance). Coming next from Jim will be appearances in Drowning in Gore, Full Moon Slaughter, Trashed, another collab novel Lycanthroship, a host of undisclosed projects, as well as follow-up books to Plebs and Rejected For Content 4: Highway To Hell (editor).

He is currently working on two new novels with plans to wrap them up before beginning further instalments of both the Plebs saga and The Zombie Trigger.

http://www.amazon.com/Jim-Goforth/e/B00HXO3FRG/ref=dp_byline_cont_ebooks_1
https://www.facebook.com/JimGoforthHorror
https://twitter.com/jim_goforth
https://www.goodreads.com/author/show/7777382.Jim_Goforth
https://jimgoforthhorrorauthor.wordpress.com/
https://plus.google.com/+JimGoforth/
https://www.facebook.com/PlebsHorror
https://www.facebook.com/pages/Rejected-For-Content/1601557196779520
https://www.facebook.com/WetWorksJEA
http://www.jellingtonashton.com/jim-goforth.html
http://www.crystallakepub.com/jim-goforth.php

STRANGERS IN A HALL

MARK LENEY

Mord Liutson studied the throng of warriors that surrounded him. He was a guest in the hall of Jarl Waltheof Hedinson. As such, he sat at the top of the table near the great chieftain. All around Mord there was much merriment, for Waltheof and his warriors had recently returned from a successful vik.

Beside the noble Jarl there was an open chest, heaped with treasures brought back from raiding the Christian monasteries that were sprouting up like vile weeds all across the Viking territories. When Mord had arrived, Waltheof had been dipping into this chest and handing out gifts to his men. Mord had been welcomed with all the hospitality that Norse tradition dictated and given his seat of honour beside their chief. Many of the gathered warriors had glanced questioningly at the bundle that Mord carried slung across his back; however, he had freely given up his sword at the door and so was allowed to keep his curious secret. Weapons were never a good thing to bring to a Norse feast. With mead and wine flowing as freely as rain, fights were inevitable, and so it was only a wise precaution that anything bigger than a eating knife was left at the door before entering.

Mord observed one such fight across the corner of the great hall. Two burly ruffians had set eyes upon the same comely serving girl and had come to blows. Mord suppressed a grin as a third suitor lured the pretty blonde slave into a dark corner while the first two pounded lumps from one another until they were pulled apart by their oar-mates.

The fight over, Mord returned his attention to the other guest in Jarl Waltheof's hall, sitting opposite to him. This was an old, grizzled looking white haired man, built like a wrestler despite his age and wearing a tunic and breeches of wolf-skins. The man's craggy face was made all the more remarkable by a white burn scar that ran from his lower lip on the right side of his face, across his cheek, and stopping just short of the blazing blue orb of his eye. This man had arrived before Mord, but the young warrior had not been surprised to see him. Rather, he had expected it… hoped for it.

Mord had not touched any mead or wine since he had arrived, though it had been freely offered. He had drunk only water and he hoped that his refusal to drink anything stronger did not offend his honoured host. As he took one last look around him, he made his decision and rose from the bench, tankard of water in his hand.

"A toast to our honoured Jarl, Waltheof Hedinson, for this magnificent feast and his unrivalled generosity!" Mord bellowed across the hall to those assembled. He downed the contents of his tankard in one and slammed it down on the great oak table. The warriors all cheered and took the excuse to drain their horns of mead or tankards of wine, banging the receptacles on the table when finished.

Waltheof raised himself from his chair at the head of the table and raised his powerful arms into the air in acceptance of this praise.

"Thank you, my friends! May I say that you have all more than earned the generosity which I am praised for? There is not a man of you here that I would not claim as my own son. Though young Mord here would honour me more were he to make his toast with a man's drink. Water is for ships to sail on, boy... not for drinking!"

There was a chorus of raucous laughter from the warriors.

"Perhaps later, my lord. I would ask you, though, if I may honour this hall with a story to entertain you all?" Mord asked.

Waltheof's answer was to sit down and nod his head. He slammed his fists on the table.

"A story!" he roared and that was all the prompt that young Mord needed.

Mord stepped up onto the great table as if it were a stage and whirled around once, his arms outstretched, encompassing his entire audience before coming to settle his eye upon the great Jarl and the old, grizzled guest at his side.

"Many years ago, in a hall just like this one, there was gathered a mighty assembly of warriors. They too had returned from a successful season of Viking off the eastern shores of England. In celebration of their successful return, they held a great feast and the Jarl rewarded his oar-men and warriors with many great gifts from the treasure which he kept hidden behind a curtain, in an alcove that lay just behind the Jarl's chair. That evening saw the arrival of a stranger to the hall. A trapper and fur tradesman who had travelled to the village to pedal his wares and, arriving late, sought food and shelter in the great hall, as was his right according to our great Norse tradition of hospitality to all travellers." At this, Mord bowed once again to his host in acknowledgement of his status as guest in the Jarl's hall.

"The trapper was given a seat next to the Jarl. A position that was only shared by the chief's wife and son. The son was a boy of but twelve winters and still longing for the day when hairs would grow on his chin, like moss grows on a troll's back. His mother, the Jarl's wife, was more beautiful than the goddess Freyja herself, may Odin strike me down if it were not so." Here he paused, arms outstretched and looked up as if waiting for the one-

8

eyed king of gods to smite him. When no blow came, he winked and grinned at the assembled warriors, who laughed heartily before allowing him to continue.

"With the honoured guest so seated, the feasting and merriment carried on well into the darkest hours of the night until eventually, weary from too much food and drink, everyone dropped off to sleep. Many slumping where they lay, on the straw strewn floor of the great hall or across the table at which they sat. It was a slumber from which none of them may have awoken, if not for the scream of one hapless warrior. Such a scream had never been heard by any of the men assembled, save in perhaps their direst nightmares of Helheim, the domain of Hel, whose mortal kiss all Norse-men fear. What those gathered warriors saw when they awoke to that scream made each man fear that they all dwelled in the same living nightmare. The screaming man was dangling in the jaws of a monster that towered over even the mightiest of those assembled. This beast was not a wolf, though it had a face like one. Nor was it a man, though it did stand on two legs, with terrible feet that ended in claws, longer and sharper than any seax. Its naked body was covered in long white fur, matted now with the blood of the fallen warrior, who no longer screamed, for no man can scream long without a throat. The varulv, for that was what it was, dropped the dead warrior, and before a blade could be drawn, it was among them. It had meant to send them all to Hel's hall while they slept, three mangled corpses spoke this tale, but the fourth had awoken and his wail of terror had given the alarm. Even had those brave men been wielding more than just eating knives, it would have made little difference. Does a warrior still go to Valhalla when he is sent to his death bearing only the knife which previously had sliced his bread and meat? I can only hope so, because it was to be a fate shared by one and all in the hall that terrible night!

"The Jarl could see how things were turning. He grabbed up his son and thrust him into the treasure alcove, behind the curtain. 'Stay, boy, and do not come out whatever happens!' they were the last words the young lad ever heard his father speak.

"Having slaughtered every last man and slave in the great hall, the varulv pounced towards the chief and his wife. The noble Jarl would have protected his wife as he had done his son. Being lord of the hall, he alone had retained his sword. He held it now, keeping his beloved behind him. The boy watched from behind the curtain and felt hope as he saw his father's blade enter the monster's chest. A blow that would have cloven the heart of any man in two. The point burst forth from the beast's back in a spray of dark blood. So stricken, the varulv staggered back, wrenching the sword from the great Jarl's hand. The Jarl did not long mourn the loss of a blade that he could retrieve soon enough from the carcass of his vanquished enemy. Only that was not to be. The wolfish features of the beast twisted into what could only have been a smile and a barking laugh escaped mockingly from its lips. Taking firm grip of the sword's handle in its terrible clawed hand, it wrenched the blade free and tossed it aside as if it were naught but a splinter. The terrible wound in its blood caked chest closed up before the eyes of those living that beheld it, as if it had never been there. For the noble Jarl it was doom. He never got the chance to recover from the shock of what he had seen.

"The boy behind the curtain could not look away; not even when his father's head flew across the hall and bounced off the wall mere feet from where he hid. Nor could he tear his eyes away when that fiendish monster caught his mother, pinned her down and violated her with its obscene, bloated member. The ferocity with which that thing raped his mother was such that she was probably dead before it ripped her throat out with its teeth.

"Now only the boy lived. As he watched his mother die, he felt his fear melt away into a red rage. He knew the varulv would be coming for him next. He was the only thing between it and what it really wanted… his father's treasure. The boy reached out behind him and felt for a weapon, determined that he would not die without a fight. Once armed, he braced himself for the beast's attack.

"As the creature tore through the curtain, the boy swung his makeshift weapon at its face. The weapon was a large silver cross, no doubt looted from an English monastery. Not much of a weapon to use against such a monster that his father's sword, one of the finest ever forged, had failed to fell. The effect of that cross upon the beast when it connected, however, was unexpected to say the least.

"The fur on the creature's face burst into a white flame and the beast flew back against the wall, knocking loose a torch from its holdings and causing it to fall upon the straw. It did not take long for the fire from the torch to take to the straw and spread quickly across the hall, devouring anything in its path like a fiery serpent. The varulv looked long and hard at the boy, as if its eyes could burn hatred into his soul. Then it bounded across the hall, through the flames, and out of the door into the night.

"When men from the next village came to investigate the smoke and fire, they found the hall a blackened shell. Outside the ruin of his former family home sat the young chieftain's son, cradling in his arms the very thing that had saved his life… the silver cross of the white-Christ.

"On that night, he swore that he would hunt down the varulv and claim his blood price for the evil that had been wrought that night. Some say he is still out there now, searching for vengeance." As Mord brought his tale to a close, there was a chorus of rowdy appreciation from the assembled warriors. Only his fellow guest did not join in the vigorous table thumping.

10

"It seems to me that you are ill-mannered to tell tales of hall-burnings when you are the guest in the hall of another. Perhaps your tale is in fact a veiled warning of your own intent?" the old stranger growled.

Mord had ignored the scorn of his grizzled heckler as he strode down the length of the table, bowing and soaking up the praise that was bestowed upon him. He strode back up to the table's head and stopped to look down on the old man.

"Perhaps you have another, better tale that you would like to tell? Of how you came by that scar, mayhap?" Mord challenged, his young face dark and serious despite his smile.

The stranger scratched the scar absent mindedly as he considered his reply.

"These fine warriors would be bored to tears to hear tell of an accident I had when I was a bairn, helping my father – a blacksmith – when I fell whilst holding a red hot soldering iron."

Jarl Waltheof rose from his chair.

"I fear you may be right. Look!" he gestured sweepingly around the hall. "Many of my men already fall asleep at the mere suggestion of it!"

There was a ripple of laughter from those still awake. Mord turned to the Jarl and nodded before turning to jump down from the table and return to his seat.

One by one, the revellers tired and fell asleep.

Mord unslung his mysterious bundle from across his back and laid it before him on the table. He rested his head upon it and closed his eyes.

The warriors had not been sleeping long before they were woken again.

It was Mord who woke them, for he had not been sleeping. Without warning, he had leapt back from the bench, taking his bundle with him. That was not the noise that had roused the warriors, however. It was the sound of splintering wood as the clawed hand of the varulv from Mord's tale had been driven into the table where the young warrior's head had previously lain.

The gathered warriors looked on through bleary, sleep heavy eyes. They must have believed that they dreamt when they saw before them the very monster that Mord had described to them in his saga earlier that night. They also saw their doom, for what else could their fate be, but to be slaughtered by this invincible creature. The varulv regarded them all with its malevolent yellow eyes, its snarl made all the more terrible by the white scar on the right side of its lupine face.

Off in the shadows there came a whistle that drew the attention of everyone, not just the beast it was meant for. From these shadows stepped Mord, unwrapping the bundle that he had worn across his back all night. It was a great warhammer, worthy of the thunderer Thor himself, its hammerhead had been forged from pure silver and was etched in runes of

11

power. Mord uttered no words as he wielded that mighty hammer and ran at the varulv head on.

The beast raised its claws and leapt to meet him with an almighty inhuman howl.

All those gathered cheered when the fiend was sent sprawling back onto the table, which splintered beneath it, blood and broken teeth and smoke billowing from its hideous mouth as it fell.

It struggled to get up from that fell blow, but Mord stepped up and swung the hammer again, knocking it once more to its back. Mord trod upon the creature's chest. It yet lived and would have got up again if Mord had not rained the hammer down, spreading its brains among the straw and table splinters with three mighty strokes.

The hall was silent. Not one of the warriors there assembled tried to stop Mord as he slung the great hammer, now stained with black ichor, across his shoulder and stalked out of the hall into the night without looking back.

Only when Mord had disappeared from sight did the men return their attention to the vanquished monster, to find the naked corpse of the old stranger lying there with his brains and blood pooled around his ruined head.

BIO: Mark Leney is from the UK and lives and writes in Bromley with his wife Nicola and his daughter Sacha. They did used to have goldfish, but they have since been replaced by robots. Mark looks forward to the day when wolves and dragons become a viable option as a household pet.

LALUPA

VERONICA MAGENTA NERO

It's that time of month again and rent is due. Evening is falling fast, drowning the city in dark hues of purple. I'm starting to get a little edgy, a little nervous, as I walk to work. Every night is my first night, every night is my last night.

From outside it looks like any other exclusive strip club. Black painted walls and door, no signs, no neon. I've certainly done a lot worse. At least there are no homeless junkies sleeping out front.

The guy at the door gives me the once over and a nod of approval.

"Have a good night, sweetheart," he says politely as he opens the door for me. He has a neck like a tree trunk, a black tee shirt clings to pumped up muscle.

***

Inside it's tasteful enough. The furnishings are plush red and black. Not too big a space, which is good. I like an intimate audience.

A cute blonde girl is stocking the bar. She smiles and waves at me cheerfully.

"The dressing room is through there," she shouts.

In the dressing room, which is in fact a storeroom crammed with furniture and boxes of stuff, I meet Candy and Amber. There is always a Candy and Amber in every club. I put my bag down on a brightly lit table, glance at myself in the large mirror and sigh. I begin to unpack some things when Candy comes over for the standard welcome.

"Hi, I'm Candy," she tells me. Her icy blue eyes sparkle. She stands too close to me, one hand on her hip. Her nails are long oval points, painted white. She is wearing a tiny silver dress; her fake breasts look painful and her skin is a baked orange colour. I stare back at her, bored. It's that time of month. I'm cranky and hungry. I've skipped a few meals lately.

"This is my table. You can use one of those over there." She points to the cluttered corner.

I get a flash of her gutted from neck to belly and I can't stop my

15

eyes from twitching. She says something else but I don't catch the words; I have to concentrate, slow down my breathing. Amber comes over to mediate.

"Don't worry about Candy, she's just very territorial."

Amber smiles warmly at me and gives Candy a nudge, unsettling her on her platform stilettos.

"I'm Lalupa," I say.

"La what? Is that, like, a Mexican name?" Candy chuckles to herself and wanders over to a clothes rack to flick through costumes and lingerie.

"Have you met Andy yet?" asks Amber.

I shake my head no.

"Well, you should get dressed and go meet him. If he doesn't like your look, he won't let you work tonight."

I nod and start getting changed.

Amber sits down at a table nearby and begins to style her long red hair. Soon a few other girls arrive. Chatter and laughter fills the dressing room.

I keep to myself, hoping not to get drawn into conversation. I don't want to make friends and I'm eager for the night to get underway. I hate hearing the same old stories. I don't care that you are stripping to pay for your law degree or that you have a happy husband and two kids waiting for you at home. I'm here because I like the thrill and the cash. A girl's got to eat.

***

A wave of nausea rolls through me; my skin prickles with heat. There's a stabbing pain building in my head. I take a few more deep breaths.

I prefer to wear a vintage style. Black lace corset, fine seamed stockings, shiny black patent heels – I hate those horrendous stripper platforms. My glossy black curls bounce around my pale face as I inspect myself in the mirror. Candy glances at me then mutters to her pals and a round of giggles erupts. Let them laugh. While they can.

***

I find my way to the manager's office. He's chatting with a guy sitting by his desk. I stand in the room, still and silent like an ornament, waiting for him to acknowledge me.

They're both wearing tailored grey suits. Merino wool, I can smell it. Silk ties and crisp, fine cotton. Their short haircuts are gelled carefully to appear casually tousled. Thick designer cologne cloaks their skin. A fresh ocean scent with base notes of vanilla and spice. Beneath the cologne is the

16

distinct stench of their sweat. Lean, firm flesh, rippled with fine streaks of fat. My mouth begins to water again.

Finally, he looks over at me.

"Nice outfit, honey," he says, "but I hope it comes off pretty quick, this is not a burlesque club!"

He laughs a dry, cruel chuckle and the other guy chimes in. Flesh taut with obsessive exercise and a diet of fine food, tears off the bone in thin strips.

"House takes fifteen percent?"

"Straight down to business. I like it. That's right, honey, House takes fifteen percent, the rest is yours. Pretty generous for a classy place like this. Tonight's a trial shift. If I like your routine and you're hot on the floor, you can come back tomorrow night."

"I'm always a crowd pleaser."

"Are you now? Well, good for you! You're on after Candy. She's a hard act to follow."

Now it's my turn to laugh, which confuses them for a moment.

"What's your name again, honey?"

"Lalupa."

"Lupa? Okay, have a good night, honey, milk 'em dry." They both chuckle as I turn to leave.

***

Things start to heat up as the night rolls out. I stand at the bar, trying not to shake or twitch, and watch the patrons come in, waiting for a likely hit. I watch the other girls too, as they saunter, smiling, chatting. They look delectable.

I set my sights on Mr. Average White Collar and strut over casually. He is self-conscious and uncomfortable and will easily blow all his cash on me.

I give him a sweet, girl next door stripper smile and ask if he wants a dance. He nods and throws back his Scotch as I step in close and begin to sway and swish, swivel and shake. He pays generously but I decide to keep moving; his anxiety is irritating. I circle the floor, bidding time, choosing the men I want to dance for and chat to. I ignore the ones who are too obnoxious or rude. Andy is poised at the bar, watching me and frowning.

Candy comes on stage to cheers and whistles. With a beaming white smile she waves at the audience, blowing kisses, striking provocative poses. Obviously the darling of the club but I'll soon change that. I head to the dressing room to freshen up.

***

17

The moon is full and high in the sky. I can feel it, gleaming, beckoning. It's making me tremble.

Finally, the DJ cues my music and I take the stage, happy to be in the limelight.

I love working the pole; I have a real talent for it. My unnatural dexterity gives my routine a flowing ease. I radiate confidence and power. Men sense it, they sit up in their seats, intrigued. Soon all eyes in the room are on me. The men are under my captivating spell – the women glare at me jealously. I'll be cleaning up tonight. I'm going to empty their pockets. As I dance I'm checking the exits, scanning the room with all my senses. There are never too many for me to handle.

I can feel it coming as I spin and twirl, bubbling under my skin, beginning to shiver through me, a blissful terror. I get so excited I grit my teeth to hold it back. I like to hold out as long as possible, give them a bit of a show first. After all, I'm a really hot dancer. I stretch my fine limbs, shimmy and slither. With legs wrapped around the pole, I use my free hand to unhook the corset and flick it off. Men cheer. I flex and hang upside down, spinning slowly. I close my eyes and enjoy the rush. It's that time of month and I can't resist it anymore. The moon is singing to my soul and I need to respond. A growl builds in my throat as I embrace it. It is so close to the surface now, about to burst out of me.

***

The men in the front row see it first. Something strange is beginning to happen.

Hair sprouts, thin and fine, along my forearms and thighs, on my chest. It spreads slowly until a dense fur covers me.

A few men chuckle thinking it is part of the routine. I can see Andy, still standing at the bar, looking really pissed off. I can make out the confused faces of the women, frozen in mid lap dance, staring at me. My body buckles and shakes, I can no longer hold it back or slow it down. I love this part, morphing from an object of desire into an object of terror. I love seeing their faces change, from lust to disgust. I drop from the pole to the floor as the bestial force surges. I begin to convulse. Nobody comes to my aid. Everybody watches. I can feel their bubbling fear, their fascination and perverse satisfaction.

My knuckles bust through skin; tendons bulge. A wail of pain escapes me as I paw at my face with bloody hands. My head is down and they can't see my jaw stretching, sharp fangs painfully pushing out of tender gums. Thick whiskers sprout on my cheeks and chin. My black curls stream down my back in a heavy mass. The crack of joints and stretching bones, each vertebra popping, the wet, sticky sound of elongating sinews and muscles, resounds in my ears.

18

Finally, it is complete and I crouch, heaving from the exertion. My breath begins to slow down as I settle into my new form.

There is complete silence in the club. The DJ has stopped the music, the patrons and staff stare at the creature on stage.

I lift my head and they see me for what I am. I watch them with eyes glowing yellow. I raise my snout and sniff deeply; terror, glorious, delicious terror. And a comforting, familiar smell; my pack. They are here. They have entered the club and are manning the exits.

I stretch, throw back my head and howl – a maniacal call. Screaming begins and in that fantastic moment, as hysteria breaks out, I plunge.

I take out the line of guys down front, one after another, with fast swipes. Shredding them easily, ripping chunks out of their chests and thighs as I take their wallets. Green bills flutter and float, drifting down into growing pools of blood.

There is no way out; my pack closes in. They are crouched, snarling, snatching the runners and pinning them down. The thick smell of slaughter erupting is intoxicating.

I leap from the stage and land on the bar. I can hear the bar girl, curled underneath the bar, sobbing. I glare at Andy as I crawl towards him slowly. He doesn't move as I sniff his chest. I can hear the frantic beat of his heart. His eyes are wide with shock. I bite off one of his arms. He begins to emit a high whine, not quite a scream, a peculiar dying noise. I take a chomp out of his chest, snatching out his heart, and gulp it down greedily. He drops to the floor and I on top of him.

I leave my pack to finish off the crowd. I am drawn by another exhilarating smell. Several dancers have locked themselves in the dressing room. I can hear their hysterical, muffled tears.

***

I tear the door off its hinges and they burst into screams, scampering into the corner. They dare not glance at me. My beauty is of another realm. Covered in coarse hair, mangled claws for hands and feet, sharp-pointed ears and snout, breasts hanging long and loose. I roar at them and they shriek, huddling closer like mice.

I can no longer make out individual faces. I scoop up one of the girls, collecting her by the scalp. I lick her skin. She is coated in so many strange flavours; sweat, tears, alcohol, makeup, deodorant, talcum powder.

I bite into her neck and shake her vigorously. Each taste makes me more ravenous. I eat quickly, snapping spines, crushing skulls, crunching bones, guzzling organs. A decadent blood drenched mess surrounds me.

***

19

It's that time of month. I am not quite myself. I am more than myself. The full moon is glowing as bright as the sun; it makes me ache with rage. I howl a blissful song but my hunger is far from satiated. I leap at the small window in the room, tearing away the bars and bricks. I bound out into the warm night; the city is a feast waiting to happen.

BIO: Veronica Magenta Nero is an author and poet. She spins dark tales weaving threads of Gothic horror, fantasy and erotica. Her work has been published in Sanitarium Magazine, The Sirens Call and in many anthologies by James Ward Kirk Fiction and JEA Press. She hails from Italy and currently resides in the Northern Rivers, Australia

REVENGE

MICHAEL NOE

It all comes back to her every time she closes her eyes. The sounds of their grunting intertwining with their laughter. She's asking for it, grab that bitch. That word, *bitch*. That was far far worse than the laughing and the grunting. Not once did she cry. Not once did she beg for them to stop. Instead, she stared at the three of them and committed their faces to memory. As she stared, she refused to be a victim. That's what they wanted. They expected her to enjoy this at some point. It was rape, not love. No matter how much they tried to convince themselves that she wanted this, the truth was that she didn't. There was nothing in any of her actions that said otherwise. Three men? One right after the other? She wasn't some dick addicted porn star.

When she closed her eyes she could feel their hands, all over her. The stench of cheap beer and motor oil assaulted her senses. That smell caused her to gag. When she closed her eyes at night it all came rushing back. Amy could pretend that she was fine, but in the darkness there was no escaping the truth. She would fight back the tears and smile instead, because they would pay for what they did to her. Every single one of them. One right after the other. Revenge wasn't best served cold, it was best served piping hot, and they would soon realize that they had gotten in way over their heads. How many other women were there? Were they hiding in their apartments, afraid to come out? Were they wondering if maybe they had done something to warrant the assault?

Amy watched the cloudless sky and felt a smile begin to form. This wasn't a smile of happiness. This was a sadistic smile that held many secrets. Secrets that the human brain couldn't comprehend. There were things hiding in the darkness, just waiting to burst free. Amy knew the darkness well. She wandered down its tangled pathways. The darkness didn't frighten her. Those men didn't frighten her. Soon, they would know the true meaning of fear. They would embrace it and maybe even make love to it. She had seen the devil and lived. These thugs were shit on the bottom of her shoe. Just little boys pretending to be men. It happened all the time. It was embarrassing to the real men that existed. She didn't hate men, and she sure as hell didn't fear them. That would give them power over her. No man had that kind of power over her.

She moved away from the window and felt the familiar twitch in her skin that told her the time was closer than she had thought. She had let her mind run away from her and here she was, naked, staring at herself in the mirror. She stroked her breasts and ran a hand down her smooth, tanned thighs. This was all just a shell. Just something that made her unique. Was it her fault she was pretty? Was it her fault that she had been running late for work and ended up taking a left instead of a right? Life was full of little coincidences. Thinking back, she could see how her life had maybe led up to events that seemed out of her control, but what if she had been guided by some unseen force? Her being disoriented that day may have been a catalyst for everything else, and these had led her to something much bigger? If she played the victim and allowed herself to be afraid of those little boys pretending to be men, then what? She could go ahead and be afraid of her own shadow or she could do something about it.

Amy thought about that day and was amazed by how normal it was. She had overslept, which meant that there had been no time for coffee, so she figured she'd stop in at Starbuck's and then head to the office. She had dressed in a simple black dress with red around the neck and sides. Her black hair hung loosely around her shoulders as she walked. If she hadn't been texting her assistant, she would have seen them standing outside the garage. Instead, she only heard them whistling and catcalling. She tried to ignore them and instead focused on the intersection ahead. It was almost nine and at that hour there weren't many cars going through it on their way downtown.

She was just one step away from passing them when one of them punched her on the side of the head. She lurched forward as her purse and coffee tumbled slowly to the ground. Everything from that moment on slowed to a crawl. When it was over, they left her on the sidewalk as if she were garbage. She knew that she had been dragged into a garage. One of the men was wearing tan, grease stained overalls and wore a backwards Cleveland Indians baseball cap. He rushed in to take her first, and as he thrust himself inside her, he squealed like a pig.

Amy couldn't remember going home. All she could remember were their faces and where they assaulted her. She had come back just to see if they were still there. She committed their smells to memory and it would guide her to them. These smells would come in handy later. It was their unique stench that would seal their fate. She dressed quickly and knew that what she wore wouldn't matter. That's why she always chose baggy sweat pants and a loose fitting t-shirt. These were clothes that she wouldn't miss later. She had learned this lesson the hard way. It was the kind of lesson that you didn't learn at school. No one could teach someone instinct or even survival. Those were things you just had to learn on your own.

She went down the narrow staircase and into the kitchen. Tonight had to be perfect and it would be. This was the first time that she had actually looked forward to the change. Once upon a time she had feared the change, but this time she welcomed it. Of all those years hiding it, she never thought that it would help her. Funny how things worked out. The one thing she was most ashamed of could now be used in a way that ensured that she was in control. She had power. Power was a wonderful thing, and she welcomed the upcoming change and the freedom that it provided.

She was born into a family of werewolves. Her parents had moved around a lot, afraid that their secret would be discovered, but thankfully it never had been. They had lived on a sprawling farm surrounded by lush woods that provided the family enough food to keep their neighbors safe. It was interesting to hear the fictitious accounts of what she was, but she kept her mouth shut. Let them believe whatever they wanted. If they wanted blood thirsty beasts, then she would give them exactly what they wanted. There were other wolves in the area, so she was able to get by on human flesh, and for shits and giggles, she would infect those who she found to be offensive.

The books were only half right. Silver could kill her, but the main cause of her condition was in fact hereditary. They never would have guessed that people they worked with were blood thirsty killers when the moon was full. It would have been far more romantic if she had been bitten or drank rainwater from a paw print. People actually did that. They wanted to be just like her and often put themselves in harm's way. They had no idea how hard it was just to bite someone without stripping flesh from bone. It took a huge amount of willpower. Most wolves didn't have it. Amy barely had it herself. She wasn't like her parents. While they were content to slaughter deer or bears, she preferred humans. An ex-boyfriend was way more fun to hunt than a defenseless deer.

These poor men had no idea what they had unleashed. She headed out the front door, whistling Werewolves of London. It was a horrible song, but one that had somehow gotten stuck inside her head. She didn't carry anything with her because it would soon get lost just like her clothes. Werewolves on television were much more glamorous than in real life. That was the only drawback aside from finding yourself miles from home, naked and unsure of where you were. It made going to college a bit difficult, but she had managed, and when she returned to Ohio, she knew exactly where she was at all times.

In the morning, she always ended up back in her house. Sometimes she would wake up in the living room, sometimes she would find herself in the back yard as if she were too exhausted to make those final steps. Each time she woke up, there was just a small amount of fear that she was followed and now at her most vulnerable she would be killed. That wasn't a rational fear because no one gave a shit about werewolves. They were fictional creatures that existed in horror novels. If they had a chance to see her up close they would believe, but the odds of their survival were pretty much nonexistent.

The legend of the wolf was steeped in a lot of bullshit, too much for her to even try and sort it out. Even if she had taken the time to trace her roots and history, there would still be a lot that she wouldn't know. Did she really want to hear how her ancestors were slaughtered because ignorant townsfolk thought that they were all demons sent from hell? No, she didn't, so she half listened to her family's stories about where they came from and how proud they should be of what they were. Pride, it seemed, was something her family really had for themselves and their ancestors, but she didn't feel the same way.

For Amy there was no pride. Every full moon she turned into a ferocious beast. That made it a little difficult to have a social life. Getting her period was bad, but having the ability to murder your boyfriend was a lot worse. How in the hell do you explain to someone that you wouldn't be able to go out due to the unfortunate habit of shredding people like roast beef? This wasn't something she could be proud of and thought of it more as a curse. It was a curse that she liked to pass on to others. Nothing made her happier than biting unsuspecting people and changing their lives forever.

Now she could see why this was something to be proud of. As she passed by a group of sweaty teens playing basketball in the park, she wondered if any of them shared her secret. There were groups, of course, but most of those people turned out to be whiny vegan types that hated the thought of killing anything. How in the hell could you be a werewolf and hate killing? It wasn't like there was a choice in the matter. When the moon was full, people or animals died. Didn't matter if it were a cat or a cow. It was food. Wolves hunted. They didn't garden or attend tea parties. Lives didn't matter when you were a wolf. White meat, dark meat, it was all the same. The brain wasn't a brain anymore, it was just a snack to tide you over until you found something else to chew on.

The one thing that Amy learned was that there were no rules. No matter how much she wanted to be someone different, it wouldn't change who she was. There were two choices. The first was that she could just accept it or she could refuse to accept it and go insane. There was no cure for what she was. The only way out was a silver slug to the brain. That would make her a coward, so she just accepted it even if she didn't want to. It didn't mean she had to like it though. She didn't date, and as far as friends went, they were few and far between. Wolves were attracted to other wolves, so the pack mentality was created out of necessity. The packs provided normalcy.

She walked toward her destination, feeling the familiar itch that always came before the change. The pull of the moon created an itch that came deep below the skin and became a part of her being. It rumbled in her muscles and tendons, filling her with a hunger that no food could satiate. Once the moon rose there was only minimal control. Amy was on autopilot until the sun rose in the morning. There was a feeling of freedom that no one normal could begin to comprehend. Now, as she headed to the place she was assaulted in, she could feel a smile creep onto her face. This would be fun. The streets were desolate as she made her way to the garage. Amy cleared all of her thoughts and focused on her surroundings. Later, it wouldn't matter because she would be led by instinct. Her mind wouldn't be her own. It was a pleasant release that was far better than any orgasm she ever had.

As she neared the garage the businesses seemed to dwindle. There was an antique store with soaped up windows and a sun faded sign that said 'coming soon'. The garage was right in the middle. The small parking lot had a couple of cars parked but she didn't have to worry about being seen. The business was closed for the day. The street itself was desolate. It was as if fate had intervened and allowed her this moment to do what needed to be done. She had spent the last week following these men. They were lazy and shiftless, with routines that never varied. That was important. It made what she was about to do that much easier. It shouldn't have been this easy. Not that she was complaining, of course.

A bell jingled, announcing her arrival. A voice from the back assured her that he would be right there. *Take your time, it's not like you have much left.* The front part of the store was simply decorated in a style that could only be described as male. Shelves that housed various car parts lined the walls behind the counter. Worn out leather chairs sat by the gleaming store front window. She eyed the swinging door that led to the garage and heard the distinct clatter of metal tools. Her anger rose as she remembered the feel of their hands on her body. The way they laughed and cajoled as if she were a piece of meat.

Time seemed to crawl as she shuffled her feet impatiently. She had about ten minutes before she changed. She urged the fat fuck to hurry up. Amy wanted to see his face as she morphed into the wolf. There was no way out for him. There was no way he could outrun her. Once she blocked his escape through the counter, his only option was through the swinging doors that led to the garage. He was trapped.

"Can I help you?" His eyes widened as recognition crossed over his face. His hands were grease stained, and fidgeted nervously at his sides. He regained his composure and smiled lecherously as he stared at her. He was wearing the same grungy overalls. She could smell a mixture of grease and stale body odor roll off his obese body.

"I think you can. I wanted to see you without your friends," Amy purred seductively. She unzipped her hoodie and took two small steps forward. She would be changing soon. She stroked his cheek and motioned toward the garage. "We should head into the back. I have a surprise for

27

you."

He stumbled over his feet as he headed toward the dark confines of the garage. The only lights were weak bulbs that hung overhead. There were windows in the garage door but they obscured the view of the parking lot. It was perfect and assured her that they wouldn't be disturbed. "Oh really? Look, I'm sorry about what we did." He frowned and looked as if he wanted to say something else, but the words just weren't coming out. He was too busy watching her slowly remove her clothes. There weren't a lot of places they could go and she could see his mind trying to sort out the details.

"Shhhhh. Don't talk about that. I am going to give you a night to remember." She groaned as the change hit. Her eyes went from a bright, clear blue to a dull, dingy yellow. Her teeth elongated and pushed out of her pink gums. He stared at her open mouthed as thick gray fur began to explode from her now naked body. Bones shifted and popped out of place as they reformed, giving her a hunched over gait. She dropped to her haunches as her face rippled and disappeared, forming a smooth snout. Amy growled and lunged.

The man screamed and backpedaled into a yellow Mustang. Warm piss filled his coveralls as she pounced with fluid grace. Her razor sharp claws sank into his shoulder, removing it cleanly. Muscle and blood poured from the stump. She ran her cold, wet snout into his face. She could smell the fear rolling off him in pungent waves. She licked his grimy face affectionately and then sank her teeth into his throat, ripping it open like a gift. She lapped at the gore and growled as her teeth explored his body. She clawed her way inside of his stomach, exposing the tasty treats inside. She ate until the body was a hollowed out husk. The stench of gore was overpowering as she slowly sauntered into the night.

***

Bobby rolled a cigarette and placed it into his mouth. Cash had been a bit short and losing his job had seriously put a dent in his beer drinking. That was where Nick came in. He was always around despite the fact that he was a pussy. Bobby only allowed him around because he was gullible. Nick should have known that he was being used, but thankfully that hadn't happened yet. Nick kept the party rolling and that was always a good thing. He drained the last of his beer and sauntered into the grimy kitchen for another.

The small apartment smelled like stale cigarettes and onions. Bobby didn't feel compelled to shower much and his cleaning skills were lacking. The dirty dishes in the sink were encrusted with food and the trash was overflowing with beer bottles and cheap TV dinners. In the living room, the sounds of Hank Williams Jr. reminded him of his station in life. He could blame others but the state of his life was his own doing. He was lazy and had an attitude that kept him from keeping a job for over a week. At twenty-nine, he was on the list of people that died young through bad decisions.

He thought about Nick and how he had cried the entire time they were raping that bitch. His dick got hard just thinking about it. What kind of shit was that? Why didn't he just say no and get the hell out of there? Did he really need their friendship that badly? Nick truly was a far bigger loser than they were. He went along with whatever they said without complaint. Maybe he was just that stupid, or maybe he was just desperate to fit in. He grabbed two beers out of the empty fridge then headed into the living room. They needed to get out for a while. Raise a little hell. Carl should be home by now, so maybe they would pay him a visit. See what was shaking. There was the strip club they always went to. If they played their cards right, maybe they could all get their dicks sucked.

The sound of breaking glass dragged him from his thoughts. He stopped walking and peered around the corner as if he were a child looking for the boogeyman. The beer slipped from his hand, exploding onto the floor in a bomb of glass and foam. His mind couldn't decipher what he was seeing. The room was dripping with gore. There was a low growl coming from the corner of the room. Something rolled toward him. He watched it and whimpered as he realized what the round shape was. *Nick's head! That's Nick's fucking head!* It stopped right by his foot, leaking blood on the already stained carpet.

Bobby stood there, paralyzed. He could see Nick's body impaled on the leg of the coffee table. The body was bent at an odd angle. His neck leaked gore, his legs bloody stumps. There were shards of glass everywhere he looked. The couch was flipped over, the cushions leaked foam. He could see it falling like confetti. The growl grew louder as something moved toward him. It was staring at him, licking its lips. There was blood coating the coarse gray fur. Bits of flesh hung from its muzzle. *What the fuck?* It was a wolf. He inched backward slowly. His eyes stayed locked on the beast that eyed him hungrily.

There was no way he was going to end up like Nick. *Where the hell are you going to go?* That part he hadn't quite figured out. The wolf growled louder this time, causing Bobby to move faster. His foot slipped on the spilled beer as a shard of glass slammed into his naked foot. He looked down for just a moment to see how much damage it had caused. His hands were shaking too badly to remove the offending obstruction. The wolf was still moving towards him. Slowly as if it were taunting him. It seemed to dare him to move, but the glass in his heel made it impossible to move very fast. Each time he took a step, the wolf moved one step closer.

If he could make it to the back door, he could maybe escape. The basement was out. The windows were too narrow to escape from and the door was too flimsy to keep the beast out. If he could just make it to the door, there was a chance he could make it to his car. Bobby thought that maybe he would be safe. The wolf couldn't rip off a car door, could it? He needed to decide, and quick. The wolf was getting closer. He could smell the stench of rotting meat on its breath. Shards of glass twinkled in its fur like Christmas lights. Bobby felt as if the wolf somehow knew him. That was impossible, of course. It was an animal. Animals only know what they're taught. Werewolves only existed in horror novels.

The wolf lunged for him and Bobby ran. The shard of glass sank deeper into his heel, sending lightning bolts of pain shooting through his leg. He could feel the blood pooling from the wound. It only seemed to excite the wolf, but at that moment, new pain sent his frightened mind into over drive. Sharp claws ripped into Bobby's back, severing the spinal cord. The pain was suddenly gone, but the relief he should have felt was replaced by the realization that he was falling. His legs no longer worked. Bobby fell like a sack of flour. He screamed as he tried to crawl to the back door. His legs felt like tree stumps.

"Please! No, just let me go. Nice doggy." The wolf pounced once more and flipped Bobby over onto his back. The wolf's teeth bit into his chin, removing skin and several teeth. He tried to scream, but the wolf bit deeper into his mouth, severing his tongue. It chewed it quickly and removed more of Bobby's face, exposing the blood stained skull beneath. The wolf still chewed at his neck, severing the vocal cords as if they were pieces of yarn. The coppery odor of blood mixed in with the wet fur smell of Amy's pelt. Her eyes glazed over as she ripped his arms from their sockets, discarding them like garbage. The smell of urine and shit exploded into her snout as she sank her sharpened teeth into his stomach. She howled and backed away, leaving a gore stained husk. As a final insult, she pissed on his steaming body to mark it as her territory. It didn't matter that he wouldn't be around to feel it.

She could hear sirens filling the night air with their symphonic urgency. She eyed the carnage with indifference. As a wolf, there wasn't any pride in what she had done. It was all instinct and the need for revenge. They had asked for this. The sounds of their screams must have been heard by the neighbors. Usually in this neighborhood, no one wanted to get involved. Of course, this time things were a bit different.

There would be pride in the morning when she relived their screams of agony. She would remember the way they looked in their final moments of life. It was a beautiful sight to behold. They wouldn't hurt anyone else anymore. Once she was a safe distance away from the carnage, she looked up at the full moon and howled triumphantly.

BIO: Michael Noe is a horror writer from Barberton Ohio. He is the author of Legacy, The Darkness Of The Soul, and the upcoming short story collection Insecure Delusions. When not writing he reviews books on his website Slaphappy Fun Time and collects vinyl records. You can find him at

https://www.facebook.com/michaelnoeslegacy/

As well as:

http://slaphappyfuntime.blogspot.com/?zx=9dcec248a7c0b9ba

FREEDOM IN THE BEAST

W. POTOCKI

London—1882.

"And I say to those who hear the siren call of justice, that good intentions are not enough. No, you need three things if you are to succeed. First, you must possess a mind open to the possibilities a criminal pathology presents. Next, you need courage to confront the fiendishness evil breeds. And, finally, you need an indefatigable strength, for it is *you* who will drag the wicked from their lairs and into the bright light of day."

The man in the smoking jacket paused, posing in a three-quarter profile for his young assistant Todd Spenser to admire. It only took a second for Todd to break into wild applause.

"Mr. Dearing, that was the best speech I ever did hear!" the twenty-two-year-old with brown hair neatly parted on the side praised. "That graduating class is in for a treat—you mark my words!"

The thick cockney accent hid a fertile mind, one Lucius Dearing was shaping by teaching Todd all he could about the fine art of deductive reasoning. If all went well, the apprentice would follow in Lucius' footsteps and run his own private detective agency someday.

The sharp ring of the doorbell interrupted the conversation—and the morning.

"We have a visitor, Todd. You didn't forget to write down any appointments, did you?"

"No, sir, Mr. Dearing. No one's scheduled."

"Then kindly see who darkens my doorstep."

As Todd did as bidden, Dearing's curiosity got the better of him. He moved to the bay window that allowed a glimpse of a slender woman gracing the landing of the front steps. Her back was to him, but it was a shapely back indeed.

The rustling associated with a woman's petticoats preceded the unannounced arrival, as did the faintest note of an intoxicating perfume. It was coming from just beyond the door of his study.

"A Mrs. Annabelle Hinton is here to see you, sir, on what she says is a personal matter," Todd stated upon re-entering.

"Personal, is it? Well, then, show her in."

When Todd left to escort the woman into the mahogany-paneled room, Dearing seized the opportunity. He smoothed back his hair and snuck a glance in the mirror that hung on his wall. It wouldn't do to not be presentable. He swung around and took in the full view of his guest.

An involuntary sip of air punctuated the silence, but then he hadn't been prepared for one so lovely. With skin the color of the finest pearl, the richness of the young woman's dark hair offset any thoughts of sterility and imbued a striking contrast. The eyes... penetrating, rich, and green... they were marked by thick, black lashes and eyebrows that arched like raven's wings. The brows provided a perfect canopy for the circles of perfection to rest beneath. A full mouth stained in red drew outward at the corners, revealing two rows of gleaming white teeth.

"Mr. Dearing, I apologize for visiting unannounced, but I feared you wouldn't see me—and you're the only one I can trust."

There was the faintest trace of French locked in her inflection.

Her long reply gave him a chance to recover. He grasped her outstretched hand, acknowledging her with a nod and formal bow. He would have liked to do more, but it would be unseemly to let the desire welling inside be displayed.

A spark of irritation crossed her face as she took the chair indicated. Dearing hadn't been given a medal of commendation from Scotland Yard for no good reason. It was he who had solved the most diabolical string of murders in London's history, so deciphering her expression was child's play.

"Mr. Spenser is my associate, Mrs. Hinton. He records salient details that I can study at my leisure. Let me assure you that anything you say will be held in the strictest confidence."

At the mention of his name, Todd suspended all movement, an awkwardness bathing him in vulnerability. She relented.

"Very well. I am no one to question your judgement."

With the matter concluded, Todd seated himself, preparing to record the conversation.

"Now, what is this about, Mrs. Hinton?"

"My husband, Bernard."

"Do you suspect infidelity?"

"No."

The answer surprised him. Nine times out of ten, it was why the female of the species paid detectives a visit.

"Then what? What do you suspect him of?"

"Murder."

Dearing exchanged a look with Todd. With a flurry of strokes, Spenser noted the response.

"Murder, you say? Who do you believe he's killed?"

34

"Four people to date, but there will be more in the future… *if* he's not stopped."

There was a slight tension in her neck and jaw. She was becoming agitated… nervous… and Dearing wondered why.

"How is it that you happened upon this information, Mrs. Hinton? Did your husband Bernard confess to these crimes?"

"N-no."

There it was—a falter. The head coiled in tresses of ebony dropped as her skin, seemingly fashioned out of wax, flushed with shame. Her eyes were no longer direct but avoided confrontation by roaming about. The detective waited until they settled. Until her tongue stopped probing the corners of her lips. Until her fingers quieted and no longer tapped the purse in her lap. "This is why I didn't write you… this is the part I don't know how to express—without you thinking me mad."

Dearing's wheels were spinning. The opinion he held of the woman with military bearing was challenged.

"Is that why you categorized this as *personal* and not *professional?*"

"Yes."

"Perhaps tea would help. Let me ring for—"

"No."

The sharp rebuff harkened her eyes' return. Focused, they were as compelling as before—such an uncommon shade of emerald. Dearing had never before waded in such a contemplative pool.

"This is difficult," she struggled. "I-I've seen what Bernard does… in my dreams."

The titter came from his charge's lips. Dearing motioned with his hand, stilling the taunting. He would not have a client ridiculed. If she were mad, she deserved sympathy—not derision.

Todd settled down. Chastised, he intently listened, but the damage was done—the tenuous cord of trust was severed.

"I will pay you for the time I've wasted and not bother you again," Mrs. Hinton apologized as she pressed to her feet.

"This is time well-spent," Dearing assured. "Now, please sit and tell me about these dreams."

"Yes, the dreams."

She descended into the vacated seat as her eyes drifted towards the heavens. A bite to her bottom lip caused a white impression to appear where the blood had been pressed away. Her eyes pinched closed as she rubbed her brow with a gloved hand.

"They started about three… no, four months ago," she continued. "They begin with me waking in my bed to a clock striking midnight. For some reason, I'm frightened by the sound… and by the night. I turn for

35

comfort, but my husband is not next to me. I rise, calling out his name, but there is no response.

"The curtains are open and allow me sight of the most haunting full moon. I'm hypnotized by it and feel a pull… a stirring inside. It's a wild place, a place of animalistic desires and immense longing. I stare… consumed… when I notice someone running from our house and into the woods… and it looks like Bernard.

"Without donning my robe, I rush down the stairs and out into the night, trying my best to follow. I scream out his name, but there is no reply. There's danger abounding on all sides, but I must find him, and so I choose a path and am about to go down it when I hear a wolf's howl.

"I can't describe the panic. My pulse is so strong that my throat throbs and my chest aches. I want to retreat and hide, but there's Bernard to consider. I must find him and so I head towards the sound of the cry.

"Thorns tear at my gown and branches at my skin, but I persevere until I penetrate the deepest part of the woods and come upon a clearing. My heart skips when I see a body on the ground. It's too dark to identify, so I creep upon it, praying it's not Bernard the animal has killed.

"When I am near enough to see the mangled throat and blue of the victim's eyes, I breathe a sigh of relief, knowing that my husband's eyes are brown. But before I have time to think, there is hot breath on my neck. I spin around and look into the face of the beast, but it's not a beast. It's Bernard… *he* is the wolf.

"Somehow, he has changed into this, this, this *creature!* I am horrified and fascinated all in one breath. But there is a passion that arises in the place the moon has awakened and I know he means to bite me… to turn me into the monster he's become. The strange thing is, Mr. Dearing… that I welcome the bite. I know it's unforgivable, but I do so knowing that the man lying on the ground is not his only kill.

"I prepare for the inevitable and unbutton the bodice of my gown, letting it slip to the ground. I collapse to my knees and await the teeth sinking into my flesh… I await becoming a wolf."

***

"But, Mr. Dearing, you can't believe her story! You can't!"

Todd was excitable, but it was to be expected given his tender years. It would take time to harness youth and its fulsomeness of expression.

The carriage rocked as two white horses galloped through the countryside at an eager pace.

"Todd, I believe in what I professed in my speech," Dearing admonished. Dressed impeccably in a three-piece custom-tailored suit, he prided himself on sartorial correctness that reflected his elevated position.

"An *open mind* is what is needed. If you disallow what is spoken, you miss fascinating connections."

"Such as?"

"Such as four deaths attributable to wolf attacks outside of Helmsley in North Yorkshire—all committed under a full moon."

"Helmsley? That's where she lives."

"Yes, it is, Todd."

"And why we're traveling there to talk with her husband?"

"Yes, with her permission, of course. However, we must stick to our cover. We are there to protect her, nothing more."

"Understood, but four killings? Well, I'll be... but have you considered she'd be aware of the attacks? Maybe that's why she had the dreams."

So naive. The audacity of youth in thinking one perspective summed up all life's probabilities.

"And maybe it isn't. An *open* mind, Todd. Remember that and it will serve you well."

***

The Hinton estate was impressive, a massive home that stretched into twenty-two rooms. The woods skirted the boundaries of the rolling lawn. While Dearing had been in many fine estates, Spenser had not, and so it was with trepidation and a mouth agape in wonder that he trailed behind the butler that led them into the inner recesses of the manor.

A flaccid man of medium height and florid complexion waited at the end of the hall.

"Mr. Dearing?" Mr. Hinton greeted.

"Yes, I am, and this is my assistant, Todd Spenser."

"Goodtomeetyousir," Todd spurted in one breath.

There was humble—and there was subservient. Todd really did need to get a handle on feeling less than those in lofty positions. Dearing made a note to bring him to his private club. There was nothing that would rid him of the impression that others were better than rubbing shoulders with the undeserving.

"I must say I was surprised to receive your letter requesting to see me," Hinton began. "Surely you didn't travel all the way from London just for a discussion with me."

Bernard's voice was neither deep nor high. A pair of reading glasses magnified his large, protruding eyes, while a moustache and sideburns tried to define the indistinguishable features.

"No, not entirely, Mr. Hinton," Dearing replied as he and Spenser took seats in the parlor.

Hinton remained standing, puffing out his broad chest and even broader stomach.

"Well, I hope it isn't because of another killer on the loose. I read about your exploits in the Eastman case. Imagine a scholar turning out to be the fiend that killed twelve children. Did he really expect his own son to come back by skinning his victims?"

The Eastman murders. It was Dearing's most celebrated case. While the ones preceding it had built his reputation, it was the arrest of Tolliver Eastman that made him famous, but he had no intention of stopping there. He wanted his name known round the world and synonymous with excellence.

"No, not through the flaying. It would be through the sewing of the skins together. After he fashioned a body, his son could use it to return from the grave—or so he believed."

He would never dispense such details in a lady's company, but with three men present, the grisly facts became fodder for discussion.

"Such an evil man," Bernard excoriated. "What possesses some to engage in such acts of cruelty?"

"There is no solution to that, but one day, science will give us our answer."

"You really believe that? You have that much faith?"

"I am more than certain. But it is fortunate that you brought up the Eastman case because it's killings that bring me to Helmsley."

"Killings? Helmsley has had no murders—at least none that I'm aware," Bernard stated before sitting down. A groan accompanied the movement, but then his waistband was entirely too tight.

"Not murders. Attacks."

"You're referring to the four-legged scavenger that has found a home in our woods? The hunters will take care of whatever it is that's been attacking the locals."

"*Scavenger?* Then you don't agree that it's a wolf?" Dearing probed.

Hinton's face contracted as he shook his head.

"I neither agree nor disagree. Any large predator could inflict such damage… and no one's sighted the beast."

"Then you're aware of the injuries?"

"No more so than anyone else that cares about his community and family."

"And you do care for your family?" Dearing asked.

"Why, of course! Why would you ask such a thing?"

"Because your wife is the reason I'm here. She feels she is in danger."

"She feels in danger?" Hinton repeated. "I don't understand."

"I mean that she is frightened… uncontrollably so. Why do you find that so unusual? There have been four deaths."

"She told you that she's frightened by the attacks? This is preposterous!" Hinton blurted.

Dearing and Spenser were confused by the reply and by the bland man darting across the room. A tapestry-covered footstool was used to reach the top of a cabinet and retrieve a book that he shoved into Dearing's hands. Todd craned his neck to see.

"*Freedom in the Beast: The History of Lycanthropy,*" Lucius read aloud.

"My wife purchased it without my permission. I lost my temper rather badly and snatched it away. I didn't want things to get worse."

"What sorts of things?" Dearing asked as he leafed through the pages that contained text and a compendium of engravings of the mythical creature made throughout the ages.

"All number of fantasies, but this," the husband sputtered, pointing at the book in the detective's hands, "*this,* she's become obsessed with. It led her to make the most wild of accusations. It's why I was surprised by your statement."

"*Accusation?*" Dearing repeated, exchanging a look with Todd. "Do you mean to imply that she accused you of being a werewolf?"

"Me?" Hinton said, touching his chest and scoffing. "No, you've got it all wrong. She thinks *she* is!"

Dearing and Spenser bolted upright, Dearing's blue eyes rounding from the shocking admission. Perhaps his associate had been right in thinking Annabelle Hinton mad. He caught himself and followed his own advice in remaining open—even in the midst of damning evidence.

Hinton placed his elbow on the mantel above the fireplace as his eyes anchored on the landscape outside.

"It started five months ago," Hinton explained. "Annabelle was being impossible and said it was the lack of excitement and travel producing it. It was true that we hadn't traveled since our honeymoon, so I acquiesced to her demands. We spent a weekend in Marseilles. It was quite splendid, but on the last night, she complained of insomnia and said only a walk would cure it.

"It was late and a ridiculous idea. I forbade it, but after I fell asleep, she did as she pleased with no regard for my explicit instructions. I awoke around midnight and found her gone. I dressed, and I was no sooner outside than I heard her scream. I ran as fast as I could and found her stumbling out of the woods, bleeding from her arm. When I asked what happened, she said a wolf had bitten her."

Hinton turned his back, then pivoted around.

"I should never have let Francois talk me into marrying her," he segued, veering into personal territory. "Francois was my wife's father. He

39

was so worried about her behavior that he arranged for a suitable husband before he died. But he was honorable and admitted that she was willful— so willful that she'd run away… several times. It's why I was reluctant at the proposal. I feared her *innocence* might not be intact."

"Do you mean her virginity?" Dearing asked.

"Yes," Hinton admitted with a derisive laugh. "But I found out on our wedding night that I needn't have worried.

"You see, Mr. Dearing, I want children. In fact, I insist on it, and although she allows my husbandly duties several times a week, there is no participation on her part. She abhors the sexual act, and I suspect her coldness as the reason for her failure at pregnancy. I discussed my supposition with our primary physician, Dr. Woolcott, and he agreed with my assessment. It's why I arranged weekly sessions with a Dr. Taylor."

"And Dr. Taylor is?"

"A psychiatrist."

"Your wife is seeing a psychiatrist?" Dearing queried.

"Yes," Hinton responded. The man's brown eyes locked onto the frosty blue of the detective's.

"Because of her disinterest?"

"Not disinterest—frigidity. It's the term Dr. Taylor used, but it's not the only one."

"What are the others?"

"Delusion, paranoia, hysteria… she exhibits them all. Taylor recommended hospitalization, but I would be betraying Francois… and I promised to take care of his daughter."

Dearing rose and approached the distraught husband. The detective's six-foot frame was several inches taller than the man under such stress.

"Mr. Hinton, your wife only involved us for the purpose of protection."

Hinton nodded, his face a mixture of conflicting emotions. There was a strange gleam in his eyes.

"Then she… she didn't mention me?"

"No," Dearing lied. "It's why I'm having this discussion."

"I see."

"Please, Mr. Hinton. Let me have a talk with Dr. Taylor. You must understand that even if the bite she suffered yielded only a scratch, it could have severely compromised your wife's mental stability."

"You believe that's it?"

"It's possible," he replied, placing a hand on Bernard's shoulder. Yes, there was something about those eyes—something Dearing didn't trust. "I'm only here to protect her, and there is a full moon coming up in a week. Let's wait and see, shall we? What we find may make the decision easier for you."

"But wolves don't care about phases of the moon—people do."

"That's exactly right, Mr. Hinton. That's why I agree with your wife."

"That a werewolf is behind this?"

"No, that a person is."

***

"Thank you for seeing us, Dr. Taylor," Dearing began.

It took three days to arrange an appointment with Annabelle's psychiatrist. Dearing wasn't happy with the time wasted, nor with having to fight the impulse to see Annabelle again, but he would have to see her, if only to rebut what her husband professed.

"You're most welcome," Taylor replied. His sharp-featured face was crowned by thatches of gray, while tufts of silver sided his face and drew attention to eyes better set in an eagle's head. "It's been one crisis after another. I should state at the outset that Mr. Hinton gave me permission to circumvent doctor-patient privilege. It's the only reason I'm discussing any of this with you."

"We appreciate your discretion. You see, Mrs. Hinton has expressed a fear of the recent wolf attacks and contracted our services to help protect her. A full understanding of her opinion on the matter would help."

Taylor leaned back, placing his hands at his stomach and clasping them.

"Yes, Mrs. Hinton made mention of them. She was frightened and implied her husband was somehow responsible."

"She stated that? That her husband was responsible?" Dearing asked.

"Yes… in so many words."

"Did she ever mention that *she* was the cause?" he pressed.

"No, I don't believe so. Besides, how could she be? A woman of her size?" Taylor asked.

"She couldn't—obviously," he stated as he moved onto the next subject. "Did Mrs. Hinton ever mention being bitten by a wolf?"

"Bitten? By the wolf they're searching for?"

"No. While she vacationed in France," Dearing replied.

"France? I have no idea what you're speaking of. She was here every week and I saw no sign of an attack."

Taylor pulled out a pocket watch to check the time.

"I see. Then she only mentioned her husband as being responsible for the attacks and that she was frightened?"

"Yes," Taylor replied.

"With no reason given as to why?"

41

"No, but it's easily understood."

"How so?" It was Todd this time, getting his feet wet and asking the pertinent question.

"Because Mrs. Hinton does not respond favorably to sexual relations. Mr. Hinton hoped I could discern what in her psyche fought the idea of surrendering to passion."

"And did you uncover a reason?" Dearing asked, taking back over.

"I attributed it to the fear of death. Under certain circumstances, the succumbing to passion and death become entwined... inexorably linked. It's due to confusion and fear of losing one's self. Hysteria is associated with the syndrome, and Mrs. Hinton suffers from it."

"Is that all?"

"No, there is also a deep-seated resentment towards her husband that I don't fully understand but recognize. When the attacks started, it only became more pronounced, but it is logical... from a psychological perspective."

"Might you explain?"

"Well, these attacks involve biting, which subconsciously translates to penetration. So the animal attacks that resulted in death were interpreted by her mind as sexual in nature, and since she is married to Mr. Hinton—"

"She became fearful of him and made him responsible."

"Exactly," Dr. Taylor stated.

"And it's because of this delusion that you recommended institutionalization?"

"No, I never recommended it. Mr. Hinton asked about the appropriateness, and I advised that if Mrs. Hinton's condition worsened, then it would be a viable option—and it has. That's why he's made arrangements to have her admitted to Wilshire."

"Wilshire Asylum?" Dearing asked.

"Don't say it like that, Mr. Dearing. Surely we no longer cast the mentally ill in such a negative light. It's an excellent treatment facility and will do her a world of good."

***

"Someone's lying," Dearing summed up in a whisper. It wouldn't do to have someone in the household overhear.

"Yes, but who?" Todd retorted.

"That's what we're here to find out."

A day had passed since speaking with Taylor. The two waited on a velvet-tufted sofa, but not for long.

Dearing was unable to wrench his eyes from the woman wafting down the staircase. The wide skirt was lifted too rapaciously by delicate fingers and allowed a glimpse of a stockinged ankle that drove him wild with desire.

Gray suited the mistress of the house. On some it might be considered drab, but Annabelle brought it to life. It made her hair darker, her skin all the more translucent, and her eyes… it made her eyes dance with glorious abandon.

She led the men into the library before sliding the doors together and securing privacy.

"We've found some discrepancies in your statements, Mrs. Hinton. It is imperative that you be completely honest with us if we are to help," Dearing began.

"I have been!" she swore with an impassioned plea. "Please, what have you discovered that has caused you to doubt me?"

"Todd," Dearing prompted.

"Yes," his assistant said, clearing his throat. "You said that you thought your husband was a werewolf, but in speaking to him, he swore it was you that alleged that you were one."

Her lips parted as she started to object. Dearing's finger pressed to his lips, quelling her response. Todd waited a moment before proceeding.

"And there was a book you purchased," he continued. *"Freedom in the Beast: The History of Lycanthropy.* You didn't tell us you bought it."

Dearing nodded to Annabelle to begin her defense.

"I did not purchase that book!" she vehemently denied. "My husband did! He left it on my pillow, and when I confronted him as to why, he ordered me to read it, saying that it would explain what he'd become."

She buried her head in her hands, trembling from emotion. Dearing reached out a hand to comfort her but retracted it. She was, after all, a married woman, and someone else's property.

"As for me thinking I'm a werewolf, the notion is ludicrous and stretches credulity. Why Bernard would allege such a thing is puzzling, but perhaps it is to cover up what he said and cause doubt. You know more about the psychology of the mind than I do, Mr. Dearing. Could that account for such a lie?"

"If it is a lie," he retorted. While he wanted to believe her, it wasn't that simple. Nothing was.

His response disturbed her composure, but it was all part of uncovering the truth of what was transpiring. He caught Todd's eye. Spenser grasped the papers, reading off the next item.

"Your husband recounted a wolf attack… in Marseilles."

"Yes," she sighed. "That is the truth. There was an attack, but it bolsters my contention, not his."

"How?" Dearing asked.

"Because the attack changed him into the creature he is today."

Dearing lurched forward.

"But he swore *you* were bitten—that *you* were the one attacked."

"Liar!" she exploded as she leapt to her feet. Pacing the room, she wrung her hands as she mumbled under her breath, "Why? Why? Why is he doing this to me? He knows he's the one that's responsible and yet he's involving me."

She turned to the two men seated, who were watching her every move.

"I don't know what to say to make you believe me. Bernard was the one that was bitten. The last time we traveled was on our honeymoon, but that ended in disaster. He accused me of flirting when I did nothing of the kind, but then, he's always been jealous of me. We haven't journeyed anywhere since, but I convinced him to go to Marseilles.

"It was horrible. He complained about everything, including insomnia. He took to prowling the woods at night. I warned him not to, but he wouldn't listen.

"One night, I awoke and found him gone. It was midnight and I was frantic. He came back, bleeding from the arm and telling me he'd been attacked by a strange wolf. He said it was bigger than any he'd ever seen." She paused, her eyes narrowing and her hand going to her throat. "It's like my dream, isn't it? Oh, I see! You think I'm confusing my dream with what happened, but I'm not! There *was* an attack, and it was Bernard that was injured—not me!" She moved in a circle, her body graceful and precise. She stopped short. "I know! You can go to Dr. Woolcott! He can tell you! He treated Bernard upon his return home. His office isn't too far from here and—"

"Mrs. Hinton, Dr. Woolcott is dead," Dearing interjected. "Did you not know that he was the last victim claimed?"

"Dead? Dead, you say?" Reeling, she staggered to the nearest chair, using a table to keep from toppling over. Collapsing on a divan, she burst into tears. "No, I didn't know! Bernard never told me! Dead? He could have confirmed it was Bernard, but now? Now I have no one... no one!"

"Mrs. Hinton, please," Dearing said as he got up and offered a linen handkerchief. She took it, dabbing at her face and eyes as he sat next to her. "Did you know your husband has arranged to have you placed in a hospital?"

"A hospital? You mean, a mental institution?" Her face drained of expression. "Well, that's it, then, isn't it? My life is over... because my husband is making me out to be insane... and maybe I am," she hissed.

One brow raised as a smile emerged. She stood, stretching out and rocking in place.

"You see, I didn't tell you everything about my dreams, but I will now," she confessed with a giggle. "The dreams don't end with the shedding of my gown... they go on." Spoken in a hushed tone, she ran her hands the length of her body, lingering on her breasts and hips.

44

"After my gown falls to the ground, I stand naked, awaiting the bite, but it is my husband that forces me down. When I am on my knees, he goes behind me, and with one arm squeezing underneath my belly, he pins me in place. Without consent, he penetrates me, pushing into me until I scream. But I don't scream because of the pain. I scream because of the pleasure.

"Never have I felt such release! It is intense and comes from fornication with a beast! I know it is forbidden, but this beast is my husband, so how can it be wrong?

"I revel in the passion, Mr. Dearing. I revel in his strength and power. Even his fur touching my skin excites me and so I bury myself in it… rubbing into it and feeling his body's heat.

"Sex was why my husband sent me to see Dr. Taylor. Bernard blamed me for not conceiving a child because of my distaste for it, but I tried. I was as any other obedient wife and tolerated the couplings, but it wasn't enough for Bernard.

"Dr. Taylor gave me medication… opiates to relax me, but that was never the problem because it was the sex in my dreams that I craved. That was the real reason I wanted to be bitten. When asleep, I was convinced it was the only way I could be free, and now my conscious mind agrees. Do you understand? I want to be free… or perhaps I should say *freed*."

With the feverish speech over, civility caused embarrassment to flourish. She rushed into Dearing's arms and then fell at his feet.

"What did I say? I don't even know! Please, Mr. Dearing! I'm begging you to help me before I am locked away!"

Dearing dropped to his knees, one hand going underneath her arm.

"Opiates, you say? Mrs. Hinton, I will help, but you must stop ingesting the medication. That is what is confusing your thoughts."

"But the doctor… he told me to take it."

"And I'm telling you to stop. Todd, help me lift her."

The two men half-carried her to the couch. Dearing gave her a moment to collect herself.

"Mrs. Hinton, someone has taken advantage of your suggestible mind, and there are two ways it could be have been accomplished. One is by seizing an opportunity, and the other is by transporting a wolf to do his bidding."

Spenser's eyes widened.

"You think it's her husband, don't you?" Todd surmised. "Yes, he could have brought a wolf to Helmsley. Maybe he trapped it in Marseilles. It might be how he got bitten. It only left putting ideas in his wife's head, and Taylor's prescription made that easy. But the question is why?"

"For the money, Todd. I inquired—very discreetly—about Mr. Hinton's finances, and I found that it was through marriage that he acquired wealth. The house that they live in is hers, or would have been.

45

Unfortunately, they married two years before the 1880 Act allowing women to keep property was enacted, so when Mrs. Hinton's father died, it passed to him—not her. Isn't that right, Mrs. Hinton?"

"Yes, yes, it is right," she concurred. "So Bernard was after my money? And he was willing to do this to me to get it?"

She burst into tears, burying her head in Dearing's chest. He cradled her, soothing her as best he could, while Todd poured a glass of water and presented it to her. She drank deeply, spilling a bit down her chin.

"Mr. Dearing, I can't thank you enough. I feel better even knowing how I was betrayed, but it is conjecture, no? Do we not need proof?"

"And proof we will have," the detective replied.

"But how?" It was Todd this time. His face a mixture of admiration and confusion, Dearing replied.

"By catching Bernard in the act. *Tomorrow* is the night of the full moon, and it is *tomorrow* that we will be glued to Mrs. Hinton's side."

* * *

"I still can't believe it, Mr. Dearing, but I knew you'd help. I knew you'd be the only one that could."

Annabelle placed a hand on his arm in gratitude, and even that simple gesture sent shockwaves of electricity surging throughout his body.

The eroticism of her dream echoed in his head. He would love to see her naked, and perhaps he would. Her husband would be put to death for this scheme. Dearing would see to it.

"I'm only glad I was worthy of your trust," he replied as they heard Bernard's heavy footsteps in the hall.

"I'll see where he goes," Todd whispered. He opened the door to the room where they hid by a slit, making sure the coast was clear before slipping out. Dearing moved to the window and beheld the moon, full and bright. He was eager for the chase to begin.

"Here," Annabelle offered as she held out a drink. "I thought we could use this."

"Good idea," Dearing responded. "To a fruitful night," he toasted before they downed the sherry. The door burst open.

"He went into the woods! I think we should hurry!"

Dearing and Annabelle discarded their glasses and followed Todd out into the night. Both he and his assistant were armed just in case Hinton didn't capitulate to their demands for surrender.

Annabelle's caplet fluttered in the night's breeze.

"This is the path he uses," Annabelle said as she took the lead. "I hear him!" she urged as she picked up her skirts and broke into a run.

"Wait! You're going too fast!" Dearing cautioned. "We don't want to lose sight of each oth—"

It was too late. Annabelle disappeared around the corner. Dearing and Todd sprinted, trying to catch up, when they heard a woman's scream. They made the turn, but the woman they were protecting was gone.

"He's got her, sir!" Todd cried. "No wolf could have pulled her off the path that quickly!"

"Yes, but a man could! It proves I'm right! We need to find her!"

There was rustling from deep within the brush—accompanied by another cry.

"You go that way, Todd! We'll meet in the middle!"

Todd took off as did Dearing, but he was tiring more quickly than was normal—and his balance was off. Out of breath from the exertion, he commanded his legs to obey. Through strength of will, he adhered to the pace set. A third scream pierced the night, but this time, it was a man's.

"Todd!" he yelled at the top of his lungs.

If anything happened to his assistant, he would never forgive himself. Never!

Seconds seemed interminable as his feet pounded into the dirt, but no shots were fired. Why hadn't Todd used his gun?

The path Dearing followed led to a clearing. The moon shone upon it, the light illuminating two bodies in the grass.

"No!" he cried, realizing he'd lost them both.

It had happened too quickly. Too quickly to stop the carnage. He neared, not relishing viewing what was done.

The evening flipped. From pleasant it dove into macabre. Terrified, his sense of duty called, but he was tired—exhausted enough for his vision to become blurred. He put a hand to the heart he feared was giving out.

Shadows. Moving. Faint sounds. And from in the shrubbery—growling. He froze in fear as the brush shook. His hand went for his pistol as the wolf emerged, towering over him. Its eyes glowed yellow and the gray of its coat glistened. Its muscles rippled as a long red tongue swiped at pointed fangs, but it was all wrong. Wolves don't stand on their hind legs, yet this one did.

He lifted his gun to take aim as the lethargy overwhelmed him. He struggled to keep erect, but there was no strength left to stand—or pull the trigger. His knees buckled and he fell to the ground.

***

The faint light of morning turned black into a drab shade of day.

Consciousness seeped into the holes of Dearing's memory. He'd passed out … but not before seeing that beast. Hinton was a werewolf. Why hadn't he kept an open mind?

Dearing's mouth was full, his tongue constrained by something pressing down upon it. As his eyes fluttered open, he used his hands to

47

remove the heavy object held between his teeth. Irritation turned to horror. It was a human arm—one pulled unwillingly from its socket.

He gasped as he spat and threw it to the side. The body of the person next to him came into focus. He stared into the light brown eyes of his assistant. Todd was dead. It was his arm that had been in Dearing's mouth.

"Todd!" he shouted before pressing his palm against the torn and bloodied jacket.

The debilitating fatigue made every movement an arduous task. He lifted his torso, turning away. But the adjustment only brought on another nightmare—one as disturbing as the taste of flesh and blood that lingered on his palate.

Bernard Hinton was to his other side and as dead as any corpse Dearing had ever viewed. His body was mauled, ravaged, and barely recognizable as human.

Human.

The thought was barely conceptualized when soft gales of laughter blanketed him in an audacious dismissal of the lives taken, but it wasn't enough. A cruelty propelled it to continue.

"Good morning, Mr. Dearing."

A voice.

The voice was recognizable, and one he'd never expected to hear under these conditions.

"Annabelle," he whispered as he looked up.

The woman he'd lusted after was nude and pointing a gun.

"Yes, it's me. Bernard told you the truth. I am the werewolf. I was the one that was bitten."

"I don't understand."

"You should, Mr. Dearing. As you know, it was my father that arranged my marriage to the very boring Bernard. My father was controlling and put my life into the hands of another who sought to control me. But it was *my* money and *my* house, and so I sought a remedy to the problem. The attack in Marseilles proved a Godsend. I finally possessed what I needed to rid myself of my jailer."

Her head was thrown back as she spewed hysterical laughter. The gun was held lazily; if only he could move. She caught the impotent attempt.

"Poor Mr. Dearing! Still not able to function? I forgot to mention that Dr. Taylor gave me a sleeping powder. I put it in that drink I served you last night."

"The sherry," he murmured.

"Yes. All that's left is to shoot you. It will look as if you were responsible. Your bite marks are on Spenser's arm—and on mine," she said, turning slightly and putting it on view. He moaned in despair.

"Then that's why you sought me out? That's why you trod on my good nature?"

"I needed a scapegoat, Mr. Dearing, and your ego and your obvious attraction made you the perfect choice. While you were not the only one I could have gone to, you were the only one arrogant enough to blind yourself to the truth. I followed the Eastman case and recognized the ambition in you. It burns brightly, but the fame you desired will turn to infamy.

"It will appear that you tried to attack me, and that I had no choice but to defend myself using your assistant's gun. And you? You will go down in history as the detective that fancied himself a werewolf and killed his own apprentice. You will be a mockery—a scourge—and quite possibly be refused burial in decent cemeteries. Quite a legacy, no?"

He was a proud man and would be turned into a laughing stock for an eternity. It wasn't fair. It wasn't right. He had to stop this. Using every ounce of fortitude, he battled to his feet, tottering as he inched forward to strangle her.

"The book was right, you know. There is *Freedom in the Beast*, Mr. Dearing. Too bad you found out too late."

The slender white hand aimed; the one shot passed through Dearing's brain.

Annabelle bent over and retrieved her clothing from the ground as he fell atop the other two bodies, but it was right to be stacked like trash.

After all, he was just another victim to the woman dressing herself in gray.

BIO: I live and write in NYC. If that's not scary enough, I write in the genre of horror. I consider horror to be an art form, and I try to do it proud. I'm the author of eight books and won the honor of being named One of the Top Ten Best "New" Horror Authors by Horror Novel Reviews.

I'm naturally humble ... love coffee, animals, and chocolate, but not necessarily in that order. Deal breakers for me are cruelty to fluffy, four-legged creatures and children.

If you want to keep in touch, it should be easy since I'm splattered all over the web. Here are some of my lairs:

Mailing list: http://bit.ly/1lGwkDm
FB: http://on.fb.me/1oOawJO
Twitter: @WPotocki
Website: http://wendypotocki.blogspot.com/

FULL MOON CRAZY

SK GREGORY

"This is going to be a crazy night," Adele Cooper muttered as she stared up at the full moon. She had been working at Mercy Hospital for five years now, as a nurse, and she had seen a lot of crazy.

Drug addicts, criminals, even a guy with a gun once. The emergency room was a nightmare, but always more so on a full moon. She read once that the moon could affect people like it did with the tides. There were certainly more accidents.

Taking one last drag of her cigarette, she flicked it off the edge of the roof and headed back inside. She had the night shift tonight along with Kerry Jones. Kerry had been in nursing for over thirty years and made sure that everyone knew it. Adele had even heard her contradicting some of the doctors when they gave a diagnosis. She liked to start nearly every sentence with 'In my day,' or 'In my experience.' She was a nightmare, and the sooner this shift was over, the better.

As she entered the emergency room, she heard a man yelling and screaming.

"We've got a live one," Kerry said, moving her ample frame out from behind the desk and down the hall. Adele hurried after her, hoping it wasn't another tweaker.

The man was, in fact, a teenage boy, around eighteen, who was fighting against two orderlies.

"I can't stay here, it's too dangerous. They're after me," he screamed.

"Now, boy, that's no way to behave," Kerry said. She placed a hand on his shoulder and pushed him down on the bed. Her girth worked in her favor and she pinned him easily.

Adele loaded a syringe with a mild sedative and passed it to her. Once the sedative took effect, the boy stopped struggling.

"Please don't let them get me," he whispered.

"Who is after you?" Adele asked.

"Hunters," he muttered.

"Hunters?" Adele said. What did that mean? Was it some new street term or the name of a gang?

"Ignore him, he's out of his gourd," Kerry tutted. "Behave yourself now, or we'll have to tie you down."

As the two of them left the room, Adele asked, "Should I call Dr. Bishop for a psych eval?"

"Rehab is what that boy needs. In my day…"

Luckily, she was interrupted when an eight year old boy threw up all over her shoes.

"Urgh," she groaned.

Grinning, Adele gave the boy a thumbs up and headed off to find one of the cleaners.

***

Van Gerrick trampled through the woods, not bothering to be stealthy. After all the trouble the boy had given him, he wanted him to hear his approach. Wanted him to know that his time was coming to an end.

He had avoided him this far and Van Gerrick had to give him some credit for that. It wasn't often that a Were could outsmart him, but this one had. All the more reason that he needed to find him and kill him quickly. He couldn't have the rest of them thinking he was losing his touch.

The rest of the team were spread out to the east and west. They would box him in and terminate him before the night was over.

Van Gerrick stopped and looked up at the moon. He should hate the full moon for what it unleashed, but it unleashed something in him too. The thrill of the hunt. Knowing that he had power over these animals, that he could crush their kind under his heel was better than any drug.

I'll find you, boy. And when I do, you're in for a world of hurt.

He ploughed on through the tree line, one hand on his gun. He didn't plan on using it, he wanted the boy's death to be slow, but it was better to be prepared, in case the kid decided to do something stupid, like try and ambush him.

Right now, the boy would be feeling the beginning of the change. It would start to take hold soon and he would turn. The process was slow, and from all accounts – excruciating.

Van Gerrick could hear something up ahead. Was that a car?

He emerged at the side of a busy road to find his team already there.

"What is it?" he asked Temple, his second in command.

"I think I know where he might have went, sir," Temple said. He pointed out across the road.

Van Gerrick climbed higher to find a hospital on the other side of the road.

"He wouldn't," Van Gerrick said.

52

"He was injured, he's desperate."

"If he turns in there, then he will be breaking the cardinal rule of the Pack. We can't let anyone see him turn; if everyone finds out about them, there'll be major panic. Find him, kill him fast."

***

Adele heard a low groan coming from the room the boy was in. He had a cut on his forehead and was favoring his ribs, but he wouldn't let anyone look at him.

"Can you tell me your name?" she asked.

He wouldn't look at her. He had dark brown hair and brown eyes. Skinny, he looked like he hadn't eaten a good meal in a while.

"Look, we can contact the police if someone is after you," Adele offered.

"No. No police. I need to get out of here."

"Not until the doctor has a look at you."

"I'm fine," he argued, but winced as he tried to sit up.

"My name is Adele," she said. If she could get him to open up, then she could figure out what was going on with him.

"Tom," he said softly.

"Okay, Tom. How about I clean that cut for you?"

He nodded slowly and she started cleaning the wound.

As she was placing a bandage over the cut, Tom doubled over, clutching his stomach.

"Are you okay? Are you going to be sick?" she asked.

He was breathing heavily, sweating.

"I need to leave," he said, trying to get off the bed. Instead he fell to the floor.

Adele rushed to help him up. "I'll get a doctor in here," she said as she helped him back onto the bed.

"No, I have to get outside."

"What's going on here?" Kerry asked.

"I think you should get the doctor. He's in a lot of pain," Adele said.

Kerry made a noise in the back of her throat and glared at Tom. She obviously thought he was faking it.

"The doctors are all busy. Someone will see him soon," she said.

Adele followed her out. "I really think something is wrong."

"Please, he wants another fix. Damn drug addicts, keep an eye on him or he'll probably try and steal them."

Adele rolled her eyes. She knew working in the ER could make a person cynical, but Kerry was taking it to extremes. She didn't know why, but she felt for the kid. He really was scared.

53

If Kerry wouldn't get someone to look at him, then she would. She found Dr. Kennedy stitching up a little girl's knee.

"Dr. Kennedy, I have a teenage boy in cubicle 4. He's experiencing abdominal pain and appears to be in a lot of pain. Could you take a look at him?"

"Yes, nurse. I'll take a look when I finish here," he said.

How hard was that? Adele thought.

There was a scream from Tom's room and Adele raced back to him. He staggered past her and fell onto the floor in the middle of the ER. On his hands and knees, he reared back and Adele heard the distinct sound of bones breaking.

"Oh my God," Adele said, she tried to get near Tom, but he lashed out and she fell back into a wheelchair.

She watched as his back arched in an unnatural angle. What the hell was happening to him?

Adele looked up to see Kerry watching too. Kerry crossed herself and backed away. Clearly this was something she had never seen in all her years of experience.

Dr. Kennedy came charging across the room, flanked by two orderlies.

"Hold him down," Dr. Kennedy ordered. He was going to administer another sedative, but the first one hadn't done much good.

The two orderlies attempted to pin him to the floor, but he kept writhing in agony. As Dr. Kennedy closed in on him, Tom struck him in the chest, sending him skidding across the floor on his ass.

Tom's right hand twisted and his nails began to grow in length until they resembled claws. He slashed one of the orderlies in the chest. The second one scrambled to his feet and ran.

Silence had descended on the ER as everyone watched the boy twist and change. He was growling and moaning, making an inhuman sound.

He twisted his head in Adele's direction and she fought the urge to scream. His face was distended, almost resembling a snout. His eyes had widened and were a sickly yellow color.

"Stop looking at me," he roared, but she couldn't look away.

It wasn't a boy before her, but something else. He was changing into something new.

His clothes shredded as his body expanded. Coarse black hair sprouted across his skin as his teeth fell onto the floor. In place of them were long canine teeth, wickedly sharp.

The whole transformation couldn't have taken more than a few minutes, but to Adele, it felt like an eternity. Finally, the moaning stopped and Tom rose up.

A monster stood before them, a beast.

54

It opened its enormous jaws and roared. People scattered, screaming, running. Even the orderly who was slashed managed to stagger out of there. Adele couldn't move. Her whole body was trembling, heart racing. This couldn't be real.

It turned toward her, saliva dripping down its face. As it took a step toward her, Adele had only one thought. *This is it, I'm going to die.*

An explosion of gunfire ripped through the air. The beast jerked wildly as bullets struck it. Blood and flesh spattered the floor and it fell, crashing onto the ground.

Adele was curled up into a ball now, not daring to move.

A group of men clad in black stepped forward, guns still drawn. They weren't cops, who the hell were they?

"Check it," one of them ordered.

A man crouched beside the beast and checked for vital signs.

"Dead," he confirmed.

The body spasmed and he jumped away.

"Relax," the apparent leader said, "Its reverting back."

Adele watched as the beast vanished and Tom reappeared, his body full of holes.

"What the hell was that?" Kerry demanded, standing up from behind the counter.

"It was a stunt. A trick, by a very dangerous man," the leader said.

"No," Adele whispered.

He looked down at her, "Excuse me?"

"No. That wasn't a stunt. He really changed into a monster," she insisted.

"No, ma'am. He used a special gas to create a hallucinogenic state."

Why was he saying this? Adele knew what she saw was real; it wasn't a hallucination or a man in a costume.

He kneeled down beside her. "Ma'am, I'm sure you understand how insane that would sound, if you were to share your story with the media. I'm sure you enjoy your job, your life as it is? What do you think would happen if you told your story?"

His voice was calm, but Adele knew a threat when she heard it. And he was right, who would believe her?

There are no such thing as werewolves. Right?

The men moved quickly and within fifteen minutes they had the body removed and the floor cleaned up. By the time the police arrived, they were gone.

Kerry helped Adele off the floor.

"What do we do? What do we say?" Adele asked.

Kerry shrugged helplessly, "It *will* sound crazy, if we tell them what we saw."

The police approached them. There were other witnesses, one of them was going to talk, but it didn't have to be her. She wasn't going to risk her career over this.

The full moon really did bring out the crazy, she just didn't want to be it.

BIO: S.K. Gregory was born in Lisburn, Northern Ireland, in 1985. She studied Media Studies in college and worked for a local magazine after leaving school. She now works for a television company. Her debut novel Daemon Persuasion was published by Mockingbird Lane Press, in 2013.

She has been writing since she was a child and loves the horror/fantasy genre. Her favourite authors are Kelley Armstrong and Stephen King.

REJECTED

JACK BANTRY

It had been one hell of a day for Tim. He arrived home from work at three in the afternoon, and went about his rituals. He took a can of Stella out of the fridge, cracked it open and took a swig of the cold amber liquid before making his way through the single storey bungalow he shared with his mother, to his bedroom at the rear of the property.

Once inside his den, he put the can of beer on the bedside cabinet and kicked off his work boots. He moved his Vans trainers out of the way so he could open his wardrobe door and grabbed the bong which was hidden away at the back. He retrieved his baggie of weed from a small pot on a shelf next to a Han Solo figure, and chucked it onto the bed.

Tim moved to his turntable on top of a cabinet containing his large collection of punk vinyl. He pulled out the first Rancid album and placed it on the turntable, lowered the needle and climbed onto the bed as the record crackled to life.

After loading up the bong, Tim took a hit and blew the pungent smoke out the window, then rolled onto the bed and laid back, head against the pillow.

He couldn't believe it. Fucking Blackie was back in the office. The bastard was laughing and joking like nothing had happened. Tim was pissed off. He wanted to punch the fucker's lights out. Fellow postman, Martin Blackwood had returned to work. Blackie had been suspended a month earlier after Tim's friend Rachel had accused him of rape. Tim couldn't get his head around how Blackie had gotten away with it. She wouldn't make it up and everyone knew Blackie was a pervert, bragging about bonking all the time. Tim hadn't spoken to Rachel since the incident, but there were no secrets in the office, the manager couldn't keep his mouth shut. It had been her day off work, and when Tim had returned from delivery, a policeman had been in the manager's office with Blackie. He was suspended, until today. Shit, Tim was furious. Rachel wouldn't answer her phone or return his text messages. She quit work and left town. The rumour was she'd moved to her parents down South. Supposedly, Blackie had left the office one morning to deliver the mail and had instead driven round to Rachel's.

When she answered the door, he had apparently forced his way in and attacked her. Blackie had denied it, said he never went to her house. *Why would she make it up and why would they believe him?*

Tim felt the effects of the weed. His body relaxed. He took another, longer swig of the beer and melted into his pillow. It wasn't long before he fell asleep.

***

Tim woke to the sound of his mother calling, tea was ready. Thursday evening was darts night, so after tea, he skinned up a joint for the journey into town, before walking the scenic route, along the river. A full moon illuminated the way. He passed a dog walker before taking out the joint and lighting up. It was a cold night, autumn had arrived, Halloween only a month away. Christmas would be here before long, bringing with it the busy period at work.

He savoured the weed, feeling it go to his head.

That fucker, Blackie, was still playing on his mind. Life wasn't fair.

Tim heard a rustling in the hedgerow to his left and could see a dog watching him pass. He hid the joint down by the side of his leg, looking around for the owner. The moon had disappeared behind some clouds so it was difficult to see, but the dog looked like a German shepherd. Tim hated dogs, being a postie it came with the job.

The canine started to growl. Could it smell that he was a postman? He often thought they could.

Or were they psychic?

The big German shepherd came towards him, growling that deep, feral growl from the back of its throat.

He could do without this!

Tim looked around, hoping the dog's owner would come to his rescue. The huge dog leaped at him. Tim panicked - a stoner's reflexes are never the quickest – and the dog impacted against his chest, knocking him to the floor. His first thought was he'd lost the joint, then he realised the dog was still coming for him.

The dog bit into his left shoulder before quickly backing off out of reach.

Fuck. You bastard!

It growled again and he prepared for it to pounce, but the dog turned and disappeared into the darkness.

The night was still, silent. Tim remained on his knees. He inspected his shoulder, feeling the bite. It was sore, tender. His favourite darts shirt was ripped. He could feel a sticky dampness where the dog had drawn blood.

Darts was off. He was shaken and needed to get back home to see

60

what damage had been done. Hopefully he wouldn't need stitches. He could do without a trip to the hospital.

Tim found the joint. A little crumpled, he straightened it out, sparked it up and cautiously made his way back along the river, towards home.

He couldn't believe he'd been bitten by a goddamn dog. They would take the piss at work.

***

When Tim got home he was fussed by his mother, she insisted he would need to go to the hospital, he was adamant he wouldn't.

He had a tetanus injection when he was bitten at work a few years earlier. All he needed was a hot bath. He would clean up the wound with some antiseptic cream. His mother worried, but it was only a dog bite.

Tim persuaded her to ring work in the morning to let them know he would be having the rest of the week off. He went straight to bed. Once in his room, he put on a Black Flag record and scrambled around in the wardrobe for the bong.

***

A month after the dog attack, Tim was back at work and all was forgotten – except when he encountered dogs delivering the mail. He spent the afternoon listening to records and getting stoned. After tea he showered, changed and headed out to his friend Stan's house, taking his darts and a 4-pack of Corona. On the way he passed trick-or-treaters. It was dark out. He could see the stars in the sky, and a full moon glowing above the houses.

There was a biting chill on the wind and he could see his foggy breath before him.

Tim walked down the driveway to the back of Stan's house. The garage light was on, meaning Stan would be in the garage, connecting his laptop to the sound system.

Tim pulled up the garage door.

"How's things?" asked Stan.

"Good, man. Looking forward to some arrows," replied Tim. "It's bloody cold tonight." He put the beers next to a pumpkin and got his darts out.

"What you been up to this week?" asked Stan.

"Nothing, just working," said Tim, "you?"

"Same. Got some cool tunes downloaded."

"We'll have to have a listen."

Tim preferred darts at Stan's to the pub. They could have a smoke with their drinks and listen to some cool tunes.

"You'll like these, Flamegriller." Stan proclaimed. It sounded a bit like Eminem to Tim, but with a West Yorkshire accent. Stan skinned-up a joint and Tim cracked open a bottle of beer. The top bounced on the concrete floor.

By nine o'clock Tim was winning 5-2. It was getting warm in the garage. He took over the laptop and put on some punk.

After a couple more games, Tim was feeling hot and started to itch. He needed some fresh air.

"Just gonna go to the toilet."

Tim lifted open the garage door and was met by the biting cold autumn wind. He went into the house to use the toilet before returning to the garage. He must have been coming down with something, he felt nauseous.

"You okay?" asked Stan.

"Feel a bit sick," replied Tim.

"You're not chucking a whitey?"

"Nah, don't be fucking stupid," he said. "I don't whitey!"

He didn't, not ever.

Stan laughed.

"My blood sugar must be running low," said Tim. "Do you have any Coke in the house, or anything with plenty of sugar in it?"

"Yeah, we should have. I'll go and have a look."

Stan returned with a Pepsi and a Mars bar. Tim consumed the fizzy drink and chocolate while Stan rolled another joint. Energy levels restored, Tim had a smoke and felt much better.

***

Another month passed and Tim sat on the patio in the back garden. His mother had gone out for an Italian meal with some friends from work. There'd been a few local drug busts and he couldn't get any weed so he sat with a can of Stella, watching the stars.

He stood searching out the North Star and the Plough. It was easy to locate the north because the London to Edinburgh train passed the town.

He heard a rustling in the shadows between properties, it sounded like it was over the fence, probably the neighbour's cat.

All of a sudden he began to feel hungry, starving.

God, am I gonna puke?

He was drained of energy.

Tim doubled up in the back garden under the twinkle of the stars.

He bit back a scream. It felt like his spine was breaking.

Holy Shit.

A feeling of terror washed over him.

The muscles along his back stretched, seemingly to breaking point, at the same time his spine changed shape. A sharp pain shot through his body. He fell down to all fours and stifled a moan. His hands elongated, the back of his hands and his fingers stretching out. The finger ends sprouted claws and the backs of his hands became thick with dark, bristly hair.

His ripped clothing fell from his body.

Tim felt a tension in his head, like it was stuck in a closing vice, a sudden bolt of pain between his eyes. His nose stretched out before him. God, he couldn't see anything. His head hurt. His vision came back, blurry at first. When it cleared, the whole perspective was wrong.

He felt like his body had been set on fire.

Tim felt exposed in the yellow glare of the outside light. He ran for the shelter of darkness and jumped the fence into next door's garden. Standing on the cold grass, he could feel the icy wind against his fur. His snout sniffed at new scents, feline. A cat sprinted across the lawn. He just stood and watched it go.

Tim slowly walked through the garden and out onto the back lane.

He took off through the shadows, squeezing past bushes, oblivious to the rose thorns scraping his sides, and on to the Flats - an area of fields that skirted that side of town, leading down to the river.

Tim's senses were on full alert to other animals in the darkness.

He was confused at what he had become, uncertain, hesitant. He shook it off and let himself run through the fields, a power flowed through his body.

Before he realised it he had come out at the other side of town, across the road from suburbia.

He heard the sound of a car approaching, it drove past without slowing. As it passed under a streetlight, he recognised the figure behind the steering wheel.

Blackwood.

It was a small town after all.

Tim chased after him, along the quiet street. Ahead, he saw the red brake lights appear on Blackie's car. It turned into a driveway.

Tim came to a stop in the next garden. The driver's door opened and Blackie climbed out. He was unaware of Tim standing in darkness, watching. Blackie smelled like he needed a shower, he'd probably been to the gym. It was something he bragged about at work.

Tim approached.

He hated Blackie more than anyone else on the planet. Tim could imagine the tears in Rachel's eyes when Blackie forced himself on her, the pain and humiliation. He wanted to gut the bastard.

Blackie was rummaging around in the back of the car. He pulled out a sports holdall. Tim leaped, pushing off his powerful hind legs. He slammed into Blackie, crashing into the back end of the car. Tim went into a frenzied attack, thrashing at the man. The sharp claws lacerated Blackie's chest, neck and face. Before he knew it he was guzzling on Blackie's throat, chewing on the flesh and slurping the warm, coppery blood.

***

The following month he didn't change. *What was happening?* Tim was confused. He expected it to be a full moon thing.

Had his encounter with Blackie really happened? The rumour was he'd been attacked by a wild animal.

Stan hadn't been able to get any weed all week and Tim needed a smoke. He walked down the back lane feeling anxious, not knowing whether he would turn into a man eating werewolf, or stay his super cool dweebo self. He'd been sitting at home watching re-runs of *Cheers* on TV when he started to feel hot despite the below zero temperature outside. When he started getting all itchy, he put on his Vans, grabbed his coat, and made his way to Stan's. *Hopefully he'll be getting some weed tonight.* No way did he want to hang about at home with his mother in the living room watching TV. He couldn't take the risk in case he *did* change.

Tim walked down the street, past the houses decked out for Christmas. He suddenly doubled up in agony. He arched his back as his spine cracked and changed shape. Tim managed to stumble into the shadows of a garden. His body burned. It felt like lava was flowing through his veins. His muscles stretched and his shoulder joints dislocated. Tim was thrown onto his knees, onto all fours, in time to see his hands shift into the paws of the beast that haunted his nightmares.

Once the change was completed, Tim flexed his new body and sniffed the air for any signs of danger. He ran through the bushes going from one garden to another, finally finding himself in the back driveway of Stan's house. The garage stood in darkness. Tim could smell the faint odour of his friend. He could also distinguish the scent of a dog. The scent was weak. Stan's neighbour had a dog, but there was no sound of its movement in the yard, it would probably be inside in front of the fire.

Stan's kitchen light came on. Tim slunk into the shadows of the driveway just as his friend stepped outside, triggering the outside light. Stan locked the back door.

Tim felt a desire burning up inside him. He lusted for something, his body craved it. Stan walked in Tim's direction. A fear suddenly broke out in Tim. He knew what he was about to do, but couldn't stop it. He tried to reel it in, to shout out a warning, but it resulted in a menacing growl. Stan looked up, seeing nothing in the darkness, but fearing the sound. Stan stepped back defensively, but he was no match for the beast. Tim leaped out of the shadows, knocking Stan to the ground. He lunged for Stan's throat, biting hard and ripping out his windpipe. Tim stood over his friend, flesh dangling from between his teeth, with a feeling of regret. He quickly threw

64

it off before feasting.

When he was finished, he turned his back on Stan and fled over the back fence, heading for the solitude of the Flats.

On all fours, he walked through the empty field which led to the river. No farm animals grazed here. It was a common place for dog walkers and he could smell the discarded faeces which lazy owners hadn't bothered to pick up. In the wind, he smelled a human and his canine. The wind was blowing in Tim's face so he knew where they were, but he didn't know which direction they were headed. He could feel the boiling blood flow through his body and his heart rate increased.

He set off in pursuit.

The frozen ground was hard under his padded paws, yet he hardly felt it. The wolf was an agile beast. The man and his dog had no chance against such a predator.

He could smell they were close.

Suddenly, Tim was distracted. There was something else out there with him, neither human nor canine. Tim was confused. Maybe a cow or sheep had escaped from a neighbouring field and wandered over to become supper. A fattened up sheep with its belly full of lamb would be a better alternative to the dog. Perplexed, Tim sensed danger. The hairs rose on his back. He growled, warning the other of his presence. He could hear movement, the padding of paws on the hardened earth. It was over near the road. Tim pursued his prey. It wandered onto the road. *Fleeing*? It could probably sense danger. When it passed under a streetlight he saw it was another wolf.

Was this the one which had changed Tim? The one he'd mistaken for a German shepherd?

He followed it over the road and through a garden, coming around a house. Tim went down the driveway and out on to the back lane. He was greeted by the flashing blue strobe of a police car. The street was busy. Tim sensed many people. He was back at Stan's. Tim had momentarily lost track of the other wolf and could hear people shouting, cries of terror.

He heard a gunshot, followed by a sudden pain in his hip.

Tim limped across the road and down another driveway. He could hear the pounding of feet on pavement. He'd quickly become the hunted. He needed to get through the garden and out onto the adjacent street.

Tim leaped over the back wall into another garden and made his way towards home.

***

The wolf was looking down at him, but Tim didn't feel threatened. For some reason he knew it couldn't get him.

Tim was dreaming.

If I'm stoned the wolf can't get in. I won't change. It suddenly dawned on him.

He awoke, laid in a puddle of blood on the kitchen's cold linoleum floor. There was a sharp pain in his hip. He was naked.

Back in the real world he found his mother, in her dressing gown, kneeling at his side.

She looked extremely worried.

The blood – his blood – was from the gunshot wound.

"Tim, what's happened?" she asked, verging on hysterics. "Have you been shot?"

"No mum," he lied. "How would I get shot? We live in Thirsk!"

"Goddammit, Tim! Don't lie to me. What have you been doing?"

Maybe he should lie to her; she sure wasn't going to believe the truth.

"I'm going to ring for an Ambulance," she said.

"No, please don't," he said, sounding desperate. "It'll be okay. The bullet went straight through."

She looked at him in disbelief.

"You've been shot!"

"Honestly, it'll be okay," he tried to reassure her. "It'll heal quicker than you think."

His mum looked confused.

"I need to put some dressing on it and get dressed. Then I'll explain everything."

And he did.

Tim started by telling her he was a stoner, which to his bemusement she knew already. Mothers weren't stupid. He told her about the dog attack, which she also knew about.

"What does this have to do with you ending up naked and all shot-up on my kitchen floor?"

"I'm getting to that bit, mum, but you need to hear it all."

He told her about the dog bite and how it healed miraculously, how he started to feel strange. He changed into a werewolf on a full moon and attacked a man, killed him. Then last night he changed and killed his friend.

"I've killed two people."

She was speechless and didn't seem to know what to make of it.

"When I was attacked, I was stoned. The werewolf didn't kill me. For some reason it didn't like the THC in my blood and it spat me out, but because I was bitten I was infected with the werewolf virus. When I'm stoned on a full moon I don't change, but the two times I killed, it was because I couldn't get any weed. Somehow the effects of the pot stopped me from changing."

His mum looked dumbstruck.

"I'll put the kettle on," she said.

66

Tim's father had died in a working accident eighteen months earlier. The company was found to be negligent and Tim's mum got a healthy pay-out. She didn't want to lose her son too, so they came up with a plan. She had used some of the money to pay off the mortgage, and she offered Tim the rest to flee to Amsterdam before either the police caught up with him, or he killed again.

That's how Tim ended up in the Dutch city. He arrived 2 weeks before the next full moon with enough money to tie him over for 6 months. In that time he had to find a job.

On arriving in Amsterdam, he worried the strain of cannabis would be different from that in England. In Thirsk, it was basically home grown. In Amsterdam, the weed was top grade. Would the skunk have the same qualities to regress the wolf?

That first full moon was the test. He spent the afternoon in a couple of coffeeshops, mingling with the tourists. It was January, the weather was cold, and in mid-week the city was quiet. Just as it started to get dark he walked to a *Wok-to-Walk*, for some noodles. He'd need all the strength he could muster. It could be a long night.

After his meal he walked down Warmoesstraat, looking just like any other English stoner visiting the city of sin. He stopped at a bar for a glass of Heineken.

He was thirsty.

Halfway through his drink a rowdy group came in. They were visiting Amsterdam on a stag weekend. He quickly drank up and vacated the bar.

Once back on the narrow street he looked up. The sky was clear. Stars twinkled. The ominous full moon glowed. He stepped up into another coffeeshop, the Greenhouse Effect, and bought a bag of the strongest weed and a couple of pieces of space cake. Tim wasn't taking any chances.

Two hours later, he found himself sat in the window seat, totally wasted, watching the world go by.

So far so good, but it was only 10pm, he wasn't tempting fate. He got up and staggered to the back of the room to get the water bong. He stumbled into a man sat at a table half way down.

He *was* stoned.

He got the bong, ordered a coffee and sat back down to consume more drugs.

At midnight, the bartender called time. Tim quickly loaded up the bong and took a hit before returning the smoking device to the bar. Amsterdam was awesome. He had no trouble getting any weed, unlike back in Thirsk. The memory of home brought back what he'd done to Stan. *Fuck,* he thought. Tim pocketed his lighter and the near empty bag of weed.

Outside, it was bitterly cold. He pulled the collar up on his denim jacket and stuck his hands in his pockets.

The other bars and coffeeshops had also turned out and, as he passed, he saw the staff sweeping up and wiping down. Tim passed Chickita's Sex Shop with its gaudy neon sign. Amsterdam was a different world, with a distinctly dirty undercurrent.

He walked down the dark street towards his flat.

Where had everyone gone so quickly?

Tim heard a muffled sound. He was walking past a cobbled side street. Someone huddled in a shop doorway, a vagrant. The person fell backwards into the street, flattening their cardboard box in the process. Something jumped out of the shadows onto the homeless person. *Someone was beating up a tramp*, thought Tim. He'd heard of homeless people getting beaten up for fun, but the attacker wasn't what Tim first thought. It let out a feral growl as it lacerated the vagrant's throat. *Jesus*, thought Tim. It was a big fucking dog. The beast must have heard Tim stumble in the street. It turned and moved towards him, allowing Tim a better view. It was fucking huge.

It was a wolf with a large snout, dripping blood and saliva.

Shit.

Tim turned and ran down the street, his feet pounding on the pavement. He chanced a look back to see the beast in pursuit.

He'd run away to Amsterdam to escape the beast within, but instead he'd run into another, only this one was a hell of a lot bigger.

Tim took a quick right and ran down an alley, only to find it ended in a closed courtyard used as an outdoor seating area for a restaurant. He looked around for a way out. *No! Shit, shit, shit!*

He turned around to face the wolf which slowly padded towards him. The wolf's head was low, lips drawn back to reveal razor sharp fangs. Red eyes pierced the darkness.

Change! Come on. Tim shook his hands, willing them to elongate and sprout thick bristly hair.

Dammit.

Nothing.

Please, he begged.

He set his legs apart and concentrated with all his will. Please, change. It was no use, he had a high concentration of THC flowing through his veins.

The creature was still creeping forward, it crouched low, ready to pounce. Tim readied himself for the inevitable. He just hoped this one would reject him like the one before. Only one way to find out.

BIO: Jack Bantry is the editor of Splatterpunk Zine. He works as a postman and resides in a small town at the edge of the North York Moors.

WOLFSKULL

JUAN J. GUTIERREZ

I am a Lonely God

I bled this world of wolfen gods,
Beneath a weeping crimson moon.
This night I hold an ancient skull,
Whose primal secrets by moonfire blooms.

I hear the olden howls through fractured bone,
Transforming by nocturnal light.
Recounting secrets by dead-speak told,
Of magic born in moonlit night.

Wolfskull of my mother goddess,
Whom held me deep inside with love.
Only I can hear her lunar doctrines,
Ways of the Wolf, by the gods undreamed of.

I listen to every ghostly word
I, apprentice of this skull's mystique,
Bow my head and whisper
'Speak Mother, speak …'

You were the Master of the Moon

BIO: Juan J. Gutiérrez lives in Desert Hot Springs, California with his loving wife and daughters. His poetry and stories have appeared in anthologies published by Static Movement, Horrified Press, Sirens Call Publications and Dead Guns Press. He is the Assistant Editor for Barbwire Butterfly Press and is overseeing the Robert E. Howard inspired anthology "Barbarian Crowns." He has appeared most recently in the horror western anthology, "Badlands," by Dead Guns Press. You can find him on his facebook page:

www.facebook.com/deadgrinwriter

PERSPECTIVE

ROMA GRAY

John stepped up to the wrought iron gate, staring up at the ancient old house. He absentmindedly ran his hand along the gate, barely acknowledged the rust and peeling black paint that cut into his skin. Harsh memories had flooded into his skull and to all else he was blind.

Forty-five years ago—no, fifty! —this house appeared huge and terrifying. This was the local haunted house that lurked in the nightmares of every child within a ten-mile radius. Now, it just looked like an empty, old Victorian home to him; maybe even a good fixer-upper. His perspective had completely changed over the many long years.

Of course, that was what had brought him here: Perspective.

John released the gate and walked past the house. The house didn't interest him; what he came for lay beyond. He followed the sidewalk for another twenty feet, then turned to the right, taking a dirt path that led behind the house and down into a deep ravine. As he descended into the forest, he held to his chest a large photo album. His grip grew uncomfortable, but he continued to cling tightly to the album as though it were his life preserver. In many ways, that's what it was—or rather soon would be.

He remembered the day he and his friends decided to explore the house, the week before Halloween. He was eight years old, and they had planned this for weeks. *Silly, who goes to a haunted house before Halloween?* he thought. *What did we think they were going to do on Halloween to top that?* He couldn't recall. But that's how it all played out. So stupid. His mom caught him in the driveway before he even got inside. With a vice-like grip on his ear, she pulled him away from the house and lectured him about disobeying her for the entire block and half walk home. And that, as they say, was all she wrote.

Or so he had thought...

His friends hid, several in the house, but not Franky. He ran into the forest, down the very path John traveled now.

Shadows grew long, and the air turned colder as he walked down the steep grade. In the distance, he heard the gurgle of a stream, hidden beneath the lush verdure. The loud crunch of his feet on the gravel path raked at his nerves; the last thing he wanted to do was announce his approach.

The day after their adventure at the haunted house, all of his friends were at school, excitedly talking about what they'd seen. A creepy portrait of old Prof. Black, staring down at them from above the fireplace; a red stain (blood from one of his victims?) on the bedroom floor; dead rats the size of small dogs in the basement; and Pete even claimed to have seen a ghost of the professor himself. All of them chattered endlessly—that is, all except Franky. He remained stone-cold silent.

As a child, John barely noticed. He was in little kid heaven, listening to the creepy stories, never imagining anything was wrong. But now, as an adult, John realized that while the other kids were only spinning tall tales, something had actually happened to Franky; he was the one with the real story to tell.

Perspective. Amazing how much of a difference something as simple as a change in perspective could make in one's life. It told you things, important things. Perhaps even things you didn't want to know.

John reached the bottom of the ravine and had to stop, his lungs aching from the effort. A ragged cough ripped through his chest, and he dropped the photo album to the ground. Staggering over to a nearby tree, he let the coughing fit exhaust itself. As the painful choking subsided and his lungs began to work once more, he continued to lean against the moss covered bark and examined the forest around him. It was here somewhere, just as Franky's sister had described to him on the phone the previous night. But where?

Over the years, Franky changed from being a happy, gregarious kid to being a withdrawn loner. A few more years passed and at the ripe old age of twelve, he started sneaking bottles of alcohol to school. By the age of fifteen, his locker was filled with harder stuff requiring pipes and needles. Franky never made it to adulthood; he died from an overdose three months before his eighteenth birthday.

John didn't understand the change in his friend at the time; in fact, he barely noticed. He was too busy battling his own case of depression. That's just what happens to kids when their mother suddenly disappears off the face of the earth.

It was Halloween, and when he came home after school, she was simply gone. Recently baked cookies lay abandoned on top of the stove, and a bowl of cookie dough waited patiently on the counter for their turn in the oven—which the police noted had been turned off. No sign of a struggle, the car was still in the driveway, and her purse sat untouched on the entry table. The police never found anything.

John's mind returned to the past few nights: long hours of research on the internet and calling Franky's relatives until he finally found one who

74

would talk. It fit, all of it. The local disappearances and strange animal attacks over the past fifty years, Franky's depression, and John's mom vanishing—it all fit.

He forced himself to push free of the tree, and he slowly walked up to the photo album lying in the dirt and gravel. John took in several deep breaths to steady himself and then bent over to pick up the heavy book. As he did so, to his surprise, he felt a cool breeze brush his cheek and he looked up. A fern frond waved gently in the breeze. He picked up the photo album as he slowly walked toward the fern, reaching down to pull loose a clump of long brown hair. The hair strands felt thick and course.

John nodded. He found it; this was where Franky hid that day.

He stood for a long moment, staring at the moving fronds, knowing his last chance to change his mind had arrived. He could be wrong about how this would turn out; in fact, there was a very good chance he would be wrong. And if he was wrong...

Still comes down to perspective, he reminded himself. *Even if you're wrong, what do you have to go back to? Your fate is the same either way.*

John pushed forward through the shrubbery until he located what he knew he would find: the opening of a cave. Just as Franky's sister described to him last night, and just as Franky had described to her fifty years before.

Within the cave, he could make out several tall boulders, but beyond that only darkness. Somewhere in the mysterious depths, the sound of running water echoed against the rock walls. A cool breeze, no doubt generated by the running water, carried a musky canine scent. The smell, more than anything, confirmed he had found the right place.

As his eyes adjusted to the dim light, he noticed movement. Shadows with angry red eyes took shape among the tall boulders, and a chorus of throaty growls began.

"My name is John Niles! John Brian Niles!" he shouted into the darkness as he pulled out a flashlight, turned it on and pointed it into the cave. "I'm 58 years old, and I used to live up the street!"

The light struck the first creature; a large wolf head snarled back at him from behind the rocks. More wolf heads emerged. He could see a hand as well, a human shaped hand covered in fur, with deadly, black talons on the end of each finger.

"Fifty years ago, my friend Franky hid down here when my mom showed up to pull me away from the old house up at the top of the ravine," he continued, expecting the cowering creatures to come out. They didn't, but the growls persisted. "He saw a man down here, tied up and helpless, surrounded by a group of men and women. Then he saw the people change, turn into werewolves and tear the man apart! You're the reason we've had disappearances in this area for over two hundred years: the lost children, runaway teens and missing homeless—it was you!"

The growls escalated, and one of the creatures rose above the rocks, standing on two hind legs like a human. Around the creature's neck was a startling flash of color. John focused his flashlight beam on the object; a collar made of braided blue and white material.

John briefly smiled. The braided collar and neatly tied knot indicated intelligence and awareness. This was a good sign.

"I never understood it, never got it until I was babysitting my granddaughter two weeks ago," he said, feeling his voice breaking as more of the creatures rose. He moved the flashlight from wolf to wolf. Green cloth collar, yellow cloth collar... "It was her birthday, and she didn't come home from school. I knew where my granddaughter was, she had snuck off to her boyfriend's house again. So I grabbed my keys to go get her and then I stopped..."

John gasped and held the flashlight steady as the beam hit the pink color. He stared at it a long time: a pink background with red and white flowers. Memories fade, but he wasn't wrong, he knew it. The braided material was from his mother's favorite apron—the one that his mother always wore when she baked cookies.

"And that's when I knew...I knew what had happened to you that day, mom," John said, stumbling forward. "I came home late from school on Halloween. I never told dad or the police; I didn't want to get into trouble, and I didn't think it mattered. But it did matter. Because you must have thought I returned to the old house, so you came to get me. Instead, they caught you and took you away from dad and me. I thought maybe they had killed you, but I knew there was a chance—the slightest chance, but a chance—that you became one of them. And I was right! I AM right!"

The growling began to die away, slowly replaced by a startling new noise: crying. Not just from his mother, but from several of the other werewolves as well. Shocked, John looked at each one, realizing only the ones wearing the braided fabric collars were crying. The others simply bowed their heads or grumbled in apparent disgust. John now understood.

They all had families, somewhere out there, somewhere lost in the past. And all had been forced to walk away from their loved ones when they became werewolves. Some of the werewolves, the ones without collars, had accepted this and moved on. But not the ones with collars. The braided fabric wasn't just a souvenir from their days as a human: it signified mourning for their past lives.

John imagined what it would have been like for those in mourning. Living away from society, living in the darkness of the cave, with nothing to think about except what they had lost. No doubt each one spent many long hours fantasising about encountering their children, husband, wife, mother or father again. And now, probably for the first time ever, their fantasy became a reality. John arrived, looking for his mother.

His arrival, surely, was both Heaven and Hell to them. The joy of seeing their friend reunited with her son, intermixed with the pain of it not being their own child.

John suddenly realized he had a new problem.

He had won over the werewolves with collars, he harbored no doubt about that. But the other werewolves now eyed him with resentment.

What was his arrival to them? Having lost all hope themselves, listening to the whining of the others in their pack, must have been irritating, even aggravating. Unfounded hope can be poison, and, no doubt, the pack had struggled with this problem for years. Now what would happen? Would some of the pack fall into a deep depression? Worse, would some of them try to leave and reach out to their own relatives?

Without meaning to, John had dropped an emotional bombshell on the entire pack, igniting an already volatile situation. This could completely destroy his plans.

For a moment, he almost laughed. Of all of the challenges he expected to face—being attacked by the creatures, his mother not recognizing him, not finding his mother at all—social dynamics was the one challenge he never, ever, would have anticipated.

But it was too late to go back now...

Returning the beam to his mother's face, she turned away, shaking her massive head.

"Grrooo. Go," she said, pointing to the mouth of the cave. "Can't herllp...me..."

"Mom, I'm dying," said John, walking toward his mother, who turned back to look at him, shock etched in her eyes. "And I've read the old Native American legends in this area. They knew of your kind and said you were immortal. It's true, isn't it?"

"Nrrot worth...yrou will become murrdererr...," she replied, beginning to back up into the cave.

John moved faster, not allowing her to increase the distance between them. "But there haven't been any disappearances in years. You've found a way to curb your bloodlust, haven't you? I suspect it has something to do with one of the missing victims cashing out a very large savings account a few days after she was reported missing. What is it? Special herbs or potion? Chains to prevent you from going on the hunt? A cooler of sirloin steaks? Something sure changed. That kind of money can make a lot of difference, can't it?"

A few of the werewolves nodded, and his mother ceased her advance into the shadows.

Am I reaching her? he wondered. *Can I sway her?*

"I cashed out my 401k and sold the house months ago when I found out I was terminal," he continued. "It's all in my checking account. I can get the money anytime."

This caught all of their attention; hopeful eyes turned to John's mother.

Again, his mother began to shake her head. "Nrroo, trapped…like us."

"I know—I know I will never be able to return to my old life. That's why I brought my life with me." John held up the photo album. "Let me stay here, let me become one of you. Mom, I can show you your grandchildren, and your great-grandchildren! We'll spend eternity together, going over old photos, living the life you gave me when you pulled me from this place."

His mother gasped, and the other werewolves began to cry harder, which soon turned into a deafening chorus of howls. Then suddenly, the howling stopped.

A footfall. Soft and stealthy. Someone had just entered the cave behind him.

John whirled around. Standing in the doorway was the largest werewolf of all. Covered in black hair with an enormous build, this one was clearly the alpha male. The creature didn't growl or cry; he merely looked down at John quizzically.

Holding his ground in the middle of the cave, halfway between the alpha male and his mother, he stated with all of his strength and conviction: "I'm not here to threaten you or your pack. I came to be with my mother. Turn me as you have turned the others. I promise to obey your wishes."

At first the alpha male said nothing, staring hard at John. The small human directed his eyes down; knowing to make eye contact could be perceived as a challenge. The alpha male then gave a slow nod and moved toward John.

John smiled, knowing he had succeeded and patiently waited for his fate. Joy filled his heart as he realized he would be with his mother now. All the missed opportunities to tell her he loved her, all the lost years, all the pain and regret—none of it mattered anymore. He could say it all, tell her everything. They had eternity together, and nothing would get between them again.

Caught up in his joy and triumph, he didn't detect the swift movement from behind. With a loud snap, his neck was broken, and darkness fell like a curtain.

***

Julie, now in human form, leafed through the photo album, touching the face of each of her relatives and reading the descriptions under each photograph. She spent fifty years wondering about them, believing in her heart she would never know what became of them, and now...

A tear drop landed on one of the plastic-covered pages, followed by another and then another. A small pool formed over the smiling face of her son, John, the tears magnifying and distorting his features. Julie roughly wiped her hand across the page and then across both of her eyes. As before, she forced an expression of cold determination on her face and focused her mind on the album

"They have taken the body of your son out into the woods to bury," said Amanda, accusation in her voice.

"You're surprised by my decision," said Julie, not bothering to look up. "Say the words, Amanda. You cannot hurt me today. I'm...beyond feeling now," she said, knowing only too well that her earlier tears revealed the truth.

"He made his decision!" argued Amanda, sitting down next to her on one of the smaller boulders. "His money would have made the pack stronger, and he wanted to join us! But you killed him, killed your own son! How could you do such a thing? What gave you the right?"

"What gave me the right?" Julie let out a strangled, half manic laugh, as she turned to look hard into Amanda's perplexed eyes. "We live in hell, Amanda! We're trapped in this pack for eternity, howling at the moon and hungering for human flesh! I know he thought he made the right decision but he didn't know, he didn't understand. Having lived it myself for the past fifty years...," she paused and then finally added. "I guess I just had a different perspective."

BIO: Roma Gray began writing at the age of 8 and wrote her first novel when she was 13. Her two published books are "Gray Shadows Under a Harvest Moon" (short story collection) and "The Hunted Tribe: Declaration of War" (novel).

Her favorite holiday of the year is Halloween. This is why she writes what she refers to as 'Trick-or-Treat Thrillers', stories with a Halloween feel about them.

She lives in Oregon with her two cats, dog and parrot.

Please visit her website (http://trickortreatthrillers.com) to see her list of published books, short stories and upcoming novels.

OF GODS AND BEASTS

KEVIN CANDELA

Pan was coming.

The word had spread quickly, and just like that the Lupercalia had quadrupled in size. After all, it was one thing to see the masters at this three day event: Zeus Lykaios, the great Zeus (he was simply called Zeus because he was master of all things), Apollo Lykaios, even "plain" Apollo (Apollo meant caretaker) – these supernatural beings were expected to roam around at the festivities. But the goat god's promised appearance heralded rare, strange things.

Not that strange wasn't already present at the gala in abundance.

Zeus and Apollo were discreet, at least by the standards of their animalistic counterparts. Neither tended toward violence, but then again, when your own will can bend that of lesser beings, physical force hardly need come into play most of the time.

Most knew why Pan was due: this year the Lupercalia fell during a full moon. All things here that were normally extreme would be even more so. Pan was an experimenter. He wanted to see how far humans would go. Under the light of a full moon and the lust of Lupercalia, well – anything was possible. And Pan wanted to see it in half-person.

What he'd seen before, in those ages-ago times, the days before the people had been taught by the gods how to draw the metals from the ground and cut and grind the stone to shelter themselves, was contained in the goat god's nearly perpetual Mona Lisa smile. Once in a while he'd grin, showing the whitest teeth imaginable, stained lavender with Bacchus' elixirs, short bone-white horns gleaming under the blazing moon. But mainly he just sort of smiled.

His arrival could be heard across the silvery meadow in the form of a breeze-like commotion passing through the expectant partygoers. As he passed by them, slowly, each woman he made eye contact with shed her clothes immediately and displayed herself before Pan – and indeed all – as though for inspection. A few of the less heterosexually inclined men disrobed as well, even though not one of them had caught Pan's eye.

Pan would occasionally nod approval to a nude female figure, but so far he hadn't.

He moved along in silence on glistening ebony hooves, making his way to the sacred steam pool at the center of the gathering of hundreds. Coming to a halt a few steps shy of the pool's edge, he turned to see the half-naked partygoers closing in around him. Many of their faces were smiling and vacant.

But not all of them.

Nyctimus made sure to stay well back in the crowd. Beside him his sister Olivia, fully clothed, surveyed the crowd, studying what almost seemed to be mass hypnosis.

"I shouldn't have brought you."

"What do you mean, brother?"

"I didn't know Pan would be here."

Olivia's slender young face was still quite appealing despite being crimped with confusion. "Is that bad?" she said. "Should we go?"

"Perhaps," Nyctimus said. He took hold of his younger sister's hand and edged back, drawing her gently with him.

They both bumped into people at the same time.

"Hello, Nyc," Garimon said. "You're not leaving, are you? Pan just got here."

"Yes," Harimus said. "And your sister here sure can't leave. Not until Pan meets her."

Nyc swallowed hard. He was as tall as either of his peers but both of them were sailors and as such, sea-hardened and muscular. Neither one was making eye contact with him because both were making no bones about looking Nyc's slender and tender teen sister up and down like one of the nearby spit-roasting sheep.

Mustering all the authority he could, Nyc tried to get the lustful young men to quit sizing Olivia up.

"Hey," he said, "we weren't leaving. We just couldn't see too well from here."

Olivia had moved up to Nyc's side and was lightly pressing against him. Her hand felt cold in his. Harimus shifted his gaze and took a gander toward the pool, where half a dozen nude women were lining up in hopes of being chosen by Pan as "first" for the night.

"I can see just fine," he said.

"Yeah," Garimon said, imitating his buddy. "Me too."

"She's a lot shorter than us," Nyc said.

"Fine," Garimon said, and he lunged quite abruptly at Olivia.

She squealed as his strong hands seized her slim arms before a surprised Nyc could even react. In an instant she was hoisted off the ground, whirled around – Garimon was a beast – and set down across his broad shoulders. She wriggled hard but he held her firmly there as the crowd found a new – if momentary – focus for their lascivious curiosities.

"There," Garimon said. "Stay still, girl. You can see what's going on now."

"Oh, to have a mouth in the back of your neck right now, eh Garimon?" an obviously envious Harimus said, making Olivia wiggle even harder.

It was right about then both young men realized that even Pan was staring at them.

Garimon showed less concern at having drawn attention from the god than most of the others there might have in the same spot, but then again he was known for being tough, not wise. Still, Pan was hardly the kind not to appreciate a lustful male "celebrating" Saturnalia by the forceful taking of a girl perhaps not yet even familiar with mystique of sex.

"Excuse me, O Great One," Garimon said. "Got carried away with Lupercalia."

After a devastatingly silent second or two Pan relented. He grinned.

He even did a wondrous goat laugh that resonated throughout the valley.

The crowd loved it.

Olivia found herself stuck, pressured by the crowd and Pan himself, albeit indirectly, not to keep fighting to get off the hulking young man's shoulders. After all, he wasn't trying to fondle her up there – at least not yet. She reluctantly settled down, glaring at her helpless brother, and as soon as she wasn't bucking around up there anymore, Garimon slipped his grip down to her pale upper legs just above her knees.

Pan went back to his show, approaching each of the women in turn – there were at least a dozen now – and sniffing them over from neck to thigh.

Olivia tolerated Garimon's kneading palms and fingers, even as they slowly worked their way back up her legs. Nyctimus stood by, staring at those greedy hands, knowing they could just as easily kill him. And here at Lupercalia, murder, like other carnal indulgences, was generally considered "heat of the moment" reaction and thus overlooked. He wanted to protect his sister, but not at the cost of his life.

Pan was checking out a rare blonde, obviously one down from the northern provinces of Italy (or the mountains beyond), when a great howl caught his attention as it raised gooseflesh across the entire gathering.

Zeus Lykaios was coming.

To meet Pan.

This would be the supreme moment of the event if such occurred, and it would indeed be very rare in that the festivity was just beginning. This was the first night. Normally a meeting between the host and his most special of guests would be saved for the final night, or at least the second.

The implications left the crowd muttering uncertainly as the resonant wolf bay faded away.

Zeus Lykaios was an enormous being. More than anything he appeared to be the Great Hairy Man of legend, the primitive root of all human beings. His great mane of thick, curling black locks and his equally dense beard made the near giant's head seem even huger than it was, and beneath this mountainous peak of hair and broad features swayed an exaggerated form of sheer muscle and sinew, covered in at least half an inch of hair from neck to toe.

Zeus Lykaios never wore clothing, and his great masculine appendage commanded almost more respect than the god's face as he strode down from the southern crest of the valley wall toward Pan and the pool.

Old god and new god met at the center of a warily respectful and thus quite wide circle of humans. There was no contact, merely a standoff "duel of nods."

"Old friend," Zeus Lykaios said. "Thank you for coming."

"With all due respect," Pan said, "I haven't yet."

Lykaios roared with laughter.

Garimon's fingers crept in toward their common target.

Lykaios walked up to the row of volunteering women and seemed to relish as they backed away from his approach.

"You've made fine selections," Lykaios said to Pan. "May I have one?"

"Of course, old friend," Pan said. "Your choice."

Lykaios moved slowly up the line, looking over each woman in turn. He didn't take the most attractive, nor did he take the most admirably built.

He took the most fearful.

The crowd gathered around the terrified redhead, clutching at her nude body and pressing her toward the broadly grinning Lykaios.

"She already tastes delicious," he said. "Thank you."

He stepped up and snatched her effortlessly away from her detainers. She screamed.

His body hair grew. His "godhood" became lethal.

His face stretched.

The crowd moaned with awe. King Lykaios' head was that of a huge, snarling wolf: a monstrous wolf, with a maw wide enough to fit a head into it.

That's exactly what happened. He waited until his "chosen one" was at her most terrified, shrieking her lungs out and casting spittle into his long, toothy snout, and then he crammed that screaming head right into his mouth and bit it off.

The woman's neck pumped blood like a fountain as her body convulsed in Lykaios' grip. The crimson spray doused the beast god's face and he reveled in the fountain, shaking his brutish head and flinging droplets of spilt life fluid across those in the front of the crowd.

Lykaios raised the body and devoured one of the dead woman's large breasts, ripping it away and swallowing it in a single bite.

The crowd went wild.

Harimus dropped back behind Garimon, seized hold of Olivia and jerked her off his friend's back. Garimon's fingers had just reached their destination, fighting off Olivia's all the way. Neither expected her to be pulled away and one of them was quite angry about it.

Garimon spun around, his eyes full of rage. Harimus had one big arm wrapped around Olivia and he was ramming his tongue down her throat while his free hand did a lustful survey of her small but flawless breasts through the flimsy fabric of her tunic.

"Hey!" Garimon bellowed. "MINE!"

He tried to pry her away but Harimus held him off with that same free hand and looked him right in the eyes.

"Share?" he said.

"NO!" Nyctimus and Olivia yelled at exactly the same time.

"Back off, Nyc," Garimon said. "Your sis will love this."

Nyc wasn't about to back off. He grabbed hold of his sister, a third pair of hands on her, and put all his effort into freeing her.

Garimon pulled out his father's war dagger and stabbed Nyc in the gut.

Olivia screamed.

But there was screaming all around. Lykaios and Pan had started something, and it was sweeping through the crowd.

Amok time. Mayhem. Grab what you want, no regrets.

One handsome, innocent looking young man near where Nyc fell saw him but could do little to help because five women twice to three times the teen's age were ripping his clothes off and fighting for control over his genitalia. Next to that scene, Nyc saw before things began to swirl, two young women were sexually assaulting a third who didn't seem too happy about it. A naked young man rushed up and threw himself bodily into that scrum, apparently wanting to help the two women out with the third.

Nyc looked back to where Garimon and Harimus had been fighting over his sister like two hungry dogs over a bone, but they had all vanished.

Then the world faded away.

But not for Olivia.

Garimon and Harimus were looking for room. With people flopping all over the ground, in piles (and in some odd cases alone), there was nowhere nearby. Pulling Olivia along between them with death clamps on her wrists, they ignored her bawling and cries for her fallen brother and focused on finding a place where they could savage the girl at their leisure for as long as they wished.

Lupercalia, you know.

Olivia's eyes, blurred with tears, locked onto the moon. It was so immense. So commanding of attention. She was set down on cold ground but she didn't notice the damp grass on her back and butt because the moon was holding her in its grip.

She felt her clothes being pulled away, more and more of her body being exposed, but it didn't matter. One of the men pressed his weight down atop her, and all she did was move her head to one side so that she could continue to stare at the moon.

The other man was behind her head, holding her wrists together between his knees. Olivia didn't know if that was Harimus or Garimon and it didn't matter. The one on top of her was forcing her bare legs farther apart.

And then she howled.

She was barely aware of anything. Just the moon. But something was happening. The bulk of either Harimus or Garimon was suddenly off her, and both men's voices came to Olivia's ears, soaked with fear.

Olivia was on her feet.

She saw Harimus ahead of her. He was running...away.

Away from her.

She spied Garimon a moment later. He was even farther from her, and staring back over his shoulder at her with a look that could only be described as mortal dread.

Some kind of strange instinct took over then, nothing the young adolescent had ever felt before. She went after them.

She had always had speed. She could run like the wind.

She hadn't always had power though.

The next thing she knew Olivia was on Garimon, taking him down while her erstwhile assailant could do little but slap at her and scream hysterically, his voice screwed up high like a little girl's.

Her claws slashed at his torso, shredding his flesh. She lunged down. Her fangs ripped into his face and came away with a good portion of it while his screams drowned in Garimon's mouthful of blood.

The moment she could tell – by *feel*, in fact – that Garimon wasn't going to get back up, she was up and off him and after Harimus.

Slowed noticeably by a shocked erection that had just suffered a last-second derailment of the worst possible kind, he was no match for the galloping Olivia. She took him down, flipped him over and in a single bite removed Harimus' still half-swollen member and associated hardware as well. He shrieked, but not for long because her next bite ripped out his throat.

She left him dying like Garimon and rushed back down to her brother.

Nyc was dead. She was too late.

86

She let out a plaintive howl so potent as to actually interrupt the combination "take your pick" orgy of sex and/or blood.

Pan and Lykaios came over to her.

It was at that moment, as she saw both deities approaching, that Olivia realized that her entire body was covered in dense canine hair. Her form had solidified as well, slim and elegant sinew and muscle replaced with the hard body of the human-shaped wolf she had become. She looked down at her bloody claws, tasted the salt on her broad lips and realized at last the change that she had undergone.

Lykaios smiled at her. He raised one hand.

"Hail sister of the Fold," he said. "I regret the loss of your kin, yet such is the way."

Standing beside him, fully erect and not a bit abashed, Pan was grinning at her.

He raised a hand as well and Olivia instantaneously morphed back into the form of a young girl, albeit one whose lower face, hands and wrists were painted in blood that glistened in the moonlight.

"Impressive, my dear," Pan said. "I too mourn the loss of your brother. But tonight you have found yourself."

"What do you mean?" Olivia said. "I just killed two people."

"Wolves defend themselves when attacked," Lykaios said. "It's natural. How did it feel to you?"

"What do you mean?"

She'd forgotten all about him being a god in her confusion, and was in fact treating both of them more as peers than the special entities they were, but neither god seemed too upset about the lack of respect.

"I mean did it feel wrong?"

To her own great surprise she wasn't able to say yes, as she surely thought she would. She in fact didn't say anything.

"From this day on," Lykaios said, "during the three days of the full moon you will be able to assume the form of the lycan and thus be endowed with the spirit – and shape – of our animal kindred. You can't control it yet, so you will have to be careful because the transformation is rooted in emotion. But soon you will, and then it will be a great asset to you. It will protect you. It simply wouldn't do for a daughter of Lykaios to have to tolerate ravaging from mere mortals, after all."

"Agreed," Pan said. "She'll have to find a worthy ravager out there."

Processing it all at once, or trying to, it took Olivia a moment to fix upon one word of Lykaios' in particular.

"*Daughter?*"

Lykaios smiled. "Your mother is a fine woman," he said. "We had a moment. Apparently it has produced something of both great beauty and potential."

Olivia looked around them. The ground was covered in revelers, some spent, others still spending. There were no wolf-people anywhere in sight.

"What is this all about?" she finally asked the deities standing before her.

Pan and Lykaios looked to one another momentarily; then Lykaios turned to her.

"Mankind fights its own nature," he said. "In trying to leave behind the animal, they leave behind too much. Lupercalia reminds them of the importance of their animal nature, how critical such things as lust and release are to their essences. It is the rebirth of desire, and as you have just seen, it is not all love and kindness."

"Why am I the only one here who became – whatever I became?"

"These are not all my children," Lykaios said. "Only you are that. As your offspring will be as well. You will have to teach them. You can teach them – when they reach adulthood, as you just have – and you can guide them to good or evil at your whim. None of us – not Pan, not myself, not even Great Zeus – influence or indeed tend to concern ourselves with such things. You are a standard bearer, daughter. You and your lineage will embrace the animal nature of your being, even as those around you grow ever more insulated from it with each passing generation."

"I…" Olivia said. "I didn't ask for this."

"Are you certain of that?"

"What do you mean?"

"I mean, my dear, that you will know more in due time: tonight has been enough of a revelation for you as it is. Bathe yourself clean in the pool and then take some time to walk around here and study the humans. Learn them. Prepare yourself to live among those whose connections to nature are not as strong as yours. Remember as you look upon them that they are weak, and decide soon if you would use this weakness for your own ends or put your strengths to use defending them from those who would."

Olivia's pretty brow furrowed. "You encourage both those who would prey on the weak and those who would defend the weak against predators?"

Pan and Lykaios looked to one another again. Both shrugged.

Pan turned to Olivia. "That's the way Nature works," he said. "Balance."

Lykaios nodded, looking at his daughter as well.

"Indeed," he said. "And there exists a third path as well."

Olivia's perplexed look was threatening to become permanent.

"Really?" she said.

"Yes," Lykaios said. "After giving it a reasonable amount of consideration, you can simply choose to bypass both predating them and defending them and just ignore the fools."

BIO: "We're all part one animal and part another, I think," Kevin Candela says. "Some of us may even be several kinds of animals, tossed in together mind-wise a la Being John Malkovich...if not indeed body-wise as well. Maybe that's how DNA works." Reaching back to the roots of lycanthropic legend for his tale Of Gods and Beasts, Candela says he was trying to get a handle on the entire modern werewolf phenomena...its various facets, its offshoots, its possibilities. A big fan of mythology since he had the strength to haul his grandparent's encyclopedias down off the bookcase and peruse them, he "went for the big picture before it got too big." His favorite lycanthropy movie is An American Werewolf in London, "because the star and I looked a lot alike at the time" he jokes. "But the Wolfman--Lon Chaney, Jr., that is, the way I always picture him--has always been one of the coolest monsters." In addition to his Dragon's Game Trilogy, featuring Mushroom Summer, The Ballad of Chalice Rayne and Dragon's Game, Candela's expanding catalog includes Sinbad and the Argonauts, Sinbad and the Winds of Destiny: The First Six Voyages and More (a tribute anthology he assembled and edited), Weedeaters: The Complete Acropalypse, the horror collection A Year in the Borderlands and quite a few short stories featured in sf, fantasy, horror and comedy anthologies. Upcoming releases include Sinbad at the End of the Universe and Little Women With Big Guns.

ALICE & THE WONDERWOLF

T.S. WOOLARD

"Why can't I see Lizzy? I'm getting tired of being told I can't see her," Alice lashed out at the doctors and orderly wrapping her arm around her back in a white, canvas jacket. The multitude of buckles and loops told her it was the same garment they brought her to the therapist's office in: the straightjacket.

That damn jacket followed her all over the institution, it seemed. It came in with her three years ago, and it travelled with her from one hall to the other. It wasn't a fashion choice, either.

"We have worked and worked and worked for you to forget all about Lizzy. We're not about to jeopardize that with letting you *see* her."

Alice thought the therapist was rather more hateful than he needed to be. She knew her chances of seeing Lizzy, her sister, were very slim, but she had to give it a shot every time she got the opportunity.

More than anything, she wanted a serious answer about why they weren't allowing her to see her sister. It made Alice angry, but it also pained her heart. She missed Lizzy—her evil little grin, bright eyes that had a world of mischief in them, and her warm, protective hugs. She needed her sister in this moment of uncertainty and fear more than any other... maybe.

"It's time for you to go back to your room, Alice, but you won't go back to Lizzy." The therapist cackled, a crazy noise, a *mad* noise.

***

Wonderland was in great shape, as per usual when Alice needed it. An individual's personal paradise, or Happy Place, as it came to be commonly known, would rarely be in disarray. It mattered for it to be in pristine condition. The landscape's purpose was for calming the person who visited. They needed it.

The flowers of Wonderland bloomed. Big and beautiful buds peeled back and displayed their vibrant purples and yellows and teals. The wild wisps of grass spouted from the ground like water in a fountain. The air sparkled with magical grain of pollen floating through invisible currents

91

of wind.

The creatures still had their incredible lore dancing upon their existence. All of them were normal creatures, with the Wonderland twist. Butterflies with keys or trinkets for bodies, bees with bulbous jars of honey under their tiny, curious faces, stinging ants with small tufts of fire shooting out of their rear ends when their thin legs flurried away from a threat.

All the weird little intricacies of Wonderland always put a smile on Alice's face. So strange, yet so pretty, all of them. The place was like running through the imagination of a six year old little girl. If you could think of it and toss in some explosive colors, you would have Wonderland. It was perfect. It never let her down.

Slipping into Wonderland saved her on several occasions. Most doctors thought she fell into deep sleeps or even some sort of mild coma, but it was escaping the world that was so cruel to her she needed. Alice's Wonderland was her personal safe haven. She could never thank her uncle, Lewis, enough for imagining such a place for her.

Alice made her way through the twisting, wandering paths and cut outs of Wonderland. She began to skip after a while, her little blue dress hem flipping up in the back off her heels. Faint scents of her favorite smells found their way to her nose. Clusters of honeysuckle, fresh blueberry muffins, and the clean, crisp smell of the tzatziki sauce she tried when she last spent time with Lizzy nuzzled themselves into her airway.

It took her a while to realize, in her Wonderland bliss, but she had skipped her way right into a blood-soaked lair made of low hanging forest. Crimson blanketed the ground and painted the tree trunks well above Alice's head. Some brown-black dried spots, long since used for whatever the hell did whatever here, crunched under the girl's feet. Some gooey spots shined from the small bit of Wonder-sun leaked through the foliage.

"Oh, dear," breathed Alice. Such a simple statement, she thought, for the calamity she felt within.

She moved across the ground, careful where she placed her feet with each step. Sometimes she slid, scared to death of falling in the foreign blood. Her heart pumped with a crazy rhythm, which left her lightheaded.

The scene made things worse. Fleshy strips of meat hung from some of the sturdier of Wonderland's plant life. Some of the chunky remains were dried out. Some were still pink and spongy. All of the pieces were nasty and scary.

Alice hauled ass out of there, back the way she came. She saw enough—enough gore and blood—to know she didn't want to hang out to find out what the hell was going on. She didn't like it. It wasn't the Wonderland she loved.

As Alice marched her way out of the blood marsh, she ran into an unfamiliar face. It shocked her. She thought she had seen every inch of Wonderland (after all it was her private place) and met everyone who lived there. In the last ten minutes, though, she had found two things that escaped her knowledge for fifteen years.

"P... please..., Aaah! Help!" the man grunted. He wore shorts made of antelope hide and brandished an overly hairy chest. Wily hair jutted from his chin and curled away from his body.

Alice backed away but couldn't leave the man in such obvious pain. "What's the problem, sir?"

"I can't... grrr... I can't change back!" he spat.

"Change back to what?"

"I'm a werewolf.... I'm stuck in human form." His body quivered as he spoke, and his eyes bulged when he tried to swallow his pain.

"I wouldn't want you to change over, either—not before me, at least." Alice shook her head.

"Easy, lit...tle girl. I... I was chasing a hare when I came upon... grrr... a... a mad fellow in a grandiose hat, having tea." The man lurched as though he may vomit and shook his head, pushing it back. "Peculiar time of day, b... but I had hunted that hare all mid-afternoon and was parched."

"Chasing a hare, you say?" Alice questioned. The situation all but spelled itself out to her. "Was the mad man's tea party in that direction, by chance?" She pointed in the direction of the Mad Hatter's mansion.

"Y... y... yes, it is. Help me, little girl. It hurts so." A whimper slipped through the man's lips. His eyes bulged again, like the pressure from the pain pushed them outward.

"I'll be back soon, sir. Hold tight."

Alice shot down the path leading to the Hatter's patch of Wonderland. As she transitioned over from the unspoken for property to the Hatter's area, everything changed in appearance. The plants were made of metal, and squeaked when the breeze blew through their leaves and petals. Instead of the orange and yellows of changing autumn leaves, rust splotched them in places. The rocks and pebbles on the little footpath were titanium marbles and steel ball bearings from long since forgotten pieces of machinery. And, finally, the sign that welcomed her: Hatter's Hallucinating Hut! Welcome. You may not be mad now, but you will be when I'm through!

A grin stretched across the young girl's pretty face. She hated the runaround the Hatter always gave her, but time always made her think fondly of her experiences with the loon. There may be a good chance she would be mad—crazy or angry—when she left his estate. She knew it to be true as her little feet pulled her up to the mansion door.

She tugged the string attached to a bell fastened to the wall, and the Hatter's voice rang from the center of a flower bloom by the porch. It was big enough for Alice to sit in, even curl up and take a nap.

"Who rings the things with strings?" he sang. "Mayhap I nap without a tap, tap, tapping?"

"It's me, Mr. Hatter." Alice made sure to remember her manners. They went a long way with the man, even if everything he did tried to break her from using them. "I need to speak with you about a traveler I met on the way here."

"Alice!" he yelled. The inside of the flower scratched from a static noise, and a small, blue eye spun around its center, spying Alice top to bottom and side to side. "Come, come, dear!"

The door of the house clicked and swung open. Alice stepped through into a room that looked like a library. As she knew it would, the door shut of its own accord behind her. The library walls and ceiling crumbled away, and the twinkle of early evening stars gleamed in the sky. The marble floor melted and became a tight-napped rug of English Moss.

In the center of the once-was-room, a high-glossed table ran the length from one end of the cutout area to the other. The top was laden with dirty dishes, sticky spoons, half-dissolved sugar cubes, and spills of tea in various stages of age.

The Hatter danced around in his weird swooping, twirling spins, cradling a tea pot in his hands like it was his soul mate. At the far end of the table, the March Hare laughed so hard his bucked-teeth popped in the front of his mouth, and the table vibrated from his jumping belly pressed against it.

"Alice is here, Alice is here, Hare! Can you believe she's back?" The Hatter didn't even notice her standing there. "We need tea for her—a celebration, yes!"

"I won't be long, Mr. Hatter. I just need to ask for some help."

"Alice! You are here. Mine eye did not deceive me. In all your glory, in all your beauty, you're really here!" The Hatter's joy threatened to infect Alice. "Hang around, my dearest Alice. Tea is coming shortly."

"I just need to ask you about the guy on the road."

The Hatter turned serious, and the March Hare's ears drooped down around his chubby cheeks. They looked like pigtails.

"What must you know about him?" said the Hatter.

"How did he end up in the state he's in?"

"Ah, dearest Alice, what must you know about him?" repeated the Hatter.

"I just asked: how did he end up like that?"

"No, no. You are asking a question but not listening to the question." The Hatter waved his finger in front of him and stole a quick, jovial glance at the March Hare.

"What should I be hearing then, Mr. Hatter?" Alice sighed in frustration.

"What *must* you know about the man on the road?"

Alice pondered on the question before she spoke. She forgot how precise she must be to get what she needed. Even then there was no guarantee he would help in anyway—maybe just more chasing white rabbits down rabbit holes.

"How do I fix the man on the road?" she said, and smiled at herself.

"Now, there's a good liddell Alice. Using your noggin, you are." The Hatter broke into another overdramatic dance.

"Mr. Hatter... the answer, please?"

Slowly, the Hatter turned his head to Alice. He appraised her for a moment before speaking. "How does one fix what seems unbroken upon inspection?"

"He needs fixing, Mr. Hatter, and seeing as how you two are the ones who broke him, I thought you'd know."

"Ah, but how do you know he is, indeed, broken?"

"He's broken inside. You can feel it," said Alice. "His true self is being hidden."

"So, he's still being, but not being himself?"

"Precisely."

"Sometimes leaving well enough alone is fixing the problem, my dear Alice."

"Mr. Hatter," she breathed to calm herself, "are you going to help me or not?"

"My dear, what more do you want from me? I've helped so much already." A whistle from a tea pot cut through their back and forth. "Oh, tea time! Care for a spot, Alice?"

"I've got to be going, Mr. Hatter. Good to see you again."

"As always, my dear, it was my deepest pleasure." The Hatter bowed to her as she walked through the doorframe sticking up from the ground.

The moment she stepped out the other side, the Hatter's house re-materialized behind her. She always made sure to turn and watch the tiny pixels build an amazing, gothic mansion. It always took Alice's breath away, and one of the small wonders of Wonderland.

Because she was in no particular hurry to get back to the werewolf to inform him she had no answers for his condition, aside from she knew who was responsible, Alice took the long way back. The steel ball bearing path transitioned over to cobblestones. In a pattern, the bricks outlined a rectangle with a heart painted in the middle. Thick, thorny leaves spouted and curled over, pushing a thin stalk supporting a flower blooming in the shape of a heart, which thumped with a miniscule pulse that was almost invisible to the naked eye. The ruby colored petals dripped with a viscous liquid of the same shade.

Alice saw the Queen of Hearts' castle—the peaks of its roof, the flat places where they met on the main structure—in the cloudless sky. It decorated the horizon with sharp, jagged angles and beautiful, strict lines. The projecting towers on the edges of the castle had an ominous look to them, like shadow encased missiles.

A *ho-hum* rumbled from the other side of a fence made of the same brick and design as the cobblestone walkway. The Queen of Hearts' card men worked on something and sang their slave song.

"Who do we do all of this for? The one who tells us to do more." Their songs were always so depressing to Alice.

"Card men!" Alice shouted over the wall.

The singing stopped.

"Hey, can anyone over there help me?"

She heard a clattering of a wooden ladder slapping against the brick. A black, angular head peered over the wall. The eyebrows, hovering just above the face, rose even higher into the air, like an ant's antennae.

"It is her!" the card man called over his shoulder before hopping over the wall. He floated in a sweeping motion on the edges of his card body.

"Hi, Five, it's been too long," said Alice to her old friend.

"So it has, my dear." Five bowed to her, showing the crease in his body from doing it so many times. "What is the help you request?"

Alice wondered how to phrase her dilemma to the five of hearts. The words perched on her lips, but, when she spoke, they came out in a haphazard, jumbled mess.

"Werewolf in the woods, Hatter's and Hare's fault." Her face reddened, and a flush of blush flooded her cheeks.

"Oh, the werewolf is still here? We've been hiding it from the queen, but she grows suspicious of our whispering."

"Why? Is the queen scared of him?"

"Well... wouldn't you be?" asked Five.

The question made so much sense, therefore Alice's reaction did not. Why didn't it bother her to help a werewolf? Why did she run from him if she wanted to help him, in turn? Her actions didn't even correspond with her desires.

"I believe you're right, Five." Alice tapped her finger to her chin as she thought. "Maybe I should be more concerned than I am, but he still needs help."

"Quite right, as usual, Alice," said Five. "You've always had the purest intentions about you, regardless of the consequences. It's the quality we all love about you. Some are even jealous of it."

"Do you have any idea how to help?" she asked.

"Of course, but just as much as the Hatter and Hare wish for him to remain harmless, so do we."

"So you can't help?" Alice knew this was part of Wonderland politics. You ask a question several different ways until you found the right one.

"I cannot, but I can tell you how to fix the problem."

That was easier than Alice expected.

"Fantastic. What do you have?"

"Four, bring me the leaf." He called over the brick wall. The pair waited a moment before the four of clubs crawled over and met them on the road. Four handed Five a black, fibrous roll. It looked like a long, fat sushi roll. "Here you go, dear."

"What is it?"

"A club leaf. Have you ever wondered where the nickname 'puppy dog tracks' came from?"

"Can't say that I have, Five. It's one of those things you think you just understand without explanation."

"No one can truly understand anything, even with explanation, without being."

"Well, explain anyway. I'll try to wrap my head around it."

"Club leaves are used to treat Lycanthropia. It can cause the change between phases, and, when brewed into a tea, it eases the effects of the wolf phase. Fancy trying to get a werewolf to drink tea, though."

"I wouldn't want to try," admitted Alice. "Thank you for your help, Five."

"It was lovely to see you again, Alice. Don't be such a stranger. Wonderland needs you."

"I'll keep it in mind." She gave the card a wink as she turned around to go back to the werewolf.

When she reached the bloody swamp, the man was crawling on his hands and knees. Tears filled his eyes, and he whimpered like a dog being kicked.

"Mr. Werewolf-man," said Alice, "Are you okay?"

What a foolish question. The man was in obvious pain and torment. It couldn't have assaulted Alice and been clearer. Heat warmed her face from the inside.

"W… w… what do you th… think?" The wolf sounded irritable. Alice understood why. "Can you h… help me yet?"

"Yes, sir, I can. I need you to eat this. I will—"

The man ripped the rolled club leaf from her hands with a violent snatch with his teeth. It scared her, but not as much as watching the man transform did.

Skin peeled away from muscles. Hair sprouted from lean, red meat. His face elongated, and his nostrils widened into holes as big around as Alice's wrist. His feet erupted from his flimsy shoes, claws digging themselves in the ground. Giant, ivory canines protruded from his jaw, and drool seeped from his lips. The monster's eyes burned a brilliant orange-yellow. The club leaf did its job; the man was a werewolf again. And he was hungry.

His intense stare settled on Alice's beautiful blue eyes, pure as the sea and scared as a baby bird in a lonesome nest. He wanted her, and he closed in on his dinner.

"Mr. Werewolf-man," began Alice. Her voice trembled. Her legs felt like they may betray her at any moment. "It's me, Alice. Remember? I helped you, got you back proper."

The werewolf snarled at the girl, lips vibrating from the violent exhaling. He took a step closer to her, and she took two steps backwards for an answer.

"Please remember me, Mr. Werewolf-man. Please. I need you to remember me." She backed up some more but bumped into a slimy, blood covered tree. There was no more retreating. If Alice didn't know any better, she would've sworn the werewolf grinned at her dilemma.

He pounced. She moved, and the werewolf slammed, snout first, into the trunk of the tree. When he turned to face a scurrying Alice, a crimson smear ran up his muzzle.

Alice ran as fast as she could through the Wonderland forest. Branches and razor sharp leaves cut her skin and ripped her nice, frilly blue dress. Each new wound caused a gasp of pain. Soon, before she ever made it back to the Hatter's section of Wonderland, she was out of breath and lightheaded.

When she looked back over her shoulder, Alice saw no sign of the werewolf. Nothing, no dust, no disturbed ground, no swishing tail, no wolf. It was an eerie sight and feeling. She knew he followed her. She could feel his gaze on her, tangible as the blood leaking from her cuts. He was there… but where?

Creeping around, trying not to attract too much attention just in case she had lost him, Alice slithered toward the Hatter's mansion. The path pebbles transitioned over to steel ball bearings, and the plants were made of sheet metal. She was in his domain and inching ever closer to his quarters. She had to make it there before the werewolf stuck his head out.

Finally, the peak of the Hatter's roof angled in the sky and waved through trees. Alice thought she may have never been happier to see the mansion. It symbolized safety, survival, relief.

Her legs trembled with a veracity making it nigh impossible to continue. Her heart pumped so hard she could feel it beating in her carotid artery. It scared her, feeling like it may rip the tissue apart from the pounding floods of blood coursing through her body. Tears leaked from her eyes, although she wasn't crying. The wind in her tear ducts made them overreact.

But she was too close to stop now. And just when she thought about taking a moment to gather herself, a feral howl echoed off the metallic plants and danced on invisible fret bars carrying it through the clear Wonderland air. It punched her right in the nether-regions, and got her moving like an Olympic runner.

"Mr. Hatter!" shouted Alice, praying she was close enough to be within earshot of the crazy fellow. "Mr. Hatter, I need you!"

She could hear growling, and a few teeth-popping nips at her heels. Each time the wolf's jaw snapped, she jumped in surprise. Alice wanted to look back but knew the view was one she would regret.

She plowed forward, too winded to call out for the Hatter again. One time, the wolf swiped a giant furry paw at the girl but missed. On his second try, he connected with her tiny ankle bone sticking out above the strap of her buckle-front shoe. The girl's leg swung and collided with the calf of her other leg. It tripped her, and she face planted right on the ball bearing path, her teeth *clacking* when the little steel balls smashed into them.

The beast straddled her. Thick strands of saliva hung from his lips. The short fur on his muzzle clung to foam from his mouth, and his hot breath smelled like a butcher's parlor. The rumbling in his chest vibrated within Alice, too.

"Alice, is that you calling?" the Hatter asked from around the wall of his mansion. A few silent moments went by while the werewolf waited for the man to give up his investigation. "Going once, I won't ask twice. It's time for tea. Isn't that nice?" he sang to no one in particular.

A mumble broke his little ditty. The werewolf turned his head sideways to listen. His tail wagged in quick jerks, like he was intrigued by what he heard.

He backed away from Alice, still careful of where to step, trying to remain as quiet as he could. Like a predator in the weeds, he prowled over to the edge of the mansion.

Alice turned on her side and even thought about yelling out for the Hatter to be careful. Before she would have mustarded up the courage, however, The March hare hopped into view.

The wolf took off at a dead sprint for his prey. The Hatter saw the massive brown blur after his friend and yelled.

"Quick Hare, behind you! Run, rabbit, run!"

***

Alice lay in her bed. It was an uncomfortable, a stiff hospital number with minimal support, and less covers. The draft from the hall blew in on her feet. Goosebumps raised on her pale legs. The answer, then, hit her.

He is a wolf in a man's skin.

BIO: T.S. Woolard lives in North Carolina five Jack Russell Terriers. For more of his work look for Lovecraft After Dark by jwkfiction, Suburban Secrets 2: Ghosts & Graveyards by J. Ellington Ashton Press, Horror From the Inside Out by Whorror House, Siren's Call 'eZines #17, 18 & 20, and his short story collection, Solo Circus. To connect with him, follow on Twitter @TSWoolard, or visit tswoolard.wordpress.

PARDOSA

DONA FOX

As I grew older, I realized I wanted to be normal despite my parents, so I built myself a small cabin, far away from the town but close enough to watch how normal people lived. I believed that was the larger part of me, the better part of me. I had never learned how to shift; indeed, I hadn't known that my parents were shifters.

I didn't want to kill, my parents taught me to kill, and by the time I realized what I had done, it was too late, but I had to eat so I hunted other animals. I was obsessed with skinning the beasts and cutting the skin into small squares. The animals were dead, it mattered not to them what I did with their hides. I hung the squares on the tree outside my door to dry.

I've worn animal skins before without incident, so I think the magic was from the tree. The oak tree was two hundred years old, hollow in the center, and once burned out, yet still green tips appeared at the end of the twigs each spring and acorns fell in their time.

The highest twigs were almost out of sight, that's where I hung my tiny squares of hide– and skin. The tree connected to the bits I hung, ran her sap into them, and kept them fresh. They never dried as I'd originally intended. The squares fluttered in the wind as beautiful as any other leaf in the forest.

One day, after I'd climbed to hang another, the breeze picked up, and one of the hanging squares of hide pressed against my arm. I felt a quick impression of the creature whose skin lay next to mine. I almost fell from the tree. The impression was fleeting. I told myself it was my imagination.

I chose another limb, another bit of hide that had fed from the tree. I had a similar experience, but of another creature. I remembered the hunt for that one, the kill. I was stunned.

I started experiencing other hides gradually, tentatively. I almost shifted. I felt myself on the edge. A slight push would achieve that final pleasure.

I needed to find a way to get beyond that barrier.

Until I breached that gap, the visitations were still a thrill, as if the animals' consciousness was for an instant inside my brain, it was quite a giddy feeling. In that way, I was not entirely alone. The bits of skin, the quick glimpses into other souls, those were my conversations. I held them as my friends, yet I was lonely.

Sometimes I was stuck. I felt as if it was getting harder to come back to myself. I needed someone else here when I took my little glimpses into other's souls.

I cut pieces from my thighs and tucked them in the hollow of the oak. If I had my own skin handy, perhaps it could save me. Assuming I was able to reach out from the haze and grab the bit of my own skin to rescue myself. Might I be safer with a trusted friend, or a lover?

I met her dog first.

To me he was just another animal. I didn't know. I would have killed him for food but he brought me a small red ball. He dropped the ball at my feet and sat down. I didn't know what to do. He nudged the ball toward me with his nose. I watched him. He picked the ball up and dropped it on my feet. I thought that was odd. I backed up. He picked the ball up and nuzzled my hand. I took the ball right out of his mouth. He ran several yards away from me, then he bounced up and down. I laughed and threw the ball. He jumped up in the air and caught it, then he ran to me and dropped it at my feet again. We played this strange game until he lay panting beside me.

"Loki! Loki!"

He jumped up, grabbed his ball, and ran into the trees.

Loki came to play with me often. Sometimes he came to my cabin and spent the day following me around as I did my chores. He'd touch me with his nose; always letting me know he was there beside me.

I spied on the girl. She was my age. I watched her grow up running through the woods with Loki but I never let her see me until the day I heard her sobbing.

I found her holding Loki's limp body.

I helped her bury him. I insisted on a shallow grave.

I never told her my secret.

Pardosa left the forest and forgot me. Eventually, it appeared she forgot Loki for she quit visiting his grave. That's when I dug him up, cut out his bits of skin, and hung them on the tree.

It was several autumns before I finally saw her again in the town, walking with her parents. Pardosa was a woman now. With her long white hair, she stood out as if a light shone on her and her alone.

I began to brush against her in crowds, to whisper her name, to draw out her breath and play it back to her as she slept until my touch alone set her on fire. For a week, I handed her one pink rose as I passed. The next week, I gave her a red rose each day. The next, she looked for me. I was not there.

102

At the end of the month, I stepped from an alley and slid my arm around her waist. Pardosa gasped as I pulled her willingly back into the dark with me, but then I disappeared.

I know she longed for me for she followed me into the forest.

She didn't remember me from our childhood.

Pardosa was inexperienced but she was willing and she liked to play games.

I'm a bit embarrassed, considering my parents and the part of me I wish to deny, but in her favorite game, I crawled silently through the brush. She would lay on her back, hidden in the tall grass, trembling in anticipation. I would find her, and then pounce.

I remember the day everything changed.

"You made it difficult, hiding the blush of your cheeks, among the wild roses, so I couldn't smell you; let me taste your lips."

"No!" She covered her mouth as she rolled away.

I was stunned. "You always let me taste before. You liked it."

"That was before I knew my lips were dirty." She looked away.

I eyed her appraisingly, *who told her she was dirty? Is there someone else here? Was it her parents?* Even so, I was hungry for her. "It's just your skin that is dirty, my dear, and I can relieve you of that."

I should have been suspicious when she laughed; the balance of power was changing. I watched her closely after that but she never left the clearing. The only third party in our relationship was the oak.

She watched me as I tended the tree and never drew closer than necessary to go about her chores.

I went into the forest alone now to use the bits of skin. It had become an addiction. If I went a day without visiting my friends I felt a gnawing in my stomach, bugs crawled on my skin. I needed the visits to release the pressure. I had a dream that one day I would cover my body with the bits of skin. Maybe I would sew the skins onto myself. My difficulty coming back continued to increase. I would not ask her to help me; I didn't trust her. I couldn't sleep.

Stark moonlight shone into the bedroom, painting an icy pallor on her skin. She lay naked and still, as if on an altar, her body the sacrifice in an ancient rite. As I let her white hair spill through my fingers, I itched to take on her skin. Shadows cast by the twigs in the oak scratched lines across her body. We both wanted her, the oak and I, no, we ached for her fresh skin.

I slipped from the bed. My bare feet padded silently on the cold floor as I left the cabin. I climbed into the tree, plucked random skins, and pressed them to my body with the night's dew as I ran into the trees.

What had never happened before came about under the moon that night.

My shoulders and hips spun in their sockets and threw me to the

103

ground as the bones in my hands cracked and hit the earth. My throat whipped out and back, throwing my face to the sky as my ears pulled up and out of my head. The pain was hideous as my nose and jaw ratcheted forward. The noises, the sounds, the howling in the night, everything was so loud. I had the worst headache of my life. I looked around me. I could see, but the view was odd. The night looked different. The smells repulsed me as they attracted me. I spun in place, sensing danger and fear. Was the fear from within me, or did I smell it on another? I raised my leg and pissed.

Then I ran. Running felt so good.

Something fled ahead of me. I chased it. Almost without trying, I caught it. I loved small prey.

The heart was alive as it pulsed in my mouth. The meat was springy and tough; with every bite, warm blood poured down my jaws and pleasure spread through my body.

Buoyed by the fresh blood from the beating heart, I was shifting back. I would be human again. I ran home and slid into my bed.

I woke from the hunt to find her bending over me. Her white hair glowed in the moonlight. Ropes bound me to the bed.

"You're covered in blood," She said.

My skin tightened, I attempted to draw away from her, "What have you done?"

Pardosa laughed, "What have I done? You come home covered in blood and you ask me what have I done? Whose blood is this? Who have you killed?"

I had no answer to her question so I held my tongue, which only fed her wrath and heightened her hysteria. As the civil dawn approached, she cycled down. Once she wearied and her rants became weak and sporadic, I found a gap between her outbursts and I whispered the words that would save me, for now.

"I can bring Loki back."

I heard the flap of a fly's wing, the boom of a mote of dust against the floor, and the swish of her eyelashes in the silence as she raised her eyes to look at me, "What?"

"I can bring your dog back, for brief visits only, but there will be a price."

"No price is too high."

From the hilltop above the crossroads, I saw two people take the turn that could only lead them to my cabin. Pardosa had kept her part of the bargain; she had summoned her parents to me. I needed an older male and a female.

I took a shortcut through the trees. I would be waiting for their arrival. I would catch them off guard.

As I watched her parents on the road, I remembered the day that still haunted me.

I was a brave child. I woke in our darkened cave, in the hours just before dawn, at the sound of soft paws and the faint click of a claw on stone. I used my natural talents of quick reaction and deadly aim to drive a wooden stake through my first victim's heart.

Yes, first the female, for I thought she was just another wolf come into the cave to shred me with her snapping incisors--how she howled as I drove the point between her furry ribs; then the male, as he came bounding, snarling, ready to kill me to protect his mate, but he was too late. For my first spike had found its mark in the female's heart.

The second spear ripped open the male's belly, his warm bowels drenched me, and then his body fell on me, his now useless claws, fully extended, clattered on the stone floor.

I grabbed hanks of his fur for purchase, pulled and pushed to free myself from under the beast. The fur slid from my hands as a snake slides back into its hole. I grabbed for his fur again but my hand found only skin. I could not grab onto the skin for the blood and sweat that ran down the sides of the creature. I slid easily from beneath the slippery beast.

I had no time to wonder, it was time to take my prize as my parents had taught me. I grabbed the hair at the top of the male's head, yanked his head back, and slit his throat. I knew pure rabid blood lust for the first time in that moment. Bouncing on the balls of my feet with sheer adrenaline, I did the same to the female.

I threw back my head and howled to release my lusty fervor. I grabbed my hatchet from my belt and hacked their heads from their bodies. Never once questioning that they were no longer wolves, I smeared their blood on my body, grabbed the two heads by the hair, and carried my prizes to the opening of the cave.

The sun rose and poured blinding light into the dark cavern.

I held the heads of my parents in my hands.

I skinned them both, cut their skins into tiny pieces, and hung the bits to dry on the great oak that stands outside my door where I carefully guarded my parents' skins.

When I realized the power the oak conferred on the bits of skin, the power to shift, I waited for my chance to find another male and female of the correct age.

Pardosa would do anything to have Loki back. She cared about him, after all. I shook my body and wagged my tail. It's getting much harder to shift back from being this dog. I won't do it anymore after today. I won't have to.

I've found I can't go back to being myself at all now without my own skin. I just have time to run home and get the bits I hid in the hollow of the tree so I can shift back before they arrive at the cabin.

105

Now I can make amends, I will apply my parents' skin to Pardosa's parents' bodies and my own parents will return to me. I will bring my parents back, and then I will deal with Pardosa.

As I neared the cabin, I saw smoke.

A fire that smelled of hide and skin raged in the oak tree.

Oh how Pardosa liked to play games.

BIO: Dona Fox published in the original issue of Cemetery Dance Magazine. She has since published with J Ellington Ashton Press and James Ward Kirk in the States and Dark Chapter Press and Horrified Press in the United Kingdom. She has won four Editor's Choice Awards from James Ward Kirk Publishing. She released a first single author collection of short stories, *Dark Tales from the Den* in 2015 which was mentioned in Ellen Datlow's The Best Horror of the Year, Volume Eight, and a second collection, *Darker Tales from the Den* in 2016. Dona is a member of Horror Writers Association. Dona blogs at donafox.com. Connect with Dona on Face Book at www.facebook.com/donafoxAP and follow on Twitter @_DonaFox.

WOLF COVE

MATTHEW WOLF KANE

A rocky and abandoned cove, tucked away on a rocky, treacherous coast line hides a wolfie secret. Locals know...sailors know...but this new breed of water loving adventure seekers don't know. Surfers, kayakers, they don't know, but soon they will be forced to know the secrets dwelling in the craggy caves of Wolf Cove.

What awaited them was death; vicious death by the claws of the werewolf that lived in the cave. It was once a human until its sixteenth birthday, when it changed to the werewolf that killed people from outside town. When the surfboards and kayaks started to appear upon the shores of the less secluded coves with pieces of gristle and bone embedded into them, and huge rents where claws had grabbed a hold of the unfortunate occupants, the townsfolk hid the boards and pleasure craft, but one day, into town strode Tommy Doyle. Tommy was a spoilt rich kid, used to getting what he wanted, and what Tommy wanted more than anything right now was Krista Myers. Blonde, lithe and beautiful, Krista was an enigma; man, did he want her. But Krista Myers had disappeared, off the waters of Wolf Cove, and Tommy wanted to know why...

He went around town with a photo of Krista; half of the locals would not stop when he asked if they had seen her around. He walked and walked until it got dark. He spotted a woman acting oddly with a sack over her shoulder.

Tommy ran up behind the woman and grabbed her by the shoulder with the thought to spin her around to face him. Next he knew, he was laying on his back at the feet of a woman that could have at one time been stunning, except now half her face appeared missing, a slit for a nostril, a lidless eye that was opaque with blindness, and a ragged hole where the other half of her scarlet lips had once been. Tommy looked up and anger mounted.

"The fuck did ya do that for?" he shouted at the stranger. "Stupid bitch, coulda broken my back!" The woman looked down upon him, and spoke with a voice that was as melodic as the dawn chorus.

"The information ye be seeking lies within yonder ale house, laddie. Not many folks around here will be tellin ye the truth, but Sid, he

109

will. He claims to be a direct descendant of Rodmar and Asgot. He'll be tellin ye the truth such as 'tis. Ye be tellin' him Milly sent ye. Now away with ye now, get your mission done on this night, for the morrow brings the full moon, and ye dunnea wanna be here in Wolf Cove then..."

Tommy jumped up, holding his nose as he backed away and watched the woman walking off with her sack.

Tommy nicked a small boat from the harbour and made his way out to Wolf cove. The sea was covered with a fog forming in front of his eyes; he could feel it coming from the sea as he lost sight of the town. There was no turning back now, even though he was scared of what he might find at the end of the fog. Through it he could see the near full moon. He wished that he brought his fur jacket with him on this trip to keep him warm. Tommy let the boat sail as he tried to rub his hands together to warm them back up.

As Tommy sailed further out to sea, the fog thickened, he was wet and freezing cold…and bloody hell! There was a hole in the damn boat! Tommy reached down with his hands and attempted to propel himself faster. As he did so, suddenly the fog parted slightly, and Tommy was startled to see a surfer pulling moves out on the water.

"Mate, hey mate!" he yelled, but the surfer ignored his calls. Tommy paddled closer to the surfer and tried again. "Oi, what you doing out here in this, you nutter?" he called, still no answer. Anger filled Tommy at this ignorance, and he finally reached the surfer, but when he did, he wished he hadn't. This surfer was dead, or rather undead, or a spectre of a surfer or something not of this world; possibly a demon surfer, and reminiscent of the strange woman with the stinking sack. This dead guy, who was somehow fucking surfing while dead, only had half a face, but his had not healed. Tommy could see brains, skull and a pierced hanging eyeball!! Screaming now, Tommy plunged into the icy water, and started to sink beneath the waves. As his lungs took in water and he began to sink, he fancied he could see Krista's beautiful face waiting for him. He was drifting into oblivion when strong hands yanked him from his watery near grave and dumped him upon the shore.

"Ye silly little fucker!" shouted the gnarled and grizzled man who was now pumping the water from Tommy's lungs, "Di'nt Milly tell ye to stay away from the cove? Ghosts out there laddie, and ye nearly joined them this night"...

"I be Sid," said the man, throwing Tommy over his shoulder, "And ye, silly wee fucker, are coming to my ale house with me 'n' I gonnea tell ye a tale."

The grizzled man gave Tommy a boating sheet to wrap around him and keep warm. He watched the guy boiling some water. A few times, the guy would look right at Tommy and smile at him with no front teeth.

110

"Who are you?" Tommy asked, as he reached a hand out to take hold of the cup of hot tea.

"I be t'watchman, for years I've watched over the cove," the old man replied.

"Many years ago, thousands, in fact, two brothers sailed into these parts and settled, but here there be monsters and strange 'appenins, and they two brothers, they both wanted to be the better, they parted ways, bitterly. Rodmar was walking one day in the woods and was bitten by a wolf like creature. He thought nowt of it til next full moon, when he turned into a part beast with bloodlust, but Rodmar was inherently good, and tried to keep away from folks when he did the shiftin', but what happened to his brother Asgot was entirely diff'r'nt laddie. Asgot was inherently bad." Wide eyed, Tommy was enthralled by the watchman's tale.

"What happened to Asgot?" He blurted through chattering teeth.

"Well, Asgot was attacked by a thing called a Draugr on an island of death. It was him and three people that escaped with their lives. But, they had to fight against the sea, and the sea won and sent them overboard, to be washed up and rescued by village people." The watchman took a sip of his tea and started again. "Slowly, one of them changed into a monster and killed for blood to make him stronger than before. Soon, they all went through the changes and they too killed for blood, Asgot was the last; he killed the leader of the village. Not a lot is known where they went after. He was heading home to his father. Wherever he went first, he got worse as a monster. He wanted to know why his father chose his brother over him."

Tommy was completely enthralled by the watchman's tale, but he was also still wondering about Krista. "Look, mate, please, nobody else will help me; most won't even answer me. Have you seen this girl? She will have been missing exactly a month tomorrow / today; whatever the fucking day it is, I need to find her, I must." Sid took the photo from Tommy's hand and looked carefully at it.

"Pretty wee thing, your intended?" he asked Tommy.

"Nope," replied Tommy. "Intended lay maybe," but he immediately felt contrite for his crassness.

"I fancy there may be a deeper feelin' in yer heart for this 'ere lassie than ye be lettin' on boy," chuckled Sid. "I'm sorry to be the one to tell ye, but chances of yer wee lassie bein' 'ere in t'cove still are slim. There be strange 'appenins 'ere abouts to this very day. Cove history holds nowt but tales of monsters and bloodshed. Ye see that there lassie you got flipped onto yer arse by? Milly? Ye caught a whiff of her sack? Yup, thought ye musta, she does that every other night, to appease that which lives in the caves of the cove, mutations and inbreedin' between the monsters down the generations have led to the horror ye will find in yonder caves t'day. Descended from generations of cross breedin', we have a monster so terrible, none but me speak of it, 'n' if the bonnie wee lassie in that photo

111

has been yer 'n' disappeared, there will be no hope for her. I'm sorry laddie, but she will likely be dead 'n' eaten now." Tommy stared at the old watchman in disbelief.

"You fucking crazy old man!! You want me to believe you have some Viking werewolf/vampire cross creature living here, killing these surfers? How can you say shit like that? You chatting shit man!" Sid looked at Tommy not unkindly, but spoke with more conviction than before.

"Boy, what I tell ye be the truth. I know it to be so, because yonder monster is none other than my own child! The were curse skips a generation, my own father was a lycanthropic vampire, and so is my only child."

Tommy jumped up and grabbed hold of the watchman's throat.

"I want you to tell me where Krista is." His grip was getting tighter. "Are you going to tell me where Krista is?" the watchman nodded at Tommy. "Good. You better start talking, old man."

"This lassie ye spoke of is likely in t'cave just up t' hill from here with my son. She may still be alive if ye hurry now, laddie, fir when that hand hits midnight, t'woman ye love may…just may, be turned like my son so's he can breed children what be just like him." Tommy could not hold back his rage anymore, so he slapped the watchman across the face, and then heard a howl echoing through the night sky.

"I don't think that will be happening tonight, mate." Tommy noticed an axe hanging proudly on the ale house wall. "And I can use that to kill your beloved son before he touches her."

It was not even hard to find the cave when the howling was echoing through the air and guided him right to the entrance. 'Krista, just hold on, love. I'm coming to save you from this monster,' Tommy thought in the back of his head. 'Your knight is going to fucking save you and we will live ever happy with our children.'

As soon as he set foot into the cave, he could hear the watchman shouting at him not to go any further in. He swore he heard something about his death, but Tommy was not going to stand around and listen to him, no, he had to go and save the woman he loved from this monster that wanted to turn her like it.

He knew he was getting closer as the howling was getting louder. It was then that he saw a shadow of something run in front of him that made him step back, and he felt something on his shoulder. Tommy turned around and used the top of the axe to hit whatever was behind him. Tommy had knocked the watchman to the floor of the cave, his nose bleeding.

"Ye must turn back now…before he sees ye an' kills ye for gettin in the way of his desires."

"Shut your god damn mouth! I've come to find the woman I love, and take her back home where she belongs."

"It's too late now…once the clouds move out of the way of the full moon…it will start and there will be no way of stopping this."

112

Tommy clapped his hands over his ears. Between the howling, the crashing of the sea and the old watchman's entreaties, he was getting a crushing headache. He slowly turned a corner in the cave which then opened up into a chamber, and lying face down on the floor, wearing just a bikini top and nothing else, was Krista. At first, he though she was dead, and he staggered back stunned when he saw what had happened to her beautiful face as he turned her over. Krista was missing half her face. Tommy screamed his distress and then caught his breath as he saw the smallest movement of her chest as she breathed shallowly. Tommy prepared to hoist her over his shoulder and get her out of there, when he heard the old watchman scream!

Placing Krista back down gently, he ran towards the sound. The watchman was there, his face was half gone, and there was a nightmare creature hunched over him. When the creature spotted Tommy, its blood soaked maw opened wider, in a suggestion of the evil it intended to do here this night. Tommy scrabbled around behind himself until he found the axe from the ale house wall. Adrenaline running wild in his veins now, he chased the man beast to the next chamber. Fury ran through Tommy as he thought of the beauty that had been stolen from Krista, and through that fury, Tommy Doyle found the strength to repeatedly swing the axe into the body of this werewolf/werevampire being, dismembering it so thoroughly that its parts were scattered all around the cave chamber. He dropped the axe and was about to make his way back to Krista, when he heard a sound that made him freeze in disbelief - howling! A different pitch of howl this was, but a howl all the same, and it was close… by heck was it close!

Tommy rounded the corner back into the first chamber and screamed. The once beautiful Krista was hunched over the now definitely dead watchman, dragging out entrails and consuming them. The half of her beautiful face not missing was now covered in a grey fur, her cherry red lips were now an elongated snout, and her remaining eye was wild with the madness. There was a flicker of recognition as she looked at Tommy, and Tommy took advantage of this and slipped out of the cave. As he went, he picked up the axe, the sack he found laying on the floor, and made his way back down the treacherous cliffs to the shore. He then turned and headed for the ale house.

So now, when travellers or adventure seekers come to Wolf Cove, it is none other than Tommy Doyle who draws them a pint of ale and tells them the tales of why they should avoid yonder cove and its mysterious caves. It is Tommy Doyle that now helps Milly collect any roadkill they can find, for Milly to deposit outside the cave in her stinking sack. Tommy Doyle must now pay the price for falling in love, for in yonder cave dwells the object of his affection. Every full moon, she howls the night away, and Tommy Doyle, watchman of Wolf Cove does what he can to protect the

113

adventurers that will surely meet their deaths, if they don't respect the evil, that is Wolf Cove.

BIO: Kitty Kane, AKA Becky Brown is an emerging horror writer that hails from the south of England. Kitty is a lifelong, avid reader of horror fiction. Her influences over the years are wide spread but include James Herbert, Clive Barker, Edgar Allen Poe, Jack Ketchum and the late, great Richard Laymon. Although writing has been a pastime that she has indulged in for most of her life, she is currently lined for her first published works as part of several collections for J.Ellington Ashton Press, as well as interest in a forthcoming novella. Her style ranges from more traditional short horror stories to bizarre fiction and poetry. Kitty is also one half of writing duo – Matthew Wolf Kane, alongside another emerging talent, Matt Boultby. Their joint venture has already seen them published twice, with subsequent works due for release.

Kitty's Facebook
https://www.facebook.com/becky.brown.560272?fref=ts

Matt's Facebook
https://www.facebook.com/boultby13?fref=ts

INDUCTION

JUSTIN HUNTER

A youth, slight in stature with ghostly pale skin, limped his way down the dimly lit suburban streets. He was nude to the waist, wore faded jeans that were ripped at both knees and brown with dirt. Shoeless, his bare feet made soft padding sounds on the dry pavement. He clung to his sunken stomach with both hands. Sweat beaded off his pimply brow. Every once in a while he would turn his gaze upward and the light from the looming full moon would reflect off his yellowing eyes.

He walked several blocks, retracing his steps as he made his slow way down the twisting avenues. The homes, depressing in their sameness, hulked like beige, upper-middle class fortresses. The boy stopped and turned sloe eyes at a two story split level home. He spied a small, dripping red X marked under the bottom front porch step. The others told him that this would be the sign they had left him. His prey was inside. His initiation into the Midwest chapter of the sanguisuge order had begun. The trial that faced him was as mysterious as the order itself. He had been assured that he would not be partaking in this induction alone. He would be watched and assisted if events turned sour. He hoped he would not fail the elders of the order.

He stepped onto the precision manicured lawn and moved toward the building, knelt by the mark and put his lips to it, sucking at the lines, allowing the salt tinged with metal ichor to roll around in his mouth. He swallowed. Bliss marred by ravenous hunger shook his meager frame. He ascended the front steps. The front door opened easily. The youth stepped inside.

His nostrils flared upon entering the home. Scents of shampooed carpet, cinnamon-apple air freshener and bleach came heavy into his olfactory senses. Below the overpowering detergents were more shallow smells; burned chicken, dirty laundry and something else. Something feral.

The youth found the door that led to the basement. He tried to open it, but it was locked, as he knew it would be. He raised the index finger of his right hand. The nail was elongated, thin and sharp. He put the nail into the lock and turned it, unlatching the door. He stared down into the dark

117

recesses of the cellar. Somewhere below would be the man that the others had promised him. A man whom he would kill. A living soul in whose veins ran several quarts of fresh, teeming blood that would satiate his hunger and etch his place among the most ancient of races. The elders had promised a captive. It had been days since the youth had been bitten and turned. He was ravenous. The youth vaulted the steps and landed cat-like on the cellar floor then froze as he gazed upon the monster before him.

The creature rose to its ponderous height. Its heavily muscled shoulder blades scraped the ceiling joists. Emerald light from the beast's eyes flashed out from the opaque blackness of the cellar. Its neck jutted aggressively straight out from above its breastbone, holding an elongated head of thick, matted fur culminating in long, open jowls, dense with jagged teeth. A copious white foaming glut of saliva caked its mouth at the edges. The werewolf's substantial arms hung to just below its knees, ending in splayed fingered hands bearing wide claws.

The creature dug deep furrows into the concrete cellar floor, lolled out a long, grey tongue and licked its chops. The beast had eyes for the youth and nothing else. Its broad chest expanded with each lushly rasping breath.

"Not what you expected, boy?" The werewolf's voice sounded like a metal file scraped over a concrete slab. "I was much weaker when the old ones came and captured me. Come and meet your death."

The werewolf lunged forward. Its shoulders smashed through two support beams as its bulk swarmed over the vampire. The youth opened his mouth, exposing twin long canine teeth which he bit into the werewolf's chest as the animal landed upon him. The werewolf gripped the vampire by the shoulders and tore his arms off with one quick wrench and twist. Then it stood, the vampire dangling from his chest by its teeth. The werewolf pressed both hands on the vampire's head and slammed him onto the floor with such force that it crushed the youth's skull and shoved the demolished head to the boy's chest cavity. The werewolf snapped its jaws closed around the vampire's hips and shook its head violently, tearing the undead creature in half.

Crouching down and raising his blood sodden visage toward the cellar ceiling, the werewolf loosed a howl that shook the very foundation of the home. The beast turned its head down toward his prey and began to feed, tearing the necrotic flesh and swallowing the severed vampire in gulps without chewing. The werewolf sprang upward, smashing through the floor and landing in the middle of the decimated living room, then crashed through the large front bay window and escaped into the night. As it ran, the beast felt bits of the vampire moving around in its stomach. The corners of its mouth turned up in a grimacing smile.

The werewolf tore through the streets with blinding speed, its head bent low to the ground, its nails digging trenches into the concrete with

118

every bound. The beast left the suburban sprawl, heading away from the city. When it reached a vast expanse of farmland, it sidelined into a deep field of ready-for-harvest corn. Several acres within the crop, the creature's track could only have been seen from above by the quaking stalks as he passed.

From high above, figures swooped down, trailing their tucked leathery wings back on their streaking descent. Seven in all, as large as full grown men, with skin the color of burned maize they came. Their bodies were supple and thin. Their backs were curved between the shoulder blades from severely bent spines. Their hairless bodies and rent, hideous wings made them look like Satan's angels at the fall.

The seven landed as one upon the werewolf. The deep roar of the angered beast culminating with the piercing shrieks of the ancient vampires silenced all creatures for miles around. Blood fountained in a torrent. Heavy thumps, tearing flesh and gnashing teeth filled the night sky. The violence was wicked, ending as suddenly as it began. The farmland was crushed in a wide circle. The werewolf sat on its haunches. Deep, open furrows were slashed into its hide. Several puncture wounds were visible on its arms, chest and neck. The vampires flanked the werewolf in a semi-circle. All were grievously wounded. Many had lost wings, arms or legs from the attack. Their faces were grim. Their visages were even, except for a seething hatred for their foe.

The werewolf wiped a bloody paw over its muzzle. "Fools. You cannot defeat me. I could kill a hundred of you before I fall." The vampires looked on, not answering the taunt. The werewolf rose to its full height, towering over the aged undead. It reared back its head and flexed its broad chest muscles. "You die. Now!" It sprang and swiped with one razor clawed paw, cleaving the head off the nearest vampire. His second swipe came from above, attempting to sever the next vampire in half, but his strike was checked. The beast looked in awe at the engorged blue veins, pulsating along the parch-skinned hand that was clasped around his wrist.

"How?" the werewolf said and then looked at the sky. A light blue haze was coming over the horizon. The full moon had fallen. The vampire stabbed its long fingernails into the werewolf's wrist and bit deeply into the open gash, feverishly sucking at the wound. The arm was losing its muscle. The matted fur faltered and crept back into its skin. The other vampires sensed their prey weakening and launched themselves upon the beast, biting and devouring its blood. The vampire youth tore the werewolf open at the stomach with one of its severed limbs, its body parts falling out of the beast amidst a pile of guts and offal. One of the vampires took its compatriot's severed head and put it on the pile of gore. The head of the undead creature began to feast, the blood it drank from the werewolf's innards draining out of its severed neck and wetting the field below with blood. The werewolf had turned back into a man. The vampires continued to feed, crawling over the man and draining him of his incredible vitality.

The rising sun peeked over the horizon, igniting the ancient vampires in a cataclysm of raging fire. The man's eardrums ruptured at the sound of their dying shrieks. The vampires ended their vengeance with death. The sun took its place in the sky. A new day dawned, sending the things of nightmares scurrying back into their dark quarters, waiting for the next night to come.

BIO: Justin Hunter has seven published novels and over thirty short stories in anthologies. His publishers include Severed Press, Morbidbooks, JWK Fiction, J Ellington Ashton Press, Strangehouse Books, NoodleDoodle Publications, Great Old Ones Publishing, Cedar Loft Publishing, and many others.

CALENDAR CURSE

DONALD ARMFIELD

Cobblestone walkways glistening in the moonlight,
the roaring, torrential downpour calming to a fine mist.
My cue for home bound to outrun the second drenching.

Reverberating sounds from my hurried strut,
bouncing off the mid-town dwelling structures.
Low-hanging clouds befog the glow of the streetlights.

An uncanny howl lingers overhead, alarming my surroundings.
The hairs on my arms raise and pinch my flesh with fright.
That sudden feeling of being watched heightens my senses.

My hurried strut, increasing to a full on dash,
but freeze before I caught wind, at the pair of eyes ahead.
The red lustrous pair stares dead, placid of all ocular movements.

A growl portrays a need, a hunger to feed under the full moon.
The glowing eyes become a ponderous shadow, lurking.
A deathly prowl drawn to my sudden raising pulse rate.

The beastly creature hurdles out of the darkness, to maul its prey-
Me; the frightened one. Ensnared under its elongated claws,
with superior strength, licking its chops exposing razor-sharp fangs.

I remember closing my eyes to accept fate, a pillaging of my soul.
My astral body unwillingly leaving behind my solid form as the living.
Looking down from above at my remains, knowing now what's after, Life.

The gaping wound in my chest cavity, chunks of viscera, my gory remains
ravaged by the wolf-like creature, salivating & munching on my corpse.
Running off back into the shadows, its drab silver fur drenched in my blood.

What happens next? I feel empty, lacking of something, a strong desire to
     feed.
This calendar curse is overwhelming; I can no longer fight this dread inside
     me,
the lunar phase will be completely illuminated tonight. A feast it should be.

BIO: Donald's active imagination gathers in a heap of words....and after a few days of organizing and a short nap, his dexterous writing abilities compile a masterpiece. (well....that is what he likes to think.) Donald's short stories and poetry have appeared in multiple anthologies, blogs and e-zines. Follow his Facebook page (http://www.facebook.com/donald.armfield) to stay updated on future projects and exclusive content.

Donald lives somewhere in New England, with a wife & four daughters and soon to own a shotgun

SOMEWHERE WE SHOULDN'T BE

ESSEL PRATT

Cold autumn winds fluttered through the shrubbery outside a typical suburban home. Two cars in the driveway, outside the closed garage doors, staked lights lining the walkway up toward the concrete front porch, and a single light illuminating the deep red doorway that kept the nighttime creepers from allowing themselves inside. From the outset, it looked eerily similar to every other house that lined the dismal street. If not for the brightly shining gaze of the full moon, differentiating details would have been lost within the darkness.

Within the darkness shadowed by the house's front façade, a young black man, in his early twenties, approached the front door. His sweater hung loosely upon his lanky frame whilst he meandered as he ascended the two steps before ringing the doorbell.

Inside, the bright lights signaled someone was home, yet there was no signal that anyone was inside. It was quiet; no television, no stereo, and no banter between adults or kids, just an unnatural silence. The young man, looking back over his shoulder, pressed the doorbell again, bending his finger in the process, to ensure it triggered the tintinnabulation inside. He could faintly hear it ring, so he pressed it repeatedly, at least ten times.

Shadows flickered within, a few bodies vaguely distinguishable behind the thick curtains moved to and fro, seemingly approaching the front door, hesitating just before vanishing behind the home's walls. The young man rang the doorbell again, letting the occupants know he was not going to give up until they answered.

The brass doorknob jiggled back and forth as the deadbolt unlatched. With a noticeable hesitation, the door opened a crack, revealing a thirty-something white woman within. "Can I help you?"

Her voice was low and quivered as she spoke.

"Sorry to bother you, ma'am," said the young man. "My car broke down on the corner and I was hoping you had a phone to call a tow truck."

"Don't you have a cell phone?" she asked, her eyes revealing that she was busy with something more important.

"Yes, ma'am," he said, "but, it has a dead battery. It will only take a moment. This has happened before and I have the number memorized."

The woman sighed, "I'm sorry, I just cannot help. I am just getting the kids settled and have a lot to do before bed tonight."

The young man looked back toward the road. "Thank you anyway. I understand, but I wish you would reconsider."

"No, I'm sorry," she said with her hand on the door, ready to close it. "But I just cannot help tonight. I wish I could."

The young man smiled at her, as though to say good bye, while tapping his left foot on the cold concrete porch. The woman started to say goodnight, but the young man's accomplice, a white male about his same age, ran from around the corner, revealing himself from the darkness, and thrust his shoulder against the door, snapping the chain lock from its mount and smashing his way inside. The woman fell to the floor, but the young black man picked her up and held a gun to her head as the pair rushed inside, shutting the door behind them. She didn't scream, she knew better as her jelly-like legs barely kept her afoot.

"Where is everyone?" asked the white male. "Tell them all to come here."

"In the dining room," she said with a shaky voice. "Please, just leave. It will be better for everyone."

"Says you, bitch," said the black male. Since they are all in there, let's go to them. Keep the element of surprise, okay?"

"Please, I beg you," she said.

"The women always beg me, but you are too old and wrinkly for me. You got a daughter? Maybe I'll let her beg."

"Man, we ain't here to fuck bitches," said the white male. "We're here for the jewelry and other shit we can sell."

"We don't have anything of value," said the woman. "We just moved here and none of our stuff has arrived. See, there isn't even any furniture in here."

"Fuck you, bitch," said the white man. "Let's just get in the dining room with the others."

The black male followed the white male toward the dining room. The hallway was dark and quiet. The woman's deep breaths seemed to echo within the corridor. The darkness made the hall seem to stretch on forever and made the black male feel uneasy.

"Damn, Jimmy, this shit is creepy as hell," he said.

"Fuck, Damon," said Jimmy. "Why the hell you use my name? Fuck, no names."

"Shit, this bitch won't say anything. Will you, bitch?"

128

"I won't say anything," she said with a quivering voice.

"See," said Damon. "The bitch won't say anything."

"Quit playing around," said Jimmy. Where the fuck is the dining room?"

The woman pointed to the end of the hallway, where it turned to the right. She didn't say a word as Damon shoved her forward while the two intruders hurried their pace and stormed around the corner, with guns pointed, ready to pop some caps.

A glimmer of light materialized as they approached the turn, a sharp contrast to the dark hallway. The men hurried their pace some more, nearly dragging the woman alongside them as they attempted their surprise entry.

Inside the light's glow, Jimmy pushed open the doorway, revealing himself to the people within. "What the fuck!"

"Oh damn, this is fucked up," said Damon. "What the hell did we walk into?"

"I told you to go," said the woman. "There's still time."

"Fuck this shit," said Jimmy. "I came here to get some shit, and I'm gonna get some shit. There has to be something worth money in this empty-as-fuck house."

No one else spoke as the boys stood there, looking at the strange scene they happened into. The room was empty except for two chairs. There were four people in the room. One was most likely the woman's husband, another was a young man about their age, probably their son, and the other two were a young set of twins, probably about six years old, one boy and one girl. Both were tied tightly to the wooden chairs.

"Seriously," Damon broke the silence. "Is anyone gonna explain why those two kids are tied to the chairs? Did we fucking interrupt an abduction or some shit?"

"Fuck, who cares," said Jimmy. "If these sonovabitches are taking these little kids, they won't tell the police we were here. It's a fucking win-win situation."

"Yeah, you're right," said Damon. "Fucking score!"

The man of the house spoke up, "Gentlemen, I would suggest you leave now. You don't want to be here any longer than necessary."

"Fuck you," said Jimmy. "I ain't gotta listen to you. We'll leave once we get the goods. Ain't no rich people gonna leave their jewelry with the movers. It's here somewhere. Damon, take her and find the jewelry and shit. It's gotta be here somewhere."

"No, please, just leave," said the woman as Damon shoved her toward the stairs at the right of the room. "There is nothing here."

The woman sobbed, tears streaming down her face, as Damon followed her up the stairs. Her husband tried to go to her rescue, but

Jimmy pointed the gun his way. The man stopped, instead remained standing with his hands folded in front of him.

The twins sobbed in their chairs. Jimmy didn't know if they were scared because he and Damon were there or if it was because their parents had them tied to the chair.

"What's up with them?" asked Jimmy. "That bitch said she was putting the kids down to bed. She didn't say anything about strapping them to a chair."

"It's for the best," said the young boy.

"That's fucked up," said Jimmy. "Who are you people, anyway?"

"We're no one," said the man. "We just want to be left alone."

"Tell me where the valuables are and we'll go," replied Jimmy.

"We already said, there is nothing here," said the man. "Just us, we moved in only today."

"Fucking shut your mouth, old man," said Jimmy. "This is a fucked up family."

Jimmy pace the room, pointing the gun at the man and his son as he did so, staring at the twins. The silence in the house was both awkward and eerie. The only noise was that of the sobbing twins, each tied so tightly they could only move their heads. Each time he looked at them, he became angrier than the last.

"You," he said waving his gun at the boy. "Untie those kids. That's fucking bullshit; you can't treat little kids like that."

The boy looked horrified as he glanced toward his father for approval. His body shook like he was out in the cold and sweat gathered on his brow. He waited for his dad to nod yes, but it didn't come. Instead, he stared into his blank eyes, unsure what to do.

"I have the fucking gun here, not daddy," said Jimmy. "Untie the kids!"

The boy walked to the twins. They followed his movement with their heads, still sobbing in fear as he approached. He stood in front of them, then crouched down, his knees bent but not touching the floor, and struggled with the knot at the little girl on the right's ankles. He fumbled with the rope, seemingly taking his time.

"Come on, hurry up," said Jimmy. "Let the kids go."

The boy fumbled faster, loosening the knot at her ankles enough for her to move her legs. She kicked forward, frightening the boy as he stood to move away from her jolting legs. As he stood, he lost balance, stumbling backward toward Jimmy.

Jimmy, unsure if the boy was falling or attacking, reacted in the only way he knew how. He pulled the trigger on the gun, sending a bullet right into the boy's throat. The bullet went straight through, lodging into the rope that held the little boy tightly to his chair.

The older boy fell limp to the ground, blood spilling onto the tan plush carpet. His voice gurgled as blood filled his throat. His father ran to him, holding the boy in his arms.

"No, oh please no," yelled the father as his son died in his arms.

As the father sobbed, Damon and the woman ran down the stairs.

"What the fuck was that?" yelled Damon.

"No, Frank, what happened to Stephen?" yelled the woman as she cried out loud, falling down next to her husband and son.

"Shit, man," said Damon. "What happened?"

"He fucking came at me," said Jimmy. "Ain't no one come at me without getting some lead in 'em."

"Shit," said Damon. "That is hardcore as fuck, but what now?"

"Get the valuables and get out of here," said Jimmy.

"There's nothing upstairs except a roll of toilet paper in the bathroom," said Damon. "Every other room is completely empty."

"Damn," replied Jimmy. "Maybe these mother fuckers told us the truth. Still don't explain why they tied up these little kids."

"Maybe we untie the kids, tie them up, and then call the cops when we leave," said Damon.

"Nah," said Jimmy. "Then they'll tell the police we were here. They won't have a reason not to."

As the two discussed the situation, neither saw the man and woman crawling toward the dark hallway, until one of the twins made a whimpering noise that was much deeper than the crying sobs. Both of the intruders looked up, just as the couple reached the hallway. Both raised their guns toward the mother and father.

"Where the fuck you goin'?" yelled out Jimmy.

"Get your asses back here, you deadbeat mother fuckers," yelled Damon.

The parents rose to their feet and walked back into the room, careful not to make any sudden moves; each keeping their eyes on Jimmy and Damon, as they moved behind the pair of chairs, waiting for their next command from the intruders.

"Now, untie the little kids and let them go. What kind of parents are you?" said Damon. "That shit's fucked up beyond anything I've ever seen. My poppa beat the shit out of me daily, but he ain't ever tied me up like that. He taught me to fight like a man, not to be submissive like a bitch."

"Hell yeah," said Jimmy. "Fucking pitiful twats."

"White people be crazy as shit," said Damon. "Ain't no black folk get away with this shit."

"Hey, I'm white," said Jimmy.

"Yeah, but you grew up in the hood," said Damon, patting him on the back. "You're an honorary brother."

As the boys joked, the father slipped a small knife from his pocket and started to slice away at the ropes of the little boy on the left, cutting them just enough that they remained together by just a few small threads. He then moved to the young girl on the right and did the same.

He looked up at his wife as she sobbed, "I'm sorry, honey. We have no choice. I love you."

As the last word left his lips, he buried the knife's blade into her temple. She gasped before falling to the ground behind the chairs, her life gone before her body impacted the floor.

"What the fuck?" said Jimmy.

The man held his hands high into the air. "It had to be done, there was no other way."

"What the fuck you talking about?" said Damon.

"This man is crazy as hell," said Jimmy. "Fuck, he ain't leaving us no choice."

Damon raised his gun and pulled the trigger without giving it a second thought. The bullet hit the man right in the center of the forehead. Their eyes met for a second before he fell limp to the floor next to his wife.

"Well," said Jimmy, "That's that. Now what?"

"Let's get the fuck out of here and call the police from a payphone," said Damon.

"Where the fuck we gonna find a payphone?" asked Jimmy.

"I don't know, but we gotta call anonymously," said Damon.

"Should we untie the kids, or keep them there so they are safe?" asked Jimmy.

Both twins broke free from the ropes, snapping the few threads that held them in place, and growled their displeasure in being tied up for so long.

"Shit," said Jimmy. "That scared the hell out of me. Looks like the old man did untie them."

"Yep," said Damon. "That answers that question, let's just get outta here and call the police."

The boys started their way to the hall, but the twins blocked their path.

"Alright kids," said Damon. "Move out of the way while we go get help."

The kids growled at them, their eyes angry as spittle expelled from their toothy expression.

"What the fuck," said Jimmy. "They retarded?"

"No man, look at their faces," said Damon. "That's some fucked up shit."

The faces of the twins started to pulsate as they began to change shape. Both dropped to their knees, crouched on all fours, their bodies mangling as the full moon's light strayed in through a crack in the only window.

The boys were shocked as they walked backward away from the hallway, ready to bolt up the stairs, their only escape. As they moved away, they tripped over the son's corpse, falling to the ground as they slipped in his blood. Not wanting to remain still, they continued their recoil in a crab walk fashion.

The twins continued to change. Their faces grew elongated like dogs as their gnarly teeth threw spittle from within, pointed ears sprouted upon their head, and fur emerged from their bodies as their clothing ripped from their growing frames. The transition from child to wolf took only seconds as the children howled in pain.

Both skulked toward Damon and Jimmy, each appearing rabid with hunger as they approached with a hunter's focus.

Jimmy and Damon were backed against the wall, in the corner, with no escape possible.

"We fucked up, man," said Damon. "We fucked up bad."

The wolf children were right upon them, their steamy hot breath slapping the boys in their faces.

"This can't be real, man," said Jimmy. "Where are we?"

"Somewhere we shouldn't be," replied Damon as the wolf children lunged atop them.

BIO: Essel Pratt is from Mishawaka, Indiana, a North Central town near the Michigan Border. His prolific writings have graced the pages of multiple publications. He is the Author of Final Reverie, ABC's of Zombie Friendship, and many short stories.

As a husband, a father, and a pet owner, Essel's responsibilities never end. His means of relieving stress and relaxing equate to sitting in front of his dual screens and writing the tales within the recesses of his mind.

Inspired by C.S. Lewis, Clive Barker, Stephen King, Harper Lee, William Golding, and many more, Essel doesn't restrain his writings to straight horror. His first Novel, Final Reverie is more Fantasy/Adventure, but does include elements of Horror. His first zombie book, The ABC's of Zombie Friendship, attacks the zombie genre from an alternate perspective. Future books, that are in progress and yet to be imagined, will explore the blurred boundaries of horror within its competing genres, mixing the elements into a literary stew.

http://esselpratt.wix.com/darknessbreaks
EsselPratt.BlogSpot.com
www.facebook.com/EsselPrattWriting
@EsselPratt

SABINE BARING - GOULD AND THE WEREWOLF

ROY C. BOOTH

Sabine Baring-Gould and the Werewolf was first published as a cover story for **Necrotic Tissue #8**, October 2009, Stygian Publications. This version has been further modified.

    Recently it was drawn to my attention of a letter sent out by Vicar Sabine Baring-Gould to Dr. H. Philpotts, the Bishop of Exeter. This letter, among many other of Dr. Philpotts', had recently been discovered, not in the Bishop Philpotts Library in Truro, Cornwall, but in the archives of the Devon County Library. As Dr. Philpotts at the time was in his late 80s and was harangued by the increasing agitation of his opponents for his many spurious pamphlets, this letter was among many that the Church of England had carefully archived, yet not opened.

    The beginning may perhaps be familiar to the reader as it was recounted later in Baring-Gould's much larger and longer work, published in 1865 as <u>The Book of Were-Wolves</u>. *The letter in full has been carefully restored to the best of my ability (the original was damaged over the past 150 years or so, and I have tried to piece it all back together, but, alas, I am a historian, not a writer), and submit it now to you, the reader, in its entirety.*

    – Christian Royce, Historian, London, 2008.

***

To his Eminence the Bishop of Exeter, Dr. H. Philpotts,

    I most humbly submit to you a request to review a most bizarre occurrence of the unnatural kind that had happened to me, while I was investigating a cromlech at Vienne, France this spring. It has shook me to my very essence and I must request from you assistance in understating the importance of this strange event that befell me that one fateful night.

For your perusal I have diligently copied for you the excerpt as it appears in my diary. I have kept nothing back and I have simply told the tale as it has unfolded to me.

My interest in the supernatural has been sparked by this miraculous event, and I would be most appreciative to hear what you, of your stature with and as a worldly man of your character would truthfully think of the matter. While it seems that the supernatural has been, in this enlightened age, relegated to the old wives tales to frighten children and simpletons, there nonetheless – I fear might be the possibility that these creatures equally do exist here in the British Isles, and that if that were to be true, what manner of safeguards should be emplaced to guard our very souls.

Your ever faithful servant,

S. Baring-Gould

***

I shall never forget the walk I took one night in Vienne, after having accomplished the examination of an unknown Druidical relic, the Pierre labie, at La Rondelle, near Champigni. I had learned of the existence of this cromlech only on my arrival at Champigni in the afternoon, and I had started to visit the curiosity without calculating the time it would take me to reach it and to return. Suffice it to say that I discovered the venerable pile of gray stones as the sun set, and that I expended the last lights of evening in planning and sketching. I then turned my face homeward. My walk of about ten miles had wearied me, coming at the end of a long day's posting, and I had lamed myself in scrambling over some stones to the Gaulish relic.

A small hamlet was at no great distance, and I betook myself hither, in the hopes of hiring a trap to convey me to the posthouse, but I was disappointed. Few in the place would speak French, and the priest, when I applied to him, assured me that he believed there was no better conveyance in the place than a common *charrue* with its solid wooden wheels; nor was a riding horse to be procured. The good man offered to house me for the night; but I was obliged to decline, as my family intended starting early on the following morning.

Out spake then the mayor: "Monsieur can never go back tonight across the flats, because of the...the..." and his voice dropped; "the *loups-garoux*."

136

"He says that he must return!" replied the priest in *patois*. "But who will go with him?"

"Ah, ha! M. le Curé. It is all very well for one of us to accompany him, but think of the coming back alone!"

"Then two must go with him," said the priest, "and you can take care of each other as you return."

"Picou tells me that he saw the were-wolf only this day se'nnight," said a peasant; "he was down by the hedge of his buckwheat field, and the sun had set, and he was thinking of coming home, when he heard a rustle on the far side of the hedge. He looked over, and there stood a wolf as big as a calf against the horizon, its tongue out, and its eyes glaring like marsh-fires. *Mon Dieu*! Catch me going over the *marais* tonight. Why, what could two men do if they were attacked by that wolf-fiend?"

"It is tempting Providence," said one of the elders of the village; "no man must expect the help of God if he throws himself willfully in the way of danger. Is it not so, M. le Curé? I heard you say as much from the pulpit on the first Sunday in Lent, preaching from the Gospel."

"That is true," observed several, shaking their heads.

"His tongue hanging out and his eyes glaring like marsh-fires!" said the confidant of Picou.

"Mon Dieu! If I met the monster, I should run," quoth another.

"I quite believe you, Cortrez; I can answer for it that you would," said the mayor.

"As big as a calf," threw in Picou's friend.

"If the loup-garou were only a natural wolf, why then, you see" – the mayor cleared his throat – "you see we should think nothing of it; but, M. le Curé, it is a fiend, a worse than fiend, a man-fiend – a worse than man-fiend, a man-wolf-fiend."

"But what is the young monsieur to do?" asked the priest, looking from one to another.

"Never mind," said I, who had been quietly listening to their patois, which I understood.

"Never mind; I will walk back myself, and if I meet the loup-garou I will crop his ears and tail, and send them to M. le Maire with my compliments."

A sigh of relief arose from the assembly, as they found themselves clear of the difficulty.

"*Il est Anglais*," said the mayor, shaking his head, as though he meant that an Englishman might face the devil with impunity.

A melancholy flat was the marais, looking desolate enough by day, but now, in the gloaming, tenfold as desolate. The sky was perfectly clear, and a soft, blue-gray tinge; illuminated by the new moon, a curve of light approaching its western bed. To the horizon reached a fen, blacked with pools of stagnant water, from which the frogs kept up an incessant trill

137

through the summer night. Heath and fern covered the ground, but near the water grew dense masses of flag and bulrush, amongst which the light wind sighed wearily. Here and there stood a sandy knoll, capped with firs, looking like black splashes against the grey sky; not a sign of habitation anywhere; the only trace of men being the white, straight road extending for miles across the fen.

That this district harbored wolves was not improbable, and I confess that I armed myself with a strong stick at the first clump of trees through which the road dived.

Upon that road I set myself to walk.

The path itself became as I progressed more weed choked, and darker. The moon bringing deep shadows and brilliant highlights against a road that shone with a queer eeriness.

The sandy fens soon turned to heavier bushes as the water wound itself farther from the road. The forest fell soon silent as the bulrushes and frogs were left behind. The thicket, for that is the only way it can be called, became an impenetrable mass of sharp and thorny protrusions that would at times seem to leap against my arms, seeking to scrape against the skin.

The journey itself was not difficult, but for my lame leg, which caused me first to use my strong stick, not as a protection from the creatures of the night, but rather as a walking stick. At times, I would have to stop, for I had not prepared myself for this long a journey. My case that I had jauntily decided to take with me, weighed quite heavily and I had to adjust the heavy strap many times.

During these periods of waiting, I heard the soft breaking of the branches along one of the hedges to the road.

"Who goes there?" I cried out in French.

No response did I hear.

"I am armed!" I shouted, brandishing my makeshift club at the hedges.

I waited for quite some time in that position, fearful that perhaps my unknown assailants had not heard me, or, worse, ignored my threats.

Nothing stirred and after a while my ears became accustomed again to the night noises that are so prevalent along this road. I have to admit I felt quite foolish there; having stood with my stick in the air, shouting hoarily at what could only be the machinations of an over-eager imagination, one fueled by rustic French stories of wolves that could be were-wolves.

Shouldering my pack I continued down along the path. At times I had to steady myself for the path itself was, while straight, quite fraught with unfilled potholes. The shrubs loomed much closer as the fields, too, were left behind, until all that was ahead of me was simply dark and forbidding thickets from which the occasional shadow of a tree would darken my path.

138

At first I thought it was a night creature that had perhaps become agitated by my near proximity to its realm. But as I continued I became increasingly aware that there was something following me.

I could feel its presence near me. Occasionally it would make a noise as it pressed its way through the undergrowth. At those times I would stop and look around me, my cudgel raised, but it never did show itself at that point. I continued to be wary and look around me.

I was in such a distracted state that I was unaware of the poor repair of the road. I lurched and fell on the ground, my pack striking me with its odd angles. There I was on the ground, when something dark fleeted across the thicket in front of me. It was as large as a man with wide haunches and a lumbering gait. Its eyes flickered towards me, strange, penetrating, golden slitted orbs, before disappearing back into the darkness.

I clambered up on my feet, my foot aching in protest as I gingerly put my weight on it. The night air that seemed so crisp moments before turned clammy against my skin. I scrambled for my stick that was but a dark shape against the road and had clattered far from me. I could hear the thing padding along in the brush, seeming to weave in and among the bushes.

There was a fright about me for the sound of the creature had masked itself in the many night noises and I knew for a certainty that it had followed me since Vienne. The creature kept coming closer; its breath obvious behind the thickets.

My foot protested for but a moment as I fled off the road, catching a glimpse of the creature for its great hairy bulk came into the view of the moon. And then it was hidden away by the brush as I ran through the thicket ahead of me.

I ran frightened through the thicket, branches clawing at my clothes, lashing out at my face. I could hear the crackle of the thicket behind me as the creature seemed to rush ever closer. Just when I thought this would be my end, the thickets ended in a clearing of stones; an ancient stone fence loomed across from it. The cairn stood white across a landscape of weaving claw-like shadows. I ran, not heeding my own safety, perhaps in a distant part of my mind I thought that possibly a heathen circle would in some way protect me from my aggressor, or that it would slow it down enough that I could cross the fence to safety.

The monster crashed through the thicket, and within a few leaps it was upon me as it slammed into my back, the white stones on the ground coming dangerously crashing towards me. My lungs exploded from the impact, I desperately scrambled for some purchase as the creature ripped at my back. A large stone came to my hand as I twisted to look up at the creature for the first time.

It had eyes like a wolf, white, sharp teeth. The wind whipped through the thicket, rattling sharp branches against themselves, cheering on the beast. It gripped me in its talons, dragging me up to an open mouth. It

139

looked at me with an evil cunning; with hellborne intelligence. I suspected it wanted me to scream as it salivated for my flesh, an opening course to an after theatre dinner. Instead, I bashed the rock in my hand hard against its head. The strike was not Herculean, but I wounded it just the same – it howled as it flung me across the cairn with a thud, my case cracking and spilling against the rocks. I took off the case, flinging it at the dark shadow that was spreading across the rocky white face towards me.

I clamored across the white stones as they clattered angrily against me, my feet bleeding from the sharp edges. The wall was in my grasp when the creature nearly had me. Climbing over it, I was at a narrow crossroads, on one side did it end in hedges and in another was there a bit of ancient wall and a metal gate.

I flattened myself against the wall as the creature leapt over it. I gasped for a moment before scrambling towards the metal gate. Its paws thundered across the road towards me. I grasped the gate, praying to the All-Merciful Father in Heaven, feeling years of rust aching against my straining physique. It groaned enough that I was able to slip inside.

Sharing the gloom with me was an effigy of Christ our Savior, and a smaller statue dedicated to Saint Christopher, the patron saint of travelers and sailors. I hid, placing my back against the cool darkness of the back of the shrine. The creature thundered toward me and against the gate, smashing into it with its full weight, snapping what was once open now to become closed. It glanced through the bars at me with luminous eyes and snarled, spittle coming from its mouth. It grabbed the gate with its mouth and rattled it, but it stood still against his trespasses.

I prayed for deliverance as the whole shrine seemed to shake from his anger, its prize only a mere few feet away from it. Finally, it let go of the gate, glaring long and hard at me with fierce eyes. It was not an animal look, it was more that of a murderer who had decided that here was a marked man that could not be reached because of divine providence, but like the devil it was, it would soon have me in its clutches. It gripped the gate once more, but then stopped, looking past me. It hesitated, as if transfixed for but the moment, and let go. Then it left me, alone with the night and the moon.

That is how the peasants found me, curled up in the shrine, covered in blood. I was taken to safety, laid out on the farm table as a priest was sent for. All the while the peasants would mutter among themselves, but would not talk directly to me, eying me with great suspicion. I could make scarce understanding of their patois, except here seemed to be an argument of sorts going on with the owner of the farm and the growing mass outside. From what I gathered, they were arguing over whether I was the fiend itself!

Before they could decide on my execution, the very kind Monsieur C. Lermarchant arrived. He turned on the people who seemed so brave moments before, and made them take me to his house where his serving woman dressed my wounds and carefully listened to my tale.

140

It would take two days before I was well enough to rejoin my family. During this time I thought about the queer situation that I had become drawn into on that one fateful night, and the only conclusion that I could draw was that it was the power of Christ who was able to deliver me from what could have been certain death, and that if I had not been so firm in my faith I would have surely perished. However, while we were waiting to depart across the channel back to England, I was approached by a rural priest who had heard my tale and had sought me out. He explained to me, in very hushed tones, that it was the statue of Saint Christopher that had saved me, that the saint himself had been born a Cynocephali, a dog-head, a were-wolf named Ruberus, and that his conversion to Christianity appeased his once bestial nature. The statue dedicated to him thwarted the beast, and thus I was left further unscathed, for exact reasons untold. I am now filled with a need to scholarly pursue some answers to this priest's allegations, and of the ordeal of which I survived – perhaps in the research to come I shall find enough lore and information to write yet another book, who knows, for it seems that very scant has been collected on the subject of were-wolves. Beyond that, I do not know what further can be lead from this tale, but that it is certain that we must prepare ourselves against the devil in whatever form he takes, whether were or wolf.

BIO: Roy C. Booth is a published author, comedian, poet, journalist, essayist, and screenwriter/doctor (w/. screenplays optioned). Internationally award winning playwright with 57 plays published (Samuel French, Heuer, *et al*) with 810+ productions in 30 countries and in ten languages. Check out his books on Amazon, Nook, Goodreads, and elsewhere.

www.amazon.com/author/roycbooth

WOLVES AT THE GATE

KERRY E.B. BLACK

Darkness blanketed the woods around Ward's house. He patrolled the fencing, assuring himself the wood remained impenetrable. His diligence revealed strong workmanship and solid materials. Still, gooseflesh rose on his arms and chills raced along his spine. A wind carried the smell of an approaching storm. Worse, primal calls echoed through the trees. Hidden in the forest, wolves yipped and answered, and then the pack unified in a chorus of howls.

From within the cottage, his baby boy let out a terrified cry.

Ward backed away from the fence as the wolf song crept closer. The gate swung open, pounding against itself with a bang. *No!* Ward surged forward to close it. His fear-slowed legs felt heavy as tree trunks, hampering progress. Emerging from the trees, wolves appeared, snarling. Their eyes glowed golden, reflecting the harvest-heavy full moon. He froze, fascinated by the deadly beauty.

A gentle hand on his shoulder made him jump. A soft voice whispered into his ear, "Ward, come away. Lock the gate. There's my good boy."

"Momma?"

He whipped around, but instead of his mother, he found his sister, Nina. She laid on a litter, crippled legs twisted at unnatural angles. Her face shone pale and pained in the moonlight.

The wolves slunk from the tree line, closing on the fence. Their bellies dragged the ground, and their rumbling growls addled his thinking.

I could run. I'd make the door.

Nina rested her head and closed her dark eyes. Shallow breaths made her chest rise with erratic haste.

How can I get Nina to the house? She can't walk on her own. If I pull her along, surely we'll both be devoured.

The baby's cries sounded distant, an enticement to hurry home.

The muscles beneath the wolves' fur tensed and rippled, prepared to jump.

143

If I left her here, she'd be a distraction. The wolves would attack her, which would allow me to get away.

As though hearing his thoughts, Nina said, "Leave me, Ward. Save yourself."

All his life, he was told to protect his sister. His knees ached to run. He ran a hand through his hair, looking from the open gate to his helpless sister. At the window of the cottage, his wife held the baby, watching the drama unfurl. *How'd the house get so far away? It'll take every last piece of strength I have to get away.* The baby pounded the window glass. *What kind of example am I setting for my boy?* His wife mouthed his name. *Will my wife respect me when this is over?*

The winds picked up, bringing the first cold, cutting onslaught of rain.

The wolves snarled and lunged, pounding over the ground as though thundering through violent water. Ward watched, fascinated by the slow-motion progress. Gray and black fur slicked as they closed in for the kill. *I'm going to die because of my own indecision.*

Clouds moved from the face of the moon. In the silver light, Ward's mother stood. Rain slicked her hair to her scalp and forced her clothing to cling. Tears mingled with the precipitation, and a resolve set her jaw in stubborn lines. She dipped her chin before pushing the entry. The gate slammed shut. The iron lock crashed into place.

No!

Snaps and snarls mingled with her screeches. Sloppy tearing agonized. The rain abandoned them, amplifying the sounds of death.

Nina sobbed and trembled, curled into herself like a newborn. "Momma."

Ward wheeled on his sister, looming over her. His grip on her litter tore the fabric. "It's your fault! She'd be alive if it weren't for you!"

Nina recoiled, pulling further into a ball, and whimpered.

His skin itched and his breathing came in deep gasps. His shadow blocked out the moon, plunging Nina into darkness. "I hate you."

His joints ached as though stretched. Rage overtook him, and he pounded on her bed. She bounced around, defenseless. Quivering, fighting to control himself, he shook and stepped away.

He dug into his flesh, determined to relieve the burning beneath his skin. Flakes fell to his feet, revealing matted hair along his arms. Something dark dripped from his hands, tickling as it fell to the ground. He smeared it along fingernails grown thick as horn, sharp as claws. A metallic smell made his stomach rumble. His tongue danced over dagger-sharp teeth as he licked between his fingers. Blood.

He jumped to his sister. Her eyes bulged, unblinking, reflecting the glorious moon dominating the troubled nighttime sky. Dark stains along her throat soaked into her splayed hair and shredded clothing.

Did I do this? Am I responsible?

The wolves beckoned. Their voices rushing through his blood, reverberating in answering echoes. He pulled his lips over elongated teeth.

A flicker drew his attention to the house. Firelight cast his wife into shadowy relief, a wall of gold, yellow, and red consuming the interior of the home he'd built. He padded toward them, enjoying the silence of his progress.

She raised a quavering warning. "Stay away!" She hunched over the baby and backed away from him. Terror played along their features.

Ward's voice sounded thick as a growl. "Stop! The fire!"

His family retreated further from him, heedless of the barrage of flame. Their screams mingled with the wolves' cries. Revolted by the answering hunger generated by the smell of their charring flesh, Ward coursed through the gate to join the pack.

BIO: Kerry E.B. Black lives along a fog enshrouded river outside of the City of Steel and Bridges in Pennsylvania, USA. Kerry dances with words to recreate nightmarish stories that dip into the universality of fear and while some works have crept into anthologies, she also writes for www.Halloweenforevermore.com and GamesOmniverse. She invites readers to follow at

www.facebook.com/authorKerryE.B.Black, https://twitter.com/BlackKerryblick, and

https://kerrylizblack.wordpress.com/

THE FIVE TOWNS PAGEANT

JAMES H. LONGMORE

His flesh tore like rending cloth, thick fur ripped away in fat, dripping clods, viscera spilled from the gaping wounds in his belly.

No longer able to fight, the beast knew that he was beaten, felt his life pouring out in hot, gushing waves and with it, the sensation of returning to his human form.

He'd put up a noble fight - his own razor teeth and keen claws had made their mark on the other creature and he'd tasted its thick, coppery blood on his tongue before succumbing to its savage onslaught.

In the background, fading as quickly as his life as he waited for those cruel teeth to deliver their coup de grace, *he could hear the sound of many voices.*

ONE

"Ouch." Cam sucked in his breath and grimaced as the thick needle punctured the tanned skin over his lean abdominal muscles.

"Almost done, Mr. McGlamery." The Doctor in the ill-fitting shirt sounded wooden and over-rehearsed. The doctor's face was fat and waxy with piggy eyes topped off with a comb-over that reeked of hair cream and antiseptic.

Cam chanced a peek at the hypodermic sticking out of his muscle and nausea washed over him. He was pleased he'd made Josephine - *Jojo* - stay in the waiting room; the last thing he'd want was for his girlfriend to see him faint, cry or pee his pants - or quite possibly all three.

He'd harbored a phobia of needles from the age of nine when one had broken off in his arm during a routine allergy shot. They'd had to surgically remove the inch or so that was embedded beneath his skin and worse, the allergy shots hadn't even worked; Cam still spent a goodly part of Spring indoors, terrorized by the insidious yellow pollen that smothered everything outside.

Doctor Pollard finished squirting the rabies vaccine into Cam's belly and withdrew the needle, nice and slow.

Cam winced and studied the twin puncture wounds that oozed blood and were bruising up a treat on his six-pack. The two shots today - the dour-faced Doctor had explained – were one dose of immunoglobulin and the first of the four-part anti-rabies course. The first shot was to make the vaccine work; the second to ensure that Cam didn't die in some slobbering, manically aggressive heap in one to three months. As for the injections yet to come, Cam put those down to pure sadism.

It wasn't as if the tetanus shot hadn't been humiliating enough. The nurse at the town's ER had insisted Cam needed one, so he'd stood there with his shirt sleeve rolled up and Jojo holding his hand.

"You're gonna have to drop 'em." The nurse had informed him with a wicked smile.

"Excuse me?"

"This goes in the glute." She'd replied as if this was all just some great big joke. "If you'd prefer the young lady wait outside -?"

"She's okay," Cam had said. He hadn't wanted to be left alone with the skinny old nurse and her evil syringe. "There's nothing she's not seen before." He grinned and took some delight at the nurse's discomfort because perhaps Nursey got her jollies by pantsing jocks in her little curtained-off area. Besides which, Jojo *had* seen it all before. Hell, she'd had most of it in her mouth at one time or another.

After sticking the needle in Cam's ass, the nurse had referred him to the bigger hospital in the next town over for rabies shots.

And to Cam McGlamery this had all seemed like a ridiculous amount of fuss over such a small bite.

TWO

It had been Jojo's idea to visit the mall's pet store to look at the puppies. Cam would often wonder if his girlfriend's predilection for baby animals was the beginning of a premature and impending broodiness. This worried him a tad, having just finished high school neither of them were ready to even *think about* babies.

Michael's Pets - along with the rest of the mall - had been gaily decorated in advance of the upcoming Five Towns Pageant with foil bunting, garish posters and balloons. It was the same every year as the stores milked the occasion the way in which they would commence their Christmas promotions the second the kids began their Fall semester.

Cam and Jojo had sauntered in, oblivious to the heads that turned at the arrival of such a handsome couple - it was just something they'd gotten used to. In any given John Hughes movie, Cam would be the popular quarterback who swam against the crowd and was loved by all. He was dark haired, six feet four inches, had an incredibly toned body and was good

148

looking in a way that made the girls swoon. He played sports, of course - excelled at them all - and had maintained a 4.0 average through high school.

Jojo Merle stood at five feet nothing *sans* heels but was as pretty as Cam was classically handsome. She was a petite size six with perky breasts and a round face with sharp, angled cheekbones. She dyed her hair blonde to mask the plain mousey-brown she'd always hated and wore contacts that accentuated her dazzling sapphire eyes. In testimony to her beauty, Jojo had been chosen to represent the town in that year's upcoming Miss Five Towns Contest which was a part of the annual Pageant that included the ubiquitous parades, cook-offs, sports events, fireworks and general gaiety that small town America does so well. Jojo had been particularly proud to have won the vote participate in the contest, especially so because she'd done it on her own merit and not because Daddy was the newly elected Mayor.

Their trip to the mall that day had been to pick out Jojo's swimsuit for the contest - something not too slutty to court disqualification (at least two of the other villages involved were quite puritan) yet not too demure since she wanted to catch the judges' eye. Jojo had settled on a black one-piece (bikinis were *so* clichéd!) that cut high on the thigh and accentuated Jojo's shapely, dancer's legs and plunged down to the navel to show off a daring amount of boob. The halter-neck suit had no back whatsoever and scooped so low that there was a danger of Jojo revealing serious butt cleavage if she so much as *thought* about bending over.

Cam had loved the suit. Far from being jealous of his girlfriend being ogled by strangers, the thought actually turned him on; in fact, he'd sported quite an erection in the clothes store during the near-ritualistic *Trying-on-of-the-Swimsuits*.

"Aww he is *so* cute." Jojo had cooed at the tiny black and white puppy in the glass-fronted cage. She tapped on the glass and the puppy opened one eye and yawned; an action that had elicited another girlish exclamation.

Cam, however, had been more interested in the store's two new assistants. The owner/manager - Michael (not a consumer-friendly *Mike* or *Mickey*) - was a nondescript, average looking man of average height, average build and average hair color (next to the entry *average* in the illustrated dictionary, there'd be a picture of this guy). It was perhaps because of this that Michael employed such babes.

One of the girls was breathtakingly stunning. Her naturally platinum blonde hair contrasted exquisitely with honey-tan skin and cascaded down her slim back like some living waterfall. One side of her head was close shaven with a Celtic pattern etched into the fuzzy hair above her ear – the pattern matching the intricate tattoo that sleeved her left arm. She had a trim, firm body and magnificent breasts that strained against her white shirt and jiggled playfully as she moved.

149

By contrast, the blonde's colleague had delectable porcelain-white skin and ink-black hair that was cut into severe, short spikes. She was petite with a young, elfin face and the biggest, brownest eyes ever. She too was spectacularly well endowed and her own white shirt - Cam presumed it corporate wear - strained at its third button as if her breasts were desperate to escape.

"Would you like to hold him?" The blonde had asked Jojo, her voice smooth and exotic.

"Could I?" Jojo had beamed, her smile faltering as she caught Cam's sideways glance at the blonde's bosom. Jojo puffed out her own perky chest, but as generous as her breasts were, they didn't come anywhere close to matching those of the pneumatic blonde.

"Sure thing, Ma'am." The assistant unlocked the cage and scooped out the puppy. It squirmed in her hand and licked her long, lithe fingers.

Jojo had giggled as the puppy was placed into her open hands. She nuzzled it and grinned the broadest grin when it lapped at the end of her nose.

"Is he a mix?" Cam asked the blonde, eager to engage the girl in some - *any* - conversation.

"Jack Russell and Doberman." The assistant had replied and Cam's mind boggled as he tried to work out the logistics of such a pairing.

"I think he likes you." Jojo had thrust the wriggling puppy into her boyfriend's hands, possibly to distract him from the blonde.

Cam had held the puppy and felt entirely unmoved. Never one for sentimentality where animals were concerned, Cam nonetheless thought it *reasonably* adorable.

"Who's a cute little fella?" Cam played along and tickled the creature's soft chin with his thumb.

And that was when the puppy had bit him.

*****

"Shit!" Cam had yelped with pain and disbelief as the puppy chomped down on his thumb.

"Aww, he *does* like you." Jojo had smiled but a worried look flitted across her face. She'd rested a calming hand on Cam's arm as a surge of rage flashed up behind his eyes. She'd seen this before; like the time Tim Gorton had picked a fight with Cam over a fumble that had cost the school team the district championship - the Gorton kid was still in a wheelchair three years on and would probably see out the rest of his life being pushed around in the thing.

Jojo had given Cam's bicep a loving squeeze and prayed for his rage to pass.

Cam had ground his teeth together and struggled against the urge to squeeze the life out of the puppy and hurl its twisted corpse across the store. Instead, he'd held it out for the assistant to reclaim and actually managed a smile through the red mist that had even obliterated his lascivious thoughts of the hot blonde and her raven-haired colleague.

"You naughty boy," the blonde had cooed as she plucked the squirming puppy from Cam's hands. She rubbed its fluffy belly. "Look what you did to the nice man."

The bite had barely drawn blood as the puppy's pinprick teeth were tiny and its jaws weak.

Jojo lifted Cam's thumb to her lips and kissed away the blood. Then she kissed his lips so that he could taste his blood on her.

It was something they did, Jojo and Cam. It was their *thing* as young lovers exploring the infinite world of carnal pleasure and all of its permutations. Through their love of blood play Jojo sported a faint razor blade scar on the top of her left breast and Cam several on his right pectoral; they wore those scars with great pride and as a declaration of their undying love.

It was astounding how quickly their relationship had veered away from the typical clumsy teenaged fumbles and into to the darker realms of BDSM and pain and rough sex. Blame it on modern culture, blame it on the extreme porn that they watched together, blame it on *Fifty Shades* if you like - but here were two like-minded souls with sexual appetites so far away from the norm who had found each other early on life's path.

Cam relished the warm, metallic taste on his lover's lips and his rage had subsided - replaced by thoughts of making love to his girl, of being deep inside her, of tying her to the bed with rough, biting rope and squeezing her throat tight as he fucked her.

Cam had broken from his reverie to see the black haired chick looking at him with an odd look in her eyes.

"Are you okay, Sir?" There was faux concern in her voice. "Would you like a Band-Aid?" She'd barely been able to suppress her smirk as she sidled up to the blonde to pet the errant puppy, her breast resting on her colleague's arm.

"I think he'll live." Jojo smiled a conspiratorial smile. *Men, eh? All of 'em really are big babies*. The unspoken words passed between Jojo and the assistants. *And if you check out my man like that again I'll rip* both *of your fucking hearts out*. "Come along, Cameron," She said with a grin, "clothes shopping awaits!"

Cam sighed and rolled his eyes in a put-upon-but-loving-it expression and allowed Jojo to lead him from the store and those impossibly beautiful girls.

THREE

151

Three days later, Cam had awoken feeling decidedly *odd*, like he had somebody else's teeth in. Also, his head throbbed and his back muscles were stiff and ached as if he'd had a serious work out the previous day instead of the laying on the couch playing *Call of Duty* he'd actually done.

Even though it had been only a quarter after six in the morning, he'd called Jojo, and despite the early hour she'd been more than delighted to go straight over.

"You really should see a doctor." She'd advised. "You may have caught something nasty." She peered at his thumb and at the barely perceptible indentations on its soft pad.

"What? From my vicious dog attack?" Cam had mocked with a nervous laugh. "I don't think it's anything to worry about." He'd pulled Jojo onto his bed. "I was only looking for a little sympathy." He slid a hand under her '*I'm Daddy's Princess*' T and she slapped him away.

"I'm serious, Cam. Heaven only knows what diseases it could have been carrying." She'd put on her *serious face*. "They breed them in puppy farms where hygiene really isn't a priority."

"It's probably just a summer cold." Cam had shrugged. "Nothing a BJ won't cure." Cam made with his best sexy smile which fell sadly short.

"There'll be nothing of the sort until you get yourself checked out." Jojo's *stern voice*. "You're not giving me *Toxocara* or freakin' Rabies."

At the sound of the r-word, Cam's libido had bottomed out to somewhere just below zero. Rabies was not something he'd even considered before then and his mind was instantly flooded with images of snarling, slobbering rage and horrendous death. Cam had even eyed with suspicion the glass of water sitting on his night stand and could have sworn that the sight of the clear liquid was making his skin crawl.

Jojo had frog-marched Cam to the ER for the tetanus shot and then the nurse had advised them to take the trip to the big hospital because she didn't carry the Rabies vaccine and it could take up to three days if she ordered it in.

"And since you've already waited three days to get yourself checked out, it would be foolish to wait *another* three." The nurse had all but wagged her finger at him. "The Rabies virus can take as little as a week to reach the brain."

And that was how Cam had found himself in a hospital cubicle, barely concealed by a hastily-drawn plastic curtain and being used as a human pin cushion by the sadistic fat doctor.

Cam had looked with dismay at the spreading purple bruise on his belly, tried to imagine just how unpleasant it would look when it turned green in a day or so. However, he *was* proud of himself for having not blubbed like a little girl during the agonizing shot.

152

"The bruising will go down in a few days." The doctor had read Cam's mind.

"Just in time for the next shot, eh?"

"Yes, there is that." The doctor had replied without humor. "You'll need to come back in five days, it's imperative that you finish the course." He'd popped the used syringe into the sharps bin and removed his latex gloves.

"Can't wait." As Cam had climbed from the bed his knees felt a little wobbly, so he'd steadied himself against the wall.

"Would you like me to call your friend in?"

"Thank you. No." Cam had brushed the doctor off, and with a deep breath, he'd made his way out through the flimsy curtains.

***

Cam had insisted on driving both to and from the hospital - he hated Jojo's driving - despite the fact that even the thought of the shots he'd faced had made him feel queasy. On the drive home Cam had been quite introspective and told Jojo that he was going to head home to sleep it off so he'd drop her off at her house. Jojo's parents were out of town and it was Sex Night; Cam wanted to be sure that he'd be in full effect for their evening's delectations.

"My poor baby." Jojo had stroked his thigh. "We could always give tonight a miss if you're not up to it?"

"No way," Cam replied – perhaps a little too forcefully. "After the morning I've had, I need me some Jojo *lovin'*." He put on the redneck accent that never failed to amuse.

Jojo was still smiling when she'd climbed from Cam's car outside her house. She'd kissed him full on the mouth and teased his lips with the tip of her tongue. "Straight to sleep, young man." She'd laughed. "No *X-Boxing* 'til you've had some shut-eye."

"Yes'm." Cam had replied with a glint in his eye.

And with that Jojo had disappeared with a wiggle of her elegantly pert behind and Cam had driven off in the direction of the mall.

Cam wasn't sure *why* he'd decided to visit the pet store instead of heading home. He wasn't even one hundred percent sure that he had actually *decided* to go; it felt more like he was on autopilot and was being drawn to the place. It was possible that it had been the impure thoughts of Blondie and Raven-hair - his modern-day sirens - that lured him - not with hypnotic song but with shirt-straining breasts.

Was it possible that he was actually even *considering* being unfaithful to Jojo - the girl to whom he'd been exclusive since eighth grade? Surely not – especially since it was highly unlikely that the two assistants would share Cam's penchant for the darker aspects of sex, as did Jojo; she

153

and he were most definitely two halves of the same when it came to exploring the depraved fringes of sexuality.

Still, Cam's legs had propelled him through the mall whilst his guilty paranoia teased him with a sickly feeling of being *watched*.

He turned the corner between the pretzel vendor and the phone case kiosk and stopped dead in his tracks.

The pet store was closed.

Not just closed, but completely gutted down to its bare walls and strung across the padlocked door hung the wasp-striped bunting of police tape.

"Police closed it up after yon incident." A voice piped up behind him, pronouncing the first word as *po-leece*. Cam turned around to face the weasel-faced guy who ran the phone case kiosk.

"Incident?"

"One of Michael's new gals got sick and went crazy." Kiosk Guy said with ghoulish glee. "She tore a customer's throat out right there in front of yon window. Poor old gal was only taking a look-see at them blue parakeets they used to sell."

Cam felt nauseous again and his abdomen throbbed with dull pain.

"You're joking?" He asked.

Kiosk Guy shook his head. "No, Sir," he said. "Happened just a coupl'a days ago, saw it all with my own two eyes." A haunted look cast over his face. "That blonde gal with the huge titties smashed up the shop and dragged the old lady to the floor and ripped out her neck with her teeth. Screamed like a freakin' banshee too."

"The old woman?"

"The blonde," Kiosk Guy corrected. "By the time the cops came, she'd eaten most of the lady's face off - and some of her arm too. They reckon Blondie was on *Smelling Salts*, or some such." Kiosk Guy rubbed his hands with sick delight.

"What happened to the other girl, and Michael?" Cam asked.

Kiosk Guy shook his head. "No idea, Buddy. The cops had the store cordoned off before you could say *exsanguination*."

Cam shuddered and walked away. Mental images of an uncontrollable, snarling rage danced through his mind, and although Blondie's breakdown most likely had been drug-related, Cam thanked his lucky stars that he'd let Jojo bully him into going to the hospital.

FOUR

Jojo licked gently around Cam's bruised belly, her soft tongue raising the gooseflesh on his skin. Cam moaned softly and laid his head back on the pillow, eyes closed tight as he lost himself in pleasure.

154

She had been waiting on her bed for Cam when he'd arrived at her home just as dusk was filling in the horizon. She'd dressed in a demure long-sleeved, white cotton nightgown that covered her body neck to knees. It had a high, intricate lace collar and matching cuffs but was otherwise plain save for a single row of pearl buttons that ran along its front. Naturally, Jojo was tantalizingly naked beneath but that did little to distract from the pure, virginal look she presented.

Jojo had spent her afternoon in diligent preparation; she'd laundered and starched the bed sheets to give a fresh, crisp feel, arranged the dozen candles that flickered and cast sensual shadows around her boudoir, and burned incense sticks that added a thick, musky scent to the warm air.

As for herself, Jojo had shaved away every last trace of body hair to leave every inch of her alabaster skin deliciously silky and smooth - just the way Cam loved it. She'd taken a long, luxurious bath with shea butter oils to slough off what little dry skin she had and upon emerging had painted her finger and toe nails a delicate, subtle pink that was almost a perfect match for her glowing skin.

At first, Cam had been taken aback. He'd become accustomed to the leather and latex outfits that populated the nether regions of Jojo's wardrobe - that and the unashamed nudity that she more often preferred. But this was new to their repertoire, and the all-covering *Little House on the Prairie* night gown was such a departure that Cam had at first struggled to attain arousal.

But then Jojo had brought out the thick, leather straps. They were - in keeping with Jojo's theme - virginal white and jangled with shining, silver buckles; Jojo let Cam know in her own wordless, submissive way that he was to use them on her once she'd finished bathing his body with her tongue.

With that task completed, and Cam's body damp and tingling, Jojo lay down and offered her wrists and ankles to each of the four corners of the bed.

Cam obliged and secured Jojo's wrists and ankles to the bed posts, taking great care not to expose her body beneath the gown, as if to do so would be to spoil the game. He then paused awhile and watched her breasts rise and fall with the rhythm of her breathing, longing to undo the gown's iridescent buttons but reluctant to undo the spell of that precious moment. Jojo looked so perfectly helpless tied to the fat wooden posts, so pure and chaste swaddled in clean white and to Cam she looked almost -

Sacrificial?

Jojo smiled and Cam could no longer hold back his animal instincts. He lowered himself to kiss her warm, soft lips and pressed his body against hers and his skin goosed at the rough touch of the cotton gown.

Jojo responded and her probing tongue pushed its way into Cam's mouth as she squirmed on the bed with an aching, wanton desire.

Cam caressed Jojo's cheek with his fingers and traced his hand down to her throat. Deftly, he picked at the first button that snuggled beneath her chin. As that button popped open, Jojo sighed and strained against the leather straps that secured her to the bed. Cam moved down to the next button, the weight of his hand resting on her heaving breast and his lips not once leaving hers.

FIVE

The weeks that followed went by in a blur for Cameron McGlamery.

He awoke in the hospital to the sight of Dr. Pollard's chubby face hovering above him. Against the stark white of the hospital's ceiling, it appeared to be disembodied.

The face to Cam's left belonged to a cop, and he swam slowly into focus as Cam's eyes adjusted to the bright, fluorescent light and until Cam attempted to sit up he didn't realize that he'd been handcuffed to the metal railings of the hospital bed, a perverse parody of his and Jojo's sex play. Cam tugged at the 'cuffs and the silver chain jingle-jangled against the rail. Beside him, the cop fidgeted uneasily in his chair and ran a hand over his sweaty face.

"Don't worry, that's there for your own safety." Doctor Pollard told him and attempted a reassuring smile.

Cam's first thought was that he'd had a bad reaction to the Rabies shot and had blacked out whilst making love to Jojo; the last thing he could recall was of unbuttoning her white night gown and stroking warm, smooth skin.

The thought also struck him that if he *had* collapsed, then Jojo would have had to have called 911 once she'd wriggled free from her bondage. Cam allowed himself a wry smile at that - he knew she would just die of embarrassment having to explain everything to the paramedics.

Only, Jojo hadn't died of embarrassment.

Officially she'd died of asphyxiation. Cam had strangled the life out of her in the throes of passion.

So went the conclusion of the inquiry into Jojo's death and they'd used the word *intercourse* in the report, a word that to Cam demeaned all of the intimate times he and Jojo had shared. The verdict itself had been *accidental death due to erotic asphyxiation* which put Jojo's demise alongside that of Michael Hutchence and David Carradine - only without the electrical flex and oranges.

Cam had attended the funeral service 'cuffed to the cop because they'd laid Jojo to rest before the inquiry was over and he was still a suspect.

156

Jojo's parents had been terribly brave and polite and had even asked Cam how *he* was bearing up during the wake at the house in which their only child had been killed.

In fact, everyone seemed painfully - impossibly - *nice* to Cam, even though he figured they must all have suspected him of some culpability in Jojo's death. And he simply couldn't escape the feeling that his girl's parents - and his own - were keeping something from him.

After the funeral, the subsequent enquiry and his final rabies shots, Cam had avoided Jojo's parents along with his own, and preferred to stay within the confines of his room along with his numbed emotions and haunted dreams.

And try as he may, Cam couldn't remember a single thing beyond the sweet scent of Jojo's body, her silky skin, the teasing, taut nipples that puckered as he exposed them and the twitching of her smooth belly when his fingertips caressed it. Cam's memory stopped right there.

Yet he had apparently (and *officially*) choked the Mayor's daughter - *his* Jojo - to death as they'd made love.

That just didn't sit right with Cam - he never forgot stuff - and the entire episode seemed to him to have been handled with an uncanny efficiency; the funeral, the quick inquiry, the absolving of all blame on his part when he'd felt that he deserved to be punished (as if losing his soulmate had not been punishment enough).

Survivor's guilt, the hospital shrink he'd seen just the once had labelled it and then assured Cam that it would pass in time.

When night time came and Cam lay his head on the pillow that he and Jojo had shared with her soft hair splayed out and tickling his face, his dreams would be of tearing flesh and hot, spraying blood that tasted of copper and looked black in the candle light; of splintering bone, stinking, slippery viscera and Jojo's gurgled, blood-choked screams.

SIX

Cam struggled to find sleep.

He tossed and turned in his bed and squinted for the thousandth time at the red LED numbers projected into the darkness on his ceiling. Time had inched along only a few tortuous minutes - to thirteen after two - since his last peek.

Desperate for sleep, Cam would even have welcomed the terrible, bloody nightmares that had plagued him since leaving the hospital, although that would mean facing the horrific dreams of Jojo's demise and the terrible, dark thoughts that skulked at the periphery of his memory.

Cam's body ached and he felt cold, he slept naked now as he'd had to discard his pyjamas as they had suddenly gotten too small for him. At first, Cam had put that down to too many pizzas and couch time but upon

157

closer inspection, he'd discovered that there wasn't an ounce of fat to be found on his body. His increase in size seemed to be muscle bulk, particularly on his upper arms, chest and thighs. This, Cam found odd insomuch he'd stopped hitting the gym after Jojo - well, after whatever had happened to her.

He turned his pillow over and hoped that maybe the cool side would help sleep catch up with him.

At least, Cam thought, he was managing to avoid the seasonal stuffed up nose that - along with the itchy eyes he'd merrily claw out of their sockets - made his life a misery this time of year. This, despite the fact that the air outside was thick with pollen as the oak tree that waved its spindly branches outside his bedroom window had coated everything in the front yard with a thick yellow layer of what was basically tree come.

Cam kicked off the bedclothes and lay on his back staring blankly up at the ceiling. Despite feeling decidedly chilly, his body was coated in a glistening sheen of sweat that glowed against the cold light that snuck through his thin curtains. Also, his dick stood tall and proud at its perfect forty-five degree angle from his groin. Cam wanted to grab the thing, slap it and hurt it like Jojo used to, but somehow the thought of doing that right now felt like being unfaithful to her memory.

Nonetheless, the arousal spread through Cam's body as if emanating from the center of the erection; a slow, creeping sensation that seemed to switch on his nerve endings one by one as it crawled beneath his skin like a swarm of miniscule, living creatures.

Cam cursed his dick, he felt even more awake now and had the old, familiar dread that once more he'd be watching the sun rise.

Suddenly Cam's body contorted.

It was a single, violent movement that was so abrupt, so unexpected, that it forced the air from his lungs in a *phoooph* sound. Cam's spine twisted, his limbs bent in on themselves as his neck threw his head back with such force that the bones popped like kindling wood.

Cam was surprised to feel no pain; in fact, the involuntary spasm that wracked his body had felt more akin to an orgasm if anything.

Cam's skin tightened as if with the heat of the sun; a burning, tingling and not entirely unpleasant prickle. Then his spine seized and curled his body forwards to double him with his arms pressed tight to his chest and his knees dug hard into his gut.

What's happening to me?

Cam's mind raced and fear overrode the paroxysms of pleasure that snaked through his body.

Am I dying?

If that was the case, how come he'd never felt more alive in his entire life?

158

Cam's back straightened out with a violent and audible *CRACK!* and his arms and legs thrust outwards and catapulted him from the bed. Cam collapsed on the floor with a thump and he feared his parents would burst in to find their precious son on all fours, rump thrust high in the air, and packing a hard-on apt to drill through the floorboards.

Another jolt of pleasure drenched Cam's brain. With it came memories of hot, naked flesh sopping with salty sweat, pliant breasts topped with hard, cherry nipples and the heady, slick wetness that oozed between spreading thighs and teased with the cloying stink of sex.

Cam felt his bones moving around inside his body, sensed them *shifting* and changing. And with each movement, every crack of loosened joints, there came yet another, almost unbearable wave of pleasure. His back arched and neck stiffened as the delicate bones in his face separated and shuffled around as if under the influence of unseen fingers; it felt like his face was melting from the inside.

Then Cam's face erupted forward with a slick, fluid movement that stretched his skin impossibly taut. There came the peculiar sensation of teeth physically *growing* within their sockets, roots snaking down to grate against his jaw bone and feel alien in his mouth.

Cam could see the end of his nose as an elongated snout complete with whiskers that snaked out of distended pores. Stretched from the freckled, upturned nose that Jojo had found *so* cute and made the target for her sweet kisses, it was now black and glistening wet like a dog's.

It was this distortion of his nose that was the clincher for Cam. Seduced by the wild, orgasmic sensations of what he was experiencing, he had not dared consider what the transformation was until now.

Hell, it wasn't even a full moon!

There were claws, of course there had to be. They forced their way out from beneath Cam's finger and toe nails which flaked from their beds and lay bloody and glinting on the hardwood floor. As each new, honed claw flexed against the polished wood, Cam absently wondered if they'd be retractable like a cat's. Alas no, they stood affixed on his broad, elongated digits like a malevolent array of knives.

The hair came next. Thick swathes of the stuff sprouted from his skin and coated his thick, taut muscles and along with it came a hellish itch that triggered the pleasure center in Cam's cerebral cortex and pushed him closer to his climax.

And then it was over.

Cam stood in transformed glory in the bedroom that had been his since he was in his crib, and he cut a magnificent lupine figure with his dark, sleek fur, vicious teeth and dripping muzzle.

The promised climax tore through Cam's new body and shook his frame. A noise forced itself from his throat; a guttural, primeval snarl that

159

sounded like nothing that had ever been human. And with it, Cam ejaculated on to the floor.

Then the pleasure ebbed like the waves of a turning tide to leave in its place an insatiable, ravenous hunger.

The beast that was Cameron McGlamery slunk from the house and out into the cool night air.

***

Cam knew the girl was in the park before his heightened senses picked up her scent. He *sensed* her, *felt* her warmth and the pulse of her quickened heartbeat through the still, dark air.

There was also another presence.

Cam couldn't determine how far away it was so he sought sanctuary in the shadows and amongst the plastic fold-up seating that had been laid out in neat, regimented rows for the Pageant. He prowled around the periphery of the park, inching ever closer to the young girl who sat alone on a swing in the kiddies' play area with her slight frame rocking gently to and fro, her dainty feet dangling an inch or so above the ground.

The part of Cam's psyche that still considered itself *human* did puzzle as to how come a young girl could be in the park at this ungodly hour. Whatever her reason, she didn't look in the least part unhappy - in fact her countenance was perfectly serene. Cam's curiosity was soon dampened by the girl's sweet fragrance which stirred within him a raw, animal hunger that gnawed deep within his belly.

Cam circled around the girl with a preternatural stealth, camouflaged by the bushes and grateful for his thick pelt that shielded against the sharp twigs that probed his body like inquisitive fingers.

He chose a place as close to the girl as he could manage without breaking cover and from there he contemplated her young, succulent body and the sweet promise of delectable flesh. She was achingly beautiful - no more than sweet sixteen - with a slender, wide-eyed face framed by shimmering shoulder-length, auburn hair. She wore a crisp, white dress that accentuated the rise of her small breasts and her feet were tiny and delicate and most delectably bare. Which gave Cam thoughts of popping each one of her tiny, perfect toes into his ravenous, snarling mouth.

And with that, he was upon her.

The girl had no time to scream before Cam seized her throat in his powerful jaws and bit down hard. A dizzying rush of gratification raced through Cam's body as the girl's larynx was crushed between his teeth and the sticky, wet heat of her blood pumped into his mouth.

Cam dragged the girl from the swing, oblivious to her flailing hands that beat at his face and yanked hard at his fur. Closing his eyes tight against her spirited onslaught, Cam shook his head side to side and heard -

felt - the rending flesh as it gave way beneath his savage teeth. The girl flew to the ground, her neck ripped open to the white nubs of her spine and the front of her dress stained a deep red that in the night looked as black as tar.

Gulping down the raw meat and gristle of his victim's throat in one, Cam paused to inhale the intoxicating aromas that spilled from her ruined body; the meaty stink of coagulating blood, sharp ammonia tang of urine and the earthy reek of her voided bowels and his animal mind reeled and raced with a tsunami of dark pleasures and the all-consuming urge to tear and rip and gorge.

The young girl was still alive when Cam tore open her belly and began feasting upon her innards.

SEVEN

The harsh morning light hurt Cam's eyes. He'd left the bedroom window wide open, his curtains flapped lazily in the early morning breeze and the window frame was smeared with dried blood.

Cam was relieved to find that the young girl's blood that had clung to his matted pelt had been confined to the window frame and bed sheets; he'd have those cleaned off long before his folks arose. It also wasn't lost on him that he must have scaled the wall of the two storey house to get back into his room.

Cam glanced down at his naked, blood-streaked body. Stretched out on the bed of his childhood, he seemed bulkier, broader, his muscles more taut and he figured that part of the transformation must have stayed with him. Cam hoped that it wouldn't fade away along with the more obvious symptoms of his lycanthropy.

He still had the taste of her blood in his mouth, as a drunk carries the sourness of his evening's libation; and with it the memory of steaming, ripped meat between his teeth, blood spattering his face and drenching his thick, black fur. Cam could still see the girl's face as he tore into her body - that look of agony and sheer terror in her final throes of life – and he knew that he should feel disgusted with what he had done (guilty even?) but no matter how hard he tried he *just couldn't*.

From his change into an otherworldly beast to the heart-thumping hunt and the fulfilment of his newfound hunger, to the insatiable lust that had pounded through his body as he'd ripped the girl apart and the sight of the thick, white ropes of his semen strewn across the girl's decimated body, Cam knew that it was all just part of his life now - of what he had become.

And it made him feel powerful.

Muscles strained and tensed beneath his skin, literally aching to run and climb and kill and fuck; Cam's body and brain throbbed with a fresh energy that triggered his synapses with input from his heightened senses - he had never felt more *alive*. Even concerns of getting caught - he'd

161

murdered an innocent girl, after all - did nothing to dampen the swelling euphoria, although Cam couldn't help but wonder if the werewolf DNA he'd left behind on the girl would match his (should he ever end up on a database) – and just how thorough had the metamorphosis been?

Sadly, that night's events had left Cam with little doubt that his poor Jojo had suffered a fate similar to the girl in the park. Cam was grateful that he held no memory of that and wished to dear God that he never would. He prayed that the process he'd been through was akin to that of a butterfly which wouldn't remember its pupal stage - when caterpillar flesh is broken down into an amorphous mush and reassembled into something altogether more elegant - there are clearly some things that Mother Nature deems it best to forget.

Easing his frame from the bed, Cam grunted at the gratifying ache in his joints. He wanted to shower and clean off the window frame before his parents were up and about; with luck, he'd have time to get his bed sheets into the washer before Mom began her chores, although he thought he could hear her moving around the house already.

Cam's bedroom door burst open and slammed hard against the wall, its handle digging into the sheetrock.

Before he could even react, Cam was wrestled to the floor by a pair of burly cops who reeked of body odor and fried food. He struggled in vain as they pinned him down with expert ease; their combined bulk on his body forcing the air from his lungs in a wheezing grunt that sounded like a sow in a slaughterhouse.

The cold, steel handcuffs snapped around Cam's wrists and he looked across the room and saw his parents in the doorway.

Dad had his arm around Mom and they both had a peculiar look on their face.

Were they smiling?

A familiar smell of greasy hair and hospitals assaulted Cam's nostrils and something sharp dug into his neck and his mind spun back to the rabies shots.

Then all went dark.

EIGHT

Cam struggled back to consciousness with a pounding in his head and a sickly sweet scent that stung his sinuses with a metallic tang. There was also the unmistakable murmur of a hushed but excited crowd.

He was still naked but no longer restrained; a blunt ache in his wrists the only reminder of the tight 'cuffs. He lay on a rough camping cot; Cam could feel the abrasive canvas against his skin and the stiff metal bars that supported it.

He cracked open an eye with great reluctance and the light stung.

162

"Hello, Mr. McGlamery." A voice from above.

Cam twisted his head and was once again greeted by Doctor Pollard's chubby face.

"What the f-?" Cam lifted his head and found that he was looking out on a small arena that had a stale, cool *underground* feel to it, so Cam naturally surmised that he was below ground.

He could also see that he was surrounded by fat, steel bars that looked like the jail cells in those old western movies. His cell had a wide door constructed of bars and had a hefty lock built into it; someone was making damn sure he wasn't going anywhere.

Peering beyond his prison, Cam saw two hundred - possibly two-fifty - people populating circular rows of flip-down seats, filling the place to its modest capacity. In the center of the circular amphitheatre there arose a tall wire cage like those he'd seen on *Ultimate Cage Fighter;* only this one was wider, the crisscrossed wire thicker and it extended all the way over the top to create a steel mesh ceiling over the dirt ring.

Cam sat up on his cot, mouth agape, and forgot for a moment about his state of undress.

Two statuesque girls strutted around inside the arena cage, spectacular bodies glistening with a heavy sheen of oil. They were clad in miniscule, latex bikinis - one black, one red - that enhanced the scant parts of flesh that they covered; high, full breasts, proud, jutting nipples and the exquisitely curved indent of pudenda. Each of the girls held aloft a white board which sported a large, black '5'.

Cam would have recognized them had they been wearing burkhas; it was the blonde girl and her colleague from the pet store.

But it was not so much the delicious young ladies that had drawn Cam's attention to that cage, but more the trio of bulky guys who were dragging out the dead werewolf.

The creature's body was bloodied and torn and it looked like mangled roadkill. Its belly had been ripped open throat to balls and the raw, red glisten of the innards made for a harsh contrast to the dark fur that lay slick and matted with clotting blood. There were savage bone-deep claw rents on the werewolf's limbs and its snout hung on by only a handful of sinews and shredded skin and Cam could easily guess at the ferocity of its final fight. A single snake of pink intestine trailed behind the dead creature as it was hauled off with little ceremony, as if desperate to keep up as the men manhandled the huge frame across the dirt floor.

The 'wolf's head appeared to Cam to have been caught somewhere between lupine and human as it lolled loosely side to side on a broken neck. Clearly, Cam mused, if you die in the beast state, that's how you stay – the same way your grandparents warned you of what happens when you pull a face during a change of wind.

163

The men manoeuvered the beast to the side of the arena and into one of four cages identical to the one Cam had awoken in. In the remaining three, there were groups of forlorn looking people standing around ragged, shapeless things that dripped blood and slop from the utilitarian cots; and what Cam saw next made him wonder if that was to be his own fate.

In a corner of the arena cage sat an immense, yellow-eyed werewolf like an obedient pet awaiting a treat. Clots of fresh blood dribbled from the creature's jaws and it snaked out a nonchalant tongue to lick at it. Aside from one superficial scratch along its flank and one ragged ear, the creature appeared unscathed.

This, Cam assumed, was the victor.

The beast eyed the pair of ring girls with a hungry look but made no move and the girls simply returned its stare with defiance. Cam noted that both girls bore a subtle lupine look in their eyes, had prominent canines and strong, lithe fingers that tapered to keen points; this clearly had the bigger beast intimidated.

"Both gals are yours if you bring this one home, son."

Startled, Cam turned around. "Dad?"

"Hello, Cameron." Edna McGlamery pushed by her husband to throw her arms around her son's neck.

"What are you doing here?" Cam drew his knees to his naked chest, suddenly self-conscious.

"We're here for the tournament, of course." Cam's father said.

"It's our first time." Mrs. McGlamery added with a grin. "We're so proud of you, son."

"What's going on, Dad?" Cam's voice came out shakier and an octave higher than he would have liked.

"It's the Five Towns Tournament, son." Mr. McGlamery explained. "The jewel in the crown of the entire pageant weekend."

"You've always loved the Five Towns Pageant weekend." Cam's Mom smiled. "It's a pity you missed it this year, but they needed time to prepare you." She sighed and her eyes brimmed with tears.

"Hey there, Cam! Good luck!" Michael from the pet store interrupted. He waved a cheery hello as he strode by Cam's cell holding a thin leather leash. Cam gawked at the black and white puppy that trotted behind him with its floppy ears bouncing up and down. The puppy was larger now, of course, but Cam would have recognized it anywhere.

Cam looked around the subterranean arena and realized that there were many familiar faces crammed into that dank, dingy space. Aside from Dr. Pollard, the pet shop staff and his parents, Cam recognized Tom Collins who owned the town's biggest car dealership, Joaney Smithson who ran the grocery store, the weasely kiosk guy, Mr. Richaux from the bank, Principal Baum, assorted members of the town council - including Jojo's father in full Mayoral regalia; he was busy mingling with the Mayors from the four

164

neighboring towns who participated in the Pageant each year (one of whom was a *lesbian* - imagine that!). Cam even espied the nurse who'd stuck his ass with the tetanus shot, mixing with the many more who Cam found less familiar. Those were the faces he'd seen once a year during Pageant weekend in whichever town's turn it was to play host.

"Mom?" Cam was spooked. A prickly chill crawled up along his spine. "Am I dreaming?"

Mrs. McGlamery perched her trim derriere on the side of Cam's cot and smoothed out her new, undoubtedly expensive blue silk dress. She stroked her son's hair, the way she used to when he was very much smaller. "This is not a dream, sweetie." She cooed. "It is a *dream come true*." Pleased with her own wordplay, Mrs. McGlamery smiled up at her husband, who in turn studied the bikini-clad ring girls with scant discretion for a married man. "For all of us. Isn't that right, dear?"

"Um? Oh yeah, most definitely." Mr. McGlamery coughed and his cheeks flushed. "We're very proud of you, son. The *whole town* is." Mr. McGlamery stared down at Cam and puffed his chest out and a father could not have looked more proud as he did at that moment.

"Your father and I were absolutely thrilled when we were selected to birth a future Town Champion." Mrs. McGlamery said.

"Selected?" Cam struggled to grasp what he was hearing.

"Every year a couple are picked to bear and raise a Champion." Cam's father explained. "And eighteen years ago, your Mom and I were chosen." A courtly smile lit up his face.

"Why did I not know about any of this?" Cam asked.

"Only the *important* people know about the Tournament." Mrs. McGlamery rested her hand on Cam's shoulder. "And the selected parents, of course."

"It's all part of the Pageant." Mr. McGlamery explained. "The parade, the tits and ass competitions, cook-offs and such keep the regular townsfolk happy." Cam couldn't remember ever having heard his father speak so crudely before, and certainly not in front of his mother. "*This* is only for the elite; it's been that way for generations."

"I've always been like - *that*?" Cam pointed across to the werewolf which had begun to pace to and fro in the fighting cage. "I thought it was the dog bite."

Cam's parents chuckled, as parents do when a small child has said something clever but inherently wrong.

"Good heavens, no!" Mr. McGlamery laughed and glanced over at Michael's puppy that was taking a pee by the exit door. "That was to get you to the hospital for the final stage of your metamorphosis." Again, vocabulary that was foreign tripped from McGlamery Senior's tongue.

"Final stage?"

"Champions are raised to be big and strong and smart." Mr. McGlamery said. "That way they make the very best werewolves. Back in the day they used to infect them the traditional way but it was all too easy for the infecting 'wolf to kill the Champion and leave the town without representation."

"That happened here back in eighteen-forty-three." Mrs. McGlamery chipped in. "And the town just about died."

Cam had learned in his Local History class about that particular year. The text books said it had been due to a number of (*unspecified*, oddly enough) economic factors that the mines had closed, the crops failed, most of the local commerce withered and died and the town had been left with less than a third of its population.

"The rabies shots?" Cam ventured.

"Like I said, raised to be smart." Mr. McGlamery slapped Cam a hearty one on the shoulder and the sharp sound echoed around the low ceiling.

"I am *so* proud of my baby boy!" Mrs. McGlamery was close to tears.

"Now then, Edna, he's not won yet." Cam's father admonished and his attention drifted back to the girls in the ring.

"Won?" Cam quizzed. "Won what?" A sick feeling in his gut told him he knew the answer before the question had left his mouth.

"This, son." His father said with a broad sweep of the arm to indicate the arena, the buzzing crowd and the snarling werewolf.

So he was supposed to fight the other werewolf and it was an honor to be ripped to bloodied shreds for the town?

"It's your destiny, Cameron." Mrs. McGlamery smiled.

"And we have high hopes that you'll break our nine year dry spell." His father added. "You have no idea how humiliating it is for the town to have not won the Tournament in almost a decade."

Cam's mind wandered to the kids who over the years had hit their eighteenth, graduated high school, and then disappeared. It had always been the biggest, fittest, most athletic boys - those who had excelled at everything the curriculum could throw at them. Cam had always assumed that they had simply relocated over the summer since the whole family had always moved away - their houses had never stood empty for long. The thought of the families of defeated – *dead* - Champions slinking out of town with their shamed heads hung low gave Cam a feeling of dread.

Cam shook his head in an attempt to clear it. He was still half-convinced that this was all some bizarre dream and he'd wake up in his own bed with Jojo curled up next to him with her head on his chest. That way the dog bite, faux-rabies shots, Jojo's death and his transformation into a murderous werewolf expected to fight for his town's honor would all simply melt away.

166

"There's someone here to see you, Mr. McGlamery." Dr. Pollard sounded full of his own importance. "Best if you stand up." He then attempted a smile which just came off as creepy.

Cam did as advised and hid his genitals with cupped hands.

"Mr. Mayor, it's so good to see you again." Mrs. McGlamery gushed.

Cam paled and turned his eyes away from the Mayor and his wife; he'd not seen them since Jojo's funeral and was not at all sure what he should say.

Gee Mr. Mayor, I'm so sorry I ripped your daughter to shreds, but I couldn't help it, you see...

"Good to see you too, Edna." The Mayor beamed. "And how's this year's Town Champion?" He held out a hand to Cam for the shaking.

"Hi, Mr. Merle." Cam stared vacantly at the man.

Mrs. McGlamery elbowed Cam in the ribs and gave him her *don't forget your manners* look. Cam selected the hand that was not directly covering his dick - his left - and shook the Mayor's hand.

"We all have high hopes for you, Cameron." The Mayor boomed. "A victory today means prosperity tomorrow!"

A well-worn phrase Cam had heard throughout his childhood; it was the town motto which he'd always assumed was a leftover from some war or other.

"Josephine would be so proud." The Mayor's wife said quietly.

"I am so sorry about -" Cam stammered.

"Nonsense boy!" The Mayor play-punched Cam's bicep. "Nothing to apologize for at all! After all, it's what she was born for."

Cam's expression must have said it all.

"You haven't told him?" The Mayor addressed Cam's parents.

"Just about to." Mr. McGlamery was painfully embarrassed.

"Good job I came along then, isn't it?" The Mayor guffawed. He slung an arm over Cam's shoulders, struggled to reach all the way around. "Our precious daughter was selected before she was born, just as you were." His voice filled with pride. "It was her destiny to be your first blood and to facilitate your transition. And I'm proud to say that she threw herself into the role with all of her sweet heart."

"She was always saying how proud she was to serve the town so." The Mayor's wife joined in with a meek upturn of her mouth.

Cam sat back down on the cot as if someone had given him a hard shove in the chest and the metal frame creaked a loud complaint.

Jojo had been a part of all this?

His dear, sweet, sexy Jojo had been nothing more than - what? *Practice*?

It did make some kind of warped sense to Cam as the memories of that night flooded back; how Jojo had been so insistent that he restrain her,

167

that she had not once struggled or cried out as he'd ripped her apart and feasted upon her as she died.

And to think that at the time he'd thought that Jojo had looked so virginal and pure in that beautiful white gown and tethered to the bed posts - that she had seemed almost sacrificial.

Because that's precisely what she had been.

A blaring horn sounded its harsh, echoing trumpet through the Tannoy and the girls sashayed from the ring.

"This is you, son." Cam's father said.

Cam glanced across at the ring, at the blood smeared werewolf that awaited him and somehow, Cam sensed that the beast was nervous.

It was *scared* of him.

In that instant Cam knew that he had a chance of defeating the creature. He felt its weakness and it was a compelling sensation that burned through him like a wildfire.

Cam felt the uncontrollable tingle creep through his flesh that was the portent of the transformation that now defined him.

Cam's parents, the Mayor and his lady wife, all stepped back as Cam dropped from the cot and onto all fours. They watched with pride as his face lengthened into a snout and long, glinting canines curved out from his jaws. Cam's spine arched and thick fur blossomed the length and breadth of his magnificent, muscular body.

Cam let out a resonant howl as waves of pleasure heralded the shifting and snapping of his joints and internal organs as they rearranged. His dick grew long and hard and the beast he'd become felt no shame because this was what he was, what everyone wanted him to be.

As Cam embraced his change into the snarling, blood-hungry beast, he felt all-powerful, invincible, and he knew that he was going to do himself, Jojo, his parents, and the whole goddamned town proud.

BIO: James hails originally from Yorkshire, England having relocated with his family to Houston, Texas in 2010. He has an honors degree in Zoology and a background in sales, marketing and business. He is relatively new to the writing arena, having only begun in earnest a few years ago.

To date he has three novels published, one out in 2017 in addition to three novellas and seven short stories dotted about in various anthologies.

James also writes screenplays and currently has three under option (a spine-chilling horror, a Tarantino-esque crime caper and an animated family movie). In 2014 he was commissioned by Spectra Records to write a biopic feature on the early life of Bob Marley, and in 2015 was writer for hire on the Kenyan sitcom '*The Samaritans*'.

As if that weren't enough, James has written and directed a bunch of short movies, winning Best Director in the 2013 *Splatterfest* film competition and Remi awards at Houston's *Worldfest* Film Festival in 2012, 2014 and 2015.

In his spare time, James pens and performs stand-up comedy on the Houston comedy circuit.

James' writing style has been described as uncompromising, unique and entertaining; he combines highly original ideas with brilliant vocabulary and highly effective yarn spinning in which the story always comes first! Be warned, his work does have a tendency towards the dark side – usually with a rich vein of humor – and there is always a delicious twist at the end!

www.jameslongmore.com

RYZDRAK THE DEMON

MATTHEW CASH

1.

Ryzdrak, pronounced *'ritz-drack'*, was a demon.

He stood not far over five feet tall, and although a native of Hell could, and did, pass as a human, albeit a weird looking one, now that he was Earthbound. His small frame was wiry but lean and taut with muscle, hair was sparse on his bat-like head, just a patch of black just above the nape of his neck which he let grow in a long ponytail. His complexion was that of someone who had spent the day in the sun, reddened, flushed. There were so many limits to being an earth based demon, he had fallen out of favour with the Powers That Be Down Below and was cursed to spend the rest of eternity on Earth.

Immortality was boring unless you had power and money. Over the centuries, Ryzdrak had gathered hardly either of these. He wished he had been given the opportunity to possess people; there were so many more avenues to explore with possession. Having a solid body, albeit fast at regeneration, with one or two basic psychic perks and the strength of three men, he was so limited. However, Ryzdrak discovered ways of enticing his humanoid shell that he never could have dreamed of back in Hell. Aside from the pleasure of tormenting lost souls in limitless ways, his ethereal form was unable to feel, but when he came to Earth, he discovered the pleasures of the flesh. A long, long time ago he realised the ecstasy in pain, whether it be inflicting or self-inflicted. Any body modifications that the twisted world of Man could invent he had endured at some point; piercings, amputation, flailing, branding and various implants and scarification. The only problem was his rapid healing. He was riddled with ancient piercings and studs that had long healed over, but his pride and joy were the one inch metal horns he'd had implanted into his head. Oh the irony. Over the years he had built his own little haven beneath the streets of the city; a dungeon where he could play and be himself and have somewhere that felt like home.

Ryzdrak turned the special key he kept on a chain round his neck in the concealed lock in the elevator and the lift dropped several storeys that

171

weren't on any blueprint. The doors opened onto a black corridor lit only with a few red lightbulbs. He hurried up the corridor, hunched over in excitement, and up to a thick metal door. The lock on this was specifically designed by himself, a concave area set in the door, and he thrust his hand into the hole. Immediately, a star-shaped piece of metal skewered his hand and took a sample of flesh and blood. He quivered in delight at the pain and as the door opened, he felt himself grow painfully hard. The door slammed behind him and Ryzdrak quickly shed his earthly garments and surveyed his utopia. The dark ceiling was so far off it was lost in blackness, a multitude of chains of all shapes and sizes cascaded from above. The ancient stone walls were long covered in mildew, damp, and human and his own detritus. What appeared to be a large bird's nest sat in the corner, the intricacy of its design made from human bones held together with leathery skin, stuck with his and other's bodily secretions. As he scuttled past it, he retched up a thick, golf ball-sized wad of greeny brown phlegm and used it to stick a wayward strand of skin down. The interior was filled and padded with human flesh and fat in various stages of decomposition. Flies buzzed everywhere, maggots wriggled and fed, continuing their circle of life. Ryzdrak yanked on a chain and from out of a hole in the floor an upside down woman slowly emerged, bound, naked, arms free, legs spread wide.

The woman's hair was matted with dried vomit and faeces from her hanging upside down. When she saw Ryzdrak, she screamed and thrashed about on the chains. He walked over to her, taking pleasure in her frightened, filthy body. He raised her up a few inches so she was at the required level and made no attempt to avoid her hands as they swiped back and forth at him, fingernails gouging into his skin. He wrapped his arms around her waist, buried his face into her pissy cunt and inhaled deeply. Ryzdrak pushed his thin forked tongue into her hole and revelled in her screams. Her fear and fighting, the shrieks and beatings of her fists against him heightened his arousal. Breaking several of her front teeth and ploughing up furls of his own skin, he forced his gnarled erection deep into her mouth and bit down hard. His teeth had been filed into the sharpest of points, his own DIY dentistry, and he tore away strips of her labia whilst she howled in pain around his violating cock. Blood spilled down over his lips and chin. He gave out an orgasmic groan as her bladder gave way and the heavy bouquet of her bowels opening filled his senses. Ryzdrak grabbed handfuls of her ample breasts and dug his claw-like fingernails into the firm flesh. He thrusted and chewed and sucked and grabbed, whilst she screamed and punched and gagged and shook. Ryzdrak felt the fire boiling in his testicles as they bashed away, blackening the woman's eyes. He swallowed half-chewed chunks of her cunt-meat and using every ounce of his arm strength, ripped off her breasts as he scalded her gullet with his hot, corrosive ejaculation. As he squeezed every last drop from himself, he carelessly threw the woman's breasts into his nest and split her stomach with

172

a fingernail. Ryzdrak pushed his head inside her opened belly and squirmed in delight at the hot pulsation of her insides. *Maybe*, he thought, *I'll have a man tomorrow*.

2.

After Ryzdrak had gorged enough on the body of Becky, he stripped her corpse of all tissue and hair, throwing the soft pulp into his nest. Her skin hung from hooks suspended above his makeshift dray like a macabre tapestry. He put her remaining organs in a cauldron where he had drained her body of any fluids, and milked her intestines of any remnants of shit. The burning coals which the pot sat on would eventually cook it into a mouth-watering stew. He curled up inside his bed of rotting gore and thought about what the next day would bring.

For years he had been searching for something to give himself a little more power, he had grown bored of the centuries of solitude and fancied starting himself a cult of sorts. Someone like him should be worshipped, and secretly he hoped if he caused enough of a ruckus, turned enough people over to the dark side, that he would strike favour with the dude downstairs and his permanent exile from his home world would be lifted. Ryzdrak had limited psychic abilities and one of these was the talent to spot and track other beings with supernatural powers or immigrants from other realms. Most of the legendary myths and monsters had some basis in truth and over his time he had met a lot of different things. Twenty-two years previously, he had spent three months following a three thousand year old vampire on the other side of the country. Even though the vampire's kiss had failed before, the bite of the vampire could give him numerous new abilities; transformation, flight, hypnotic manipulation, but it offered more weaknesses than advantages. It was a total myth that vampires loathed, or feared crucifixes, that was all down to faith. Ryzdrak himself couldn't bear to look at a cross, but he had one hundred percent certainty that there was a God. It wasn't as black and white as The Bible, or *The Libel* as he referred to it, made out, but he knew the omnipresent God was real, and the fact that he knew about the *Big Secret* between Him and Satan was the main reason he was banished from Hell. They could have erased him from existence, but they hadn't for reasons unknown to him.

But Ryzdrak wanted more power, he wanted, he *deserved* to be worshipped. Recently, he detected a new power on earth, and it was big and had endless potentials. He had located a shape-shifter. The presence had arrived so suddenly and so strong it was too good to be true, so naturally he was apprehensive to approach it. He found it a few days before and had been studying it carefully, trying to fathom out if it had ways of detecting what he really was. It seemed oblivious. He had found a wolf. A wolf with the gift of lycanthropy. Now this, despite legends, was a rarity. He had been

173

on Earth for almost three thousand years and only ever had one sniff of a werewolf in all that time; a brief knowledge of its presence before it flittered away like a sneeze in a hurricane. It had been powerfully intelligent; it had known of him immediately and vanished. But this one was different, docile even, but its powers were the same nonetheless. Ryzdrak had a theory, and judging by the habitat it had chosen to reside in, he was absolutely certain of it. The werewolf in question was in a zoo. The docility of the creature led him to believe it had chosen the form of a wolf and stayed that way for so long, it had forgotten what it was like to be human. Maybe the fear of being hunted got too much for the lycan and it chose the form for a simpler way of life. Maybe the laziness mixed with safety that an enclosure provided appealed to it. Maybe it was captured. Maybe even just a carrier of the shape-shifting virus. Either way, within the next twenty-four hours he was going to make that wolf attack him.

3.

The CCTV footage was remarkably clear, and after the Newscaster had warned that the reel would show horrifically graphic scenes, the bulletin was broadcast across the nation and even made international news. The camera showed a scrawny little balding man, with a ruddy complexion, dressed in a long black leather coat, pressed against the wolf enclosure for a considerable amount of time before he shed his coat and scaled the wire like a spider. Security had been called before he had even made it to the top of the high fence, but when he made it to the top he leapt down the twenty feet drop without hesitation. A few onlookers had given statements that the man had broken his arm so severely in the fall that bone splintered through the flesh. Apparently he had looked ecstatic at this. As soon as his bare feet hit the ground he ran into the trees. He was out of shot for a few minutes whilst the CCTV showed the keeper and security start to unlock the enclosure. Then viewers saw the men jump back as one as a pack of a dozen wolves charged towards them, seemingly being chased by the now naked intruder. He had something big and white in his arms; it was the zoo's newest habitant, an albino Siberian male wolf. Unbelievably, the little man was punching and biting at the wild animal's body, even more unbelievable was that the wolf seemed drugged and determined not to retaliate.

Then the footage showed the man's mouth come away from the wolf's side with a bloody crimson smile. The beast howled in pain and its jaws clamped round the little man's throat.

The security and the keeper got trigger happy with their tranquillisers and subdued the majority of the pack after firing one at the albino. The man dropped to the ground, his throat leaking onto the leaves, as the guards surrounded him and called for medical help. The News report then changed to a full screen image of the man's face, scarified and ugly with the surgically embedded metal horns and piercing eyes. It was a screenshot from the CCTV. The Newscaster then informed the general public that the man had survived the wolf's attack, and after attacking the paramedics and evading the police escort, vanished. He was considered a serious threat, unhinged and extremely dangerous. A number was screened for witnesses to call if they saw him.

4.

Ryzdrak noticed the changes immediately. The virus or whatever it was that passed on the shape-shifting contagion had already started taking affect. After Ryzdrak had fled the ambulance, the wound on his neck was virtually healed. The therianthropy added to his own abnormally rapid healing process was phenomenal, and he even felt physically stronger. When he had slaughtered the tramp in one of the city's dark alleyways, biting through his filthy throat and stealing his hooded coat, he felt invincible. When he left the alleyway dressed in the vagrant's rags, he forgot himself momentarily and passed by St Andrew's church with none of his usual repulsion or anger. Normally, when passing a church or any holy building, he would feel his stomach churn, his head pound and his eyes begin to boil. He wondered if the church had been defiled in some way; the last time he had been able to stand even walking on the same side of the road as a church had been two hundred years ago. A small white church in little village in England called Beaumont had been desecrated by a sect of Satanists holding a Black Mass. He visited the building afterwards; the stink of its corruption had been sublime.

Ryzdrak backtracked to St Andrew's church and laid a palm against the door. Nothing. No reaction whatsoever. For the first time in two centuries, Ryzdrak pushed open the door of a holy building and crossed the threshold.

The church was surprisingly empty for a place of worship in a busy city centre, a few elderly people shuffled along the central aisle, other than that it was deserted. Ryzdrak scowled from beneath the stinking hood of his stolen coat at the murals, etchings and artwork of lies. Saints depicted in coloured glass, and the epitome of the biggest farce in the universe - the Nazarene. And to think a moniker for his Master was the Father of Lies. He wanted to destroy the place, burn it down, fill it to the brim with barbaric acts of cruelty. A large, elderly woman with big, drooping, pendulous, breasts that seemed to mould and melt into her waistline crinkled her nose in disgust at him, her toothless mouth puckering like an arsehole. He grinned at her and flicked his tongue like a snake. He considered taking her but it wasn't worth the effort. He passed the grumbling pensioner and sat at a pew near the altar. Ryzdrak stared up at Christ on the cross, expecting the sudden wave of stomach churning nausea to return with a vengeance, but it

175

didn't. He smiled maliciously up at the carved effigy of the so-called Messiah. It was rare for anyone to make Ryzdrak jump but the sudden voice beside him made him jolt in surprise.

"I'm sorry for startling you, my son." The Priest said, taking a seat beside him. Ryzdrak recoiled, wide-eyed at the young priest to his left. The priest paid no attention to his dirty, dishevelled appearance or the rancid smell coming from him; he had obviously seen it all before.

"Do you have shelter? A place to stay?"Ryzdrak continued to stare in bewildered amusement.

The Priest smiled warmly and took Ryzdrak's silence as humbleness. "Would you like a drink, something to eat? You are welcome to sit for as long as you need to; everyone is welcome in God's house." The Priest reached out and shook Ryzdrak's dirty, long-nailed hand. Ryzdrak boiled with rage and, still holding the Priest's hand, rose to his feet, staring down in pure hatred. "This is no house of God! It's a mockery of stone, fused together by the blood of hundreds of deluded half-wits." The Priest whimpered as Ryzdrak squeezed the bones together in his hand, the bones audibly crunching. Ryzdrak twisted the Priest's arm round, sharply dislocating his shoulder, and pushed him to the stony floor. He grabbed a fistful of the Priest's brown hair and ground his face into the cold ground. The Priest groaned and pleaded as he tried to look at Ryzdrak, his nose squashed and bloodied. Ryzdrak sneered at the cowering Priest, "pray to your imaginary God, Priest, but I am the real God around here, and you are fucked." With one swipe of his hand, Ryzdrak ripped off the Priest's trousers and underpants before dropping the dirt-caked tracksuit bottoms he'd stolen off the tramp. Ryzdrak clutched hold of himself and gasped in genuine horror. His penis was shrivelled and lifeless. This was also a first time experience, whether it be with man, woman, child or animal, nothing ever dampened his ravenous sexual appetite. The Priest saw Ryzdrak's impotence and increased his plea for mercy.

Ryzdrak had never felt such anger. Pushing his long-clawed fingertips together, he brought his elbow backwards and then thrust his arm forwards with as much strength as he could muster. His fist drove inside the Priest's anus up to the elbow. The Priest's screams echoed around the church as Ryzdrak split his insides, grabbed a handful of his guts and tore them from his rectum.

Footsteps rapidly approached, attracted by the Priest's cries. Ryzdrak spat on the dying Priest and walked up the central aisle, his arm dripping brown and red.

The ultimate test, Ryzdrak thought as he ignored the sudden shouts of whoever had found the disembowelled Priest. The stone font was filled with supposedly holy water. He still had scars from the 15th century from holy water, a white pock-marked splatter across his back when he had been captured in France by a dozen armed men and publicly flayed in front of a small town. A local clergyman splashed the stuff over his bleeding back. That had been the only time he had cried out throughout the ordeal. Before that, he had laughed and shouted French obscenities at all who could hear; he had enjoyed the pain up until then. But the splash of holy water burned so painfully, he had summoned up his last reserves of strength to break his bonds and escape. Within a week, he had wiped out the whole town. Ryzdrak hesitated, his fingertips mere millimetres above the water, the Priest's gore dripped and swirled it into brown cloudiness. Ryzdrak dipped a fingertip into the water and gasped, it was cold. He began to laugh as he dunked his filthy arm into the water; the laughter filled the church and almost drowned out the distant scream of police sirens.

Ryzdrak left the cowering parishioners who he knew huddled out of eyesight below the pews near the dead Priest. Let them bear witness, what would they say, and who would believe them? Ryzdrak left the church and slipped down a dark alleyway beside it.

5.

Back in his lair, he cackled with delight and all the excitement of the day had made him ravenous. He scoured the chains hanging down from above and yanked on two of them. Two naked, bound figures rose upside-down from pits in the ground. A man and a heavy set woman. The woman's ankles looked extended from her weight and the duration she had been hanging. Ryzdrak really hoped she hadn't died already. The man opened his eyes as though he had just woken up. For the first few seconds before coherence settled in he looked puzzled, but when he saw the demon's upside-down snarling grin, the expression of confusion soon turned to fear. Ryzdrak ignored his feeble protests and promises and prodded a finger into the fat woman's flopping stomach, hard.

"Ah still in the land of the living. Good." Ryzdrak greeted her after her eyes snapped open.

He considered starting on the woman, to skin her and suck at the delicious lumpy fat would be a delicacy like no other, but he wanted the man first. He wanted to gorge on the pair of them until his stomach burst. He reached a hand up towards the man's pectorals and a sudden wave of unpleasant light-headedness overcame him. *This isn't normal*, Ryzdrak thought as he rested his hands on his knees, he was strong, immortal. "The wolf bite, of course." He couldn't expect his body to just accept the supernatural virus without a fight; he had already noticed his increased strength and immunity in the church, so this was how his body was reacting. Ryzdrak crawled over to his nest and made himself comfortable amidst the putrid offal. He would rest, let his victims have a brief glimmer of hope before he finally tortured and devoured them.

He felt warm and blissful as he slowly awoke from slumber. He opened his eyes and stretched out his limbs, feeling rejuvenated and rested. He pushed himself up on the soft pillows and sat up. *Wait a second*! Ryzdrak screamed inside his head as he sprang from his nest of bone and gore. His pit of stinking flesh, fat and offal was gone and had been swapped with luxuriously soft eiderdown pillows, animal fur blankets and silken sheets. He stared in horror around him. It was still his den, the walls were still plastered in a combination of his own and numerous people's excretions but someone or something had tampered with his nest. Who dared infiltrate his sanctuary? Then he noticed the man and woman had vanished. How long had he been asleep? Nothing made sense. He bent down and snatched a pillow for inspection, no labels or anything to detect where it came from. That was when he noticed his fingernails and the hands they were attached to. His usual thick, yellow, horny talons had transformed into crystal clear, perfectly manicured, spotlessly clean fingernails. His rough, scarred and calloused hands were smooth, pink and blemish free. Something was wrong. Something was dramatically wrong. His arms were the same; clean, lean and covered in fine golden hair. Ryzdrak stared down in horror at his transformed body; he was pristine, like some perverted holy rebirth. It must be the therianthropy virus, it had affected him, had changed him.

Ryzdrak slowly raised his newly manicured hands to his face, the skin no longer pock-marked and scarred from wounds and inflictions that he refused to let heal. His metal implanted horns had gone completely but the most disturbing thing was that he had a full head of hair.

He screamed in frustration and grabbed for his strewn coat to cover himself. He needed to see his reflection. He needed to see what he had turned into. Luckily, whatever stupor he had been in hadn't led him to throw away his stinking clothes. The sodden trousers that he wore came just below his knees, telling him his metamorphosis had affected his height too.

What the hell had happened? With most shape-shifting cases that he had studied, blackouts were commonplace, but the last thing he expected was this, waking up in a pile of gore that for once he didn't remember creating was more to his expectation, not this...this abomination. He ran barefoot into the lift that would take him up to civilisation and caught his reflection in the mirrored walls. He stood well over six feet tall, his eyes shone with blue serenity. Lustrous golden locks curled atop of his scalp like he was some Greek Adonis. His torso, what he glimpsed before he closed the coat, was hairless and immaculately chiselled like a male stripper. Ryzdrak punched his new fist into the mirror, shattering the facade and shrieked in rage when the glass didn't even break his skin.

Something was wrong. Surely the fact that he was demon incarnate would eradicate most of the lycanthropy, therianthropy or whatever the hell it was that the wolf had infected him with. When he had tracked down a nest of vampires during the Second World War in East Berlin, he had forced one to bite him even though the weaknesses of the vampiric curse offered more disadvantages than not. The vampire had burst into flames within minutes, the demonic blood that it had imbibed had proved instantly fatal. And the zombie, well patient zero of a mutated virus that had the ability to be a fantastic global epidemic of ravenous resurrected flesh. The virus had put up a good fight against his own remarkable immune system, the least he hoped to gain from it was to be a carrier of the new plague, but that too had failed. His demonic fucking lifeforce had given the fucking would be zombie his own immunity. What a joke that had been, having to hire a hitman to take care of his fuck up with a bucket of holy water.

He knew he was on the right track with lycanthropy, he knew it was a raw, more primal condition, shape-shifting was one of the oldest of the earthly based supernatural powers, he knew it would have some effect, but not this. The Siberian albino wolf was obviously more powerful than him, or at least on par. Ryzdrak scowled at his shattered reflection. He needed to find that wolf.

6.

After what had happened at the zoo, security was doubled but the episode was deemed a likely one-off. There had been national uproar when the word got out that the wolf would be exterminated, put down for attacking its attacker. The world, not just all the animal activists, wanted to save the Siberian albino wolf. He had been protecting the pack, and there was enough CCTV footage to prove that the wolf's attack on the intruder was totally provoked. It had remained docile up until the man had ripped a chunk of its flesh and fur out before snatching its jaws at his neck. The twenty-four hour global protestation could only end in one result, Aziraphale was saved. A heartwarming video showed the look of sheer exaltation on the wolf's Keeper when the news of his safety was announced. Tears streamed down the grey-haired lady's face as she went into the enclosure and the wolf nuzzled into her like a domestic dog. Nobody expected the second break in.

The blackout affected the majority of the town, so no one was overly surprised when the zoo's electricity went down. Normally, the backup generators would kick in; there were animals and creatures that relied on electricity around the clock, as well as aquariums and special enclosures for certain things that needed to keep their body temperature at a particular level. Because of the catastrophic coincidence that the zoo's generators chose that night to malfunction, most of the out of hours hubbub was focused on getting them to work and to make sure the creatures that relied on the power weren't in any immediate danger. The animals that lived in outside enclosures weren't paid much attention to, other than the routine circuits of the park that the security would make on the hour in their zebra-striped carts. With the power off and no CCTV cameras, nobody saw the tall, good-looking blonde man move stealthily through the velvet blackness to the wolf enclosure.

Ryzdrak kicked off his dirty boots and hooked his toes and fingers into the chainlink fence. His new body felt just as powerful as before, except the pain when he shredded the flesh on his stomach on the razor-wired barricaded top hurt more. The pain wasn't enjoyable at all. He hoped this new skin would harden to his usual abuse after a few weeks. He dropped to the grass and crouched down. The wolves knew immediately that there was a stranger in their enclosure. Slowly, they came through the trees towards where he stood. Lips drew back over teeth as they saw him squatted naked on the grass. Ryzdrak snarled at the pack, there was about a dozen surrounding him, but none were the albino Siberian. He moved on all fours, cautiously towards the centre of the pack despite the low growls coming from their throats. He didn't think that they would attack, they weren't stupid creatures, they knew he was superior to them, however a couple showed surprising bravado. A large, dark furred male stepped towards him and barked aggressively, possibly the pack leader. Ryzdrak mimicked its growl and leapt at the canine. Teeth bit and grazed his shoulder but Ryzdrak grabbed the wolf round the neck and twisted sharply until a loud, hollow snap made the animal still. He straightened up and hurled the broken pack leader at the others and lunged for the next closest. The others having had proof of his strength backed off, the one whom he had captured struggled to free itself. Ryzdrak didn't care how many he would have to slaughter before the albino showed up. He forced his fingers between the wolf's salivating jaws and prised them open to unnatural capacity. A new, more powerful growl came from behind him and he knew the albino had arrived. He wrenched his arms apart, tearing the wolf's lower jaw off, spun and flung the injured wolf at the albino's paws. The albino Siberian wolf looked pitifully, if a wolf could look pitifully, at the dying wolf on the ground and lowered its mouth to its bloody throat. With one snap of its strong jaws, the albino tore the throat out of the dying wolf and roared at Ryzdrak. Ryzdrak laughed at the albino, sprays of arterial blood stained its fur like ink around the white fluff of its muzzle and chest.

"Show me your true form before I kill the rest of your pack." Ryzdrak spoke and spat on the ground. The albino wolf growled. "Show me your final form!" Ryzdrak screamed and took a step towards one of the albino's retreating pack members. The wolf began to change. The albino Siberian pressed itself against the grass and whined as it began its transformation. It slumped onto its side as its spine stretched, cracked and elongated. All over its body, the white fur began to recede rapidly until it was naked and pink. The bones and cartilage warped and shrank and buckled and redesigned themselves into a more humanoid form. Ryzdrak stared as blonde, seraphic hair sprouted from its newly formed scalp and took a step back as the figure slowly stood on two legs. He knew what it was.

The thing that was once wolf must have seen Ryzdrak's expression of realisation because a bemused smile cracked it's flawlessly asexual face. Ryzdrak shook his head. The last traces of his denial, his hope that he was wrong were extinguished when the figure turned its naked back to him, stretched out its arms and laughed at the sky. A sound like ripping leather and two white feathered wings grew like saplings from the angel's back and matured into a ten foot wingspan. The angel turned and glowed with an ethereal light. It smiled sympathetically at Ryzdrak. "Your time has come, Demon."

Ryzdrak tried to move, tried to escape, but his body was no longer under his control. A tingling sensation tickled his shoulder blades as wings burst from his own back. "No," he whispered.

The angel silenced him with a raised palm.

"You of all of the Creations should see the irony of your pleas. We have no use for you anymore, your exile is over. Once the transformation is complete you will be an empty vessel, without thought, memory, or free will. You will be as you were before the Great Divide." Ryzdrak screamed and pleaded regardless.

"I know the Great Secret; I could have destroyed religion with my knowledge. Please, show mercy, send me back to Hell, I beg you." The angel shook its head and rolled its eyes heavenward. Ryzdrak snarled and shouted obscenities at the angel as his wings began to beat and his feet left the ground. All around the mythological pair, the wolves gathered in frightened wonder and howled their mournful chorus.

"No." The angel said, "Your time is over. Ryzdrak, demon, your time has come."

A bright, blinding white light a-washed them as Ryzdrak rose above the angel and wolves. It was beautiful, welcoming, wonderful, he hated it. He felt the glory of God on his face and then nothing.

BIO: Matthew Cash, or Matty-Bob Cash as he is known to most, was born and raised in Suffolk; which is the setting for debut novel Pinprick. He is compiler and editor of Death By Chocolate, a chocoholic horror anthology and has numerous releases on Kindle and several collections in paperback.

He has always written stories since he first learnt to write and most, although not all, tend to slip into the many layered murky depths of the Horror genre.

His influences ranged from when he first started reading to Present day are, to name but a small select few; Roald Dahl, James Herbert, Clive Barker, Stephen King, Stephen Laws, and more recently he enjoys Adam Nevill, F.R Tallis, Michael Bray, William Meikle and Iain Rob Wright (who featured Matty-Bob in his famous A-Z of

Horror title M is For Matty-Bob, plus Matthew wrote his own version of events which was included as a bonus).

He is a father of two, a husband of one and a zoo keeper of numerous fur babies.

Www.facebook.com/pinprickbymatthewcash "

THE END

URWIN BOWER

When you have been through a number of life sentences, you never expect a day out, so this makes a change. I had been dragged from my cell, and taken to a room. It felt like being back at school, except my legs were clamped to the chair legs, and chains on my arms gave me some, but not much reach on the desk. I giggled to myself at the fun I had before I got here.

Looking around there was the usual scum, all chained to their chairs. Well, we are all classed as the scum of the earth; actually I would class myself more of an artist. There were nine of us in total, most people think that those on death row are constantly locked away, when in fact we are shrinks' wet dreams. They want to study us, at least it did not mean dissecting us. I laugh at the thought comparing what I had done. I think if they were allowed, they would take our brains apart to see why we are the way we are.

This had to be another one of the shrink's tests, another way to find out why we are sick. To be honest, people need to know why we do what we do; is it childhood? Is it the environment? Is it in our genes? No, for me it was because I liked it, loved it, needed it. I loved the tests, an easy way to fuck with the establishment. Now, was it going to be another Rorschach? I loved them, every spot was a different blood pattern to me, well, not really, but seeing the shrinks' eyes light up was a buzz.

Then she entered the room, I could smell her, a killer's scent is always heightened like an animal. I closed my eyes, and took in the smell, letting it drift up my nose, tasting it as it went down my throat. I could also smell her fear, she used the perfume to try and hide that smell, the sweat. I could imagine the cortisol surging through her blood stream. Was she getting ready to run? She was standing in a room with the worst killers in history, the best of the bunch, the worst of the worst. She was slim, her long, pure blond hair tied back, a black pencil skirt, and a tailored jacket. She was trying to give off an essence of authority, total bullshit. They all do that, and it does not work. They are all the same when you slice into them. She was the kind I would hunt, the ones who thought they were untouchable. I have

183

to say, she did not give off the usual sense of a quack, there was something different about her. She seemed younger than most of the ones we saw. Even though she was young, she gave this feeling of authority. If I was not chained to this bloody desk, I would show her who had the authority.

I was called the lonewolf; I loved the name the papers gave me. I hunted women, like a wolf would hunt his prey. I watched them, waited, then killed. I shredded them like paper, basking in their body heat as my claws ripped through their bodies. I was accredited with twelve kills, well that is what they know about. I always took part of the kill home, like a wolf. I killed for a purpose; apart from the joy of the kill, I killed to feed, hoping one day I would become the wolf- A real wolf. I had read all there was about werewolves and tried all the tribal stuff, and knew the chances of getting bit were rare. I knew all the films were bullshit; I knew there had to be some truth behind the legends. I didn't want to be bit and become someone's bitch. I would become a werewolf by killing, but before I could I was caught. One of the bitches I hunted survived and pointed the finger, hence why I am sitting here and being a shrink's bitch. I missed my claws; I spent ages making them. It made Freddy Kruger's fingers look like picnic cutlery. I had fangs fashioned to make tearing at the flesh easier; I was as near to a werewolf as there could be.

Well, it beat sitting in the cell wanking all day, sharpening my nails and hoping one day to be free. If they considered me sane, I could get out. I took my attention back to the woman who had just entered the room. You could tell she was anxious as she walked to the front of the room. She took each one of us in. In her arms she hugged a stack of envelopes to her chest, another bloody inkblot test. As she spoke, I could hear the fear in her voice and also a stab of excitement.

"The guards are going to pass out these tests. All I want you to do is read the instructions. Once finished, just put the paper back into the envelope and seal it."

She passed the stack of envelopes to the guards, the guards walked between the tables passing out the packages. On the front of mine was a list of instructions…

This was like being back at school. We had two hours to finish the test, there was a pen enclosed in the pack. No wonder our arms were chained to the desk. The things we could do with a pen, especially to her, the damage I could do; well, I could take that image back to my cell with me.

I took the paper out of the package. At the start there was the beginning of a story, all I had to do was finish the story in my own way, basically pick my own ending. Now, this was so different from what I was used to. What were they trying to do? Well if they want an ending, I would definitely give them one. Ok here we go, here is how the story started….

"Once upon a time, a lonely girl was on her way through the woods. She was picking flowers and looking forward to getting back to the cabin.

184

She was not far when she heard a sound, something behind the trees, something that cast no shadow. She quickly picked up her pace and headed for the cabin…."

Now this is where I take over. This was going to be so good. I could feel the presence of the woman in the room as she walked between the rows, watching as we all began to work.

They wanted a story so I would give them one…

"I was the shadow behind the trees, I was the thing that watched the woman pick the flowers, I was the thing that made her breath heavy, I was the thing that made her pick up pace and head to the cabin. I followed close behind, making sure she could not see me. I watched her enter the cabin, and heard the bolts slam into place."

"I could feel my body begin to change, every muscle in my body pulsing. I was becoming invincible. I was becoming the entity, part wolf part man, and I was unstoppable. I could still smell her even though she was in the cabin. I placed a paw against the cabin wall. I could feel her heart beat. Her heart was racing, and I could not wait to hold that heart in my paw…"

I looked up from my work and could see all the other freaks were engrossed in their stories as much as I was, they were scribbling away like lunatics. What am I saying? They are lunatics. The woman was watching us intensely. I saw a look in her eyes which I recognised. I had seen that look before; when I glared at my prey I had the same look. Well, let me give her a little surprise. I bet she would love to read my stuff and realise that I had made her the subject of my little fantasy. She would be the woman in the cabin, I would be slicing her up. So, back to the story…

"I watched her through the window. I knew she could sense something was not right. I watched as she checked all the rooms. She knew something was there but could not find it. I had to pick the right time to pounce; I had to enter without her knowing. I wanted to build her fear up, take her at the right time, and this was like an obscure type of courting. I watched as she entered the bathroom, and the shower began to run; this was the time. I approached the bedroom window. I could see my reflection. I was magnificent. My eyes were wild with blood lust, my fangs, my mouth salivating with the need to kill, to feed. Would I make her mine and let us run together, or just kill? I would know when I looked into her eyes. I was majestic, a combination of animal, man and god, standing on my hind legs, the dark fur emphasising my strong muscles. I pushed on one of the panes, it pushed through very easily. These cabins were so easy to get into. It was a cinch from there to swing the window open and enter…."

I could feel myself getting hard under the desk. I looked up and she was staring at me, looking deep into my eyes. Did she realise it was her I would be ripping apart in my story? It would be her heart I would be holding in my hand. That would teach the bitch a lesson. I am not a Guinea pig, I am a man. I am not to be messed with. Now to the best bit of the story, the bit where I tear her apart…

"I just followed her smell, I could hear the shower. I slowly crept forward. I loved the thrill of the chase, and I could just see her in the shower, naked, her hair clinging to her back, as she slowly soaped herself down. I couldn't help but get aroused, which animal would not, but was she worthy to be mated with, make her like me, run together? Or was the hunger, the need to feed more important? I liked to watch, but she turned and saw me and screamed…"

I stopped writing. My erection was getting very intense, and the woman was still staring at me. Did she realise that I had an erection? She seemed to be intensely interested in me in particular. Well, that made the ending of the story easier...

"As she screamed, I had to pounce. She was not the one to run with me. I needed the kill, I needed to hold her heart in my hand, I needed to feed, I needed to kill the bitch. The shower was still running. I like to kill slowly, seeing the hope in their eyes that it will be quick, but that is not me. I grabbed her hands and pulled her off her feet, the water dripping both off her and me. I licked down her neck, tasting her fear. With one claw, I traced the heart on her chest. Taking a paw back, I plunged hard into her chest, pulling her heart out, and watching the hope drain from her face.

The end

I was so engrossed in my story that I didn't see the woman at the front indicate that the two hours were up. I followed the instructions, taking the paper, putting into the envelope, licking and sealing it. As it was taken off me, I hoped that the dumb bitch would be reading it and realising that she was in the story. It would wipe that strange smile off her face.

We were escorted to our cells. Not my usual cell, this looked more like one of those cells that they take lunatics to, padded, for those who spend their time bouncing off the walls. I settled on the bed and went to sleep, to dream of what I would like to do to that dumb bitch.

I was woken by screams, screams that I recognised, screams of pure terror. There was more than one scream. I looked out of the window in the door, and saw the guards standing by the walls with their fingers in their ears, staring at the floor. The bitch was at the end of the corridor, an eerie grin on her face. What the fuck was going on?

Then I felt it, I sensed it behind me. It was huge and the smell was awful. I could hear it breathe. I knew what was going to happen; I knew what she had done. I had created my own ending. Standing behind me was the beast I had always wanted to be, the beast I admired so much. I was going to be my own victim. I slowly turned, and there before me, was my own creation; the werewolf that I had tried to be. The beast was going to take me, not make me; it was going to tear me apart. I was going to be a victim of my own fantasy.

186

She knew what each cell was going to be like when she opened it. This was a new way to deal with criminals; let them create their own ending. She could hear the guards vomiting as she opened each cell. She opened the lonewolf's cell, saw a heart placed on the bed, and embraced the look of terror on his face.

She considered this test a success, now it was time to go national.

BIO: Urwin Bower was born in the UK and has spent her time finding ways to create new nightmares.

KILLER

RUFUS SKEENS

The darkness moved with him, inside him, down where his shadow lurked, coiled like a viper around heart, lungs, stomach, loins. Wulf's times to hunt were when the winter moon was full. Sometimes, when the light angled right, his shade would spill out around his feet to mirror his steps. His stalk.

All these small country towns were the same. People roamed street and park late evenings as if there were nothing in the night to fear. And, usually, there wasn't. But then, out of nowhere, an apex predator, like Wulf himself, would step out of the dark and strike. These incautious people were dumb as sheep. Over the years, he had hunted well among their ilk, only to vanish like a wisp of smoke after a kill.

Ahead, the jogger paced her steps through Sugar Hollow Park, rapid thudding of her athletic shoes like heartbeats drumming across the wooden bridge that spanned Beaver Creek. Who she was did not matter. She was here, alone, and that was enough. When she came abreast the boxwoods where Wulf hid, two long arms sprang from the leaves with hardly a rustle, pulled the woman's struggling form into the shadows. The killer punched, punched again, and then, he lowered his sharpened teeth to the unconscious woman's throat.

***

Ted worked evening shift at Ball's, 2:00 P.M until 10:00. His was a boring job that paid a fair living. If Ted had a dollar for every aluminum soda can tab he had processed on his machine, he would have been a millionaire many times over. Instead, he made bill money, and not much more. Sometimes his life felt like a gerbil's, stuck inside that metal wheel, running endless circles but going nowhere. Only Margie's love kept him sane. He knew she was just there, waiting behind the front door. She was nothing, if not a creature of habit, greeting his shift-end and return home with a big hug at the door as if he had been gone for weeks. He would be surrounded by the wholesome perfume of body sweat from her nightly jog,

189

and the aroma of the late supper she always set the table with. Slipping his key in the lock, he turned it, and twisted the knob. There were no waiting arms. Ted stepped into an empty living room.

"Margie," Ted yelled into the dark house, voice echoing hollowly.

No reply. Ted instantly knew something wasn't right! Margie never failed to meet Ted at the door! A hard rush of adrenalin sent his heart racing, popped cold sweat out on his back to burn icily along the ridges of his spine.

"Margie!" Ted's panic sent him throughout the house, flicking on the light switch in every room. He looked in every closet. Got down on hand and knee, peered under beds. But something in his soul told Ted his wife was not in the house. There was emptiness only absence could explain. Like some psychic bomb exploding in his mind, Ted knew that his wife was gone. Taking his cell from his pocket, he pressed the numbers for 911 with trembling fingers.

***

Wulf lifted his victim from where she lay, and slipped her still form inside a large lawn and leaf bag. His big rig was parked in the patron's lot, only vehicle in the vast expanse of asphalt. Quick exits and an absence of a body were the keys to a successful hunt. No victim meant no evidence, and the on-ramp for I-81 beckoned only a half-mile south. Once he had her loaded inside the sleeper compartment, he would carefully slip the thin plastic poncho over his head, followed by the rubber gloves, and toss them into a small metal trash can to be burned at a truck stop hundreds of miles down the road. Wulf was opening the door to his truck when two marked police cars came tearing through the park entrance, blue lights flashing. A halogen spotlight centered on his bloody face.

"Stop right there!"

Dropping the body, Wulf raised his hands.

***

Ted knew his wife's evening routine. Rain or clear, she always jogged between 8:00 and 9:00 P.M. at the park. He arrived as the police officers were roughly loading a big man into the back seat of a marked Crown Vic. Ted knew the officer who came to greet him. They had played high school football together, shared an occasional beer at the bowling alley. Something tied inside a black plastic bag was piled on the ground next to a big rig.

"Rob, did you find Margie?"

"Ted, don't come any closer. Detectives are on their way...I don't know how to say this, but Margie's gone."

190

Ted's heart sank into his guts. Everything faded out, went dark.

***

Ted woke up in the ER. Rob's pale face rose into his vision, frightened, bleak.

Without asking, Ted knew. Margie was dead.

***

The next day, the killer's face was splashed across the Herald Courier's front page.

"Over the Road Driver and Suspected Serial Killer Wulf Linski Murders Local Woman!"

National network news programs flooded the small town of Bristol, many of whom tried their best to interview Ted where he lay shocked and medicated in a hospital room. Friends and family ran interference, guarding access points into Bristol Regional Medical Center, while Rob and his compatriots in the police department aggressively blocked news vans from the hospital parking lot.

That evening, Rob entered Ted's room. When his eyes met Ted's, some fierce inner light burning behind the man's pale irises abruptly stopped Rob in his tracks. Inadvertently, his police instinct made him stutter-step backward, dropping his hand to the holstered .38 on his service belt.

"Rob," Ted barked, "what did that monster do to my Margie?"

"Ted, you don't want to know."

"Rob, I need to know!"

"She died from blood loss...."

"How? Knife, gun, HOW DID MY WIFE DIE?"

"He," Rob answered brokenly, "ripped her throat out with his teeth!"

***

Wulf hunkered in his cell, dressed in only an orange jumpsuit and socks. The pigs thought him a suicide risk. What a hoot! The darkness in the cell settled around his large, tattooed form, comforting as a blanket, while his mind pondered the advice of his high-priced defense attorney whom he had consulted with prior to the morning's arraignment. Insanity. Yes, he could act crazy. Couple of years in a mental hospital upstate, become sane, and then back on the road again. Back to the hunt. He could do it. Predators are anything, if not adaptable.

191

A fever was raging inside Ted's body. He could feel the lava-like fire consuming the marrow in his bones, spreading out from his chest, following the puzzle path of joint to joint even as he lay sleeping in his hospital bed. A nightmare was playing inside his mind. It flickered and twitched like a '50's B-movie. He was tracking a wolf through dark woods. Sometimes moonlight would give him a glimpse of his prey. It walked upright on two feet, like a man, but there was nothing mannish about the beast. He could hear it growling continuously, as if it suffered some vast, all-consuming hunger. When it paused, raised its muzzle to the moon and howled, unseen women among the night-washed trees screamed with agonized terror!

"Kill it, Ted! Kill it," Margie's terrified voice rose loudest among them, *"KILL IT! KILL IT!"*

Ted sat up with two loud bangs and a roar! He was shaking, and holding something hard in his hands. Looking down, he saw that his grip had broken the plastic hand rails the nurse had raised on either side of the bed. Dropping rails to sheet, he reached up, yanked the I.V. out of his arm, and climbed out onto the cold tile floor. As he lifted his stained work clothes out of the closet, a woman's shadowed form flickered past the open doorway that led to the hall. Margie. Letting the hospital gown fall to the floor, Ted began putting on his clothes. There was something he needed to do....

***

Around 3:00 A.M. that night, there was an uproar somewhere outside the cell block. Cursing, shouts, the drunken sobs of someone who had way too much to drink. After a series of clatters, bangs, raised voices that gradually settled down, three police officers carefully carried a limp man into a cell three doors down from Wulf's, and placed him on a cot.

"I thought he was doped up in the hospital, poor bastard," one of the officers spoke softly to the other two, "he has to be out of his mind with grief! If I was him, I'd be dead drunk too, or loading a gun. I can't say as I blame him."

His fellow officers mumbled sad agreement.

"Sleep it off, buddy," one of the officers said, closing the cell door. Talking softly among themselves, the officers turned the lights off, and left.

Darkness settled in again, the block falling silent. An hour passed. A scratching, clicking noise caught the killer's attention, pulled him to full awareness. A loud clack sounded, and the cell door three down scritched open on greased hinges.

Soft footsteps moved close, paused outside Wulf's door.

192

"Do you want out of here?" a soft voice asked.

"Oh yes," Wulf replied, "very much so!"

The scratching, clicking noise began sounding from the lock on the killer's cell. With a final clank, the door swung slowly open.

"My father was a locksmith," the soft voice answered in explanation.

With a soft growl of pleasure, the killer started to rise. The sudden arrival of a hard-toed boot to the forehead shoved him into unconsciousness down a long, cascading corona of stars.

***

Though a much larger man than Ted, the killer's weight seemed infinitesimal to the manic strength coursing through Ted's body as he dragged Margie's murderer along the slick concrete floor by his long, greasy hair. Boosting the killer over one shoulder like a sack of potatoes, Ted pushed open the fire escape door whose lock he had picked earlier, and descended the steps. Once in the alley, he turned left, crossed a back street, turned right around a corner, and found his Ford F-150 exactly where he had left it, behind an abandoned building. Sensing a stir in the killer's body, Ted rolled him into the bed of his truck, hopped in behind, and savagely rabbit-punched him in the back of the neck where head meets body. The killer's from stilled once more. Stepping down from the bed, Ted opened the driver's door, felt over the sun visor, removed the spare key.

***

Ted could see them in his peripheral vision as he drove into the densely wooded ridges bordering Fire Tower Road. At headlight's edge, the shades of women would flicker in and out of the ditch line, paralleling his path. Glancing through his rear-view mirror, he could see them following, more substantial in the road's gravel dust, the darkness behind, dozens, young, old, short, tall, fat, thin.

Picking his spot, Ted pulled over, turned the Ford off. Unloading tool bag and lantern from the passenger side floorboard, he reached into the truck's bed, grabbed a fistful of hair, and slid the killer over the tail gate. Shouldering bag and lantern, Ted dragged the killer behind him into the wood, the body's jumpsuit near frictionless on fall leaves. Like black fog, women's shadows followed.

***

A bucket of cold water to the face wrenched Wulf to gasping wakefulness. He struggled to move, and found himself roped to a tree. A

193

kerosene lantern flickered, casting sepulchral light across a dark fold somewhere in the woods. Looking up, his eyes met the sad face of a man. The man was wearing a thin, plastic poncho, and rubber surgeon's gloves.

"I'm Ted," the sad face explained. "Husband of Margie. Remember her, Mr. Wulf? She's here with us now. And so are all the other women you've murdered."

"I ain't admitting to no other women, but when I get loose from here, asshole, I will show you first hand exactly what I did to your wife!"

All around the tiny circle of light, women's voices screamed at the crude sound of Wulf's denial and threat!

"Kill it kill it kill it kill it KILL IT!"

Looking at the killer's face for some sign of recognition, it quickly became obvious to Ted that only he could hear the piteous wails.

"Oh," Ted's sad voice replied, meeting the killer's glare, "there's no getting loose for you."

"Rob said you used your teeth to kill my Margie. I have these…"

A hand raised a pair of pliers, shoved them against the bigger man's lips.

"Kill it kill it kill it kill it KILL IT!"

The killer struggled mightily to keep his mouth closed, but a finger and thumb clamped his nostrils firmly closed. When the killer's mouth opened to gulp air, Ted reached in, grasped an incisor, twisted, yanked savagely. He held up the tooth, studied it. It had been filed to a shark-like point.

"Mr. Wulf, Appalachians are raised to love dogs. Occasionally, one goes bad, turns wolf and kills the sheep it's a dog's job to protect. Wolves love their teeth, you know. They like to gnaw on things. So, when the worst happens, you hog-tie the wolf dog, take pliers, and pull out all his teeth."

"No," the tied man cried, "you can't do this! It's not…!"

"Kill it kill it kill it kill it KILL IT!"

Ted grasped another tooth, twisted, yanked!

The killer was a blubbering, bloody mess by the time Ted finished with the last wisdom tooth. The tied man hung limply in his ropes, snot, tears, long strings of bloody saliva dangling from his torn lips.

"Next," Ted continued, "if pulling the wolf dog's teeth don't mediate his nature, we tie the mean critter up, and castrate him."

Tossing down the pliers, Ted reached behind his back, pulled out a large pair of knitting shears.

"Kill it kill it kill it kill it KILL IT!"

"These were my Margie's, you know. Girl could do almost anything with her hands. Cook, bake, mend. Of course, you wouldn't have known that, seeing as how you pick strangers to stalk and murder. Did you know even one of those poor women? No, I suppose not."

194

The bloody man whined and bleated in terror, much like a sheep at shearing day, but Ted would not be denied. A few deft snips, and the tied man's jumpsuit puddled to the ground around his feet. Wulf's many tattoos stood out starkly against his skin's pale background.

"You fancy yourself a hunter, huh? Well, Mr. Wulf, Appalachians are raised hunters, even though the vast majority of Americans see us as simple minded sheep. We hunt here to feed our families, to protect what's ours from harm, be it man or beast. You're just a cheap wannabe!"

Removing a piece of baling wire, Ted wrapped it tightly around the struggling man's scrotum, and knotted it with a deft twist.

"Kill it kill it kill it kill it KILL IT!"

"Wouldn't want you to bleed out, would we?"

Picking up the shears, he made a sudden, savage snip.

***

A second bucket of icy water brought the killer awake. His mouth and loins were a burning agony of fire.

"Wakee wake, Mr. Wulf!"

"You can't do this to me," the killer quaked and moaned, "it ain't human! Please…I need a doctor…."

"Mr. Wulf, you ever hear of 'an eye for an eye?' My grandpa was a firm believer. It means, you hurt me, I hurt you. You took my Margie from me and cut out my heart! How many hearts have you cut out over the years? So…."

Ted felt around scattered leaves, found the pliers, held them up in front of the killer's agonized eyes.

"Kill it kill it kill it kill it KILL IT!"

"Did you know, my grandpa trapped wolves in his day? Skinned them out, cured and sold the pelts to the county for the bounty. Nah, you wouldn't know that. How could you? I will let you in on a little secret, though. Something you definitely wouldn't know. When I was just a brat, grandpa taught me how to skin a wolf…."

When it was done, he buried the killer's skinned carcass deep in a laurel bed's heart. Tramped the dirt down carefully. Replaced moss and leaves. The silent shades gathered around his work, bearing silent witness. When he stood, finished, there was a collective sigh from the shades, and one by one, each vanished in a brilliant flash of light. Margie's soul was the last one to go, Ted was sure. Her exit was blinding when seen through tears.

Leaving, Ted dug in a pocket for his cigarette lighter. He had a poncho and gloves to burn.

***

At morning head count, running feet and panicked shouts shocked Ted from his sleep. The quiet jail had become a mad house. Cops were racing back and forth past Ted's locked cell like chickens with their heads cut off! Reeking of alcohol, Ted sat blearily up on his cot.

"Ted," Rob shouted through the bars, "did you see or hear anything last night? The monster who murdered Margie has escaped! You were too drunk to know it last night, but he was just three cells down from you!"

In the months that came to pass after Margie's funeral, Ted seemed to hold his act together. There were no more drunken outbursts. He was sad and solemn, but who in his shoes would not be? No clue to the whereabouts of Margie's killer was ever found. The police were baffled. No one took it upon themselves to question why Ted never asked the police department once for information about Margie's killer. People just understood. Some questions were just too painful to ask, or answer.

For police departments across the country, it was as if the big Wulf man had vanished off the face of the planet.

Most days, when seen around Bristol, Ted had taken to wearing a large, tanned leather vest. It had strangely inked designs on its outside. If they were located on a man's body, one might have thought them tattoos.

BIO: Rufus Skeens is a retired coal miner who lives and writes in Bristol, Virginia. Late last year his first volume of poetry, Lost for Words was published by James Ward Kirk publishing, and is available on Amazon Books in print and e-book versions. He loves words, art, and music, and works at poetry and art, while listening in rapt fascination to Pink Floyd.

WOLF, RICHARD

BRIAN GLOSSUP

Waxing Gibbous

It's itchy down there. More so now than ever before. I mean, the shit's really nothing new. I itch all the time, it's just more....aggressive. It agitates easily. I could be walking along, minding my own business and out of the fuckin' blue BAM! It's all over me. Like it takes hold of me and vigorously, angrily does the deed. Private, public...it don't matter. Shit has to be done then and there. Until some kind of relief. Some kind of comfort is achieved. Something besides this goddamned itching.

The moon is a bitch now too.

Not like I fuckin' couldn't just stay indoors, handcuff myself to the goddamned radiator in my apartment. It might help....might. Shit only lasts a little while during the full moon anyways. If I could hold off and just deal with the aggravation I'd be fine. Fighting with it I'd be risking losing a finger or two trying to keep it from eating the fuckin' cuffs. Or biting through my wrists and hands like some trapped animal, gnawing its feet off. No, fuck that. If I only had some help. Someone to lock my ass in, and leave me to the infernal itching and pain. I'd be okay, right? Right?

Anyways, there's Candy, the hooker that works the street in front of my apartments and up the block. She'd do just about anything for fifty bucks. I've seen her in a three way with a tranny and an orangutan before. And that was for twenty bucks and two lukewarm forties. Pretty sure a crumpled, blood stained Grant, that's missing a corner and may have some meth crumbs stuck to it, will get the whore to do the deed FOR me.

Or....I could just wait a few days and do the deed TO her. The moon will be full then. Telling me its perverted secrets. Telling me that it is time to. Shining down on this shitty little pathetic soul that has been chosen to carry this fucked up burden. She could be the slutty, scab ridden scratch to my overpowering, insistent, burning itch. The slut would love it. Lure her in with false hopes and promises of greenbacks earned on her back. She'd be the perfect prey. No one would miss her. Fuck, no one knows she's alive now. She has no family. And her pimp, Slim, got stabbed in the throat

199

behind the apartments over two weeks ago. He sure as shit won't be missing her. Fuckin' Slim was fuckin' dead.

It would be so easy, though. I know Candy's been staying at the motel on the corner. And I know she'd want to spend the night in a warm apartment with some scratch to boot, instead of spending it giving handjobs to crusty, old drunks in the grimy bathrooms at the recreation center for five dollars a pop. Just to get enough money to rent a room. I'd be her saint. I'd be her god damned savior. I'd be her mother fuckin' god. She could take the whole night off, even. And just tend to my simple needs. Tending to the itch.

Maybe it'd work. Maybe not. I could just balls up and be a man. Take the deed in hand and satisfy the beast within. Let the itch be scratched. Let it be done. It just has to pass, has to turn its cycle, right? Like any infection. Shit's just gotta run its course.

Ah fuck it! I'll give it a few days and then decide. No time like the heat of the moment, right? Allow some bad decision to end some bad shit. Either way something's gotta give. I'm either gonna feed it or fuck it, because this shit's getting old. Just so goddamned tired of the mother fuckin' itching! The deed will be done. Hopefully, with a little luck this will be the last time.

Nope. Fuck....this WILL be the last time. Even if I have to put a goddamned silver bullet in my brain, I'm not living with this shit through another cycle. I just want it all to be over with, yunno? Fuck it.

Now....where the fuck do you buy silver bullets?

Full Moon

It's hot as fuck up in my apartment. Had to leave the window open while I went to meet Candy on the corner. Let some cool, fresh air in. Hopefully letting some of the stuffiness out. It's also pretty musky in there, but that's just me. It gets real pungent before the change. It smells like a dirty wet dog shook itself dry right in front of your face after he had a good romp in a cow pasture and a hardy swim in a mud hole. All stinky and shit clumped fur wafting up your nose.

And balls, it also smells of balls.

And goddamn the itch is something fierce. I can hardly keep from scratching my skin off as I'm convincing Candy to come up to my apartment for some "coffee". That being her code word for sex with all the Johns. I told her the "coffee" was hot and the "cream" was cool. That was my code word for semen.

"Come on, baby." I told her. "I don't bite." I lied. Laying it down thick. "Besides, when was the last time you slept in a clean bed, huh? I have a fridge full of food." Another lie. I flashed a half false smile and said sweetly. "Take the rest of the night off and come on up."

"Richard." She says my name in a nasally, gum smacking pitch. The whore. "I can't come up to yo apartment, hunny." Her huge, floppy tits, heaving with each wheeze from the emphysema crippling her lungs. "You don't even know me. I mean, what makes you betta than all tha otha Johns? How do I know you ain't gonna rape and kill me?" There was sweat rolling down her plump face. Discolored from the layers of foundation that looks like it had been applied by a blind man with a paint roller. "Huh?" She blew bubbles of gum and twirled her hair. The bitch.

"Come on, Candy." I assured her. "You know I'm harmless." I lied again. Smiling real big, I slid my arm around her and squeezed one of them jugs with a sweaty hand. "Now, how's about that 'coffee' and 'cream'?"

She took the bait.

We walked up two flights of stairs to my apartment, because the goddamned elevator's out. Fucking landlord is a cheap fuck and won't splurge on a fix until next year. He let the building tenants know in a posted letter the day he left for his three week vacation. The dick. Guess I can use the exercise. God knows Candy's fat ass does. She was sweating like a, well, like a *her* in church. Sitting in the front pew, hearing how God felt about the faggots and the sins of adultery and such.

She grunts with each step and I have to help her with the last few to the third floor. My apartment was just down the hall. We exited the stair well and Candy had to have a smoke. Pulling shit outta her purse, looking for her cigarettes and a lighter, I watched the slick folds under her arms slide. She plucks a coffin nail from the pack after she finds it. Lights the tip and sucks the butt, then hacks half a lung out in a cloud of stink and smoke. Smiling at me, she breathes heavily. Her breath was rancid as she spoke.

"I don't do no ass play." That's fine, I thought. "And I won't kiss you in da mouth." Which was fuckin' fine too. "Everything else is negotiable. Ya dig, Richard? Can I call ya 'Dick'?" Her brown teeth pinching the cigarette as she adjusted the thong between her sweaty ass checks.

"Richard is fine, Candy." I let her know straight up, leading her down the hall to my apartment door. "I don't like to be called dick." Fumbling with my keys to unlock the door, because you keep your shit locked up with neighbors like I have, the whore lets out a bellowing, cracked cackle of laughter. She wasn't making this easy.

"You so silly, Richard." Her tits were giggling and it was pissing me off just at the sight of her cellulite formed body laughing at me. "I just might suck yo dick harder than you ever had in yo miserable lil life." I didn't doubt her skills as a whore. There was a long, thick, phlegm filled wheeze as she sucked down the last half of the cigarette and dropped the butt in the middle of the hallway. Stomping it out with her high heeled, bunion encrusted feet, she then grabs my crotch firmly. And squeezes. "You ready to have yo world rocked, hun?"

201

"Bitch." I said. "I'll take everything you can give." And that was the truth. She acted offended, but she knew she was street trash. She'd been called worse. I unlocked the door and extended my arm into my apartment. "Enter, my lady." I said with a smile. "Let the mother fucking fun begin."

Watching her waddle her fat ass into my apartment I felt relieved that the stank had almost completely cleared out. Not like I really gave too much of a fuck if she smelled it or not, just didn't want anything slowing my groove to get the itch on. But, now with the window open, it was a bit chilly in here. Candy almost immediately began rubbing her arms. Rolls forming and smoothing out with her kneading hands.

"Brrrrrrr!" She blurted out rudely as I hurried over to the window to shut it. "It's colder than polar bear's balls in here, Dick!" How the fuck would she know? I locked the window and tried to keep calm, grinning as I turned around towards her.

"Richard, Candy. Please, I hate the name Dick." My blood was on the brink of boiling, but it wasn't time. Gotta keep cool. I had to prolong the deed as long as I could. "How about that 'coffee'?" I tried flexing my arm and chest muscles. Showing her what she was in for, offering a glimpse of what she was about to get. And she laughed.

"Think I might need somethin' stronger than 'coffee', Richard." Her funky colored lips flapped. "You got any booze?" She asked as she slipped out of her slut jacket and kicked off her big slutty stilettos. "I really could use a drink before we do dis."

"Sure." I replied, clenching my teeth. Trying to hold back the urge to tell this whore if she wanted some fuckin' green she needs to be choking down a mouthful of my cock right about now, and not drinkin' up all my goddamned hooch. This wasn't a bar. I didn't have to get her drunk and trick her into fuckin' me. She WAS the trick, and she was the one that was gonna get fucked. "I have some cheap scotch." I told her, walking over to the cupboard in the kitchen and opening it and removing said bottle. There was no way in pedophile HELL I was gonna let this slut drink up all my top shelf stuff.

"Whatever. I don't care. Tha stronger, tha better." She was scratchin' at her crotch and fixin' her wig as she strolled across my living room like she was queen bitch of the brothel. "Can I use your potty?" She asks in a childish lisp. "I wanna freshen up a lil bit before we get at each other's goods, baby."

"Through the bedroom." I told her, pointing the cheap scotch in its direction. There were two clean glasses in the dishwasher and I snatched them up. Putting a little pep in my step on the way out of the kitchen. "You make yourself nice and pretty and I'll meet you in bed, Candy." You fuckin' skanky whore you.

I had to just keep calm until the moment was right, just relax and play it smooth and cool, but my goddamned stupid feet caught the shag rug in the living room. And my goddamned stupid fuckin' ass tripped into the moonlight.

Shit was instant. A beam coming through the small oval window above the sink caught me right across the face. Filling my vision with pale, illustrious shine. It was peacefully angering the fuck outta me in its beautiful rays. Then the itch surges into my brain. Standing all the hair on my body on end with goose bumps. Like a wet electric charge, blistering my skin with sensations only animals and them crusty bums downtown could ever know. My hands drop the cheap bottle of scotch and the glasses and go right to work instinctively. Scratching my chest, my arms, my back. I relieve the agitated areas quickly just short of leaving bloodied welts and others erupt in irritation like patches of scabies, or crabs. In this case, more like sonova bitchin' sea monsters. Digging fingernails into my scalp and across my face, the itch was worse than it had been in a long fuckin' time. My neck was irritated, my legs were on fire, my balls were aflame. It was an entire body itch and I didn't know if I had big enough hands to scratch it. I must have winced aloud, or the bottle and glasses hitting the carpeted floor alerted her, because the hooker heard me

WHORE! "Need some help gettin' it up, hun?" The bitch! One more fuckin' time and I gut her. But first, I gotta get this thing out.

I tear my shirt off with a pull at the neckline. One tug and the shit just splits with a loud rip. I'm all sweaty now and it's wet and I sling it across the living room. Where it slaps the wall with a sick splat and sticks. It's getting musky in here again, and I'm smelling balls. Funky fuckin' balls.

"IT'S RICHARD!" I replied with an exasperated scream. "RICHARD YOU FAT, DUMB, DEAF SLUT! FOR THE LAST GODDAMNED TIME, DON'T CALL ME DICK!!!" Kicking my shoes off I hop around in a circle tugging at my socks. My feet were alive with the squiggles of healing wounds, and pins and needles, tickled with feathers and dry skin and a vengeful ghost of a rash. It was a sonovabitch of a fuckin' moment for me, clawing away at my toes, but it was getting time. Just have to hold out a little bit longer, until the big finale. Then she's gonna get it. "AND PLEASE," I pretend pleaded with the portly prostitute. "WASH YOUR PUSSY FOR ME! IT'S GETTING RANK IN HERE!" I lied. It really didn't matter. She would be fucked before sunrise anyways, stinky twat or not.

"Watch yo dirty ass mouth, RICHARD!" She replies and I hear the toilet flush. "I may be a ho, but I'M STILL A LADY!" There was a hefty cough thick in her throat and she spits. The toilet lid clacks shut and the counter creaks as she leans over the sink, touching up that horrible paint job of a face she has, I imagine. Bitch better not be raiding my goddamn medicine cabinet. "Baby....HEY, BABY....YOU GOTS ANY RUBBERS?!?" There was rustling of papers and the smell of cloves mixing with the funky air as she began chewing fresh pieces of gum. Smacking

203

with each word that escaped her large lips. "HUH? BABY?" SMACK! SMACK! SMACK! "I'm fresh out."

Whatever this skank had crawling around in her bush or bloodstream couldn't compare to the shit I already got. Couldn't hold a candle made of STDs to it. Not even fuckin' close. What the fuck did we need with rubbers? Who was she fooling? Who the fuck was protecting who, and why would we care? Candy could have the black plague, butt fucked with the whole sonova bitchin' Spanish Inquisition infected with AIDS and this goddamned persistent fucking itch would overcome. Chew it to bits and shit out the bones.

And that was when the shit got real. The itch made the change. As I was fumbling with the button on my jeans it was howling to be set free from my boxers. Its tiny furry arms ending in tiny sharp claws scratching at my hands as I unzipped my pants and let them fall around my feet. The mother fucker was fierce, opening wounds all along my fingers and knuckles. It howled and snarled from the sinister face at the end of my fuzzy shaft. Salivating from its fanged mouth, glaring at me intensely through its savage, red eyes. The ugly little sonovabitch.

I wanted to choke the goddamned little fucker. Snap its girthy goddamned neck. Maybe hold its nasty mouth shut until it turns blue and shrivels up then falls off, if it didn't chew my fuckin' fingers off first. But I was feeling desperate. I'd do anything to cease this curse now, end its horrible shitty existence. Even if I have to bite a goddamned Lone Ranger special slug that I bought from a thug four buildings down. The guy was a part time gunrunner and gunsmith, but a full time drug dealer. I let him know I'd be back for his ass if the bullet wasn't real silver. I wasn't risking an extra hole in my head for this shit for nothing. It was ending tonight. Either this crusty cunt satiates the itch, or I'm using a serial number scraped Saturday night special on a fuckin' shitty Monday morning.

"NO, CANDY! I DON'T!" I managed to finally scream at the slut. Struggling with the beast between my legs. Stumbling around the living room like a goddamned drunk perverted penguin with my pants around my ankles. Wrestling the biting thing with both hands, keeping it from nipping my thighs or balls. "HURRY UP! GET YOUR FAT ASS OUT HERE, WHORE! NOW!" It was time and I couldn't control what I was saying or the tone of my voice. Aggression was pouring from me, commanded by that sickening demon I was cursed with so long ago. The one that was really in control. The one that took my manhood, and replaced it with a goddamned wild animal.

"Hold yo tiny dick...." Don't you fuckin' do it, slut. Don't do it! "DICK!" This dirty whore has mocked me for the last fuckin' time! This dirty whore has to fuckin' die now! Most goddamned definitely, no doubt about it!

I tripped through the living room, stumbling with my feet tangled up in my jeans. Falling into the bedroom and bouncing off of the soiled, unmade bed, and up into the bathroom door. Gripping my monstered meat firmly, I begin banging it against the frame and lock. And now I'm growling and spitting along with the little fucker. Just as angered as it is. We both were insane and ravenous, with the want of this bitch's blood.

"YOU FUCKIN' FAT SLUT BITCH!" I yell and the creature that is my dick mimics me. Snarling and scratching at the bathroom door's knob. Its claws leaving curling metal ribbons tumbling to the carpet. It's screeching seems to move through its mouth and out my vocal cords. "FOR THE LAST GODDAMNED TIME." I release the double hand hold on my furry cock and begin slamming my fists into the door. It gives a bit with every strike. "STOP CALLING ME DICK!" Enough was enough. The itch had won, it had to be scratched, and I was about to feed this whore bitch to it.

"You crazy muh fuckuh!" Candy calls to me through the cracking and splintering wood. "I knew yo goofy ass was fucked up in da head! You better watch yoself, I ain't fuckin' round!" She was pissed, not as much as me and my dick was, but seriously fuckin' irked. Fuck her, though, she wasn't shit. Let her get mad. I don't give a fuck. "Back away from tha door, you psycho fuck!" She barked. "We either gone do dis or I'm fuckin' outta here, DICK!"

"BIIIIIIIIIIIIITCH!!!" I'm screaming as I burst the goddamned bathroom door in. That was fuckin' it! Enough was mother fuckin' enough! My veiny, throbbing were-member was howling, and I was too. Both our heads crying out to the moon as we forced our way into the bathroom. In a storm of broken wood and dust. With all intentions of taking this disgusting whore apart, piece by piece.

And she's just standing there. Looking dumb. With her bare, drooping tits pointed at the tiled floor. Her caked on makeup, slightly running down her weathered fuckin' face. She wasn't startled, not at all. Standing with a liver spotted hand on her obese hip. All the attitude in the world staring from her eyes, cutting into me. I stop, abruptly. Calming down from the confusion. So was my growling dick. It quieted as we both gawked at the horrible hooker, puzzled and stupefied.

It wasn't the naked, wrinkled and aged skin that seemed to droop and jiggle as she breathed heavily that bothered us. The wiggling of the cellulite down her stomach and arms, kept in check by the bracelets of plastic on her heroin marked wrists and what little elastic still held her panties up. Not even the odd buff of the salt and pepper colored seventies bush that jutted out around the lines of her off colored underwear, which was looking like it had seen better days, maybe back when it was still a fresh pair of panties in a plastic wrapper at the store and not stretched out holding all this fat whore's nasty parts in. No, that wasn't enough to make me puke or halt me and the monster dick in our tracks. Even the blue and purple broken blood vessels that mapped out her scrawny old legs, reminding me of melting wax or badly drawn lines in crayon on a preschoolers bedroom wall wasn't bothersome at the moment.....no. Not at all disturbing.

It was the muffled snarling movement under them dirty drawers that scared me. A growling that was all too familiar and horrifying to hear for the first time. Something was seething beneath Candy's crusty cunt cloth concealment. Something that shocked me more than my own fucked up bullshit and beyond even the sickest shit the werewolf dick could even comprehend. Something goddamned diabolically evil.

And then it dawned on me....she got a wolf pussy.

BIO: Brian Glossup was surgically removed from a tumor at birth. He grew up being incubated on this plane of existence, mimicking social interaction and biding his time. Now, expressing himself with the tools of the natives he is out of control and must be stopped. If you see him do not interfere with his insanity. Contact the authorities immediately.

IT TAKES A LOT TO KILL A HUMAN

SHARON L. HIGA

Wolf shifter*

A human being - male or female - who can arbitrarily transform either their whole body or individual parts, into a combination wolf/human shape. The shifter, once transformed, has the strength and a size greater than five times that of their human counterpart. The shifter can change at any time, day or night, however – on the night of the full moon, their powers are at their peak, making them incapable of being either destroyed or stopped from annihilating their intended target on that particular night.

The blindfold had slipped a little, giving Bill the ability to see if he pushed his head way back. The vehicle was pitching from side to side, the road so bad that Bill kept slipping first to the right, then to the left. No matter which way he began to fall, he'd be grabbed and forcefully shoved back into place – seated on the cold metal floor of the van, hands and feet bound with metal shackles.

After what seemed like hours, the van jerked to a halt. Bill heard a door slide open then he felt his shoulders grabbed and hauled forward. He felt himself falling, his stomach and thighs snagging on the fender while his face, arms, and elbows hit the rough dirt ground.

A boot in his butt knocked him the rest of the way out while hands once more grabbed him - this time under the armpits - and yanked him to a kneeling position. The metal ankle cuffs were removed as he was jerked upwards, his numb legs and feet barely able to keep him from collapsing onto the cold, gravel and dirt covered earth.

Bill kept his head angled up, allowing him the ability to see a little of the ground at his feet, helping him to keep his footing while being propelled forward to who-knew-where.

The young man was yanked to a halt as the blindfold covering his eyes was snatched off, the snatcher taking a patch of his hair along with it. He flinched from the pain, then blinked a couple of times. When his eyes had adjusted, he looked around and noticed that they were standing in front

209

of a log cabin surrounded by nothing but woods. He glanced up at the night sky which was clear and bright with stars, the full moon bathing everything in its phosphorescent glow.

His arms were grabbed once more as he was hauled up the wooden steps, then unceremoniously thrown through the partially open door.

"Careful you assholes! Don't wreck the door. I just had it replaced from the last time you gorillas brought a guest here."

Harsh laughter erupted from all around Bill. He recognized the voice and looked to the right of where he and the four rough looking hoods stood by the entrance.

The cabin was an open loft design, the downstairs combining living room, office, kitchen and dining area. The spiral staircase in the center of the cabin led upstairs to the bathrooms and bedrooms (two of each). It was a small and elaborately decorated getaway and Bill assumed – correctly – that it was as far removed from civilization as any place could ever be.

The man standing next to the fireplace was heavy-set, bald and clean shaven as if he'd been born yesterday. His dark skin and black eyes spoke of a Mediterranean heritage; his family came originally from Greece. Saburo Manos was his birth-name, but everyone in the five counties that made up the city of Wolfsons Creek knew him as *Cutter*. He'd worked his way up through the ranks, starting as a low level enforcer, maneuvering his way to the top where he eventually deposed the former leader of the gang known as The Red Death.

Their name fits, Bill thought to himself as he stared at the man, *like the plague, these psychos decimate every living thing they touch.* He shook his head, which earned him a sharp cuff on the left ear by the thug standing behind him. "Listen up, shit-for-brains; Boss's talkin' at ya."

The blow hadn't hurt Bill too much, but he stumbled sideways, acting like it had. His hair was grabbed from behind and he was pulled upright as Cutter began to draw near.

Cutter waved a hand at the man while continuing to walk towards Bill, smiling. "Hold off, Sticks. There's no need for brutality just yet." He stood in front of Bill, hands clasped behind his back. "Bill and I need to have a little chat first; there's something he needs to help me understand."

He assessed both the kid and the damage his men had inflicted so far. The young man standing in front of him was twenty-seven years old, tall, wiry build, brown shoulder-length hair, the same color brown eyes. His looks were what could be classified as 'common', meaning he could walk into a restaurant, have a meal, and five minutes after he'd walked out the door, no one would remember either what he looked like or that he'd even been there.

A real loser if ever I'd seen one, Cutter thought to himself as he reached out with one hand and grabbed the kid's chin. He turned the face this way and that, noting the blackened left eye, blood trickling from the left

210

ear, swollen right jaw, the torn flannel shirt with scratches and beginning discolorations showing through the rips. Satisfied, he let go of Bill's face, and turning, he began walking into the living room, commanding "Bring him in here."

Bill was escorted to a folding chair set by the blazing fire and unceremoniously shoved into it. Cutter took his seat - a far more comfortable one than Bill's - and reached for a cigar on the end table next to him. The four thugs took their places around the room, awaiting further orders.

Cutter clipped the end of the cigar, flipped open a gold monogrammed lighter and puffed until he was satisfied with the draw. He looked through the swirling smoke at the kid seated in the chair across from him and felt a little disconcerted. Bill wasn't showing any signs of fear or terror; no cowering on the seat, pissin' his pants, no babbling bullshit – no outward signs of even caring about his predicament whatsoever. This enraged the gang leader – he was used to being the bad ass in charge, not the other way around. He set the cigar down and leaned forward.

"Well, Billy boy -do I have to explain to you why you're in this fucked up situation?"

Billy stopped assessing the surroundings and turned his attention to the man seated in front of him. Bill's response was calm and conversational, a touch of mockery coating his reply. "Is it because you're an insignificant turd who thinks he's something special swimming around in this toilet you call a life?"

Before any of his men could react, Cutter - with reflexes as fast as a rattlesnake - cleared the space between him and Bill and punched the kid right in the mouth. Bill's head rocked backwards, blood flying up and out from his split lips. Somehow, he kept himself from falling off the chair. Cutter leaned back, and pulling a handkerchief from his back pocket, rubbed the kid's blood off of his knuckles.

Bill brought his head forward, wiped his lips on the sleeve of his flannel shirt, spit a wad of additional blood into the fire, then brought his gaze back to his attacker. "Good shot - it still doesn't change the truth."

Cutter shook his head and reached once more for the cigar. "Billy, Billy, Billy. What did you think you were going to accomplish by turning the business owners against me? Did you think they were going to stand behind you and stop paying their tribute, or their protection money? Did you think they would see you as the *knight in shining armor* who would slay the bad old dragon? Really…tell me…what did you think was going to happen - other than your inevitable demise as an example to the rest of those fucking sheep?"

Bill leaned forward, elbows on knees, eyes locked on the gang leader in front of him. "Truthfully, I was thinking that you would take the hint, buy the clue, see the light - Hell, whatever you want to call it, Cutter –

211

and leave this location before you and the pieces of garbage you call a gang get taken out."

The words were said without the slightest hint of malice or emotion. Cutter couldn't believe his ears. *It's like he thinks we're discussing the football game or the races over a beer!* The thought was shocking to the man, and it fueled his rage even more. *Smart-ass don't even know he's just signed and sealed his own death certificate.* Cutter stared back at Bill, their eyes still locked. Bill refused to look away. *Okay, he's done.*

Cutter broke eye contact, stood, and motioned to the four men. "Take him out to the usual spot and make it hurt." The men sprang forward and jerked Bill up, forcing him to stand in front of Cutter once more. The gangster looked at the bloodied man being held by his goons up and down - his grin sadistic, filled with malevolence. "After all, it takes a lot to kill a human... that is, if you don't use a weapon." Winking at Bill, Cutter dismissed the group with a wave of his hand.

Bill allowed himself to be dragged across the room and out into the night. One of the thugs, who went by the nickname of Pissant, picked up the blindfold. "Should we use this again, Sticks?"

Sticks had hold of Bill's right arm while Scrip had his left. "Naw, where we're takin' him, he ain't never comin' back. Let him see what he's headed for; be more fun that way."

Pissant chortled and danced around, waving the blindfold in Bill's face. "Quit bein' a dick and open the door!" Sticks yelled. Bo had already gone around to the driver's side and hopped in. He revved the engine, lending a sense of urgency to the situation.

Sticks flung Bill toward the partially opened door, catching the kid on the hip and tumbling him into the van. Bill rolled with the blow and fetched up on the other side of the empty interior, legs pulled against his chest, cuffed hands clasped between his knees. He brought his head up slowly and deliberately. Sticks peered at the kid while Pissant and Scrip piled inside.

Bill's eyes were in shadow, but Pissant saw the slow smile spread across the blood-covered lips and chin. An involuntary shudder ran up the thug's spine. "Keep your eyes on him, fuktards. We don't need no problems before we get to the pit." He slammed the sliding door for emphasis and pulled himself into the passenger seat. Bo threw the van into gear and aimed the vehicle back the way they'd come.

Bill leaned his head against the cold metal wall. Pissant and Scrip were joshing back and forth, Bo intent on watching the road in the moonlight. Sticks let the bantering go on for a bit before he finally spoke.

"Hey, Scrip - how long did that one guy last on us? Was it two hours...three, before he croaked?"

Scrip gave Piss-ant one more punch in the shoulder before replying. He leaned back and stared directly at Bill. "Which guy? The big, fat realtor piece-of-shit, or the short, scrawny news guy?"

Pissant pounded the wall and laughed like a loon. "The scrawny news guy! The scrawny fucker! He lasted almos' four hours with us givin' him wall therapy!" His laughter reverberated around the interior of the moving van. "We still ended up buryin' him alive, didn't we Sticks?"

Sticks nodded, turning sideways so he could gauge Bill's reaction. "Well… if you could call the sounds his body was makin' still alive…yeah."

The figure leaning against the wall didn't move; not even a bound finger twitched. Sticks began to feel a little disconcerted. Usually, by the time their victims reached this point, they weren't above promising anything, including their first-born kid, to get out of the situation.

Sticks faced forward again, saying, "Scrip, explain the situation to this jack-off."

Scrip grinned and rammed Pissant into a corner, shoving a finger under his nose, indicating the cackling idiot needed to shut up. Pissant snorted a few more times before he leaned against the back doors, arms and legs crossed indian-style. Once Scrip knew he'd settled down, he turned his attention back to Bill.

Cracking his knuckles, Scrip yawned then asked, "How far are we from the gravel pit, Bo?"

The driver peered through the dirty windscreen and turned the wheel to the right, guiding the van onto another dirt road. "About fifteen minutes; time enough for you to explain the facts of life to the shitbird."

Scrip nodded and began.

"You see, Billy boy – you don't mind me callin' you Billy, do ya? Oh well…anywho, what we do for the boss is kinda different. Instead of leavin' bullets in bodies where they can be traced, or knife wounds, or DNA found on any *problems* left behind, we have, in a manner of speakin', built a better mouse trap. The elimination happens and the disposal is permanent so there is no body, no evidence, nothing to tie us or the boss to any kind of foul play. We get the chance to practice our sparring methods, and the boss gets a problem resolved. It works out for all of us – except the person in your current position." He chuckled and glanced out the window before resuming the conversation.

"Well, Billy, what is going to happen is this. We are going to be pulling up to an old, abandoned gravel pit. It's on private property – under the name of a shell corporation, so it can't be traced to the boss - n' so far out in Pittsville that I don't even think anyone even remembers it bein' here. Anywho, this is where it's the end of the line for you."

Scrip reached down to his right, and from a side pouch in the door, pulled out a pair of leather gloves. He placed those in his lap, reached back

213

down, then tossed a set to Pissant. He tapped the back of Sticks' chair. Sticks reached behind and Scrip slapped two more sets of gloves into the man's hand. Sticks pulled a pair on and set Bo's pair on the console between them. Scrip adjusted the gloves between his fingers, squeezed his hands open and closed a couple of times, then, satisfied with the fit, continued his dissertation.

"We are going to stop here at the gravel pit, and when we have picked a good place to bury your remains, we are going to drag you out of this van into a cleared area and literally beat you to death. However long it takes you to die is up to you." Scrip delivered this last statement as if he had done no more than read off a grocery list.

He peered through the darkness of the van, eager to see the response to his explanation. Nothing. The idiot didn't even flinch.

If Scrip didn't know any better, he'd swear the guy was already dead, or just too retarded to understand his predicament. He lashed out one booted foot and connected with the asshole's ankle. A slight, hissing intake of air assured Scrip that he was both alive and had more than likely heard it all.

The brakes squealed as the van came to an abrupt halt. Pissant grabbed a couple of shovels that had been bungeed down against the side wall and popped open the back doors.

Scrip pulled the side door open and snarled, "Stay there" to Bill before he stepped out. Sticks followed suit from the front passenger seat. Bo waited with their victim for the sign to bring him out. They sat in silence, Bo neither interested nor compelled to talk to the soon-to-be-dead dude in the back. A pounding on the side window broke his reverie.

"Bring him out!" Sticks motioned with both hands. Bo nodded and pocketed the keys. He worked his way over the console and crouched down next to Bill. "Am I gonna have any trouble with you?" Bill just stared at the grungy man in front of him. Bo nodded and said, "Fair enough...let's go," as he reached out and grabbed Bill by his cuffed wrists.

Flinging the sliding door open with one hand, he hauled Bill out with the other, not waiting for the man to get his feet or balance. Bill slid out, hitting the ground on his knees again, incurring fresh cuts that seeped blood into the chalky dirt beneath.

Pissant was dancing side to side, his desire to inflict harm animating his body. Bo reached down and pulled Bill up, dragging him forward into a cleared area. Bill looked around and saw that the shovels had been used as markers for his burial spot. Scrip and Sticks already had two corners of the area blocked off. Pissant took his position, and when Bo shoved Bill into the ring, he stepped behind the young man to block off the last chance for escape.

Bill stood, hands cuffed in front of him, and turned his face upwards - toward the moon - eyes closed, a small smile touching his split

214

lips. All four men watched their prey as he seemed to be either communing with the moonlit skies or saying his last prayers. *Don't matter anyhow*, Sticks thought to himself, *dumbass is as dead as dogshit anyway.*

Sticks had just taken his first step toward the immobile figure, planning on landing the first of many devastating blows, when a sudden twitching from Bill's body stopped him in his tracks.

Bill's face was still turned to the night sky, and in what the other four could only register as an optical illusion, the moonlight seemed to be focused solely on the bound figure. They looked about in confusion as the shadows darkened around them, but Bill seemed to be caught in a spotlight of moonbeams. Scrip and Bo stared in dawning fear as Bill's wounds suddenly seemed to be shrinking, the blood disappearing as his flesh, hair and eyes began to take on the marble white color of the moon. The man also seemed to be growing bulkier and – impossible as it was - taller, his whole frame beginning to change. They all stared, bug-eyed in disbelief, when the metal handcuffs that had been restraining Bill's hands suddenly snapped, the pieces flying in all different directions.

Bill brought his head back down, staring at both of his arms while he flexed his hands and fingers. Rolling his shoulders, he continued to fill out and develop thickened muscles along his spine, his thighs, his biceps. The men could do nothing but stare, their fascination and fear rooting them to the spot. Sticks, Scrip, Bo and Piss-ant shuffled closer to the changing man; a move that none of them consciously realized they were doing.

Bill brought his attention back to his captors, the chin and jaws now elongating, extending his nose, his ears laying back flat against his head and protracting into canine points. His torso began to spasm, and before the change became complete, he snarled out loud the only words since they'd put him in the van back at the cabin;

"Yeah…hmmpf… it may…huhhuhhuh…take a lot to kill a humannnnggrrr…**but I'm not humAAAAWWWWWOOOOO!**"

Pissant turned to run, but it was too late. The giant white wolf lunged forward and with one swipe tore the thug's backbone out, from ass to skull. Pissant fell, his last thought being *what the hell?* just before he spiraled down into never ending darkness.

Bo and Scrip launched themselves at the monster's back, but Bill shrugged them off as if they were flies. Bo flew fifteen feet backwards, landing on his neck and shoulders, his fall stopped by the two shovels set next to the freshly dug grave. He felt one of the handles snap and impale him through the side, pinning his left arm to his ribcage. He screamed and thrashed in agony, but couldn't get himself upright to remove the broken spar.

Scrip was snagged by the collar bone in a vice-like grip that snapped his shoulder blade and rammed his humor bone upwards into his armpit, severing the nerve bundle and causing excruciating agony. The pain was so intense, he couldn't even scream. With a snarl of pure fury, the wolf shifter grabbed the man's leg and tore it from its hip socket, subsequently tossing the limb aside and leaving Scrip to bleed out, both internally and externally.

Sticks had made it to the van, but once there he realized that Bo had the keys. Locking all the doors, he lunged toward the driver's seat and pulled the wires from underneath the dash, attempting to hot-wire the vehicle. The windshield shattered, spewing safety glass all over his back and head. A shaggy, moon-white paw with five razor sharp claws embedded itself into his back, yanking Sticks out of the van with such force it skinned him from the shoulders up.

Sticks lay flopping like a fish out of water on the hood, the skin which had separated from his back pulled over his neck and head, hands and feet thrumming a staccato tattoo on the metal. He tried to manoeuver over the side and flee but the short circuit of agonizing pain to his nervous system was too much. Runnels of blood slicked the bonnet; he slid down the front where the creature waited. Grabbing the flapping skin with its teeth, the wolf shifter shook Sticks from side-to-side, like a dog with a rag. Sticks' skin shredded and tore loose, sending the dying man tumbling across the dust and rock filled path. Sticks' mind shut down from the shock and blood loss, the agony of his live skinning being the last thing his brain registered.

Bo had finally managed to roll over onto the undamaged side of his body. Using the other shovel for support, he'd limped his way further down the road that circled the gravel pit. The blood was sheeting down his side and onto his shoes, making the going slippery and difficult to manage. He thought he'd gotten far enough away, but the sudden blast of fetid breath that encircled his head declared *no such luck*.

Bo stopped dead in his tracks and ever so slowly, turned his head to look. The beast was standing not two feet behind the wounded thug, and the minute their eyes met, the hulking creature reached forward and shoved the remaining section of wood through Bo, shattering ribs and spearing his heart clean through. Bo dropped without even blinking his eyes.

Howling in exultation, Bill – the white wolf shifter – dropped down onto all fours and sprinted away from the gravel pit.

***

Cutter was enjoying a glass of cognac by the fire, his thoughts mellow, a mood of contentment encompassing his surroundings. The abrupt chime of the doorbell broke into his reverie; he set the glass down on the mantel. Glancing at the grandfather clock in the hall, he turned the deadbolt while at the same time he called out,

"You boys made swift work of this one…"

216

He didn't get to finish the sentence. Something monstrous hit the door and a huge, white, clawed paw lashed out, catching the gang leader on the side of the face. Cutter's lower mandible sailed across the room, blood sheeting and spraying the windows on either side of the door.

The man instinctively stepped backwards, his tongue dangling in the space which his jaw had previously occupied, grunts and clicks coming from the semi-exposed larynx. Cutter threw his hands protectively over the gaping wound and staggered toward his office, the gun in the top drawer of the desk his goal.

The figure followed the man through the entryway, not bothering to disguise its approach. The shifter pushed himself upright once he got past the spiral staircase and sauntered after the gurgling human. Cutter had reached the desk but his blood-slicked hand was making it difficult for him to pull the drawer open. He stopped his attempts when he saw the shadow loom in the open doorway.

The wolf shifter was immense, having to duck its head to enter. It stood for a second, staring at the bleeding man; Cutter watched as the shape began to ripple and shimmer in front of him.

Bill now stood in front of the gang leader, naked, blood dripping from his hands and smeared across his lips, cheeks and chin. He held a hand up and casually flicked blood off onto the Persian carpet Cutter had set in front of his desk. Bill smiled, the look more predatory than friendly.

Cutter stared in disbelief, his missing lower jaw all but forgotten as Bill casually walked further into the room, his eyes never leaving the prey behind the desk.

"I can tell by the look in your eyes you've figured out what's happened to your employees. In all fairness, I did try to warn you." Bill's approach made the man start to scrabble and paw madly at the knob once more. Bill watched with disdain, his disgust and contempt evident in his moves.

With a gargled caw of triumph, Cutter yanked the drawer open and put his hand in, feeling for the gun. Before his grasping fingers could even find it, Bill had circled the desk, and with one shove, slammed the drawer on the man's hand, breaking the bones, eliciting a scream of pain from the damaged vocal chords. Bill's own hands shimmered and rippled once more, turning into the huge, razor-clawed paws they had been earlier.

The wolf shifter brought his transformed hands up and grasped both sides of Cutter's head, forcing the man upright, making Cutter stare directly into Bill's eyes. They were now literally nose-to-nose; all resistance ran out of the gangster's frame, along with freshets of blood from where the claws dug into his ears and temples. "Your ledger, you piece of shit…where is it?"

Cutter's eyes cut to the underside of his desk. Shifting his grip on the bleeding man, Bill reached below and began to feel around. He hit a

217

metal button and pressed it. A false compartment slid open, revealing a leather-bound book. Bill pulled it out, set it on the desk top, and turned his attention back to the real monster in front of him.

"After tonight, neither you nor any one of your followers will terrorize or extort the people of this city, and," the shifter's lip curled up in a snarl, exposing a suddenly growing canine, "I can guarantee that once this little story of how you all died gets around, no one else will ever come within five miles of *my* city…ever again."

The intimation was not lost on Cutter. His eyes widened as the huge paws closed together on the man's head, squeezing and compressing until Cutter's brains were leaking out of his ears, his eyeballs popped and his skull cracked and shattered into pieces. Bill released the body and it hit the floor with a small thump. The odor of urine and shit now joined the thick, coppery smell of blood.

Bending down, the shifter wiped his once-more human hands on the back of the dead man's shirt then turned to the ledger. He swiftly paged through it, noting the locations of the remainder of the gang leader's followers, his stash houses, and main warehouse. Smiling in satisfaction, he shut the book and walking to the middle of the room, began his transformation.

Once back in his wolf shifter form, Bill picked up the ledger between his canines and trotted out of the office, through the cabin door, and into the light of the full moon. As he broke from a trot into an all-out run, Bill thought to himself with an anticipatory shiver of glee, *This is going to be one heck of a fun night.*

BIO: At six years old, Sharon L. Higa became obsessed with the supernatural, compliments of an older cousin who fascinated her with stories of hauntings and horror. Travelling the world with her family, the fascination grew, resulting in Sharon creating and telling her own stories. She wrote intermittently for a number of years, but it was after she and her husband moved to East Tennessee that her family and friends convinced her to write and publish her works. She now writes full time, and has published three novels, one novella and two dozen short stories in various anthologies. Sharon specializes in horror, but also writes fantasy/action, supernatural thrillers, and mystery/suspense.

Her website is: www.leapingunicornliterary.com

She shares her home on 6.2 acres with seven cats, one dog, a vast variety of wildlife, and Mark, her patient and loving husband of twenty- five years.

THE MASSACRE AT FOREE FARM

THOMAS S. FLOWERS

The devil had a hold of Peter. He shifted gears and accelerated faster down the pot marked country road. Blood pumping dangerously high, he never felt more alive. Not since returning from Iraq, returning home with his cursed wounds from Kurdistan, when he discovered for the first time what was could never be again. All because of that *White Wolf*, he was now broken, miserably alone, and dangerous, especially when the moon was full. Glancing over the setting sun, he could feel the curse now inching towards control as his motorcycle roared, kicking up fresh dirt, laughing deep under his flesh, or perhaps it was his heart where the foul thing made its home, the home of that bastard beast with the yellow eyes and triple jointed, bipedal legs fur and teeth, gleaming and hysterical and full of terrifying wonder. Howling at the moon as if it was some long lost lover readied to ravish the night and destroy his memory.

Peter welcomed the thing inside, the monster he would turn into soon enough. He was done with hiding. Done with pretending to be something he was not. Any thought of preserving his father's estate perished with the last Foree, his mother, who died just last year from breast cancer. The once good son had done all he could to make his mother comfortable, but she went all the same, in a slow and horrifying decay. Now there was nothing for him. Not even the quiet peace the farm had afforded him in these last few years since returning home from war.

Let the Foree Farm burn, for all he cared. Peter forced his thoughts on the here and now, on those people in the once sublime Texas town of Otzberg, who were now not very far behind him.

Old friends.

Old neighbors.

For fear for their children's safety, perhaps, or simply fear itself, those neighbors now rallied together with pitchforks and torches, sheep rifles and field stalkers, long range Remington scopes with .22 caliber rounds and buck shot, and red coolers filled with Miller Lite, shouting and hollering. Giving a merry sort of chase in pickups and church vans down

221

dirt roads and pitted country routes, ready to do the Lord's work, ready to remove this unnatural thing among them.

The veteran skirted the turn onto Schiff Drive. Reaching the farm's long gravel road, he almost laid down the Fatboy. Kicking dirt and rock, the double headed motor rumbled with frustration as Peter guided the bike into the field. He wanted *them* to see the 1974 Harley Davidson. A calling. An announcement. *"Here I am. Come and get me."*

Resting the motorcycle against the large oak out in the front of the property, Peter hoped in part that they'd not only see the bike, but also that they'd leave it unharmed. The Fatboy was his father's, as the farm was once. Dad wasn't around anymore. This was one of the remaining memories of the man who'd taught him how to shoot, how to ride, and how to be a man.

Peter was more than fond of the chrome and rubber. Much more than a memento, the motorcycle was an expression of the freedom he so craved, as the farm had become a sort of refuge, a place of solitude, not just from the world and its bullshit, but himself. A place safe and private enough to keep his *other half* from venturing into the sovereignty of public.

No more of that.

Day's gone by, a man could consider his home a place where he could be himself without fear of intrusion, or of outsiders.

No more.

Somehow, someone knows what I become, when the moon is full...

And now I'm the outsider. *The* unknown. *Dangerous. Feral.*

Even before when the Otzberg folk started spitting at his feet and keeping their children far away from his shadow, Peter had a dream he kept close at heart. Freedom beyond the farm. The rolling wheels. The wind. The control and often lack thereof. No hesitations. No boundaries. That was what the Harley Fatboy offered.

But these were thoughts for another time and place.

True to their word, the angered, fearful mass of Otzberg came. Two bright white lights rounded the driveway on a slow approach off Schiff Drive. What looked to belong to an off-white, almost grey with soot, Dodge Ram Van, the kind popular with camping families back in the 1970s, or maybe even churches with those cheap Bible belt *Praise the Lord* logos stenciled on the sides. The van crunched over the gravel and dirt, moving slowly toward the farm. The van's suspension creaked despite their apparent desire for stealth or perhaps caution. Peter watched from the far side of the front of the property, near the house, lying on the ground as flat as humanly possible. When the darkness came and the moon was full, he knew they would not be able to see him until the beast allowed itself to be seen.

Another vehicle approached, a Ford F-150 with dented sides, blaring some awful country melody. Boys pretending to be men howling, mocking, and jumping out with rifles and cans of beer foaming at their feet in the dust of the driveway.

Taking precaution, as the dwindling twilight hours seemed to cast a glow on the land, Peter removed his leather jacket and Nirvana smiley-faced t-shirt and soiled his pale bare skin in mud. He was reminded, briefly, of the training his unit had undergone in the dense pine and spruce of Fort Benning before deploying to the desert. How he wished he could see *them* again, his old unit and friends, even that bastard Sergeant Ross. More than anyone, he wanted to see, at least one more time, his battle buddy Doug Reiniger, hell, he'd even take chain-smoking Private Ricky Olson. But they were all dead now, and he was still here. Alive, but not quite, somehow, at his family home. His father's farm. Facing the community that'd once called him son, but as fate would have it, now wanted to see him dead.

Why?

What had *he* done?

Did it really matter?

Maybe he *was* dangerous.

With the beast inside…

Stephen David Emge, the local Baptist pastor, who most folks in town called Pastor Dave, came into view between the two vehicles. *More were on the way*, Peter was sure. But his attention was focused on the man who baptized him when he was fifteen.

The pastor stopped at the front of the van. He turned to the gaggle of men, some perhaps desiring to wait for the full posse before making a move on the farm.

"Night is upon us, gentlemen. I fear we *cannot* delay." Pastor Dave was shouting to the small group. Arms gesturing toward the setting sun, tracing the lines of purple and red cloud.

They shifted uncomfortably.

"We cannot delay," Pastor Dave shouted again. "We are here do to the Lord's work…and to bring peace for the Foree family memory. Peter died…in Iraq, what came back, what we've seen in town is no longer the boy we all once knew, he is something *else*, something demonic and dangerous."

He's right there, Peter smiled.

They've come to set the world right…

Finish what the war started.

Let them come.

The men gathered near Pastor Dave shouted. Raised arms toasting cans of beer and firing their rifles into the dimming light. *Is this what we've become?* Peter wondered as he watched the charade. *Is there nothing left of our humanity? No room for forgiveness and understanding in churches, nothing but shadows of flags and promises from our leaders?*

Doesn't matter.

Not right now.

The only thing that mattered to Peter…

Was surviving.

And now with the sun fully swallowed by the flatlands, the moon rose and held sway over the land, glimmering pale blue and wantonly seductive. Ample. Plump. And intoxicating.

Peter Foree swallowed hard. Throat dry as sand. Sweat dripped off his chin and nose like rain as he lay low in the tall grass. Regardless of the pain, there was a gleam in his eye and a smile on his face. *You're enjoying this, aren't you?* he asked his yellow eyed monstrous other. His heart fluttered in response. Skin tightened. Behind his eyes, he could feel an inferno pouring from the pores of his flesh. His breath coming in rhythmic beats.

They came on a full moon…

Stupid.

Stupid.

Will you tear these people apart, devil?

It doesn't have to be this way.

You know.

Remaining low, Peter bit his tongue, trying to force himself to remain quiet as his skin pulled tight against tissue and muscle. He could see those familiar nails growing, stretching, ripping from his fingertips. Moaning slightly, his voice growling somewhat into a deep, pitiful lament, he muffled his pain in the dirt, clenching into the earth, tasting the iron minerals and soggy summer dew. His calf muscles bulged, spasming, he kept them glued to the ground. His jeans ripped, and for a moment he was thankful he'd removed his favorite shirt and leather jacket. He prayed the wolf would be cunning, as cunning as the White Wolf in Kurdistan, the desert beast that'd slaughtered so many and had gotten away with its murderous deeds for so long.

He moaned.

He growled.

And then the pain stopped.

The transformation was complete.

***

Pastor Dave looked upon the horizon. He knew they could wait no more. With God's providence, the others would join them soon enough. *What needs to happen must be done in the light of day. And day is coming to a close.*

"Come out, Peter. Let us end this." Pastor Dave was standing in front of his little pack of men, still holding his worn brown leather King

224

James Bible. He looked toward the house, expecting Peter to be cowering inside.

"Hey, *dog.*" One of the men shouted. Tony Buba aimed his rifle, tracing a line from the house to the shadows along the front porch, and back to the fields on his flank. "I've got some nice yummy bullets for you."

Bullets? Perhaps we should have cast silver, Pastor Dave thought. *Whatever this lowly creature Peter has become…it is inhuman. What do these men know of demons? Devils? Fallen angels? Nothing. For it is my duty to teach and guide the unlearned. But what will happen if something becomes of me? Better not take the chance of that damned creature getting close…or one of these morons accidentally shooting me in the back.*

Pastor Dave cleared his throat loudly, loud enough, he hoped, for the others to remain quiet and allow him to do the talking.

"Peter, let us end your suffering. Surely you do not want to go through life with this *curse*? This sin, do you? Let us help you, *please*. We will be merciful as the Lord is merciful. We will make it quick." Pastor Dave stretched his arms outward, gesturing a form of crucified goodwill.

***

Without forethought and unable to keep himself quiet, Peter growled. Deep inside, where his humanity slept and watched, he scolded the wolf. Quickly, the beast rolled back farther into the unseen places of the yard. Braced against low hanging fern, the wolf watched with hungry eyes as one of the drunken, angry men aimed and fired in the direction he'd just been. The bullet impacted the dirt, showering the air with red topsoil.

The wolf knew it would have to move again soon.

Tony gestured with his rifle. One of the other men, the one some of the poor white trash folks in town called Butchie, crept toward where Peter had just been.

The wolf slunk away. Smiling with sharp, gleaming teeth. Keeping to the dark. Playing. Teasing the moment.

Butchie turned his back to shrug at Pastor Dave, Tony, and the other men.

The wolf knelt.

As Butchie turned back around, peering over the brush, the wolf rushed out; sprinting as hard and fast as possible, faster than any natural born creature. The wind lashed his fur. As he passed the tubby poor white, the wolf slashed at the man's throat, taking a string of meat and tissue with him. Veins frayed out like pulled moist noodles made of some kind of purplish blue. Crimson gore gushed, ruining the man's denim overalls.

Butchie danced in a semi-circle. His eyes wide with surprise and horror.

225

The wolf skirted back into the shadows and watched, wonderfully satisfied, as the fat fool stumbled, grasping his throat in a poor attempt to hold in the life that was quickly pouring out on the ground.

Tony ran to him.

Pastor Dave held his ground, eyes wild.

Butchie fell to his knees, still clutching his mortal wound.

"Oh, Butchie, *Jesus Christ*...no...." Tony clumsily did whatever he could to hold in the wound. He pressed his large hands over his friend's throat, whimpering as more blood poured between his fingers, which were now glistening wet and black in the moonlight.

Butchie gazed with glassy eyes up at his friend, stunned and confused. Soon his hand slipped from his throat and dropped to the ground.

Tony's eyes froze in horrifying realization.

"No! Butchie, *no!*" The man shouted and shook his friend. The large, bloodied body spasmed and lay still, jerking slightly against the pulls of the sobbing man's embrace.

"Pick up your rifle, you *idiot*." Pastor Dave stood unmoved, still scanning the area, carefully keeping to the relative safety of the church van.

"He's *dead*, Pastor Dave. He's dead. Butchie is dead." The man wept inconsolably.

"*He's* still here, you dumbass, and we still have work to do."

Shaking horribly, Tony tore himself away from his dead friend. He stood, aiming wildly. "Come on, you son of a *bitch!*" he screamed.

Restraining laughter, the wolf heaved a stick as far as he could. By the sound of it, the piece of branch came down somewhere in the backyard.

Shouting hysterically, the man with the bloodied hands and tear wet face went after the sound.

"*Don't* you idiot, come back!" Pastor Dave, not wanting to lose another man, summoned what remained of his hunting party and went after the grief stricken Tony.

As the men disappeared around the corner of the side of the house, the wolf crept from his hiding place. Moving more on instinct, the creature leapt and climbed the leaf and twig covered gutters. On his hands and feet, he crawled to the top of the roof, peering down. Waiting. Shielding himself partly by the chimney flue.

"I'm going to *kill* you, you bastard, you *fucking* bastard." Tony stomped every which way. Kicking shrubs and tulips, destroying most of what remained of Peter's mother's garden.

The wolf sneered, dripped blood from its teeth, trying hard not to growl. Not to give itself away. The memory of the *other's* mother was with the creature as well as with the man. The wolf knew, just as Peter did, how hard she worked on that garden, just to keep it alive. She worked on giving life to those flowers and blooms and roses and lilies. This was *her* place. How dare they come trespassing on sacred ground?

226

"Come out, *Peter*!" Tony shouted again, firing randomly at an Oak tree.

"Get a hold of yourself." Pastor Dave was near him, standing on the cobble stones lining the garden. Just beyond was the barn where in years past, Peter's father had raised hogs. The hogs had long since been gone. Nothing remained inside but hay and chains in which the veteran kept himself locked away on full moons.

No longer.

No longer.

"He killed Butchie, Pastor Dave. I want this *fucker* dead." Tony spat on the ground, kicking another rose bush.

"You're not going to kill anything but yourself shooting off like this."

"Fuck you!"

The man snuffed out with the heel of his boot the last remaining rose from the garden. Pastor Dave stepped away, taking up perhaps his own search, giving up on Tony. Or maybe he was waiting, using the hysterical man as bait in some way. Knowing the loudmouth would be the focus of the beast's rage.

Either way, the wolf could no longer keep itself idle. It wanted to play. The garden was one of the few remnants of his other's mother, besides the few possessions in the house. The garden was different. She took care of the garden. Nursed it. Loved it. Cooed the plants as a mother would a small child. This was everything beautiful about her memory, all the veteran had left to hold onto hope or purpose. To steward the garden. To steward himself.

But no more.

These men had now taken that last vestige of humanity away from him.

Now the wolf was to have its way.

Doom will come to these men.

To this town.

Destruction and death.

Ignoring the interior pleas of his human other, eyes burning yellow, claws digging into the brick chimney flue, the wolf leapt from the roof. With a snarl, he tackled the man destroying the garden. The rifle fell from his hands and tumbled somewhere out of sight.

Some of the men shouted.

One of them fired aimlessly.

The wolf howled and sunk its sharp teeth into Tony's neck, clamping on a sizable chunk of meat. Jerking upward, he tore away flesh, muscle, and vein. The man screamed, muffled with a gurgled spout.

Blood poured and showered the ground.

227

The man fought weakly, pushing against the wolf's face. His gaze fixed in terror.

The wolf slashed into Tony's flesh, again and again, panting in song-like growls of joy. Gore stained claws soaking the ruined garden in black blood glistening in the white beams of moonlight, which sat high up in the sky, a silent observer to the horrors of the night.

One of the boy men ran away, dropping his rifle in the process.

Pastor Dave watched, frozen, perhaps incapable of thought.

Licking, tasting iron on his lapping tongue, the wolf glared into the eyes of his victim, fixated on his exposed chest, bone, rib and hacked away red meat, at the blood gushing out like some nightmarish water fountain filled with blood.

Tony uttered one last spasm, gurgling in a muddy exhalation.

Engrossed in its work, the wolf did not see one of the last men who remained scrabbling for one of the rifles which lay in the grass. Searching frantically in the dark, the short, small fellow everyone in town knew by Marty McCloskey, whose biggest accomplishment in life was getting to third base with Francine Crawford during their senior prom a few years back, took hold of the .22, aimed and fired into the beast.

The wolf howled, arching his back.

Letting Tony's blood soaked corpse fall to the wet dirt, it turned and glared at Marty with yellow devil eyes.

Licking his lips, the wolf strolled toward him on its unnaturally triple jointed legs.

Panicked, Marty cocked another round with the bolt.

He aimed.

The wolf snarled and snatched the barrel of the rifle as it went off.

The round deafened the night.

With its talon, the wolf lacerated Marty's throat in one quick motion.

Gurgling, the *once-upon-a-time* Prom King touched his wound.

He stared at his gore dripping fingers, not knowing this was his end.

The wolf slit its nails across the man's belly, spilling his guts on the ground.

Eyes rolling back, Marty fell dead.

"*Enough!*" Pastor Dave shouted, throwing his hands furiously into the air. He held the brown leather bible in front of him, gesturing for the wolf to keep his distance as if it was some kind of protective charm or held some power other than turning brother against brother.

"Enough, foul thing. God will not permit you to live. You *must* be destroyed." From his vestments, Pastor Dave produced a revolver.

He aimed, whispering, muttering to himself. "A person may think their own ways are *right*, but the Lord God Almighty weighs the heart and *your* heart, my dear Peter, is corrupt and unnatural. You are an *abomination.*"

The wolf faced him, watching in a way that mirrored the way packs of dogs circle some injured, meaty prey. With wet crimson teeth, it smiled wickedly at the pastor, dribbling on its red, matted fur.

"This is the heritage of the servants of the Lord. This is *my* vindication." Pastor Dave fired the revolver. Smoke and sulfur filled the night's breeze.

Blinded by the flash, Pastor Dave struggled to regain his vision.

He blinked rapidly.

Searching for his target.

The wolf was gone.

"Have I done *your* bidding, my Lord?" Pastor Dave whispered, thinking perhaps creatures of such impurity dissolved into wisps before being cast back into the pits of hell from which they came.

"Goodbye, Peter. May the Lord rest your soul." Pastor Dave dropped the revolver.

Something growled behind him.

The bible shook nervously.

"Peter?" Pastor Dave moaned.

Lifting him off the ground, the wolf tore Pastor Dave, splitting his torso clean from the lower regions of his body. Bones snapped with the sound of twigs under a brush fire. The already ruined ground splattered with more remains.

The wolf glared down and watched as the pastor struggled for life with a sort of amusement despite the horrible burning from his side, the trickle of blood that oozed down his furred legs. The wolf watched and laughed, in its own way, as the Holy man's eyes rolled back in a wild desperation to retain life, if only for a breath longer.

With the deed finished, the wolf arched and howled at the moon.

Miles away, the people of Otzberg shuttered their windows.

And they bolted their doors.

For the melody of the wolf carried on the wind.

BIO: Thomas S. Flowers is the published author of several character driven stories of dark fiction. He resides in Houston, Texas, with his wife and daughter. He is published with The Sinister Horror Company's horror anthology The Black Room Manuscripts. His debut novel, Reinheit, is published with Shadow Work Publishing, along with The Incredible Zilch Von Whitstein and Apocalypse Meow. His military/paranormal thriller series, The Subdue Series, both Dwelling and Emerging, are published with Limitless Publishing, LLC. In 2008, he was honorably discharged from the U.S. Army where he served for seven years, with three tours serving in Operation Iraqi Freedom. In 2014, Thomas graduated from University of Houston Clear Lake with a BA in History. He blogs at machinemean[dot]org, where he does author interviews and reviews on a wide range of strange yet oddly related topics.

HOLY BLOOD, LUNAR BLOOD

BRIAN BARR

Lord Jesus served vigil in his statue form, many feet over the front altar of Eastshire Matthew's Church of Friendship.

"That demonic blood moon signals the end, friends. Satan has returned. Armageddon has come."

Deacon Brown, ever faithful to Pastor Matthews, gazed at his leader with horrified eyes.

"We're safe here, right, pastor? In the sanctity of the church?"

"Only through the blood of the cross can we be saved from the blood of demons. They'll fly high as the moon heralds their return. The return of the snake, the dragon." The pastor formed a cross over his chest with his trembling fingers, then pressed the tips of those holy digits on the deacon's forehead. "Stay focused on our savior, and you'll be saved. All of you will be saved."

The pastor looked at what remained of his congregation. Four members left, including himself, Deacon Brown, and Brown's family, pious Ms. Brown and the teenaged boy, Keith. Everyone else left, believing Pastor Matthews to be *crazy.*

That very night of September Twenty Seventh, Two Thousand and Fifteen, would be the last night many unfortunate nonbelievers would live. Not the pastor's last followers. They were too smart, loyal to God, and not easily strayed by the secular celebrations of idiot scientists and star worshippers tuning in to enjoy that unholy red moon's rise.

With the exception of the boy, the pastor thought with a sneer. *He's like the rest of that lot out there. Heathens, all of them. Cursed and damned, every last one of those bastards. Lord, if the deacon and his wife hadn't insisted...*

A series of howls were heard from outside.

"Dogs," said Ms. Brown with perked ears.

"Damned wolves," Deacon Brown said. "Sounds like so many of them."

231

"Devils," returned the pastor, looking at the stained windows. "Fear not. No hellhound can violate the house of God. Only through Him shall we be protected and defended."

"I don't know, pastor," said Keith, Deacon Brown's teenaged son, gaunt in frame and pockmarked in the face. "Should we really believe the safety of this simple church can really protect us from demons?"

Pastor Matthews turned to the youth with a scowl. "The house of the Lord is not simple! You put the power of the unholy before the might of the Father?"

"Forgive him, Pastor Matthews," Deacon Brown said. "He's young, and not strong in his faith like he used to be."

"Your boy is a little atheist now!" Pastor Matthews shouted. "If he weren't your son, I'd have him thrown out the church. His blasphemous mind is a foul affront to our Lord."

"Forgive him, Pastor. Please. Forgive me." Deacon Brown looked pitifully to Keith. "Haven't I raised you in the word of the Lord? Didn't I make you strong? Why are you turning against us?"

"I just asked a simple question, dad," Keith said. "I don't see what's the matter. I don't really believe all this Armageddon stuff anyway. You forced me to come along, and I hate it. All the kids make fun of me at school. Say I belong to a cult, that we're the Jonestown family."

Ms. Brown slapped her fifteen-year-old son in the face, her own visage red with rage. "We didn't raise you to be so disrespectful! You see there? Those boys at his school have corrupted him! All their drinking, and smoking, and evil thoughts!"

"Thinking is good when one is endowed with the knowledge of the Lord." Pastor Matthews shook his head. "Keith. You have two choices, and you need to make one now. Either walk out that door and join the blasphemers, or stay here with your family in Christ."

"Just let him go," Ms. Brown said. "Think of all the grief he's given us. Running off at all hours of the night, hanging out with those devil worshippers."

"They're my friends, mom!" Keith shouted. "They like to have fun. Not sit in some church all day, talking about the end of the world that's never come, and ain't never gonna come!"

"Hush, boy!" Deacon Brown shouted.

"It's true! They thought the world was gonna end in the year One Thousand, and the year Two Thousand, and Twenty Twelve. Where's the end, huh? Only people that get left behind are the fearful!" Keith grinned as he held out his arms defiantly. "Well, I got a new family now! They aren't scared! They don't fear nothing!"

The pastor stabbed his finger in Keith's direction. "Your family is Satan's family!"

"Then keep Satan out your church! Hear the howl of Satan! I'm in here, brothers! Aaaaooooo! Aaaaoooooooooooo!"

The howls of the wolves from outside grew louder, closer.

"Stop, Keith!" Ms. Brown pleaded.

The boy ignored them, mimicking the wolves' calls at a louder volume.

As the pastor shivered and Ms. Brown screamed, stained glass shattered from the windows of the church. Feral beasts rushed in, sharp-haired and yellow-eyed, slobbering and mad. The outside world was no longer hidden behind them, the blood-red moon shining.

"Stop them, Lord Jesus!" Ms. Brown pleaded with frantic arms outstretched before jaws snapped into her neck.

Under the crimson moon, Keith's body began to shake and convulse, his form beginning to change.

Pastor Matthews and Deacon Brown hollered under the weight of paws, claws, and jaws, snapping their body parts like twigs.

Keith's transformation continued, all humanity void from his yellow eyes. Fangs snarled with dripping volumes of saliva, as sharp, brown needles of fur covered nearly every inch of his hirsute body, and sharp nails stretched from the ends of his fingers.

Remade in the image of his friends, Keith was free.

Keith's brethren left enough scraps for him, and they feasted on bloody stumps of hands, legs, feet, toes, and heads. Hearts and intestines were tugged by their serrated teeth, consumed with eager hunger, all under the watchful eye of Statue Lord Jesus and the moon.

Once the wolves grew bored with their meal, they left church, returning to the outside world.

BIO: Brian Barr is an American author. Brian has been published in various short story anthologies and magazines, including *New Realm, Nebula Rift, Under the Bed*, Queer Sci Fi's *Discovery, NonBinary Review*, Dark Chapter Press's *Kill for a Copy*, and *Mantid Magazine*. Brian collaborates with another writer, Chuck Amadori, on the supernatural dark fantasy noir comic book series *Empress*, along with Sullivan Suad and Geraldo Filho. His first novel, Carolina Daemonic, Book 1: Confederate Shadows, was published by J. Ellington Ashton Press in 2015. His second novel is Psychological Revenge: The First Super Inc. Novel.

Amazon Author Page:

http://www.amazon.com/Brian-Barr/e/B010Y0MEJU/ref=sr_ntt_srch_lnk_1?qid=1465147335&sr=8-1

Website: www.brianbarrbooks.com

HOMEWARD BOUND

JOHN P COLLINS JR

Despite the fact that the evening's full moon was casting a bright, silvery light over the landscape, Jacob Thompson had left the floodlights on. Harsh and artificial, the halogen lights smothered the natural lunar brilliance that he would have preferred. The electric light robbed the eyes of the land's organic beauty.

He loved the symmetry of his land, especially in the natural light. For the past twenty five years, he had worked the land hard and the land did the same to him in return. The earth had fought him every step of the way, never making his labor easy or the rewards of a day's work to be taken for granted. In hardship, he had developed a grudging respect for the land. A love for nature's resilience and sheer beauty.

The idea of leaving the flood lights on brought his temper up. The calm that settled over his land when cloaked in moonlight always left him a bit breathless. During the day, bright sunlight displayed the day's labor in its harsh, blinding rays. The sunlight signaled the time of men. A time where they would busy themselves with their daily trials and labors.

In the moon's glow, however, nature took over again. The night was filled with the music of a symphony of chirping insects. Owls would cry out after a successful hunt. The night was alive with all the life that thrived on the land, which made the darkness its home. It was the home of all the predators that balanced the night.

As much as Jacob loved his land in the moon's dreamlike glow, the flood lights would drive away the shadows, exposing the footfalls that might hide in the gloom, just laying in wait for an unexpected ankle to snap in mid step. The glare of the lights would take away any camouflage from any of the hazards that might lay in wait.

Tonight the lights were a necessary evil. Tonight his son was coming home.

After a full season had passed since he left, his son was finally coming home. In his absence, Jacob had found a sadness settle over him. He had known that his son would leave just as he did when he was the boy's age. He couldn't have imagined that his own father had felt the same searing pain that he had felt when the boy left. He knew that it would sound corny as hell but if anyone were to ask him how he felt the day after his son departed, he would have answered,   "like a piece of heart had left me." Clichéd, but still very true.

The flood light encircled his home like a halo. The corn fields that surround the house in three directions were brightened ten plants deep. Not as deep as Jacob would've preferred but it would have to do. The one hundred yard long driveway was outlined by low laying marker lights. Everything was in place. His farm was a beacon that his son would steer towards from any direction.

Standing on his side porch, coffee cup in his hand, he would listen to the music of the night. He would listen and wait. Wait for his son's arrival.

Crashing out of the wooded grove, Adam stumbled forward. Losing his battle with gravity; he crushed two stalks of corn underneath him. Spikes of vegetation stabbed into his gut and sternum, painfully forcing air from his lungs. He rolled back and forth, trying in vain to shake off the pain.

After a few moments, the pain faded into a dull throb; Adam jerked up. He quickly scanned in all directions.

Where was it? Where is the dog? He had expected for the nasty little fucker to come barreling out of the brush teeth bared and salivating, finally about to get his bone.

The night had turned to a shitshow the moment he left the roadside diner earlier that evening. For the past two months, he had been peddling his way across the states. There was always a sense of wanderlust in his blood, but the moment his father had said that he spent the summer after graduating high school hitching throughout the Midwest, Adam knew how he would be spending the summer.

He had packed his gear; a small tent, a rugged cell that he prepaid, his bank card as well as a solid, fixed blade knife. Promising not to hitch, 'the world is not the same as it was when I left high school', his father had said. His father had bought an all terrain bicycle for his graduation gift. The gift appeared to seal his plans and the day after caps and gowns, Adam had left.

Making his way across the country, he saw life open up in front of him. He slept in campgrounds, watched little league games in small towns like Beaver Creek, Missouri. He had been in time for the annual Bar-b-que festival in Lincoln County just last week.

Despite all the things he saw, he began to miss home. He felt empty every night at seven o'clock when he would sit on the porch with his father, enjoying a cup or two of coffee as they silently watched over the land. He had missed his father's mere presence, more so than he had ever thought possible. When he had awakened yesterday morning, he decided that it was time to go home. On the bike, it was only two days away.

He debated whether to make his arrival a surprise or not. His father was not one for surprises so he decided against it. After packing his gear, he called home, informing his dad that he was making his way home. It pleased him to hear the joy in his dad's voice once he heard Adam's decision.

Adam had moved on that day with little rest. He had wanted to make good time and was making good on his intention. The bike was lightweight, but solidly built. He moved swiftly and precisely through whatever obstacles were in the way. He was riding faster than he had during his journey. Sightseeing was now over, time to return to his life.

Only stopping to sleep, he awoke and started again on his breakneck pace. Making excellent time, he had expected to be home before dawn. Until the accident.

To be honest, the supposed accident. He thought, almost a little guiltily. It wasn't like him to dismiss the misfortune of others but the whole scenario seemed fake, almost put upon, an act.

He was approaching the second bend in what a traffic sign read as three bends ahead, when he came upon fire trucks, ambulances and other emergency vehicles. A diesel fueled generator chugged away, providing power to safety lighting bright enough to mimic daylight. The scent of burnt rubber lent a sense that something bad had happened.

Still, the actual visual evidence of an accident was not present. A member of the emergency personnel, a volunteer firefighter, informed him that he couldn't pass and probably wouldn't be able to for several hours. A tanker truck misjudged the turn and was overturned. A strong scent of spilled fuel and other petroleum fluids hung in the air.

When the fireman had told him that back up the road there was a trail that would help him bypass the accident, Adam's suspicion rose. *Why would a fireman direct me to a trail? In the dark, no less?* The situation felt odd and slightly off. As he popped up the GPS on his phone, he could feel the weight of the fireman's stare on him.

Technically, if there was a trail, Adam saw that it would lead him past the next bend and even more distance on top of that as well. However, trekking though the dark woods was not part of his plan. Still, it had to be better than staying here. He had a timetable that he was determined to meet.

With a sigh, he began to backtrack down the road. The moon was clear and bright; if the trail was bike worthy, then maybe he wouldn't lose as much time as he feared he had.

The trail was exactly where the firefighter had said it was, next to a slightly fallen dead pine tree. Spruce trees stood five feet apart, the top of their foliage arched towards each other, giving the appearance of a doorway.

Footing on the path started as smooth as could be, but as he traveled deeper into the wood, the path's condition began to deteriorate; foot wide holes in some spots, long, deep, snakelike rivulets in other spots. The walking became slower and more labored. Moonlight filtered in though the treetops in glowing bright ribbons, giving the pathway an ethereal quality.

Adam was hoping it wouldn't be too long until he was back on the road. That this little side trip would be over before he knew it and would become one of those little stories that he would tell one day over beers. He hoped to be back in complete moonlight and on sure footing, back on his way home.

Movement in the bush interrupted his thoughts. Low and to his left. A raccoon maybe, possibly a possum. Adam began again on his way.

The darkness was complete here. No moonbeams pierced the overgrowth, the atmosphere was complete blackout. His vision was registering total blackout, not even the shapes of the trees were visible.

In front of him, growling began to rise from the gloom.

Adam froze. Sweat broke out, drenching him in raw panic. A breeze drifted across, causing chills to run down his spine. The growling continued, the tone deep and threatening. In his travels, he had encountered large dogs. He had a familiarity with their tone, their voices. He knew when barking was just excitement or something more dangerous. Growling was never a good sign.

With a slow ease, he began to back up the path. If he could make it to the road without angering or provoking the animal any more than he had, he would be more than content to wait out the emergency workers until he was allowed to pass.

He tried to concentrate on the animal's pacing back and forth through the brush, trying hard to keep track of the animal's movement just so he could ignore the tone of the growling. He had never heard a growl that deep, that menacing. The bass of it was malevolent, a warning of its inbreed savagery. A feral promise of violence.

The growling had now made its way behind him, blocking his retreat.

Turning himself around, he made out a shape that became more outlined in the darkness. Low to the ground, Adam immediately thought *pit bull!* The growling was more thunderous now. All the small animals of the night went silent to give this creature's hideous roar the echoes and respect it commanded. If there was ever a warning in the growl then it was no longer there. Adam felt it in the base of his skull, in his goosed flesh, in his guts. This was the cry of a beast who knew no equal.

The animal's outline was becoming more defined. If this was a pit bull, then it was the biggest one he had ever seen; wide through the shoulders and impossibly getting thicker. If he had to guess, he would place

238

the animal at one hundred fifty pounds. At that size, he offered a quick prayer that the beast was indeed a pit.

The growling began to lower in volume but Adam knew it was still there. The barely audible rumble vibrated though the air, raising his hackles. His skin crawled as tiny hairs stiffened in his primal fear. His spinal cord went rigid, locked in with dread. He felt his limbs go leaden. Panic rose as he tried to shake off his rigor, to be ready to act if he needed to be.

Silence.

The beast roared a scrotum shrinking howl.

Adam took off.

Without an ounce of grace, Adam sprinted into the wood. Leaving behind his bike, his pack, his motor ran on pure survival instinct. He crashed forward, bouncing off tress and crashing through small shrubbery, he ran in whatever direction he was facing. The panic overtook his senses; he just needed to get as far away from here as possible. To put distance between this animal and himself as quickly as he could.

He could hear the animal move about the wood. First to the left, then the right and back to the left again. Steering him forward

Like he's steering me into a trap!

A wide clearing ahead, filled with bright, lunar light.

What about the trap? His mind screamed. *Impossible!*

As he broke though the tree line, into the beginning of a cornfield, a savage slash ripped through his calves, bringing him crashing into the corn, landing face first into the sharp vegetables.

He tried to find his footing and failed twice. The damage to the right calf was severe while the left felt more cosmetic. Reaching down to the right, he could feel the ruined tissue hang in shards, the pain brought tears to his eyes. The left in comparison was a paper cut.

The corn whistled under the gentle breeze that blanketed the crop. Adam listened, waited for some sign of the animal.

Movement to his left. Silence.

With a slow pained ease, he rose. He made his way toward the right. The left leg carrying the majority of his weight, he dragged the right behind. Falling twice, he continued on. The agony of his wounds kept him awake and alert. Every step shocking his system to push forward.

He knew in his heart that the animal was stalking him, pacing his every step. He moved forward. The corn was thick on all sides, a living curtain smothering his senses with its cloying, heavy smell. The stalks scratched at his bare flesh, adding to his discomfort. Insects crippled in a deafening chorus. He was running blind in every way.

Without any sign, the crop opened up. He stood in a wide space. The clearing was six rows wide and deep. A wooden post stood routed upright, riding a good six feet above the corn stalks' tassels. A smaller plank cut across the post's midsection, forming into a cross. At the base, a figure lay bent and folded against the wood. The tattered remains of a scarecrow steamed up at him.

Adam walked forward, not hearing the movement behind him.

Focusing on the scarecrows remains, he collapsed. The right leg could take no more. Using the wooden post for balance, he picked up the wire and cloth figure. The junk rattled, feeling heavier than it should have been. He felt puzzled; more questions began rifling inside his head.

That isn't a jawbone, is it?

A shadow rose in front of him. Deep growling became the answers to any question that he might have had.

The thick body slammed into him. Knocking him backwards, he was pinned to the moist ground under the beast's deadweight. Sharp teeth nipped and snapped at his face, opening small, deep wounds on his jawline. Claws dug into his collarbone as he tried to reach up and get a hold on the dog's neck. His fingers locked around a chain, a choke chain he realized. If only he could shift his weight, he might have a chance to roll over and....

Sharp tipped fingers closed over his throat, crushing his windpipe.

Fingers!?! How can a dog choke me? Dogs don't have fingers!

A wide row of razor sharp fangs smiled at him. The pressure on his neck increased, causing blood vessels to rupture in his eyes, blinding him. Multiple knives began to dig into the flesh of his throat, pulling chunks away. Adam felt his heart start to slow down as the thick tongue of the beast lapped away at the remains of his throat.

Adam felt his fluids splashed over his torso as the beast clamped down on what remained of his neck. Powerful jaws worked back and forth as Adam grew cold. As he felt his spinal column detach, his mind fled with one final question.

Why would a dog have fingers?

Jacob had grown impatient by the passing minute. He had expected his son over an hour ago. Now, three cups of coffee later, there was still no sign of him. The boy had left over a month ago with a timetable set. Set in stone.

He should have been here by now.

It was not easy for him when the boy left. He had always possessed a parent's anxiety for his son. He knew it was silly. The boy was doing exactly as he had when Jacob was his age. This was the beginning of something....

His son came out of the cornfield.

Jacob dropped his mug as he ran off the porch. Crossing the yard faster than he had ever done before, passing the swing set, he practically dove into his son's arms.

The nine year old looked dazed. Eyes focused on something far, far away. The boy shivered in Jacob's arms, vibrating through his body.

"Oh, Michael. So good to have you home."

Michael's nude body was encased in mud and grime. Dark, arterial blood caked his mouth. A sure sign of the season's feeding.

Jacob would carry him inside. He would bath him, tend to any cut and contusions that would surely be there. Given enough time, the boy will be his old self once again. In time, Michael will appreciate the family tradition and his place in it.

Once the boy was asleep, Jacob would gather the other farmers. Together, they would work the bush until they found the sacrifice. The remains would be set on the post as their yearly offering and the crops would flourish, thanks as always.

He removed the silver choker. Placing it in his shirt pocket, he would clean it later and place it in a lock box where it would wait until next year.

Scooping up the boy in his arms, he carried him inside for his bath, pleased that the family tradition would carry on.

BIO: When not terrifying local villagers, John P Collins Jr can be found wandering the back roads of Long Island, New York looking for good coffee, bloody horror films and quality fiction. Surrounded by some very patient people, he's currently working on more fiction.

WOLFHEART: CONQUER ALL

JUAN J. GUTIERREZ

All is darkness; I am nothing.

From nothing, there is a genesis. I feel the void of my spirit and it is a strange sensation. As I become aware of my senses, pulsing starfire surrounds me. Glints of foreign light give sight to my existence. Suddenly I feel it … I feel the wolfheart beating and its precious bloodlight percolating through the shadow around me. The cold light burns upon me, giving me bone, flesh, and nerve. Thus, I exist.

Circlet of Night, you rise above reflecting, not the sunlight, but things to come, images I cannot fully realize. I see the broken fangs of bloodless creatures, shattered skulls of scaled giants, and the wolfheart in my bloodied hand. A wave of battle rushes through me! My flesh burns away but my suffering remains. Weakened, I skulk and my balance falters, every step I take is blood-soaked. The starlight dies but the moonspell calls me.

Now I pulse, as I feel every breath inside of me. My bones rip through the exposed nerves and flesh. My face shatters and elongates. I feel the teeth and tissues growing. Falling on all fours, I lick my pool of blood as the biological alchemy takes hold. Flesh and moonlight become fur and claws. Behold, I am the Master of the Moon.

From darkness, there is an end. I feel my destiny and it is a strange sensation. I see the magic of the moon and its secrets; I know my secrets. Shadows are my robe and I embrace the blackness of my spirit. I feel the wolfheart beating. I know my purpose, I am a conqueror and I shall conquer all!

All is nothing; I am darkness.

BIO: Juan J. Gutiérrez lives in Desert Hot Springs, California with his loving wife and daughters. His poetry and stories have appeared in anthologies published by Static Movement, Horrified Press, Sirens Call Publications and Dead Guns Press. He is the Assistant Editor for Barbwire Butterfly Press and is overseeing the Robert E. Howard inspired anthology "Barbarian Crowns." He has appeared most recently in the horror western anthology, "Badlands," by Dead Guns Press. You can find him on his facebook page:

www.facebook.com/deadgrinwriter

WEREWOLF'S LAMENT

R.E. LYONS

Wilton Wilson had never seen a moon so big or bright in his life. He stood there mesmerized by its awesomeness. He could almost see everything around him without any trouble at all.

This is great, he thought. *This is a great hunter's moon.* No game could escape him in this light, he could hear them rustling in the distance. The area was full of them. He could go about in any direction and get all he wanted. They were all there, the small game as well as the medium and larger game. The thought of the hunt made his heart race. His eyes became bigger and brighter with excitement as he breathed in deeper and longer, preparing himself for the chase. Everything about this made him feel alive. Everything, but most of all, the kill. He did not quite understand it, but when he saw the blood flowing out from the wound he inflicted, it drove him insane with delight. The more blood that flowed from the injury, the better. He even loved drinking the blood that flowed out of the game. Drinking the spirit of the kill was the final domination; the ultimate thrill of life was to take another life. Be the top of the food chain. Then after the kill, to eat the flesh of his victim.

He listened to hear all that was out there. He heard the sound of a rabbit as it hopped close by. He listened as he decided whether he would start with that. He cocked his head toward the sound to hear more clearly and calculate the distance as well as how big it would be. He paused. No, this would not do. It was too small. He would have to kill too many rabbits to fill the hunger he had tonight. That would take too long as well. He would be starved before the night had ended. That would not do.

He listened for more game as he started to circle around the area ever so quietly so as to not let his victim be aware of his existence. He tested the air to see which way it was blowing so they could not smell his scent. He wanted to keep upwind of them. He was so into the hunt his mouth watered, sliding down the sides of his mouth, and yet his mouth became dry craving the blood. Surely there was game worthy of his ability?

A deer was sharpening his horns on an old oak tree. You could hear it scraping back and forth against the bark. It was an annoying sound that irritated him way too much. Maybe he should just kill him to stop that ridiculously annoying sound. Wilton was tempted to do just that. All that bellowing like he was in pain, but he was only horny for the does. It sounded like he was getting ready to battle the lead buck. Wilton wasn't interested in deer blood, or the meat. He needed something else. Something he just couldn't put his finger on, but something he was craving very much. It wasn't going to leave him alone until he had some. But what could it be?

There seemed to be something in the air, something out there that didn't seem right. It didn't seem natural. What it felt like was downright spooky. It raised the hair on the back of Wilton's neck. He looked about to see if he could see anything different or strange. Still nothing. And yet he knew something was different.

Well, he was on a hunt, right? So he needed to get his mind back on what he was doing. He needed to eat. The hunger was getting stronger. He feel it deep within, like he hadn't eaten for a couple of weeks. Felt like he could eat a bear whole. Now *that* was a thought. A bear sounded good. Now, would there be one around here close? He started to listen for sounds that would be connected with a bear.

He started to check the ground for tracks. Big juicy bears left tracks; beautiful, big furry beasts that put up a fight. Wilton *loved* it when they put up a fight. Made it all the better when he got the kill. The challenge was everything. Then to drink the blood while it was breathing its last breath. It was delicious. All that hot blood pumping out of the wound. It was to die for. Yes, die. The bear would die so he could drink its blood before he devoured its flesh. The more he thought of it, the more he craved it. The more he hunted for it.

As he hunted, he could still sense something was off. Something was wrong. It kept nagging at him. It was drawing his attention more as time went along, but still he couldn't figure it out. He caught himself looking for something that shouldn't be more than he was on the hunt for. Wilton didn't like that one damn bit. This was his one and only pleasure in life. How dare anyone or anything mess that up for him. What in the hell could it be anyway? There was only one thing more important than the hunt and that was the kill.

Now where was a damn bear? He didn't see anything out of the ordinary. *Everything was fine*, he kept telling himself. Maybe the moon was affecting him somehow. Whatever the hell it was, it didn't matter. He was hungry. Very hungry!

He started looking for the tracks again. He went around in a circle, going wider and wider from the center. He saw raccoons, owls, bats, squirrels, deer, possum, all kinds of wildlife, but no bears or even their tracks to be found. *That's the luck of a hunter*, Wilton thought. *When you're hunting for something, you'll see everything else before you see what you're hunting. It's just the way it is.*

Finally, he found the tracks of a bear; it was the imprints of a big bear. A good, heavy set bear. He would put up a great fight, a worthy opponent after all. Now he could get back into the frame of mind that brought him the most pleasure, testing his skills as a hunter as well as his abilities to survive. It was the highest high he ever experienced. He was hooked on it, like some drug addict needing a fix. Except this there was no cure for, he would have this need until the day he died.

He started tracking the bear. He could smell the scent of it; it had to be close with the wind blowing the bear's scent down toward him. Good for Wilton, bad for the bear. Now the hunt was on. Again his heart started to race. He tingled all over. Now his full attention was once again on the hunt. He could hear rustling right ahead of him. Now was the time to be cautious. If he wasn't careful, the bear would be attacking him in no time. If it caught his scent, he would attack and rip him to shreds.

Wilton had several advantages that the bear didn't. First, he had reasoning, so he could outthink the bear. Second, he was downwind so it couldn't smell him yet. Third, he was planning how to take the bear down. It would be surprised and react only out of instinct. He had hunted bear before and knew how they would react. Wilton was hoping that this one would surprise him with more moves so it would bring up the intensity of the battle. Now that would make the kill all the better. All the sweeter. Mmm, he could almost taste the blood of the bear in his mouth already.

He started checking the wind so he could make sure he was downwind of the bear. One whiff of his scent and it would be ready for him. You might not think it, but a bear that size could rip a man to pieces in no time without the man having a chance. Wilton smiled at the thought of the danger. It was what he was craving. The thrill, the danger. It drove him to kill that bear more than ever.

He got up to where he could almost feel the huge bear's breath breathing down on him. The bear was moving about as if he was restless, unable to sleep. This made him all the more dangerous to be close to. Yes, this was exciting. Now he could kill Wilson any second. Wilton decided he would give the bear a sporting chance. He wanted it to look him in the eyes as he pulled the trigger.

Wilton was ready for the bear to turn around. One bullet right between the eyes. That was all he needed to bring this bad boy down. He took careful aim and was ready for the bear to stand up for the deadly shot when he heard a noise. Unfortunately, so did the bear. It raised up on its hind feet, sniffing the air. It let out a snort of displeasure, coming down on all fours, and scurried off in the opposite direction.

Wilton dropped his riffle down from his shoulder frustrated. What in the Hell could have made the bear act that way? Surely he had heard sounds like that all the time in these thick woods. That was the last straw. He had been robbed of his greatest kill. He would not stand for this at all.

247

He could feel it rushing throughout his body. He had lost the feeling of the hunt. All he had now was the anger. He didn't care that now he was upwind and his prey could smell him. Let the stinking animal smell him. Let it fill his nostrils. Let it feel the fear. He wanted this. Whatever it was deserved it. Mess up his hunt, will it? He was going to let it die slowly.

As he got closer, he noticed something was different about the noises. It didn't sound like wild animals. It sounded more human than anything else. In fact, it sounded like *two* humans. A man and a woman. Yes, it was two humans. They were out in the darkness with only the moon for light, in the woods fooling around.

He could see them now; they were naked, exploring each other. Wilton couldn't take his eyes off the woman. Her long blonde hair flowed down her back like a wild animal as she moved about with every touch, every caress of the man. He was mesmerized by her firm round breasts, her bright blue eyes sparkling with delight. He continued staring, looking at her firmly toned body. He could smell her scent, oh so clear. She was so aroused by this man. The moon apparently had enraged both of their hormones to the point that they needed to come out into the woods for their sexual romp. They were going all out with their animal instincts, biting and nibbling each other, bringing them into more sexually, craving each other all the more. Wilton could even hear them growling deeply in their lust. They were becoming animals as they prepared themselves for sexual intercourse. Wilson growled himself as he watched. He felt his blood once again boil, but even though he was growling, this man and woman were so involved with each other they did not hear him.

Wilton could not take his eyes off them as the man got behind the woman, mounting her from behind. As he inserted himself into her, she groaned and her eyes rolled back. Her body started rocking back and forth, taking his manhood all the way deep inside her. The man's eyes were closed as he concentrated on the feeling of being inside her. She had brought him harder than he had ever been and he was determined to repay her with the best sex she had ever had. From the way she was acting that was exactly what he was doing. In fact, it seemed like it was the best sex either had ever had. The animal behavior they were experiencing was bringing them to the highest sexual peak they had ever known. The man's hands had grabbed hold of the woman's hips, ramming his manhood as deep and as hard in her as he could. The faster he went the more she groaned and begged for more. On and on they went, pushing themselves to the limit until, at last, they collapsed on the ground, their bodies shaking hard as they orgasmed. They were totally exhausted, pouring with sweat. Wilton watched the woman's chest as her breasts raised up and down rapidly. They were so full and desirable.

But while Wilton watched he became very troubled, where any other time he would have become filled with desire. A beautiful woman, naked, having sex in front of him. What man wouldn't, especially as sexy as she was? She was any man's fantasy, a dream they all want to come true. And yet he stood there, not desiring to have sex with her, but wanting to taste her blood. To taste the blood of both and to tear their flesh from their bones. What was wrong with him? They were human beings, for Christ sake! He was human as well. He should not want to drink the blood of a human being, let alone tear their flesh from their bones with his teeth! What in the world was he thinking? Had he become like an animal? Had he hunted so long that he had lost his humanity?

All he was thinking about was the hunt. The kill. He slowly moved back, away from them. He had to think. He had to get away from them before he could no longer fight off this urge to kill a fellow human being. This was never what he wanted. Not in a million years would he want to do that! Why did he want to? He was not in a battle for life and death. Not in a war! Those two were fellow human beings, fellow countrymen out in the woods being human, enjoying each other like they were meant to. This didn't make sense. He wasn't like that. He wasn't raised that way! Yet here he was, craving another human being's blood. Not only it's blood, but it's flesh too. Not to just hurt it. No. He wanted to kill it. To tear it up so bad that there would be no one who would recognize it. To totally destroy it. A beautiful girl like that, someone who he had always hoped to get and be married to, to fulfill all his sexual desires, to bear his children, to be with him for life. What in Heaven's name would possess him to make him ever think such a thing? What had they done to him? Nothing at all! Nothing! What was making him want to do such a thing?

The thoughts kept running through his mind. A battle was forming within him, a terrible battle that was tearing his mind... his soul apart. He fought with all his might. He would beat this thing, this evil desire. He was a hunter of animals, not humans! Animals were for hunting and eating. Was he possessed by some evil demon? What else would make him want this? Yes, that is what it must be. A demon had crept up on him and somehow entered him. It had to be, but how? How would he get it out of him? How would he fight this, this thing within him? There wasn't a priest for miles from where he was. This thing, whatever it was, was getting stronger within him. Too strong, God help him. He was losing the battle. He could feel himself getting weaker. The feeling was rushing over him like a flood. Drowning him with evil desires. His head pounded, it hurt so much. *Please God, save those two. Whoever they are and whatever they might have done, I am sure they do not deserve what is about to happen to them. Make them feel the need to get out of the woods. To get in their home safely behind locked doors! Be merciful, Oh Lord.*

Tears flowed down his face. He was fighting the need, concentrating so hard that sweat poured from his forehead clear down his body. Wilton wanted no part of this horrible thing. He hunted only to feed himself, his brother, and his brother's wife. That's all he wanted. That's all he needed. Why was this filthy desire put on his mind so?

Wait, he was at last winning. He was forcing the thoughts out of his head, gaining control of himself once again. It was working at last. *I swear I am going home as soon as I get my mind clear. Go straight home. Hang up my gun and go to bed. Sleep this horrible nightmare away. Damn this moon*! He never wanted to see such a moon again in his life. It was a curse, not a blessing! He leaned against a tree to help clear his mind. He could do it. He knew he could control himself now. It was almost completely gone from him.

Suddenly he heard them back at it again, heard their growling and groaning as they went at each other. He heard himself start to growl again. At first it was a low growl, coming from deep down inside him. It wouldn't stop. It grew louder and louder. He hurt all over and it was as if whatever it was inside him was coming out, forcing his whole body to start changing. He was no longer in control. This demon within was taking over. This time there was no way he could stop it. Why didn't they just go home? He felt the need to stand as he looked down over his body.

The growling was becoming louder from his body. It was more intense as the sound of the couple was getting louder. No matter how hard he tried to resist, his mind and body reacted to the sounds the couple made. A deep hunger was sinking down deep within him. The taste of blood filled his mouth; he felt something running out of his mouth, running down either side. Reaching up to wipe it away, he found himself salivating. Chills went down his body, filling him with terror. What was going on? *Sweet Jesus, I'm losing my mind*!

Suddenly, a long groan came from the couple and he was off running for them. He was running, faster and faster, but his mind was floating. He was losing the battle and he knew it. Heaven help that couple. There was nothing else in the way of protecting them. His will was fading fast. The beast was in control and wanted their blood, their flesh. Halfway there he was gone altogether. The beast was one hundred percent in control, bearing down on the couple.

***

The couple had collapsed after they orgasmed, still laying there, smiling at each other, holding each other's hands, feeling the love each had for the other. She was glad he had talked her into taking a walk under this beautiful moon. She turned and looked at it, marveling at its brightness. How it lit up everything all about them. She lay there, catching her breath. My, how that man could make love to her. Tonight though, it seemed as if he had extra energy, making her feel more excitement from his lovemaking than she has ever had. He had always been a good lover, but this time he had really outdone himself. God, how she loved that man.

All the while she was looking around, he was watching her, smiling. How did he ever get so lucky in finding her? She was the light of his life, his reason for doing anything. He couldn't even remember a time without her, probably because he never wanted a time without her. She was the only world he wanted to be in. He looked down her body. All those curves, those succulent breasts, that tight, firm ass, those long, luscious legs. Plus what was between those legs, so tight and delicious. He couldn't get enough of it. He rolled over to her to give her a passionate kiss.

Suddenly, they were snapped rudely back into the cruel world. For it was then they noticed the snarling, growling, fur covered beast leaping at them. It was so fast they never had a chance to react to it. She could only let out a squealing scream as the beast landed upon them, its claws out and moving like a blur, raking her firm right breast, slicing into it deep, rivers of blood streaming down toward her side. At the same time, it was clawing his left chest, making the same flowing rivers of blood on him. Then the beast sank his fangs into the woman's neck, ripping half of it open, chewing it with delight, enjoying the fresh meat.

The man looked toward his love as the blood from her neck sprayed onto his face and body. His face became a visage of horrified fear. As he tried to scream the beast sank his teeth deep into his throat, ripping it out and enjoying the mixture of blood and flesh rolling about in his mouth as he chewed it up, and then swallowed it. Blood flowed out the sides of its mouth as it chewed, enjoying the flavor, licking the blood from the neck before taking bite after bite of his fresh killed victims.

The beast ate until he had his fill, almost completely devouring both of his kills. Satisfied with what he did, the beast laid down beside the mostly eaten corpses that were only a few minutes ago so full of life and happiness. Their lives were cut short in their prime, in the peak of their lovemaking, killed and eaten by this evil creature. This creature, which, as it lay there calming down from its blood lust, began to change. Fading away was this hairy, grotesque creature, and in its place came the form of Wilton Wilson, in a deep sleep. Looking at him, you would think he was fully at peace.

He lay there sleeping until almost daybreak, then stirred as he began to wake up. His face and body were turned away from the couples' corpses, not knowing what happened the night before. He slowly rose; feeling like his body had been in a terrible fight where he had lost. He stood there stretching when he began to feel a chill. He looked down, finding he was totally naked. He started to look around to see where his clothes were. He turned around, and seeing a familiar area, he took a step to head that way. When he did he felt something at his feet and looked down. He stepped back in terror as he looked upon his sister in law Rachel's face, bloodied.

251

There, beside her, lay his brother Wilber. Both were almost totally eaten, leaving nothing but chewed bones. Only their faces were left intact by the beast.

He stood there in shock at the sight he beheld. He couldn't believe it. No, the truth was he didn't *want* to believe what he saw. His mind was spinning as his stomach began to churn. He turned just in time as he puked profusely. When he could stop puking, he wiped his mouth and turned back to the bodies of his only family, laying there. Tears filled his eyes, rolling down his cheeks. He knew in his heart somehow he was the reason they lay there, dead and eaten. He had no idea how it happened, but he knew what was filling his mind just before he blacked out. Little did he know that he had changed from a hunter to a blood thirsty beast that craved human flesh. The only thing that mattered to him then was he had killed the two most important people in his life.

He fell down on his knees, looking up the full moon, shaking his fist. He tried with all his might to scream out his anguish but all that came out of his mouth was the howling of a wolf.

BIO: A lifetime fan of horror, sci fi, the macabre, mystery, and fantasy, R. E. Lyons digs deep within his soul to write character driven novels that, while influenced by his darker interests, can also be heavily laced with fantasy, romance, mystery, history and magic. R. E. Lyons has lived his life filled with storytelling from generations of story tellers and, as you will notice by his children, the tradition continues with marvelous enchanting stories. Some stories of R. E. Lyons are Ghostly Tales of The Old West, Werewolf's Lament and Birth of a Witch to be found in anthologies from JEA Publishing. Some unpublished works include Novellas of the Werewolf, *Rogue Desires*, and an unpublished novel, *I Will Love You Forever*. He is looking forward to having them all published at JEA Publishing in the future. As well as other short stories for other horror anthologies.

FREE RUNNING

URWIN BOWER

I had better start with how I became a werewolf. Contrary to popular belief, I was not bitten, nor did I receive a curse, or an inherited gene. The way it happened was a pure accident, quite boring actually. I am one of those geeks, an old geek to be honest. I love collecting shark teeth, star wars figures, you name it, I have it. I live a boring life, I work in a call centre, and spent my life reading from a script and having people swear at me - I have learnt so many new put downs. One of the invisible people, a 27 year old virgin, I couldn't get laid in a brothel with a fist full of twenties. I am not a bad looking man, but not a good looking one at that.

Anyway, how did I become a werewolf? As usual, more money than sense. Browsing a sales site, I came across someone advertising "genuine werewolf teeth." I am not stupid, but more money than sense, the quick click of a mouse and I was holding a box with the teeth in it. Not for one second did I believe I was holding actual werewolf teeth, but thought it would be an interesting conversational piece, that is if I ever had a party or such, something to bring out and show people. Never once did I believe they were real, even when I accidently nicked a finger on one of the teeth.

Not even when I woke up one morning in the forest, covered in mud and a half eaten rabbit sticking out of my mouth did I believe. I thought one of the bastards at work had stuck something in my coffee that had sent me into cloud cuckoo land. It took a while to make the connection, but when I did it changed me in ways I could never believe, and brings me to where I am now.

I decided firstly that I would sue the guy who sold me the teeth - obviously every solicitor I went to see thought I was crazy. I even tried to stick one of the teeth into the solicitor, but that resulted in me getting a caution, a fine, and being advised by the Magistrate to seek professional help. I even went on the internet; there must be other people like me. I cannot be the only one, but most of the groups were crazy. They either dressed up in furry costumes or ran around the woods howling. It looked more like something from Disney rather than *American Werewolf in Paris*. I am not sure what was worse, the furrys or the ones who covered themselves in blood and ran around the woods naked. I realised that this was not going to be easy.

I thought that if I found the perfect woman and asked her to join me in an eternity of hairy happiness, I would no longer be alone. Let's face it, women make perfect werewolves, they already get bitchy once a month. Apart from the hairiness, nothing would change. So my next step was finding the perfect mate, also how to approach the subject?

"Hi, my name's Mark. How do you fancy an eternity of ripping the heads off rabbits and doing it doggystyle?"

In the end, I realised I was going to have to go this alone, and deal with it in my own way. I practiced my art of changing, and realised that the full moon didn't make that much of a difference, I could change at will. There were certain problems, like when the neighbourhood bitches were in heat, I had to chain myself to the radiator. I have dated some dogs in the past but that would be taking it to the next level. On occasion, I did chase the local cats; at that point I realised that I needed my freedom to free run and be me, well, whichever me it was at that time.

I have always been a loner and even before the change I had always loved the wilderness. I loved to get away, pitch a tent and forget my boring life, pretend I was Rambo - yeah I can hear you laughing - the image of me, a total dweeb in shorts, a vest, and a red sock tied around my head, running around the forest and jumping from rock to rock. I cannot tell you how many times I tripped over a weed and sprained my ankle - weeds 5, Rambo 0 - told you I was a geek.

During my many camping trips, I had noticed a group that met on a regular basis to hunt and live the free life. I had never thought to approach them, and stayed well out their way. I made sure I stayed out of their way while going through the change; the last thing I wanted to be was their lunch or trophy. I stayed invisible, why change the habits of a lifetime?

Mind you, when I finally met them I was not invisible. I happened to be taking a shit at the time and I wanted to disappear up my own arse. Well, bears shit in the woods, so why not me? Thankfully, I had not changed, the lads seemed to take it in their stride after a few sniggers and asked me if I would like to join them at their base; obviously I had to finish my shit first. Initially, when I joined them, I expected I was going to be the butt of their jokes, like asking *had I wiped my ass properly?* so I asked if one of them wanted to sniff it and make sure. After the banter had died down I relaxed, and for once, I felt like I belonged.

I soon realised that the big guy of the group, Judd, was pretty cool and all the other guys totally admired him, and that is where I met Mela. She had long, dark hair and chocolate eyes you could melt into. I knew at that moment I had met the woman of my dreams. I could tell the way she looked at me she was interested. When she walked away she always looked back, her chocolate eyes staring into mine. Major problem... Mela was

Judd's sister and he was way protective. The other guys were great and I felt totally accepted.

I lived for the times that I would be part of the group, I learnt so much from them. They were survivalists and they could deal with anything; how to find food, the best shelter. But how could I tell them? Would they hunt me too?

They wanted me to join them, become a survivalist like them and live in the forest. For Mela, I would do anything. I joined them whenever I could. The first time Mela and I sneaked off and made love, it was everything I dreamed of. Protection didn't even cross my mind. The love making was frenzied. I held onto her tight. Like me, she was still a virgin. I so wanted to tell her who I really was, ask her to join me, leave her brother and run with me through the woods for an eternity, one bite and she would be mine. I knew she loved me. She would beg me not to leave, nuzzle into my neck, but if I stayed then they would learn what I really was. So I continued to live two lives, trying to sell insurance in one life, being a werewolf and running with the gang in the other. Would Mela be happy living in a damp house in the middle of a housing estate, and surviving on my shitty wages? Could I take her away from this life of freedom?

Then finally the day came when I had no choice but to tell the group what I really was … they caught me in the middle of a change. I thought I had timed things to perfection like I usually did, but this time I did not expect them to suddenly come around a tree; the look on their faces when they realised what I really was…

Judd pointed at me and screamed werewolf, I saw Mela pass out. One minute I was a naked human, the next covered in fur. Judd nudged Mela; I saw her rouse and the tears in her eyes. What was coming next? Would they hunt me and tear me apart? Mela got up and began to walk away, the long black hair on her tail, pushed between her long strong legs. The other wolves began to trot after her. Judd just looked at me and shook his head. He was the leader of the pack. He licked his black nose and looked at me…

"I cannot believe I let you sniff my sister's butt. I even sniffed your butt… dude you have issues… "

I watched as he turned away and joined the rest of the wolves. I knew I could never come back.

That was the last I saw of them. I returned back to my job, and changed in the cage I had bought for Mela. Like I said, I knew she would never be happy here. I suppose it was back to sniffing dogs' butts and chasing cats, and cat, you may ask, tastes just like chicken…

BIO: Urwin Bower was born in the UK and has spent her time finding ways to create new nightmares.

DIARY OF A WEREWOLF

SANDRA ROZANSKI

If I had known or even suspected that my college flame was not all that he seemed, I doubt I ever would have dated him in spite of the attraction I felt. No mega-crush is worth all that followed. That one fateful night ruined the rest of my remaining college days. You know, the ones that were meant to be the best time of my life, not to mention the ruination of the rest of my life. But Derek Mayhew had swept me off my feet and, back seventeen years ago, I doubted seriously that they would ever touch the ground again. And may I also mention that he was a werewolf, which I found out the hard way, yes indeed, when he bit me, of course. No matter if it happened in the throes of passion, his husky voice whispering my name over and over.

"Alexa, I love you. I want you so bad….need you so much. Alexa."

What does matter is that it did happen and thousands of apologies could never undo it. Thus I was left to weep and wail about it and then learn to cope. Needless to say, Derek was my first 'kill' and I had no regrets. The feast was well worth it because of the hunger that was ripping apart my innards even as I was ripping him apart, the pain from it was so great. When it was over, I would have no taste for so-called normal food ever again. That fact became a real problem down the road.

I'd had the feeling after the deed was done that feasting on my former boyfriend was not going to be enough to sate my new, horrendous hunger and I was right. An hour later, I was browsing the winding lanes through the campus in the hope of finding a snack, just the right snack of course. Though I literally had not left much of Derek to be recognized as a human, disposing of the left over bones had been an unwelcome chore. I threw them in the trash, then thought better of it. I thought the best bet would be to toss them in the chute that went to the incinerator in the huge basement three floors below me, but the custodian had the keys and would be making rounds at dawn. I knew that because I had dated him for a few months my first year here. He always checked the furnace before he fired it up, and what would he think, I wondered, if he saw part of a human skull along with other parts and pieces? "It" would hit the fan in a heartbeat and the entire

259

place would be crawling with police. I ended up bundling up what remained of my paramour and tossing him unceremoniously into the trash bin closest to the Dean's office. Why not let him get tagged if they were discovered somehow? How odd, my way of thinking had completely changed. I'd never thought one step ahead before, now it was the only way I could reason. I got on with my food hunt, thinking that a football jock would fit the menu nicely.

Broad shouldered, big chested, and other meaty attributes to whet my appetite. Was that drool leaking from the corners of my mouth? Seriously? Of course there were more than a few heavy weight coeds running around campus as well. They would also suit perfectly.

Speak of the devil; here was one coming my way. She doddered along, glancing back over her shoulder now and then, looking a little nervous to be out alone in the dark of night. I wondered briefly where she had been before I approached her and smiled a big hello. She started and when she saw me, relaxed and smiled back. Being another female meant she was safe from undue harm, she thought. In a moment, her night was going to get a lot more interesting. I invited her to a hot chocolate after I introduced myself and it was her turn to drool. We headed in the direction of the all night café just inside the front doors of our great academy. Many a student spent the night there, cramming and keeping the coffee coming.

We were walking slowly, getting acquainted, when we passed by a small copse off the side of the trail. I sprung and got a good bite of her throat in my sharp teeth and lords did she taste yummy. Pasta and pizza were dominant but I tasted wine and Italian torte as well. But the meat of her was what I needed and I feasted with relish, enjoying every morsel of my newfound friend. When I finished and felt so full I thought I might burst, I piled her bones in the pillow case I had in my pocket, neatly folded and ready for bear. I made my way back to my dorm by way of the assistant dean's office and tossed her into the trash bin there. Pickup for all the bins would be made in the morning, only about an hour and half away. All traces of my deeds would be gone and I would be safe and go on as if nothing had changed. I fell into my bed, clothes still on, and slept a dreamless sleep until the clock sounded at seven-thirty. My first class was at eight.

I dressed haphazardly in jeans, sweatshirt, and sneakers, threw a light jacket on and rushed out the door. I made it to class with no minutes to spare. The professor for my journalist class cleared his throat and stared at me when I took a seat. Some sort of explanation was apparently in order for being late and then interrupting his class with my tardy bustle. I mumbled something about cramming all night and apologized. All was good again. Yet when the bell sounded and I rose to shuffle out with the others, he called out and told me to stay a minute. I supposed I would be in for a private dressing down. I couldn't have been more wrong....or right.

Before I could say a word, he was on me like white on rice; our clothes were off, we were on the floor behind his desk and I was earning my A the easy way. I was becoming quite the piece of work. Thus it went for the next two years. I was his girl of the hour. What stunned me beyond all understanding was that on the day of my graduation he asked me to marry him. He was getting the milk for free so why was he committing himself further? He clarified it for me. He had fallen in love with the 'best' he'd ever known and could not let me go. A compliment? I doubted it, but I accepted it anyway to secure my future without too much of a struggle, such as going to a steady job every day.

We married a week later, I became Mrs. Clive Porter and my life of doldrums began. I continued with my frenzy feedings when the urge struck, which it did like clockwork at least once a month. I suffered from a different curse that plagues normal women. How to keep it a secret? I thought nothing could get much worse until I realized I was pregnant. How that happened was beyond me. I believed that in my new state of being, I could not conceive and bear a child. If so, it certainly would not be more than half human. Logic rules, right? I'd be making monsters, so to speak.

I gave birth to a son, Clive Junior. A year later, I gave birth to a second son and named him Derek, in memory of my first love and murder. A small tribute for all he gave to me. A year and half later, a third son came in to the picture. Erik was premature and so small he had stayed a month in the hospital after I'd gone home. I made up my mind no more children would be baked in my personal oven. I needn't have worried because Clive took to being away from home most nights. Working late to make the money needed to support his growing family, he said when I complained about being stuck with all of the work of the children and household. When I discovered otherwise, I handled it in my own way. His paid for romances disappeared one at a time and were never seen or heard from again. My darling husband kept me well fed without a clue. I was growing tired of him and his thoughtless shenanigans. After all, I kept him relaxed, or so I thought.

A wife who never says no is the woman every man wants, does he not? I gave him three children, three of which I never wanted. They were all hellions, every one of them. I was the one who had to put up with all their nonsense, getting called to school every other week, it seemed. Cleaning up after them, cooking, bathing, the whole bit until they got old enough to take care of their own needs. I did not dare let them near the stove, however, so I kept up the meals. After all, mac and cheese is not difficult and hot dogs or hamburgers are no big deal. I packed them lunches for school every day, peanut butter and jelly or bologna and cheese. I saw them out the door every morning to the school bus and I was there every afternoon when they came home. I deemed myself a good mother.

One morning, I came back inside after they had gone to school and desperately needed another cup of coffee. I closed the front door and stood

261

a moment in the hallway, feeling tired and drained. I caught sight of myself in the oval mirror hanging there and got the shock of my life. I looked old and dowdy. What had happened to my hair, my figure? No wonder Clive had begun to roam other pastures.

I took my time showering, luxuriating in the steamy spray as I had not done in a very long while, and I enjoyed it tremendously. I dried off and dressed in what was the least shabby I could find in the closet. I bagged up what was left after I put on the low cut shirt, worn often to seduce men. It would go to the Goodwill and be replaced with the latest fashions. The clingy black skirt was a bit tight on my post pregnant hips but it would do for the purpose. I let my long, strawberry blonde hair air dry and brushed it to cascade down over my shoulders. I was stunned to see that it fell to the small of my back. Why had I been wearing a prissy tight knot for so long? I couldn't think of a single reason other than that's what I thought a respectable wife did so as not to attract unwanted attention. Fool I'd been for I could have used this look to attract my food supply more willingly. The hunt had been a trial for me for months.

I took money from the auto teller machine, a good amount, and then I dropped off my disgusting biddy clothing into the bin at the second hand store. I drove off in search of a little heart to heart talk with the first subject that came along and could fill my needs. I didn't care who, male or female…my one rule had always been no children. In spite of the fact that I often had moments of harboring the idea of 'taking care' of my sons, quickly and painlessly. Somehow, I just couldn't bring myself to do it. They were unwanted little brats but they were my own unwanted little brats. Erik had somehow wormed his way into my heart in spite of the fact that I was sure I didn't have one, or at least had not since college. Perhaps it was the circumstances of his difficult birth and ill health that forced his stay in the hospital. I hated coming home with empty arms. I remember thinking all those pregnant months and the hours of labor and nothing to show for it. Pity, yet, he was a sweet boy and kind of a chameleon. He blended in with his background, became almost invisible and everyone forgot he was there, his family included.

The teachers gave him A's every term. Clive Jr. and Derek hated him for his brains. He could make the fool of them any given second and often did. It didn't help matters that they considered him a mama's boy. He was not, of course, only in their eyes. Yet he gave me a little tug of those motherhood feelings now and then. I swung the car into the parking lot of an elite dress shop and ignored the valet as I sauntered by him, swinging and swaying; being obvious, I hoped, in my invitation. The bell over the door chimed musically as I entered. I felt myself being scrutinized by the two women behind the counter and a third pushing hangers back and forth on a rack of gorgeous dresses. I could almost hear the wheels turning in their well-coifed heads. Snobs all. They deemed me useless trash, I felt sure.

262

No one approached me to offer assistance and I was confident I would be well fed for the next several times I needed to hunt. I knew right where to come for my meals.

I continued browsing, enjoying the lush carpet under my open-toed pumps. I sunk in nearly up to my ankles. The mauve shade of it was very attractive and offset the gray walls, which otherwise would have appeared dull and depressing. The front windows were floor to ceiling and adorned at the top with poufy valences of the same in a deeper shade of mauve. Very high class, I thought as I perused. Only once did I take a garment from the rack. It was a lovely royal blue dress, knee length, with capped sleeves and a plunging bodice trimmed with delicate lace. The atmosphere in the place turned to ice. I swear I could see my breath. An impulse struck me and I decided to buy it.

I carried it to the glass counter which housed gorgeous jewelry, purses and gloves, scarves and shoe clips, all costing upward of a hundred and fifty dollars. It occurred to me then to check the price tag of the dress which I did subtly as I pretended to reach for a handkerchief. I nearly swooned and prayed it didn't show. Fifteen thousand dollars. Can you imagine the reception I got as I hurriedly placed it down on the gleaming glass counter top and said with the snobbiest voice I could summon that I would take this one though it was not what I really wanted?

The three of them put their tongues back inside their gaping mouths and checked me out in robot fashion, clicking and whirring as they went through the motions. My purchase was folded and placed inside of a lovely box lined with blue tissue paper, with a small card giving directions on the care and cleaning. I sashayed out of the shop and smiled as the bell rang its goodbye to me.

In the parking lot, the valet was waiting beside my car with a leering grin on his handsome face. He handed me the key and opened the door as I climbed in, then he passed by the front of the car and climbed into the passenger seat. I said nothing but only stared into his dark eyes. Slate colored and fringed with black lashes, topped with even blacker brows.

"Drive around the block," he ordered me. His set jaw was lightly bristled with five o'clock shadow, ordinarily a turn off, but his heavy brows and thick lashes told me he meant business. Those eyes bore right through me and I couldn't refuse even if he meant to murder me. He said his name was Lucas Black which I thought was a perfect fit.

After our session, I felt so hungry I was starved. He had taken me to his little walk up several blocks away. I thought it was typical bachelor, and more than a little shabby.

I smiled sweetly and let him have his way with me. I sneezed a few times as the dust that was coating everything tickled my nose. He blessed me with another round of wrestling on the small, rumpled bed but it was big enough for us both since we were exercising and not sleeping. I made a date to meet him that night and on my way home, I plotted my plan of attack. He would make me a delightful meal to say the least. I would insist on one more demonstration of his ardor for me. Then I'd put on the feed bag and replenish my energy.

On the way home, I stopped and bought several pair of new shoes, not quite as high heeled as I might like but very nice anyway. A pair of plain black pumps and a lovely pair of heeled silver sandals which would look very nice with my new dress. The third was a pair of boots, black leather, studded and very sexy looking on my feet. No more dowdy for me. I would take more money out of the bank tomorrow and buy a new wardrobe from soup to nuts. After all, I planned on branching out.

I wore the dress and sandals that night and when I met Lucas at the small bar he had recommended for privacy, he whistled through his teeth appreciatively and crushed me to him in a smothering embrace.

"Baby, I love your hair down like that…I had no idea how gorgeous you are and I can't wait to get lost in it. Let's leave this dive and go do some serious lovin'!"

I can't say the idea wasn't appealing and I was so hungry by now my nerves were jumping out of my skin, which felt like lava to the touch. Yes, indeed, I had very special plans for my 'love'.

After one quick brandy for me and a beer for him, we left and walked hand in hand to my car. He was humming some lilting tune that numbed my senses and made my heart race. I had not felt such passion rising within me since Derek. I had thought it dead long since and sex was a tool to be used as a means to get whatever I wanted or desired out of life. Clive had overwhelmed me with three of his brats but had never overwhelmed me with desire. He must know by now that I had abandoned ship and was never going back. I was out to see the world and take up my life from where it had been so rudely interrupted all those years ago. Lucas would be a lovely distraction for a while but also a very hearty meal for this woman in a very short time. I could not, would not allow myself to have these feelings for him roaring up from the pit of my stomach. Derek was my last bad lesson in love. Clive had been a means to a way of doing things- until I finally woke up and realized he was the worst answer I could have chosen for solving any problems I thought I might have. Instead of making him my slave, I had made myself his and he took full advantage. I was far more grateful to Derek for the gifts he gave me.

The hunt lust, the never satisfied appetite, the love of raw meat and the stalking and planning of my next meal. And, of course, my very deep love of the full moon. Even if I did not really need it to stalk my prey, it enhanced every sense and nerve in my body to the utmost. I did not mind the change as it took place anymore but I loved the horror on those faces as they realized just who, or should I say *what* it was they were playing with?

Nothing could top that, ever.

We climbed into the car and for once I let him drive. He was overwhelmed with surprise that I had deferred to him and I was surprised too. What had come over me, the one who always felt the need to be in control? This had to stop. Now.

I purred and caressed, leaning in close to him, laying my head on his shoulder. I wanted him to get a good, deep whiff of my hair as it fanned out over his neck and arms. He turned to me, buried his nose in my tresses and inhaled deeply, holding the breath. When he let it out through pursed lips, I felt the heat of it waft by my cheekbone.

Gods it was divine being a woman again, feeling like a woman again, powerful and seductive. I had him wrapped. I loved it. More than that, I needed it. I hoped that my lovely dress would not get wrecked in the melee of lovemaking. That would make me very unhappy indeed. A few moments later, Lucas pulled off the paved road onto a narrow dirt lane studded by tips of huge boulders jutting up. Some of them so large they were almost like small mountain tops. He expertly wove the wheels of the car around them and there was very little teeth jarring jostling as I might have imagined. In fact, the little bit of bumping only added to my anxious anticipation. I felt myself growing warmer as I imagined my teeth sinking into his belly and my claws digging deep into the soft flesh of his thighs, and I could almost feel the hot blood flowing down my throat, taste the chunks of delicious meat that I needed so badly. I was going to savor my fine meal tonight, more than any I'd had in a long time.

We finally pulled into a small glade and he parked among ancient, tall trees, canopied by a huge umbrella of boughs of thick leaves, leaving a little opening for the half-moon to shine down on us. The darkness was nearly complete. He roughly pulled me to him and kissed me ferociously, as if he wanted to chew me alive and swallow me whole, take absolute possession of me once and for all. He had never handled me so roughly before and I felt the passing pull of misgiving. He was a very strong man. He could easily hurt me very badly in my human state. I had to change if the need came for me to defend myself. I kissed him back, hoping to meet passion with passion, take him off guard, yet in seconds I did not have to pretend. I felt my nails growing, my teeth springing from my lips as they curled back and I moaned under his touch. The sexual need for his touch was becoming stronger than my need to dispose of him, assuage my hunger, and when I melted into him, I knew I was lost. We made love like it had never been made before.

We were naked, sprawled out on the front seat. He had put the backs down. It was almost as good as a bed. It was so inky black in these woods, we were enmeshed in its soft blanket, comforted and warm in each other's arms. My dress was neatly folded and placed up in the back window out of harm's way. He had gently removed it and made sure it was safe. I could love him for that alone. He knew what that garment meant to me.

Freedom and a new lease on life. None of it seemed important to me now. I felt I could stay right here with him for the rest of my days. Then he surprised me by saying he had a little cabin out here in these woods, just past the copse of trees and it was on a small lake.

We quickly dressed and he lifted me out of the car and took my hand in case I tripped as we walked. I had no trouble seeing well in the dark but I would not give up the helpless female act. If he guessed, he never let on to me but I could not let him know I was more than he thought I was, until I was ready. My hunger was surging with every step and I was becoming concerned I would not be able to contain it. I really hated the thought of destroying my lover, yet I knew well that I would not be able to help myself.

I could hear the scurrying of small animals in the bushes and a plan came into my mind. I asked Lucas to let me go in to the woods for a minute. I really felt the need to go to the bathroom, which was a lie but one that he readily bought and he led me to a rough opening and I felt my way to a place where I could pretend to do what I needed. He turned his back and leaned against a huge old Oak.

I sat very still, crouched down for long seconds, letting out a small sigh of relief. When at long last a small vole skittered in front of me, I snatched it up and swallowed it whole. Not my favorite choice of fare but it would stave off the insatiable gnawing I had begun to feel at my insides and hopefully keep me from doing something I would surely regret. I rose and joined my paramour, wiping my lips as I went. He smiled and took my hand again. We made our way for several yards, stepping gingerly, not speaking but both deep in thought. I had to find a way to solve this, a solution that would be perfect for me, assuring my happiness and my future and acceptable to him. I had fallen in love again, against my will and my better judgement.

Love allowed another person to claim you, body and soul. If you are unlucky as I had twice been, I knew if I stayed with Lucas as I wished, then I would have to tell him what I was or better, show him what I was and what I needed. Embrace him as my cohort and partner in crime. I couldn't begin to fathom how he would take that. All hell could break loose and rain fire down over me, sucking out every breath I drew into my choking lungs. This loss would be more than I could take above all the others.

I saw the outline of the cabin painting itself in the backdrop of darkness, slowly defining its shape in the small clearing under the black clouds scudding across the moon. I squeezed his hand in mine, more for pretense of fear than actual fear, but it was eerie standing here with mist from the lake rising around our ankles like something out of an old horror movie. I shivered and it was genuine. He held me close and then brought his lips to mine in assurance. I clung.

"I have to tell you something," he breathed in my ear. My heart thudded.

"Then you should," I whispered in answer "And when you finish, there is something I have to tell you." I answered his kiss with my own, putting my promise into it with all I had.

"I didn't want to tell you this way but I think it's the only way." It sounded very ominous and I wondered if he was married after all, cheating on his forlorn wife? I could not bear it.

"I've been tutoring a young man with a lot of problems for some months now. He's a tortured soul and feels his life is useless. I just couldn't stand by and do nothing; I had to try to help him."

Oh lord, was that all? I thought amid a scattering of thoughts that had been whirling in my head. I sighed in tremendous relief and answered him with a great hug that huffed the breath out of him in a grunt. We were still good….in fact, we were great. Now it was my turn and my news was going to be a bit more shocking to him than his was to me. I took a deep breath and screwed up my resolve.

"I've been keeping a secret from you too and it isn't easy to tell you but I want you to know."

"There's nothing you can't tell me that would change how I feel about you. You crazy dame, I'm nuts about you and I want us to get hitched."

"Well, you may not feel that way when you hear what I have to tell you."

"Don't ever think that, ever. Nothing will drive us apart in this lifetime. Not in the next one either." That was a very strange thing for him to say, I thought. I readied a reply but before I could open my mouth, the door to the cabin opened on rusty hinges and a shadow stepped out into the sudden light of the moon. A tall, thin figure stepped closer to us but his face was still hidden.

"Alexa, this is the young man I was telling you about. It is my hope to adopt him and I will be more able to do that if you marry me. We will all have the family we always longed for and never found. With each other, we will."

I was stunned into silence. I was a complete failure at my first marriage and the role of motherhood. I had no desire to go through that again. Yet, here was the man I loved beyond reasoning asking me to do just that. My hesitation was so obvious that it seemed the entire night became more silent than before. I had not had my chance to confess so now was the time. Once he knew, he would not want me. He might be so horrified that he fled, or worse, he might try to kill me out of fear. I would not let that happen. I stood frozen and mulled.

The voice that spoke out of the darkness was one I had not heard in a very long while but I knew it well. I gasped in surprise and turned to the figure standing on the porch.

267

"I think it's a great idea, mom," said Erik. He came down the steps and stood tall in front of me. My youngest son was a grown young man now. His red hair lit up the night.

"I know Lucas loves you true like dad never did. I know you had it bad when you were there. I tried hard not to add too much to the flak. You were a great mom." I could barely absorb any of this. Lucas had met Erik when he had come to the dress shop looking for me. Seems he was the only one who saw what was happening and he had followed me instead of heading out to school that day. But did he know about the other?

He stepped up and hugged me close. He was two heads taller than my five foot eight. Without a solitary thought to the consequences, I blurted everything out. From start to finish, I babbled without a breath until it was all told. I inhaled when I was done, a long drawn breath that filled my lungs and set my nerves tingling. When neither of them spoke, I assumed the worst. I had to leave. I could never harm my youngest son or the man I had gone completely gaga over. I was doomed.

"Come inside, Alexa," Lucas urged. I did not think it was good idea. I rejected it.

"Yeah, mom, seriously. Come inside, please. We have something for you. A big surprise we've planned for weeks." I took Lucas's hand and then Erik held out his hand for my other and clasped it tight. We went into the darkened cabin together.

Through the musty odor and dust tickling my nose, I was tempted to back right out again. Then Lucas flipped a switch and the room flooded with light. There was a table set with a feast of food on it, all raw and bleeding. The blood leaked over the edges of the platters and fell onto the white linen table cloth. I drooled, gods forgive me. I felt the saliva seeping out of the corners of my mouth and slithering down my chin. When I stepped closer, I saw a human heart on a silver platter, with a fork plunged into it as if waiting to be picked up and....enjoyed - which I did.

Lucas and Erik stepped up and began to pick entrails from a large bowl and stuff them into their mouths. I stared wide-eyed, open mouthed and watched them enjoy and savor what they were chewing. What the hell was happening?

Lucas grinned and his red mouth was deliciously macabre. Erik swallowed his food and grinned. I stood silently and waited. Then both of them blurted the same thing at the same moment.

"We are werewolves too, in case you haven't guessed."

I thought I could not be more surprised. I wasn't sure how I should feel but it did explain a lot about Lucas. Erik was a stumper. How had it happened? Then he told me. I had not breast fed his older brothers but because he had been sickly and premature, I decided to take the advice of the nurses and breast feed Erik to give him better nourishment. It worked like a charm and he thrived. I stopped when he was six months old, not because I wished to but because he had cut a tooth and he bit me, drew blood. It was what had passed the werewolf curse gene to him. He was early at everything, including baby teeth.

We sat by the fire that Lucas had started in the hearth and we sipped red wine from crystal goblets. In this case, it was our kind of red wine. Poured from a pitcher that had been the center piece of the banquet. I could live like this, forever. It was the nicest surprise anyone had ever given me. It couldn't be better or so I thought. Until they told me that our meal had consisted of my former husband, Clive. For once in his life, he had given me a satisfying experience.

BIO: I have been married with children for a large part of my life. My family has always been topmost of my priorities. When I picked up a pencil at the age of eight to write a gothic tale about a castle and a stormy night I had an inkling that I had just been bitten by the writing bug. All those years, along with raising our kids put that inkling on the back burner until about fifteen years ago when I picked it up again in earnest and have been going ever since. Over the last several years some of my short tales have appeared in a few anthologies. We all remember the thrill of seeing our work in print for the first time.

I am so proud and pleased that my submission for Full Moon Slaughter was accepted and I am anxiously awaiting to hold a copy in my hands and read every story by so many wonderful authors. May the writing fever stay with each of us forevermore~

Best always ♪ ~Sandy

THE LAST LYCAN

KITTY KANE

Alone, the last, his kind edging so near to past,
The Lycan sits upon his shore, knowing to his dismay his kind could be no
        more.
Without the threat of fang and claw,
The last Lycan shall knock upon Hell's door.

A sound! But where? There! A maiden fair,
With heaving bust, and silver hair.
The Lycan strains to hear again the sound,
She drops her gown upon the ground,
The Lycans head snaps straight around.

So long, thinks he, since my desire has been satiated,
Not one more moment shall he have waited.
Swiftly the Lycan seizes her around waist and nape,
Wrestles her groundwards before committing the rape.

He tears and rents, and mauls and gores,
Remembering times of past harlots and whores,
He elongates her neck, how far can it go?
Reaches around for weaponry to deal the killing blow.

But by the light of the moon,
The maiden whimpers and stirs,
Full moon lighting a path downwards,
Through oak trees and firs.
An emotion so alien to the Lycan strikes hard,
Her exquisite beauty, her warmth, and her soul now so charred.

A pity, a sorrow, a most heartrending love,
As he looked down upon her, bearing now only amulet and glove.
Flesh torn and bleeding, yet wonders the Lycan,
Could this maiden be the saviour, the Lycan race is needing?

He lifts her and drags her away to his dwelling,
Very soon the fair maiden's belly with child is swelling,
No requirement for rope or chain is there,
As oddly, his love is returned by that maiden fair.

The time swiftly passed since his night of disgrace,
The Lycan covets the child that shall save his race.
The maiden's contractions start a fortnight too soon,
The Lycan's heart drops, at first sight of that night's moon.

"Full I shall be," the lunar goddess Isis she taunted,
The small humanness left in his heart now quite daunted.
Childbirthing brings blood, and screaming and pain,
All Lycan desires when moon neither on wax nor on wane.

The maiden's loins ripple, and contract with pain,
As the full moon she rises, goddess Isis feeling no shame.
Body wracked with pain, yet mind strangely adrift,
The maiden screams now with fear,
As the Lycan begins his deadly shift.

As the moonrise completes, and pale light fills the clearing.
The child is born to parents, one screaming, one leering.
Scents of blood and fear set the Lycan's bloodlust wild,
Umbilical bond still attached,
The werewolf consumes his own child.

He chews on the cord, still attached to the mother,
Moves on to extremities, arms, legs, then the other.
The organs of the werechild pulsate as they are torn,
Violently ripped from the corpse of the newborn.

The werechild's parents stare one with horror, one delight,
As one basks and howls in, but one curses the moonlight.
The maiden seeing her child torn asunder,
Finally her mind snaps at this ultimate plunder.

As the Lycan, blood dripping from its gaping maw,
Howls at the full moon, infant flesh smothering his paw,
The amulet, she looks upon a silver chain round her neck, so doth she pull
it.
She knows what it means, this single solitary silver bullet.

The last of her twisted warped love sails like ship from dock,
Her grasping hands tremble, as she finds each a rock,
Only one chance at this feat shall she take,
To ensure its work, and the mark it must make.

She brings rocks and amulet together, with almighty sound,
And gasps, and then screams,
As the Lycan corpse hits the blood soaked ground.

An unholy love, for this man beast she knew must die,
And for her child dismembered, and for her Lycan lover she did cry.
So now, if you sail past that Lycan's lonely shore,
There sits our fair maiden,
And there she shall sit evermore.

The moral of my tale is but a warning,
To those who feel the stirrings of a new love dawning.
Run, hide, love hurts now flee,
Who needs love's scars? You? Them?
No, nor me.

BIO: Kitty Kane, AKA Becky Brown is an emerging horror writer that hails from the south of England. Kitty is a lifelong, avid reader of horror fiction. Her influences over the years are wide spread but include James Herbert, Clive Barker, Edgar Allen Poe, Jack Ketchum and the late, great Richard Laymon. Although writing has been a pastime that she has indulged in for most of her life, she is currently lined for her first published works as part of several collections for J.Ellington Ashton Press, as well as interest in a forthcoming novella. Her style ranges from more traditional short horror stories to bizarre fiction and poetry. Kitty is also one half of writing duo – Matthew Wolf Kane, alongside another emerging talent, Matt Boultby. Their joint venture has already seen them published twice, with subsequent works due for release.

Facebook -
https://www.facebook.com/becky.brown.560272?fref=ts

IN THE MOONLIT FOREST GLADE

JOHN QUICK

He'd forgotten to get ice, so the beer was warm, and wasn't that just the icing on the fucking cake? Aside from the annoyance factor, Ronnie couldn't care less. He was going to drink it anyway, and hope it would help put this godawful horrorshow of a day behind him. It wouldn't have been so bad had the divorce papers not shown up just as he was getting into the truck to come out here for his hunting trip. He'd known they were coming, and considering how vindictive his soon-to-be-ex was, it shouldn't have surprised him that she'd timed it so the process server would come while he was about to go try to relax, but when the man got out and asked his name, it still managed to all but ruin his day.

The first beer went fast, disappearing down his throat in three long swallows. He winced at the added bitterness the temperature bestowed on it and crushed the can in his fist before tossing it back into the cooler alongside the rest of the case. One or two more and he was sure he wouldn't even notice how warm they were anymore; three or four after that would let him sleep, and then he wouldn't give two shits about anything for a while.

It was the opposite of what he'd hoped for this trip to be. He'd hoped that by now he would have already snagged *something*, be it a deer, or a rabbit, or even some piddling little squirrel. But no, any potential prey had eluded him. He'd had one lined up, a beautiful six-point buck, but he'd been so excited at the thought of the coming kill that he'd pulled the trigger instead of squeezing it. The shot went wide, the buck flagged and bolted, and he'd not had another chance to fire the rifle the rest of the day.

What he *really* wanted was for his bitch of an ex to be wandering around out here instead of some kind of wild game. He knew he just wanted to smell the blood after a fresh kill and imagine it was hers to try and make himself feel better about the situation he was in. He also knew it wouldn't work, but even if it gave him a few brief moments of contentment, it would be worth it.

He tilted the second can up and was surprised to find it already empty. He grunted. Maybe he needed to drink them warm more often when he was upset; they went faster when the cold didn't make his teeth ache,

275

and he could already feel the fuzzy numbness creeping into his fingers. He tossed the second can after the first and pulled out another one, cracking the top and forcing himself to sip on it while he sat gazing across the small, crackling fire he'd meant to cook some of his quarry on.

At least it was a beautiful night. Upset as he was, he could still appreciate that. The way the flames danced and bobbed in the light breeze combined nicely with his encroaching buzz to finally make him feel like he was starting to relax. He was still pretty pissed off, but at least some of the edge was being tempered, and that was a good thing.

His head jerked up as he realized he was actually starting to doze off. Apparently, the beer was hitting him harder than he thought it was. It probably didn't help that he hadn't bothered to eat anything today, so the only thing in his stomach was alcohol. As he tipped up the can and guzzled down the last few swallows, a soft sound caught his attention. He paused, swallowing as quickly as he could without trying to drown himself, and listened.

After a moment, he heard it again: a faint snapping of twigs somewhere deep in the trees. A faint rustling as the underbrush was moved by something's passing. Still too faint to figure out exactly what it was, but he was sure that it wasn't just the wind.

He put the can down slowly and reached behind him, feeling his way around until his hand landed on the butt of his rifle. He pulled it out of the tent carefully, trying hard to keep it from brushing against the canvas sides and spooking whatever it was away. If he needed to spook it away for some reason or another, he could just fire into the air and give the proverbial warning shot. The way things were in the world nowadays, there was every chance whatever was coming his way would be another hunter who might not have his best interests at heart. But if it was an animal he could shoot and keep, either for food or as a trophy, it would be the perfect thing to turn this day around.

The soft crunch repeated itself, closer this time. Ronnie socketed the rifle against his shoulder and tried to aim with his ears, pointing the barrel in the approximate direction the noises were coming from. More rustling told him that whatever it was had to be lower to the ground. An animal of some kind, then; at least he wasn't about to shoot a person. He was on private property, so it could even be whoever owned the land seeing his fire and coming to ask what the hell he thought he was doing out here. The choice to shoot in either of those situations would not end well.

When the crunching came again, it sounded as though it was moving closer. Whatever it was sounded fairly large, based on the stride and the force behind the breaking twigs. He still had no idea what *kind* of animal it was, but he didn't plan on waiting for it to eat his face off before finding out. He quickly adjusted his aim and fired. The report was overly loud in the stillness of the night, assaulting his ears and leaving them with a faint hum, even as the recoil shoved him slightly backward. He forced himself to breathe slowly, waiting to see if anything came charging out of the woods, angered by his attempt to kill it and ready to exact some revenge.

The woods remained still, even the normal sounds of nature muted by the overpowering crack of the rifle.

As his hearing returned to something resembling normalcy, he faintly heard a light yipping sound. A dog or coyote then, or possibly even a fox. If it was a fox, he could end up with a nice trophy out of it. Not so much for a coyote, but at least it would be one less scavenger in the world to terrorize local livestock, or even thin potential prey for him. If it was a dog, just some harmless thing out scavenging for scraps, well, that would suck, but it was better to err on the side of caution.

Whatever it was, it was obvious he'd only injured it and not killed it. He sighed and stood, dropping the rifle down to a ready position in his hands. As much as he didn't want to leave the comfort of his fire just yet, he needed to head into the brush, find it, and put it out of its misery. His father always told him he should try for a clean kill and not to let the animal suffer. There were many things his father had told him that he ignored, but that wasn't one of them. Especially considering the situation he found himself in, he couldn't bear the thought of any other creature suffering.

He sighed and set off, brushing past the thick foliage that surrounded the little clearing where he'd set up camp, listening for the sounds of pain to point him in the right direction. Strangely, they sounded less like the yipping he heard at first, and more like anguished moans. Not animalistic in other words, but somehow… *human*. He frowned. He was sure whatever he'd shot at was below the normal height level of a person, so he didn't know how it was possible, but based on the sounds he was now hearing, it had to be. He quickened his pace, hoping it was possible for an animal to make the same sounds.

When he finally broke through into another small clearing, he froze, his eyes struggling to comprehend what he was looking at.

It was a woman. She was still shrouded in shadow, but enough of the full moon filtered through the trees for him to make out that she was relatively young, gorgeous from what little he could see of her, and naked as the day she was born. Her dark hair draped the ground around her like a silken blanket, giving him a clear view of the agonized grimace on her face.

Visions of prison danced in his head as he dropped the rifle and rushed to her side.

"Oh, fuck!" he cried, reaching out, yet too afraid to actually touch her yet. "I am so fucking sorry!"

She moaned and shifted slightly, revealing her hands pressed over a wound in her thigh, blood trickling around her fingers to pool on the forest floor beneath her.

Ronnie pulled a flashlight from the pouch on his belt and shined it on her injury, slightly relieved that the wound most likely wouldn't be a fatal one, but still cursing himself for shooting without verifying his target first. It was an amateur mistake, and one he knew he'd made as a result of the beer he'd been putting away on an empty stomach, but knowing that did nothing to lessen the impact of what he'd done.

"Let me see," he said, trying to keep the tremble out of his voice.

Slowly, she moved her hands away, revealing the ragged hole where the bullet punched through. Ronnie tried to ignore the proximity of her exposed womanhood and focused on studying the wound. As best he could tell, the bullet had gone through it cleanly and wasn't stuck inside her leg or anything like that. It was still severe, the blood rushing from her in a near-torrent as soon as she took the pressure away. Untreated, the best she could hope for would be an infection that took her leg. At worst, she was going to bleed out.

He'd caused this, so it was only right that he try to fix it. He pulled off the flannel shirt he was wearing, shivering slightly as the cool night air passed easily through his undershirt. He took his pocketknife and cut the flannel into long strips. He folded two of the strips into thick pads he could use to absorb the blood flow, then forced himself to meet her eyes.

They were a deep, rich brown, and thankfully seemed to be regarding him with more curiosity than anger. He swallowed hard, wondering how long it would take staring into those eyes before he became lost in them completely.

"I'm going to have to move your leg," he told her. "I'll get you bandaged up, then get you back to my camp. I've got a first aid kit there. I don't know what good it will do, but I can try to keep this from getting too infected. We're going to need to get you to a hospital, too, but let's do what we can here, first, since it's going to be rough getting back out to my truck. Okay?"

She nodded once, her eyes never leaving his face. He took a deep breath.

"Here we go," he said. He lifted her thigh and quickly pressed one of the pads against the wound on the other side of it. She gritted her teeth and moaned again, but otherwise remained silent. He pressed the second pad against the other side of her leg, and juggled the task of wrapping another piece of his shirt around them and knotting it to keep them in place. When he wound the last strip around her leg for added security, he noted that she'd already bled through the pads, leaving them sodden and a little tacky. He tied the second strip tighter than the first, making her cry out softly, and hoped it would be enough until he could get her to a hospital.

He looked back to her face, unable to stop himself from noting how high and firm her breasts sat on her chest, even while she was lying down.

"I'm going to pick you up now, since I doubt you'll be able to walk. Where's your clothes?"

She met his eyes again, studying him, then slowly shook her head.

Ronnie frowned again, wondering why she didn't just talk to him. He doubted she was mute since she'd made noises; then again, he didn't know anything about how that worked, so for all he knew she was mute. "You mean you don't have clothes?"

She nodded once.

He wanted to ask her if she was insane, especially since the night was coming off cooler than it had been in weeks, but he kept his mouth shut. If she wanted to go gallivanting around the woods naked, who was he to tell her she couldn't? Besides, he'd be lying if he said he didn't appreciate her freedom of expression when it came to her body.

"Okay, here we go. Ready?"

She nodded again. Ronnie slipped one arm gently beneath her legs and the other beneath her shoulders, then pulled her toward himself and lifted with his legs until he was in a standing position. Thankfully, she was smaller than she'd looked at first, and much lighter than he'd feared. He doubted he'd even be that winded by the time he made it back to camp.

When she wrapped one arm around his shoulders to help support herself, he became all too aware of her nakedness pressed against his thin shirt and felt a stirring in his groin. This was probably the worst possible time to be thinking about what he'd like to do with this girl, so he started walking, trying his best to put it out of his mind.

She remained silent as he carried her through the woods, only occasionally letting out a whimper when he stepped on something and stumbled, jarring her in his arms. Small woman or not, by the time he finally spotted the faint glow of his fire through the trees, his arms were starting to tremble from her added weight.

He sat her gently next to the fire, then crawled into his tent and started digging through his pack. Naturally, the first aid kit was buried at the bottom. He pulled it out, considered, and grabbed another of his flannel shirts as well. As much as he didn't want her to cover up, it would be much less distracting for him to try and help her if she did.

She hadn't moved since he put her down, and her eyes were closed when he returned from his tent. His heart lurched against his ribcage, icy fear grabbing his spine. If she'd died in the short time he'd been grabbing that kit, he had no idea what he was going to do. Finally, he saw her chest rising and falling with her shallow breaths and realized she was only asleep or resting her eyes.

"Here," he said, draping the shirt over her shoulders. "Getting cold out here."

Her eyes opened and looked back up at him, questioning, but she slipped her arms into the shirt readily enough. She didn't bother buttoning

279

it up, so his hopes of being less distracted were minimalized, but at least it was better than nothing. She shifted her gaze to the first aid kit in his hand and nodded before extending her slim leg out to the side for him to work on.

He felt his mouth go dry at the view the movement gave him, then put it out of his mind and bent to his task. He untied the strips of cloth as gently as he could, wincing himself as he heard each sharp intake of breath she made, then carefully peeled them away and studied the wound again. It was still bleeding, but not as badly as it had been, it seemed. From the way the cloth stuck to her skin as he pulled it away, he was fairly confident that it was beginning to clot. That was good; at least she wouldn't bleed to death before he could get her to a hospital for proper care.

He pulled out the little bottle of peroxide and gave her a sheepish look. "This is probably going to hurt, but it needs to be cleaned. I'm sorry."

Another of those single nods.

He sighed, took the cap off, and dumped the liquid onto her leg. It began bubbling up immediately, sending pinkish runners of partially congealed blood streaming down her thigh. Her breathing grew harder and more frequent, coming out as a pant, mixed with a low whine that was nearly enough to break his heart. He knew he was only doing what he had to do, but it still bothered him to think he was hurting her more than he already had.

He took one of the gauze pads from the kit, tore it open, and used it to clean the edges of the wound. After wiping most of the dried blood away, it didn't look nearly as bad. As he thought, the bullet had passed straight through; painful, he was sure, but she should live, provided it didn't get infected. He nodded to himself and gently turned her leg so he could get to the matching hole on the other side. He poured the rest of the peroxide over it, then cleaned it with a fresh gauze pad before evaluating it as well. As with the first, it didn't look as bad as he'd feared.

He opened up a couple more gauze pads and taped them down with the roll of medical tape in the kit. When he was done, he sat back and looked up at her again. She was studying his handiwork, a look of satisfaction on her face.

"It's not much," he said. "But it should help until I can get you to a hospital. Just give me a minute to catch my breath and we'll head out."

She nodded and looked over to him. "You helped me. Thank you."

He couldn't help but smile. Her voice was low, and thick with an accent he couldn't immediately place, but she'd finally decided to talk to him. He wondered briefly whether or not she knew he'd been the one to hurt her in the first place, then remembered he'd dropped the rifle when he'd first noticed her. He doubted that she'd ever even seen it, which meant she might not realize that her savior was the same person as her attacker. That was good. If she didn't mention it, neither would he.

"Don't thank me yet," he said. "We've still got to get you some real medical attention. Thank me after we've managed that."

She shook her head, once, firmly, the same way she nodded agreement. "No. It will heal."

Ronnie wished he could place that accent. Slavic, maybe? Her skin seemed to have a slight olive tint to it, but that could be just a trick of the dim lighting around them.

"I appreciate your confidence, but I really think we should…."

"No," she said again, more firmly this time. "It will heal. You will help it."

She seemed convinced, so he didn't bother trying to change her mind. "Now that you're talking, do you have a name?"

"Katya," she said. She was looking at him intently now, and Ronnie had the distinct impression she was actually looking for something in particular, though what that could be he had no idea. "You will help me again, now."

Before he knew what was happening or had a chance to respond, Katya crossed the small space between them and straddled him, knees pressed firmly against the outsides of his thighs, hands gently pressing on his shoulders, forcing him to lie back. His face went red as he realized that as hard as she was pressing herself against him, there would be no way she wouldn't notice the erection forming in his pants. Then again, considering what she was doing, she probably wouldn't mind all that much.

She lowered her head and began to lick at his ear and the side of his neck. Ronnie felt a shudder run through him. This was far from his first time, but something about the primal way she was lapping at him, unmindful of the sweat and grime that surely had accumulated over the course of the day, made the experience more erotic than anything he'd ever experienced before. Enjoyable as it was, though, she had just been seriously injured, and he didn't want to be responsible for making that injury worse than it already was.

Especially since he'd been the one to cause it in the first place.

"Look," he said, struggling to form coherent thoughts as she pressed her warm body against his chest. "I don't know if you should be doing this. I mean, you're hurt, and I really think you should…."

"You will help it," she said into his ear. "You hurt me, now you help me."

Ronnie felt his blood run cold, his excitement over what was happening vanishing in a heartbeat. She knew.

"For that," she went on, her voice strangely rough and melodic at once. "You will go quickly. I will try to be gentle."

She leaned back, and Ronnie blinked at the change he saw in her. Her face had elongated, her shoulders broadening as she stretched. Her fingers looked like they were longer, too. In the firelight, he could see faint

281

pink splotches on her chest, running down from her breasts to just above her belly, just visible in the opening of the shirt she wore. If he didn't know any better, he would almost swear they looked like additional nipples, but that wasn't possible. Couldn't be possible.

When she lowered her head again, Ronnie thought for sure that his mind must have snapped. He didn't think he was all that drunk, but there was no other way to explain the way her hair had expanded across her cheeks and forehead, framing eyes that glowed a bright yellow in the firelight, or the way her mouth and nose had elongated, highlighting a set of long, and very sharp-looking teeth. A soft chuffing sound escaped that terrible maw, and he had the acute sense that she was laughing at him.

He tried to sit up, to push her off of him so he could either fight back or run, but her thighs clenched, holding him in place with a grip that felt as strong as steel. She pushed him back down again, and he finally noticed the tops of her hands were now covered in a fur the same dark shade as the hair on her head, the nails extended to needle-sharp claws. She threw back her head and howled, the sound nearly rupturing his eardrums as it echoed throughout the forest.

The thought that things couldn't possibly get any worse passed through his mind, and then he heard the additional howls in response coming from all around him and realized that despite her promise to make it fast, the worst was yet to come.

BIO: John Quick has been reading and writing scary and disturbing stuff for as long as he can remember, and has only recently begun releasing some of his creations upon the world. His debut novel, *Consequences* is available now as a paperback or digital eBook, and his second, *The Journal of Jeremy Todd*, is scheduled for release from Sinister Grin Press in 2017. He lives in Middle Tennessee with his wife, two kids, and three dogs that think they're kids. When he's not hard at work on his next novel, you can find him online athttp://www.facebook.com/johnquickbooks, on Twitter @johndquick, or http://johnquickauthor.blogspot.com.

THE MONSTER WITHIN

KAT GRACEY

"Hey, jerk wad, what are you doing here?" Brandon said, thumping Tyler in the back. Tyler stumbled forward, spilling his drink on the floor.

"I was invited," he muttered, using a napkin to wipe the beer off his hand.

"I don't think so, loser. Who the hell would invite you to the party of the year?" Brandon sneered.

Tyler pulled a crumpled flyer from his jeans pocket and held it out. "It says all seniors are invited. I'm a senior."

Brandon snatched the flyer from him, crumpled it into a ball and threw it across the room. He shoved Tyler back until he hit the island in the middle of the kitchen.

"This is my girlfriend's house. And I'm telling you that you are not on the guest list."

Tyler shrank away from him, probably waiting for the next hit. Brandon wasn't afraid to use his fists to make a point. He had serious anger issues.

"Leave him alone, Brandon," I said. Brandon looked surprised to find me standing on the other side of the island. And why not, I spent most of my life being invisible to everyone including my own brother.

"Piss off, Natalie. Why the hell are you here too?" he said.

"Because Stacey invited me," I replied. Stacey was his girlfriend Lisa's younger sister and my friend. I didn't want to come to this stupid party, but Stacey insisted. She was determined to bag herself a senior. She was crazy; there was no way any of the senior boys would be interested in a sophomore.

"I think it's time you left," Brandon said to Tyler.

"Brandon, stop being a total dick," I said.

He shot me a glare. "Defending your boyfriend, are you?"

I felt my face heat up. "Shut up. Why don't you go back to drinking yourself into oblivion and leave me alone."

He opened his mouth to say something when Lisa's whiny voice cut through the air, "Brandon. Where are you?"

285

"Coming," he yelled. He gave Tyler another shove before disappearing back into the living room.

"What an asshole. I'm still hoping he was adopted," I said, "Or that I was."

Tyler attempted to smile, but I could tell he was embarrassed by the whole thing. Brandon was always picking on someone, but he took a special interest in Tyler. I lost count of the amount of times I saw Brandon shoving him, punching him or tripping him in the hall at school. Brandon was a grade A dick, I couldn't understand the hate he had for people. Guess it was part of being popular. If that was the case, I was happy to remain an invisible loser.

Tyler drank the rest of his beer. "I should probably go."

"Don't let him chase you away. Give him half an hour and he'll be passed out on the couch."

Tyler smiled at me. "Thanks, Natalie."

I took a sip of my own drink, just a Coke, hoping he didn't think that I did it because I liked him. He was a nice guy, but not my type. He was tall with sandy colored hair and brown eyes and he was the most awkward person I knew. Even the way he held himself was awkward. Not that I was supermodel status myself, far from it. Stacey called me a plain Jane. And I agreed with her. She was always trying to give me a makeover, but I wasn't interested.

"Look on the bright side, only six more months of high school and you're free of him," I said.

"Yeah, knowing my luck though, we'll end up in the same dorm room."

"I wouldn't worry about that, he told Mom the other day that he wants to skip college. She wasn't too happy about that."

"What about you? What do you plan on doing?" he asked.

"I have a while to go yet, but I'd like to be a vet."

"Yeah, you like animals?"

I nodded, "I was always bringing home strays as a kid. Mom hated it, but I call it work experience."

Tyler chuckled. He poured himself another beer, offering me one. I shook my head.

"I don't know why I came here in the first place. I guess it was a better option than sitting at home alone."

"Where's your parents?" I asked.

A dark look crossed his face and I regretted asking, "Forget it," I said.

"No, it's fine. Mom is away and my dad cut out on us when I was a kid."

"Sorry," I muttered.

Stacey came bouncing into the kitchen, her blonde hair styled to perfection; she wore a tight black dress that she had no doubt swiped from Lisa's wardrobe.

"Oh my God, Luke actually spoke to me," she said. Luke was Brandon's friend. There were four of them altogether, the other two being Shane and Tom. They were like a pack of wild animals, constantly preying on the weak. I couldn't believe that Stacey was interested in one of them.

"What did he say?" I asked.

"He asked me to get him another beer," she said, grabbing one from the cooler.

I rolled my eyes, *what a riveting conversation.*

"Stace, don't you think you would be better off maybe..." she had already left the room.

She was hopeless. Why were we even friends? We had nothing in common.

After Tyler finished his current beer, he said, "I'm going to go. It was nice talking to you."

"You too."

Brandon appeared behind him, "You're leaving?"

"Yes, okay. You've made your point," Tyler said.

Brandon laughed, "Come on, I was just kidding around. The guys and I were talking and we're going on a beer run. You should come with us."

He had a hand clamped on Tyler's shoulder. To an outsider it looked friendly enough, but I could see Tyler wince under his grip.

"Brandon," I warned.

"Relax, we're pals now. Aren't we?" he said to Tyler.

Tyler nodded.

"Good, so let's go."

He slung his arm around Tyler's shoulders and led him from the room. What were they up to now?

A few minutes later, Stacey came back into the kitchen looking frustrated, "Luke is away off with the guys to the quarry."

"The quarry? Brandon said they were going on a beer run."

Stacey shrugged, "You know how much they love that place."

I did. In fact, they loved it so much that last year they took a guy called Lester out there, stripped him naked, and left him to walk home. It was a cold night outside; if they did the same to Tyler he would end up with hypothermia.

"Stacey, can I borrow the keys to your car?" I asked. Stacey was a few months older than me and her parents had already given her a car. A Fiat 500.

"You don't have a license yet," she pointed out.

"I'll be careful. Please," I said.

Narrowing her eyes at me, she handed the keys over, "What are you up to?"

"I just need to go and check on something. I promise I won't hurt your precious car."

The quarry was a few miles outside the edge of town. It was a good place to drink or get high without getting caught.

Worried that I would in fact damage Stacey's Fiat, I drove along the road at around fifteen miles an hour. My uncle taught me how to drive when I was fifteen, but I was still nervous. The road out to the quarry was deserted. A full moon had risen overhead and it was a clear night. When I finally reached the quarry, I found two trucks already parked up top. One was Brandon's. I think the other one belonged to Shane.

Stopping the car, I left the headlights on for some light and got out. As I walked toward the quarry edge, I spotted someone heading my way. As he stepped into the light, I realized it was Tyler. And that they had done exactly what I thought they would. Stripped him naked.

I quickly turned my head away, but not before I got the full frontal. Okay, so maybe he wasn't entirely *awkward.*

Face burning, I stared at the ground. "Tyler? Are you okay?"

He stopped a few feet from me, "Natalie? What are you doing here?" he said, sounding confused and out of it. I wondered if they had gotten him drunk first.

"I came to check on you. I'm sorry, Brandon and the guys are assholes."

I chanced a look, keeping my eyes on his face. His head was bent as he seemed to realize that he was naked. When he looked up I could see that there was dried blood on his face, around his mouth and nose. They must have hit him too.

"I'll check the trunk of Stacey's car. She might have something to cover you with," I said, running back to the car. I found a wool blanket folded up in the trunk.

"This will do," I said, closing the trunk. Tyler was gone. Turning on the spot, I searched for him, but he had disappeared.

He must have been embarrassed and ran off. Embarrassed or not, he would freeze out here.

"Tyler!" I yelled. "Where are you?"

A hand clamped down on my shoulder and I screamed. It wasn't Tyler behind me though, it was Shane. His face was ashen and he looked terrified.

"Get off me," I said, shaking his hand off. "What the hell are you guys playing at?"

"It killed them," he whispered.

"What?"

"An animal, it was huge," he said. Then he dropped to his knees and slumped forward onto the ground. When I saw the deep claw marks in his back, I started screaming again. Dropping the blanket, I ran to the car and jumped inside. I was shaking so much that I couldn't get the key in the ignition.

Shane was dead. And he said that something had attacked them? *Brandon?*

He was a jerk, but he was still my brother. I started the car and took a side road that led down into the quarry. It was barely even a road and I was worried that the Fiat would get stuck, but there was no way I was walking down there.

I managed to get down in one piece. I could see a campfire up ahead. Approaching it slowly, I turned on the high beams.

Scattered around the fire were the remains of my brother and his friends. Thick pools of blood soaked the ground, there were *parts* lying in the dirt. I could see a severed arm and a string of intestines. And right next to the flames, as if on display, was Brandon's head. His mouth was open and his eyes were gone.

Bile rose in my throat and I vomited over myself. They were dead. They were all dead. I felt like I couldn't breathe, this couldn't be real. It had to be Brandon playing a trick.

A piercing howl ripped through the air, almost stopping my heart. I looked up to the top of the quarry. Something was there. Something big and covered in fur. It threw its head back and howled again.

Throwing the car into reverse, I slammed my foot into the accelerator. I spun the car, not bothering to slow down and headed back to the side road. The Fiat struggled as I started to climb. I kept the pedal pressed to the floor. If the car couldn't get back up then I was a sitting duck.

"Please, come on," I sobbed.

The car began to roll back down the hill. "No! Oh God, please," I cried.

At the last second, the tires gained some traction and it jerked forward. I reached the top of the hill. As I passed the trucks, I saw a flash of fur in the side mirror. Looking over my shoulder, I saw that the creature had dropped to all fours and it was chasing me. What the hell was it? And how was it able to run so fast?

The car veered wildly as it slammed into the side of it. Pushing the car as hard as I could, I managed to get ahead of the creature and back to the main road. It dropped behind and eventually out of sight.

I headed for the police station. Parking the car on the curb, I ran inside.

"Help me! They're all dead," I screamed.

A policewoman rushed forward. "Calm down, honey. Tell me what's happened."

"It killed them. A monster out at the quarry, it killed my brother and his friends."

I collapsed to the floor, sobbing.

***

It had been two weeks since the deaths of Brandon and his friends. The town was in shock and a curfew had been issued for everyone. No one believed my story about the monster, why would they? The police believed it was a bear or rabid wolf, although they couldn't explain how it could have done all that damage. I heard them talking with my Mom, about me being traumatized.

Damn right I was traumatized. I hadn't slept at all since that night.

Today was my brother's funeral. The whole day had been a blur and I had finally escaped the surge of family members and well-wishers to sit out on the back porch. I didn't venture too far from the house these days. Not alone anyway.

"Natalie?"

I looked up to find Tyler dressed in a badly fitted suit. I hadn't seen him at the church.

"Hey. You got home okay? The other night?" I'd forgotten all about him after…

He nodded, "Yeah, I'm fine. I wanted to see how you were."

I shrugged, "I'm fine."

He crouched beside my chair, "How could you be fine after all you've been through?" he said softly.

A sob escaped me and he took my hand.

"I just keep seeing it. It won't go away."

"It'll get easier. You just need to give it time," he said.

"You were lucky to get out of there when you did. Otherwise you could have been killed too," I said.

"Yeah," he murmured.

"Did you see it?" I asked.

"No, I didn't see anything. Brandon forced me to drink half a bottle of whiskey. I had no idea what was going on. What would happen."

He stood up. "If you need someone to talk to, I'm here."

"Thank you," I said. He didn't have to come here after what Brandon did, but he still came.

Bracing myself, I went back inside the house.

***

"No!" I cried, leaping up in bed. I switched the light on beside my bed, searching the shadows for that thing. The room was empty, it was just another nightmare. I had been asleep for less than an hour.

Mom had started taking sleeping tablets to help her. Maybe I should do it too. Anything was better than lying in the dark, waiting for it to come and get me.

I went downstairs for a glass of water. The kitchen was piled high with casseroles and pies. There was enough food to last us for the next month. The thought of food turned my stomach though. I would take a few bites out of my dinner and leave the rest.

Stacey commented that I was well on my way to a size zero, something she seemed quite pleased about. I told her to go to hell. I couldn't stand being around her anymore. She was such a vain, superficial bitch. Mom had retreated into herself, leaving me with no one to talk to.

On a whim, I grabbed my phone and dialed Tyler's number.

"Hello?" he said, sounding half asleep. It didn't even occur to me to check the time. It was well after midnight.

"Uh, Tyler? It's me. Sorry, I shouldn't have called this late." I felt like an idiot.

"Natalie? It's fine. Are you okay?"

"I just…I couldn't sleep and needed someone to talk to."

He was probably only being polite the other day when he offered.

"I can be over in fifteen minutes," he said.

"Oh, I…" but he had already hung up. I didn't expect him to come to the house.

Hurrying back upstairs, I pulled on some clothes. Dragging a brush through my hair, I put on some lip gloss too.

What the hell am I doing? I wondered. He was coming over to offer moral support; we weren't going on a date!

Wiping the gloss off, I went back downstairs. When his car pulled up, I slipped outside. I didn't want Mom to hear us, although I doubted anything would wake her, so I got into the car.

"You really didn't have to come over," I said.

"You need to talk. It's easier to do face to face."

"I guess. I haven't been sleeping. I keep having these nightmares, where that…creature, is in my room, waiting to tear me apart."

"Creature? I thought it was a bear?"

"Promise you won't laugh at me?" I asked. I had to tell someone about it.

"I would never laugh at you," he said.

"The thing that killed Brandon. I saw it. And it wasn't a bear."

"Then what was it?"

"I don't know. Definitely not anything natural. It sort of looked like a wolf, but it was huge and it could stand on its hind legs."

He was silent and I wished I could see his face. He probably thought I was nuts.

"I believe you," he said finally.

"You do?"

"Yes, I mean scientists are finding new animals every day. This could be something no one has seen before."

"I guess, but I got the feeling that it was something more."

"More?"

"It was…I know it sounds stupid, but I think it was evil."

"Natalie, I know it might seem that way. But animals aren't good or evil. They just do what comes naturally to them."

"I know that. I know. But you weren't there."

"You know what you need? To get out of your own head for a while. How about we go out? Tomorrow night, or tonight really, considering what time it is."

"Are you asking me out?" I didn't mean to sound so surprised.

"Well, I mean only if you want to," he stuttered slipping back into his awkward self.

"As friends?" I said.

"Of course. Friends."

***

Tyler picked me up that evening. It was still light out, which was the main reason I felt comfortable going out.

"Where are we going?" I asked.

"Where do you want to go?"

"Somewhere with a lot of people," I said.

"Oh," he said.

"No, I just prefer it if there were a lot of people around. I don't like going out, since…"

He nodded. "I understand. Let's get something to eat in town."

We went to a small barbecue place called The Pit. Tyler kept asking if I was okay the whole time, especially when I kept jumping at every loud noise.

"We can go if you want?" Tyler said.

"No, it's okay. I'm sorry I'm ruining this."

He gave my hand a squeeze, "You're not ruining anything."

I managed to eat some of my meal, then put my napkin over the rest so Tyler wouldn't see that I had left most of it. He was tucking into some ribs.

"How's your mom?" Tyler asked.

"She doesn't really talk to me much. She was the same after my dad left."

292

"I'm sorry."

"This is nice. You were right, it feels good to do something normal for a while."

He smiled at me, "I told you."

Tyler insisted on paying for the meal. It was like being on a real date. Glancing over at Tyler on the way back, I wondered if that was a bad thing.

Instead of going back to the house right away, we went to a small park a few blocks from my house.

The sun was starting to set, but Tyler didn't seem worried.

"The curfew is soon," I said.

"I know, I thought we could take a walk. Just for a few minutes."

"I-I don't know," I said.

"You don't have to be afraid to go outside. I wouldn't let anything happen to you," he said.

"Okay, just for a few minutes."

I followed him to a small fountain in the middle of the park. We took a seat on the edge of it. I kept glancing around me every few seconds.

"Just breathe. There's nothing here that can hurt you," Tyler said.

I tried to calm my racing heart, but it wasn't easy. It was hard to believe that I would ever feel safe again.

A yell from a house nearby almost give me a heart attack. I leapt up, ready to run. A man came pelting out of his house, a few yards from us.

"They got it," he crowed.

"Got what?" Tyler called to him.

"The bear that attacked those kids. It's huge, apparently. They've got it in the town square," the man called as he jumped into his truck.

Tyler shot a worried glance my way, "Do you want me to take you home?"

"No. I want to see it," I said.

"You don't need to do that," Tyler said.

"I have to. Let's go."

I got back into his car. Whatever they had shot, I needed to see it, to be sure.

Tyler drove us into town where quite a crowd had gathered. A group of men stood with guns, wearing hi-vis vests. Hunters. They had come out in force recently.

I got out of the car and pushed my way through the people. When they saw that it was me, several of them moved out of my way. Lying on the ground, was a mangled mess of fur and blood. It looked like the hunters had emptied every round they had into it and then reloaded. I'd never really seen a bear up close. I saw one, at a distance, on a camping trip once, but this one was a lot bigger.

I felt Tyler's hand on my shoulder, "Well?"

"I don't know. It looks different, I can't be sure."

"A lot was happening that night. You were in shock, it's not unusual for people to imagine…"

"I didn't imagine it," I snapped.

"I didn't mean it like that," he said.

With a final look at the bear, I went back to the car. I wanted to go home, where I felt relatively safe.

As Tyler pulled up outside the house, he said, "I'm sorry if I upset you."

"It's okay. I just wanted this to be over."

"It is over."

I hoped he was right.

***

News spread quickly about the bear and the curfew was lifted. I couldn't believe how easy it was for everyone to go back to normal after four teenagers were killed. Didn't they matter? Everyone was moving on. Mom even suggested that I should go back to school. I didn't think I could face it. People staring at me, whispering. It made me wish I was invisible again.

Tyler kept calling me to check if I was okay. It was sweet of him, I don't know why he cared. He asked me to go out with him again. I was hesitating about texting him back.

Mom wandered into the room like a zombie. She lifted her bottle of sleeping pills and shambled out again. She barely spoke at all anymore.

Pick me up in an hour. I texted Tyler.

I couldn't sit in here anymore. Despite what my mind had conjured up, the animal I saw had to be the bear. Hunters had been through every inch of the forest and there was nothing else in there.

Before I left the house, I grabbed a bottle of whiskey that Mom kept under the sink. I took a couple mouthfuls of it and put the rest in my purse.

"Where do you want to go?" Tyler asked as I got into the car.

"Anywhere."

"Well we could grab dinner…"

"No, let's go somewhere else. Where we can be alone."

His eyes widened, "Um, well, my Mom is out of town."

I nodded, "Perfect."

A few more slugs of whiskey and I was starting to relax. I offered the bottle to Tyler, but he pulled a face and shook his head.

"I don't really have a taste for it anymore," he said.

I remembered that Brandon had force fed him it.

"More for me," I muttered, starting to get a buzz.

294

Tyler's house was down near the ravine. His house was the last one on the block. The house was small and tidy, but it smelled musty. Tyler led me through and out into the back yard. He had a tent set up in the yard.

"I like to sleep outside most nights," he said.

"Why?"

"I don't know. I like it out here. It's quiet."

"And cold," I said, rubbing my arms.

"I'll light a fire," he said. I sat on a fold down chair as he lit a small campfire. I sipped on my whiskey. The yard was surrounded by a low wooden fence and beyond that were some trees. A breeze was blowing and I pulled my jacket tighter around me.

When he got the fire going, Tyler took a seat beside me.

"What does your mom do?" I asked.

"Mostly she drives to bars and shacks up with guys for a few days before she comes back."

"Oh, sorry," I muttered. I thought she was working or something.

"Guess we both have messed up families," he said.

"Yeah." I didn't have much of one left.

I had almost finished the bottle of whiskey. Leaning back in the chair, I stared up at the sky and the full moon shinning down on us.

"I can't believe it's been a month already," I said.

"It will get easier. The memory will fade."

"I hope so."

I finished the whiskey, "So are you going to kiss me or are we going to look at the stars all night?"

He turned so fast to look at me that his chair tipped sideways, sending him onto the ground. I started laughing and found it hard to stop. Embarrassed, he picked himself up.

"Sorry, that was just so funny," I said, doubled over.

He started to laugh himself, "I'm not always such a klutz."

I finally got a hold of myself when he leaned in and kissed me. After a few seconds he stopped.

"Are you sure about this?" he asked.

I nodded, "Yes."

Grinning, he kissed me again. Overexcited, I felt him bite my lip.

"Ow," I said.

"I'm sorry, I didn't mean to," he stammered.

I wiped at my lip, "Its fine, it's just a nip."

He put his head in his hands, "What am I doing?"

"Forget about it," I said.

He stood up and moved over the fire, the light throwing weird shadows on his face.

"I have to tell you something, Natalie."

Oh, God, he's going to tell me he's not interested in me, I thought.

295

"Look, I like you a lot. I've never felt this way about anyone. For a long time I've been searching for the right person. Someone I could call a mate."

"A mate? So you want us to be friends? Because I thought this was going somewhere else."

My lip was starting to itch; I rubbed at it, but the feeling spread up my cheek.

He carried on as though he hadn't heard me, "You don't know what it's like being trapped like this. As a gawky teenager when I know I'm so much more."

"Tyler, what are you talking about?" I asked. I was having trouble concentrating. I felt woozy from the drink and my whole body was starting to tingle now. Was I having an allergic reaction to something?

"I hate being a target. Brandon and the guys, they kept pushing. It's hard enough holding it in, but on the night of the full moon, the way they were acting? I couldn't help myself."

"What are you saying?" I asked.

He turned to look at me, "I'm sorry, Natalie. I never meant to hurt you, but your brother got what he deserved."

Frozen in place, I desperately hoped that I had misheard him. Was he actually saying..?

I got up from the chair and backed away.

"You had blood on you. I thought you got hit, but it wasn't your blood, was it?"

He shook his head, "No. They wouldn't let up. I lost control."

"What about the creature I saw?"

He held out his arms and I heard bones popping. His eyes glowed with an inner light and I screamed. He was the creature, the monster I saw. It was real. This whole time I thought he was a nice, normal guy but he had just been hiding the monster within.

I turned and ran, vaulting the fence and heading down to the ravine. I tripped over a branch and rolled down the hill, coming to a stop at the base of a tree.

Dazed, I lay there trying to get the strength to stand. My head was spinning, my whole body felt like it was on fire. What the hell was happening to me?

Tyler came toward me and I began to crawl through the dead leaves.

"Don't fight it, Natalie," he said.

"Leave me alone," I screeched.

"It's going to hurt at first, but that will pass," he said.

I rolled onto my back, "What are you going to do to me?" I sobbed.

"It's already done," he said, tapping his lip. Confused, I ran my tongue over the cut on my lip.

"What have you done?" I whispered.

He crouched beside me, "What do you have here, really? Family? Friends? There is no one worth sticking around for. We can go away together, just you and me."

I felt something snap in my back and screamed in pain.

"I don't want to be a monster," I cried.

"I'm not a monster. I'm just…different. Once you change and feel it for yourself, you'll realize that this is a gift."

My arm bone snapped, followed by one of my legs. Why couldn't anyone hear me screaming? I felt my body change, through the pain I could tell I was stronger now.

"What are you?" I whispered as I started to lose consciousness.

"A werewolf."

My entire body bent back on itself and I was gone.

BIO: Kat Gracey is an urban fantasy writer from Northern Ireland. She has been a full time writer for the last five years and writes about witches and werewolves. You can check out her website at witchesandwerewolves.co.uk.

SCAT

ASH HARTWELL

"What the fuck is that?" Scarlett stood up and peered over her shoulder, trying to identify what she'd just sat in.

"Scat." Lowell took the opportunity to stare at her cute, bikini-clad buttocks.

"What?" She wiped her hand across the tight, white material, dislodging a dark clump of dry scat.

"Animal shit. Probably wolf, looking at it," Lowell couldn't help laughing as he spoke.

"Wha... Eww, gross." Scarlett looked at the hand she'd just rubbed across her bikini briefs. "Eww, Grosser. I think I'm gonna hurl." She half skipped to the water's edge a few yards away and sank into a crouch, washing her hands in the lagoon's clear water.

Lowell admired her body from his supine position farther up the tiny beach-like inlet, shielding his eyes against the setting sun which was fast disappearing behind the wall of tall pine trees on the far side of the lagoon. She was beautiful, gracefully athletic and intelligent enough to realise the power this gave her, yet so humble and unassuming she never consciously used it to her advantage. A trait that only added to her appeal as it gave her a subtle, old-fashioned innocence so lacking in her generation as a whole, and yet, to Lowell at least, so desirable.

Scarlett finished washing her hands and stood up, turning towards Lowell. As she reached up to refasten the hairband keeping her long hair – dyed gothically black – out of her piercing green eyes, her vest top rode up, exposing her taught and naturally tanned midriff. She stopped in her tracks, arms above her head, and said, "What ya doing? You're staring at me like some creepy weirdo."

Lowell quickly looked away. "Sorry, I... I was miles away, lost in my own little world." He'd known Scarlett for almost a year but never had the courage to tell her how he felt, besides, until a few weeks ago, she and Gary Kozlowski were the hottest couple on campus. That was until he dumped her on the eve of the Summer Ball for Rachael 'BJ' Simpson. Her friends had invited her on this short camping trip to take her mind off

Scumbag Kozlowski, and as cruel fate, or well-meaning collusion, would have it, Lowell was also invited. And now here he was, alone with the girl of his dreams beside a lagoon at sunset — and she thought he was a creepy weirdo.

Way to go, Dumbass! He made a mental note to bang his head against a wall the next time the opportunity arose.

"Do you mind if we don't go back to the others just yet?" Scarlett pulled her baggy, navy coloured sweatshirt over her head and rolled it down her body before continuing, "It's a full moon tonight and the lagoon will look so beautiful in the moonlight."

When Lowell didn't reply, she mistook his euphoric silence for reticence. "Pleeease," she added, flinging herself onto the blanket next to him, a cartoon-style grin spread across her delicate features.

Lowell decided to play this for all it was worth. "I don't know, Scarlett. It will be dark soon and the others will worry. What if we lose our way in the woods?"

Scarlett remained silent. The sun finally dipped out of sight, the last rays dancing briefly on the water's surface before a dark veil crept across the lagoon, casting everything into darkness. A breeze, chilled by the night, ruffled her hair and brought goose bumps to his exposed skin. Lowell feared he'd pushed it too far.

After a while, Scarlett's darkened silhouette moved closer to him and he felt the warmth of her breath on his neck as she whispered in his ear, "Don't fuck with me, Lowell. I know you want to stay here as much as I do. Just think of me, all scared in the dark, needing a strong man to save me from the wild beasts."

Lowell felt a warm flush radiate up his face and was glad his obviously reddened features were obscured by the darkness. He swallowed hard, unsure if his voice would betray him. "I'm not fucking with you. We really should be going back." His voice was strong and confident, with none of the expected nervous croaks and squeaks.

If he was honest, he knew they should be heading back. Camp was a mile upstream, the narrow path taking them over slippery outcrops of rock and several areas where the water had eroded the bank right up to the path, not to mention the overhanging branches and often dense foliage. It would be a treacherous journey to make now the sun had set.

But to Hell with honesty. Scarlett. Sizzling fucking hot, Scarlett, wanted to stay by the lagoon… in the moonlight… with him. He turned his head and peered through the gloom at her face, trying to tell if she was winding him up. It had to be a joke, the others, no doubt lurking in the bushes, ready to jump out and have a good laugh at his expense. They all knew he had a massive crush on her; it would be just like them to tell her.

Scarlett's face had been veiled in shadow, her features hidden from him, but now the moon broke through the clouds, bathing her slightly

300

upturned face in silvery light. There was no trace of mirth in her eyes, just an intensity that made him feel uncomfortable, as if she were scrutinising his thoughts, splaying open his soul, and exposing his innermost emotions.

The clouds passed across the moon, plunging them back into darkness. Lowell wished she would speak — the silence was torturous. He heard the rustle of her clothing and caught a gentle waft of coconut suntan lotion and floral perfume, then her shadow loomed out of the darkness towards him, catching him off guard. His natural instinct was to turn away but her hand wrapped round the back of his neck, holding him still.

Then her soft lips were on his, drawing him into a kiss, tentative at first but then, as he began to respond, with more urgency and passion. After what to Lowell was an exquisite glimpse of paradise, Scarlett pulled away. She giggled nervously, "Wow!"

"What... I... I don't understand? Why wo... Why would you... do that?" Lowell stammered, his brow furrowed in confusion.

"I didn't mean it earlier when I said you were a weirdo. In fact, I didn't actually say you were a weirdo, just like a creepy weirdo. Not that you are like a creepy weirdo, I mean... Oh shit, I'm jabbering like some geeky virgin." She leant in again.

"Wait!" Lowell eased her away. "Are you making fun of me? 'Cos if you are that's fuckin' mean." He glanced around the small beach-like clearing, looking for the others, but it was too dark to make out anything apart from the general shape of the nearest trees.

Scarlett looked at him for a second then burst out laughing, "You think I spent all afternoon here with you, alone, just to pull some horrible prank?"

"Well... I don't know. You've never shown any interest in me... not in that way." The moon broke through again as he spoke.

"I was with that lowlife, two-timing bastard, Gary. Besides, you never asked me." Scarlett shrugged, coyly pushing a few strands of loose hair back behind her ear, "Why was that?"

"Because you were with that lowlife, two-timing bastard, and I thought you'd laugh at me. I'm not exactly one of the 'in' crowd and you are smart, sexy, and popular... way out of my league." Lowell still expected the others to jump out any second.

"It doesn't matter to me you're not in the popular group. You're fit, in both senses. Quiet, which I happen to like by-the-way, and respectful — even if you did stare at my tits most of the afternoon."

Lowell looked away, that telltale burn of embarrassment sweeping across his face, and mumbled apologetically, "I... I... Sorry."

"Don't be, you were meant to. I noticed you the first day of school, sat in Professor William's lecture. But I could never get you to notice me and thought you weren't interested. So I took Kozlowski up on his offer — he seemed sweet at the time — it was only when he dumped me that Claire

301

explained how you felt." Scarlett took his hand in hers, "I'm not fuckin' with you. I honestly want to get to know you, spend some time with you, that's why we're here. That's why we're alone."

"I thought it was odd no one else came to the lagoon." Then the penny dropped and Lowell added, "Those bastards all know, don't they?"

Scarlett smiled and nodded vigorously, "I'm afraid so."

He laughed self-consciously, "But I got the girl, so I guess it doesn't really matter." He squeezed her hand and she laid her head on his shoulder.

They sat in silence for a while, just watching the moonlight glint off the water's surface, before Scarlett said with a shiver, "I'm getting cold. Maybe we should head back." She kissed him on the cheek and jumped up, grabbing her jeans which she quickly pulled on while Lowell folded up the blanket, stuffing it into a large beach bag.

"Might be a good idea," said Lowell with a soft laugh. "I wouldn't like to meet the wolf that left the scat you sat in, he must be fuckin' huge." He took her hand and led her up the short, root-strewn slope to the narrow path that wound its way through the woods to the small clearing where they'd set up camp.

Lowell was glad when the clouds cleared a little, allowing at least some moonlight to penetrate the dark canopy above their heads, illuminating the pathway. At one point, he tripped over a small rock that protruded from the flattened path, nearly pulling Scarlett over with him, then, to compound his embarrassment, he caught his foot in a rabbit hole, rolling his ankle. Luckily, he'd done no real damage, although his macho pride took a beating when his surprisingly surefooted new girlfriend — he still couldn't believe she liked him — offered to carry the beach bag for him.

In the distance a wolf howled. Scarlett tightened her grip on his hand. He gave her hand a gentle squeeze and said, with what he hoped was reassuring confidence, "It's only some wild dog. Ignore what I said back there about the scat, wolves are rare in this area."

Scarlett flashed him a nervous smile, and replied in a hoarse whisper, "I hope that's true. It seemed awfully close!"

"It'll be cool. The night air makes it sound closer than it is and we'll be back in camp in a few minutes." Lowell quickened his pace and hoped Scarlett didn't notice. His theories on sound waves and the night air were, at best, sketchy and his knowledge of local wolf populations amounted to a steaming pile of...well, scat! Scarlett's fear, the darkness, and the proximity of at least one wolf — he was pretty sure they hunted in packs — were all beginning to have an effect on him. He felt the tension in his neck and shoulders, his mouth was dry, and his heart pounded loud in his ears. He knew it was a simple hormonal reaction to a perceived threat, the consequence of adrenaline coursing through his veins, preparing his body for action. But in that moment it didn't matter.

He felt scared!

Through the trees he made out the flickering flame of a campfire, the sweet, smoky smell of burning pine assailed his nostrils. He looked back at Scarlett, forcing a smile. She was staring at the distant fire, the yellow flames dancing in her eyes. "Nearly there," he whispered, more for his own benefit than hers.

Another howl broke the silence. It was closer this time, much closer.

Lowell almost dragged Scarlett through the undergrowth as he hurried towards camp.

A human scream ripped through the night. It had barely died away when another wolf howled. Lowell crashed through the bushes and out into the clearing, Scarlett a heartbeat behind him.

He stumbled to a halt just short of the tents circling the campfire and surveyed the carnage laid before him like a smorgasbord of slaughter. Scarlett, dragged downward when he stumbled, fell to the dirt at his feet.

For a moment he was too shocked to react, his eyes focused on his friend, Karl who was laid on his back in a pool of blood a few feet away. His throat had been torn open, blood soaked his torso and his head lolled at a strange angle, only held in place by a thin strip of flesh and vertebrae. Beyond Karl's crumpled body, a wolf fed from the open abdomen of his brother, Craig.

Lowell met Craig's stare and knew instinctively he wasn't dead as the wolf ripped his entrails from the open cavity, tugging his body across the ground with each torn mouthful. The wolf looked in Lowell's direction but didn't stop feeding, just uttered a low growl to warn them against trying to steal her delicious prize.

Scarlett scrambled to her feet next to him.

Spurred into action by her presence, he pulled her behind him. "Don't look!" He hissed.

She tried to evade his grasp, to witness the fate of her friends for herself.

"Don't Fuckin' look, Scarlett." He tightened his grip on her wrist and began to back away, keeping her behind him.

He kept his eyes on the wolf, trying not to look into the fire; he didn't want to ruin his night vision. As he and Scarlett circled the perimeter of the clearing, putting distance between them and the huge wolf chowing down on their friend's still warm guts, Lowell noticed Claire. She lay, sprawled face down, across a fallen log, the tattered remains of her clothes hanging from her near naked body, fresh wounds cut deep furrows in the flesh of her hips and thighs. A huge wolf-like beast stood upright on its hind legs behind her. Blood dripped from its razor-like claws, its huge erection glistening in the moonlight.

"No! Oh, my fuckin' god, no!" Lowell cried as the truth of what had just occurred dawned on him. At the sound of his voice, two things happened. Claire, whom Lowell had assumed was dead, lifted her head to look in his direction, a half-smile playing on her lips. He noticed what looked like a large circular bite mark scarred the top of her left breast. Rivulets of fresh blood still oozed from the puncture wounds inflicted by the beasts longer, pointed canines.

The second consequence of his anguished cry was far more terrifying. The she-wolf feasting on the now dead Craig looked up and fixed her large yellow eyes on Lowell's retreating form, her powerful jaws slavering with gore as she advanced a few feet towards him. The larger wolf, his animalistic desire satisfied, abandoned Claire's exposed body to take up a menacing stance, standing shoulder to shoulder with his mate a few yards in front of Lowell.

"Oh... shh...i...it." Scarlett whimpered. Lowell felt her grab a fistful of his shirt, tugging him away from the camp, away from the vicious beasts staring him down. She pushed her face against his shoulder, too afraid to look at the wolves, too scared to look at her friend's massacred bodies, and too disgusted to look at Claire, who rolled from the log to sit cross-legged by the crackling fire.

Lowell felt her body pressed against his. She was shaking, her tears dampening the arm of his shirt. He reached for her arm, trying to keep his movements unhurried, almost languid, so as not to alarm their tormentors. He rubbed her elbow gently.

"Scarlett, listen to me. We're going to have to run. Do you understand?"

She gave him a sharp nod but didn't look up.

"Keep backing slowly towards the trees. When I say *now!* Run. Don't fuckin' stop. Don't look back. Okay?" He hadn't taken his eyes off the wolves. They, in turn, hadn't taken theirs off him.

He kept shuffling backwards, Scarlett gripping his shirt. Briefly, he wondered where the others had gone. Hiding in the woods maybe? Too shit fucking scared to come out. He couldn't blame them.

The larger wolf threw his head back and howled. The sound echoed back and forth through the trees, silencing the usual nighttime woodland sounds and sending a chill down Lowell's spine. Gradually, more wolves appeared from between the surrounding trees. They too were bloodied about the mouth; one carried a severed and partially chewed arm between its teeth. It was at that moment he realised his friends weren't hiding out in the woods, that they too were innocent victims of this insatiable pack of marauding wolves.

"Scarlett?" He felt her nod. "I know this is way early, but if I don't say it to you, I won't say it to anyone." She moved her face from his shoulder and he glanced down. Tears streaked her face, but her eyes were alive with an inner fire.

"Go on." She managed to muster a weak smile.

"I love you!" He said the words with conviction, sure in the knowledge they would be his last words of note.

"I love you too." She looked genuinely happy and yet crazy at the same time. Her eyes, catching the campfire's flickering light, sparkled with excitement as she stood on tiptoe to kiss his cheek.

"Ready?" He said, trying to look brave.

"You bet!"

"Now!"

Together they turned and sprinted into the thick woods, crashing through the dense foliage with reckless abandon, running for their lives.

The wolves howled in anguish, surprise or maybe just excitement at the thrill of the chase, before leaping into the undergrowth in pursuit.

Lowell ran blindly into the night, small branches and thorny tendrils caught on his clothes or smacked against his arms and face. One snagged on his cheek, the hooked barb raking through his skin, another caught his ankle, tripping him. Off balance, he stumbled into the darkness, the excited howls of the beasts ringing in his ears.

He broke through the trees onto the narrow path and swung to his left, picking up pace on the firmer surface. For a second, Scarlett, beautiful athletic Scarlett was by his side, matching his stride, her long mane of hair trailing in her wake. Then she was gone, swallowed up by the encroaching shadows and thick bushes.

He skidded to a stop, peering into the surrounding void. "Scarlett!" He tried to whisper but he was breathing hard and the word caught in his throat coming out in a loud, strangled squawk. There was no reply, save for the fierce snarl of a wolf only a few feet away in the undergrowth.

Exasperated, tears of frustration and fear welling in his eyes, Lowell abandoned Scarlett to her fate. Hoping against hope she would somehow find a way to escape the vicious pack and make it to safety.

He ran on, legs and arms pumping, chest burning.

Still the wolves howled and bayed behind him. He could hear them crashing through the bushes, first on his left, then his right. They appeared to be toying with him, playing with their food.

Why didn't they finish him off?

Then they were gone. The howling ceased and the woods filled with an eerie silence. The beasts that moments before had thundered through the bushes, simply abandoned their pursuit. All Lowell could hear now was his own rasping breaths and the frantic, thumping beat of his heart.

He stopped running, doubling over in pain, the stitch in his side feeling like a knife slicing the flesh from his ribs. He coughed, vomited, then coughed again as he tried to suck in air to quench the burning void in his lungs.

"Lowell?"

He raised his head. *Had he heard that?*

"Lowell?" This time there was no mistaking Scarlett's voice.

"Scarlett? Where are you?" He swung round, trying to get a fix on her location.

Above him, finally, the clouds parted and weak moonlight filtered through the forest's high canopy.

"Over here. Follow my voice." Scarlett said. "I'm in a clearing just off the path." Lowell crept carefully towards her voice, pushing through the bushes. The undergrowth was less dense here, the trees further apart.

Stepping into the clearing he saw Scarlett. She was staring at him through piercing green eyes, her dark mane of shaggy hair ruffling gently in the breeze. Her clothes lay discarded on the floor, her white bikini bottoms almost luminescent in the moonlight.

With one bounding stride she was on him, her powerful forepaws knocking him to the ground, her razor-sharp teeth biting deep into his shoulder. And in that exquisite moment of release, he knew why the wolves didn't run him to ground. He was Scarlett's and Scarlett's alone.

He understood why Claire was so content following her union with the massive beast at the campsite. He'd chosen her for his own, turning her with his bite.

Lowell also realised why the pile of scat at the lagoon had been so big.

BIO: Ash Hartwell came into existence in Maine, USA but has lived in England all his life. He has had over thirty stories published in anthologies by JEA, Stitched Smile Press, Horrified Press, Old Style Press and Undead Press among others. He also released a collection of his own stories, Zombies, Vamps and Fiends thro JEA last year and his debut novel The Tip Of The Iceberg should be out late in 2016. He can be found on Facebook and twitter and at <u>Ash Hartwell | Author of horror novels</u> Enjoy your slaughter under a full moon.

ALONE WOLF

SHARON L. HIGA

The three inch claws dug into the bark of the tree, digging grooves four feet long. The bugs skittered out from the rents, giving the creature the chance to press his snout to the rips and lap up the insectile protein running around the bole.

The moon was full, the rays seeping through the burned and twisted branches of trees seen in what now passed for the world. The apocalypse had happened months earlier, and what the bombs and weapons of mass destruction did not decimate outright, it warped and distorted.

The creature had been caught during his transformation, the eye-searing blast and subsequent deafening roar engulfing him as he made a desperate attempt to outrun the all-consuming light. He made it to an old badger's den and dove in head first, pulling his legs into the damp, root entangled cave just as the evaporating wind and all-consuming blast hit his location.

He had no idea how long he lay there, only that it seemed like an eternity, his fur-covered arms firmly gripping and crushing his legs up against his chest, head buried beneath one armpit.

The silence and lightening at the den opening was what finally coaxed him out of his refuge. He almost wished he had stayed underground.

Crouched on all fours, he put his nose into the wind, lips curling back from elongated canines, scenting the air, trying to find anything familiar. The woods were gone; blackened, burned shrubs, singed grass and gnarled stumps now the only things in sight for as far as he could see.

Giving into his fear, he howled;

AAAARRRROOOOOWWWWW!

then held his breath, waiting to see if he got a reply. Nothing. Terror began to grip his brain, and in desperation, he attempted to 'change', but his body refused to comply. His desperate search began.

For the past seven moons, he'd been travelling across the country, finding some places not as desolate, others even worse than his original home. Every night, he would find the highest point and pointing his nose to the now yellow/red moon, would call out:

AAAAARRRROOOOOWWW!   AAAARRROOOOWWW!
WHUFF! WHUFF! WHUFF!

yet never received an answer. Though his brain was still human, thinking and functioning like a homosapien, his physique was forever locked into its animal state; the condition he was in the night his world ended.

Tonight, he once again climbed to the top of a barren hill, pointing his muzzle toward the moon, and began to howl, but, something stopped him cold. A smell - a scent that was similar to his - blew across his face on the foetid air. He turned toward the smell and gave out one of his most vocal bellows:

AAARRRROOOOROOOOROOOOOWWWWW!

This time, in the near distance, there was a response:

AAAAWOOOWOOOWOOO!YIP!YIP!YIP!

The *crushing loneliness* disappeared in one fell swoop. Giving out high *YIPS* in response, he bounded toward the encouraging cry - the world's loneliest werewolf was alone no more.

BIO: At six years old, Sharon L. Higa became obsessed with the supernatural, compliments of an older cousin who fascinated her with stories of hauntings and horror. Travelling the world with her family, the fascination grew, resulting in Sharon creating and telling her own stories. She wrote intermittently for a number of years, but it was after she and her husband moved to East Tennessee that her family and friends convinced her to write and publish her works. She now writes full time, and has published three novels, one novella and two dozen short stories in various anthologies. Sharon specializes in horror, but also writes fantasy/action, supernatural thrillers, and mystery/suspense.

Her website is: www.leapingunicornliterary.com

She shares her home on 6.2 acres with seven cats, one dog, a vast variety of wildlife, and Mark, her patient and loving husband of twenty- five years.

MEAN PUPPY

MELISSA LASON AND MICHELLE GARZA (SISTERS OF SLAUGHTER)

She could see him through the peephole, a walking sack of shit. He fidgeted nervously, sweat building on his greasy forehead. She could discern he was out of shape, dressed like a yuppie and perspiring like a pig at the slaughterhouse...he was perfect. She pulled the door open and small talk ensued in hushed voices, like a drug deal. She could tell that he was nervous but something in his eyes spoke that he wouldn't turn back; he had to take the risk of her being an undercover cop, his needs were out of control. He was like a junkie on the verge of a fix, a drunk urgently prying the seal from a cheap vodka bottle, a hunter within reach of his quarry...but even hunters become victims.

"I'm here about the ad online... uh, you said 200 dollars, right? And like, I can do anything? That's what it says, that I could do whatever I like. "

"Yeah that's what the ad said," Maddie answered.

Serena sits in her room waiting for aunt Maddie to give her dinner. She's wearing a tiny purple night gown. Her brown hair hangs in loose curls and waves.

"Dinner time for baby puppy," is sweetly called to her through her bedroom door. "Is my sweet little puppy ready for dinner?"

Serena smiles, aunt Maddie always takes good care of her. Her loving aunt knows that it's time for mean puppy to have meat. She always can count on her aunt to feed her well.

Serena can feel it's time to change and time to feed mean puppy. Her tiny hands pull her night gown over her head. She is being potty trained so she takes off her pull up training diaper. Serena is delighted, she didn't make pee-pee in it. Maddie would be so proud.

Carl couldn't believe his luck. How did his life come to this? He knew how disgusting he was, but he always found a way to hide it for the most part. The parents of the kids he taught at his karate class never would've guessed. He didn't shit where he ate; he kept his hands to himself though his mind did stray sometimes. He could always find some disgusting person online that would allow his perversion for drugs or money…but tonight he was getting what he truly deserved, a reward for the sins that stained his soul.

Maddie had drugged him immediately as he waddled thru the front door. The disgusting piece of shit never saw the syringe coming. Serena's aunt found the perfect hook up with a cleaning lady at a hospice home. As far as she knew, Maddie was just an addict and not using the drugs to dope the worst of society in order to feed to a tiny carnivorous beast. The lead nurse there had a craving for opiates and often skimmed them from the patients. As long as Maddie's friend looked the other way, the nurse would pass her a vial or two of something that would knock a tiger on its ass, for the right price Maddie could get all that she needed. A little bit in the neck of one of those sickos always had them seeing stars right quick. Yes, Maddie had everything lined up.

Carl was chained down to a table in the basement, the veggies were almost stewed just right. On occasion she liked to stuff them with some with carrots and mashed potatoes, shove them in there however they would fit; often it gagged the bastards while they were restrained, causing them to choke and vomit on themselves. Maddie had grown accustomed to watching them suffer, sympathy was never a weakness of hers; not when it came to those who liked torturing children. To them she was every bit a monster or more than the miniature beast that waited to dine upon them. Maddie was always looking for ways to make sure her little one was getting all she needed. Tonight would be no different.

He awakened on the table. The lights were low and the room was dark in the corners. Carl heard a soft humming. It was a lullaby that he remembered from childhood. Out of the darkness a woman came. She held a small figure in her arms; as she cooed little hands played with her long dark hair. The prisoner noticed that the little hands were covered in brown fur. There were tiny razor like claws at the end of small fingers. The woman continued to hum and stroke the little creature's back. Turning its face, he could see it was some kind of wolf creature. Drool dripping from small but powerful looking jaws. *How could this be?* He thought. Carl was beginning to realize he was in trouble. He shook the table with his body and pressed against the restraints. They held tight, there was no way to get free. His eyes opened wide as he stared. The little thing snuggled into the woman's long black hair. It made strange content coos as it was held closer to him.

"Yummy yum time, sweetie. It's time to fill our belly. Now be sure to get some veggies too."

Horrified, he was sniffed, then a little claw was dragged down his cheek releasing blood, raking away strips of his skin. It lapped the blood and he thought he heard the word "yum" come from its salivating mouth. The straps were abruptly tightened, his mouth forced open and a last handful of steaming mashed vegetables were shoved in. The young

314

woman stood over him while the little creature perched on his chest. She smirked as he choked on the scalding hot carrots and potatoes.

"As payback for raping all those little ones, I have a special place for this one," The dark haired woman giggled as she held up a very large uncooked carrot.

"Start dinner sweetie. Auntie is going to feed the girl good tonight. My little pup needs some extra vitamins, so remember, don't ignore the vegetables this time."

This time, he recalled those words over and over in his mind. It became apparent that he wasn't the only one to get what they deserved.

8 months prior

"I'm sorry to inform you of this, ma'am, but there's been an incident. I'm sorry to say your sister and brother in law are dead. Luckily your niece survived with cuts and a bite. They were attacked by a bear. Please come to the Star Valley Police Department as soon as possible. We will explain more when you get here. Your niece has been seen by doctors. She will survive but was wounded. Again, we are truly sorry for your loss. "

Madeline hung up the phone with shaking hands. Her life had changed instantly. She had lost her sister and best friend and was a mother now. Her sister Catherine made her promise when Serena was born that she would take care of the little girl if something were to ever happen. Of course she said yes at the time, and now with all the grief and shock, all Madeline could think of was the tiny girl. How terrified was she? Did she see her parents die? Knowing Catherine, she gave her last breath to make sure her daughter survived. Little Serena had always adored her aunt. They were buddies and always had the best time together. Now they would be the only family they each had.

Madeline made the drive up north to the police station in record time, anxious to hold Serena and get the whole story from the police. She parked her car outside the station and ran to the front doors. Desperation flooded her body. Madeline's heart beat wildly and her hands shook uncontrollably. A police man with a grey mustache guided her into a small room.

"My name is Jim Moran and I'm an investigator here with the department."

Madeline cut him off, "I want my niece!" she stammered.

"Oh, of course, I will have her brought in soon. I thought we should talk away from her. I don't know how much she will understand and didn't want to upset her anymore."

"Oh yes, I suppose that's better," she agreed.

"I will explain as quickly as I can so you two can be with each other. I will start by saying again that your niece is ok, but was bitten by the animal that killed your sister and her husband. Their campsite was discovered early this morning by a park service worker. The adults died of blood loss from their wounds. The toddler was found hiding beneath the camper. She had scrapes on her arms and legs and a large bite mark on her leg. We believe your sister and brother in law hid her during the fight with what we believe was a bear. They fought the animal away from the child but they still passed due to their injuries. If it helps, they died saving her. There was evidence that the bear was wounded pretty severely, so they obviously did their best."

Madeline heard the words. She had no doubt her sister did everything to save her niece. She could only focus on getting Serena home and do her best raising her.

After a few more moments talking with the cops, Madeline finally held her tiny niece. The girl looked surprisingly good for what she'd been through. She had a large bandage covering most of her leg. Madeline listened intently about the recovery time Serena was looking at. Luckily the wound, while deep, miraculously didn't appear to need surgery. And the doctors could foresee a full recovery, even though she was warned it could be quite long. Madeline could only hug the child close. They couldn't be parted. Over and over Maddie promised to love and protect the little girl forever....

The month passed and Serena did mend physically. She, in fact, healed remarkably; her leg barely had a thin pink scar. Madeline was overjoyed to have the little one, even though she was given to her under the worst circumstances. As the days went by, Serena and Madeline recovered from their loss together and life seemed to have a rhythm that they were both getting used to. Madeline did graphic design from home so she was there with the little girl always. There were times of grief and Serena didn't understand what had happened. She was often looking for her parents and asked her aunt questions that she couldn't always answer but they helped each other along through moments of endless sorrow, forming a bond just as deep as a natural mother and her child.

The nights were the worst, that was when Serena often hid from what she called Mean Puppy, demanding that Maddie close all the curtains in the house and turn on all the lights. She always did everything little Serena asked to make her feel safe. Maddie had a separate bedroom for her niece but the terrified girl often begged to sleep with her aunt because she had nightmares of Mean Puppy, Maddie would hold her close and whisper to the trembling child until she once again slept comfortably. Countless nights Madeline combated the monster in her niece's dreams by the power of her voice. She found singing the child's favorite lullaby eased her almost immediately, so from that night on during their nightly routine of bathing, brushing little teeth and laying down in bed, Madeleine would sing the song until Serena was sound asleep. She would hum the tune if the girl started to fidget or whimper and soon Serena began to sleep peacefully the whole night through. Everything seemed to be falling into place as well as it possibly could until Mean Puppy returned...

It was a typical evening for them both, though for dinner Serena only wanted the meat from her cheeseburger. Maddie didn't argue with the girl, she was only concerned that the child had filled her tummy. Next it was time for a bath and cartoons. While Maddie dressed her niece in her nightgown, she sang Serena's favorite lullaby. The girl began to dance around and make little noises that her aunt laughed at until she realized the toddler was trying to howl.

"What are you doing, silly?" Maddie asked.

"I a puppy!" Serena giggled. "Mean Puppy!"

"Not mean, you're a good little...girl," Maddie said, trying not to let her unease show.

"I a puppy!" Serena hollered, suddenly becoming irritated.

"I A PUPPY! A PUPPY! A PUPPY!!"

"Alright, Serena. You're a puppy," Her aunt said, trying to calm the little girl.

"I a puppy!" Serena giggled.

Maddie smiled back, unable to be angry with the sweet angelic face of her niece. "You're my pretty little puppy."

Serena laughed as her aunt tickled her belly, then they began running around the house, barking and howling.

They fell asleep early, snuggled up on the couch. What ended up taking place was something no one could have ever expected. Serena awoke screaming in torment. Her aunt was startled awake, horrified to see the girl's body was twisting uncontrollably. At first she thought Serena was having a seizure. Maddie reached for her cell phone when an animalistic moaning stopped her. She could see that her niece's delicate face was changing, pulling outward into a canine muzzle. She knew then what Mean Puppy was and what had killed her sister. Madeline's mind filled with questions as she wrapped a blanket around Serena, and held her as her fragile body sprouted fur and her ears stretched into points. It was terrifying, it was painful, and it set the course of life in a different direction.

As a twist of fate, it was also the night that a man named Jason Carmichael thought he was going to break into the house down the street. He had been watching the reclusive mother and her child for weeks, never once did he see a man in the house. That bolstered his confidence. No single woman could stop him from kicking the door in and taking whatever he pleased, maybe a piece of the young mother and her daughter if she didn't behave.

"I will kick the door in, I will knock them over the head or whatever, I'm the predator. I'm in charge. I will clean the bitch out. She will be lucky if I choose to let them live."

His brain raced as quickly as his heart rate. The only thought he had was to get the drugs he needed, he would do anything to get them, even rob a woman and her child. He was only thinking of getting what he wanted and in the end he got what he deserved.

The back door splintered in as Madeline watched her precious niece, who was now a tiny growling creature, pace across the living room carpet. Her mind was so shocked at what had happened with Serena she hardly registered the door breaking. The tiny wolf sniffed the air, she howled and growled and tossed a coffee table across the room. Madeline waited. She didn't understand fully what had become of her little girl but she knew for sure she couldn't hurt her even if Serena decided to eat her... she loved her far too much.

Jason strolled through the kitchen as if he owned it. He picked up a large knife from the sink and thought it would do the job, whatever he decided it would be. He could tell by the itch on his neck and the near erection he got from knocking the door down it would involve something terrible; he was just in the mood to be disgusting. The meth in his system made him feel invincible. That was the draw to the drug, that's why he would get it one way or another, even if it meant shit like this.

Madeline waited and watched as Serena's ears twitched and she growled low in her gut again. Madeline hoped she would live through the night. There was no way she could have Serena deal with this alone. Madeline had put it all together now, a reality that most would never believe. There was no bear, it was a werewolf that murdered her sister and bit her niece. She knew that once Serena was human again, she couldn't survive alone being a toddler. The little wolf huffed and sniffed; she tilted her head and stared at her aunt.

Sniff, Sniff, growl. A smell met her tiny nose, it was not her aunt. Aunty smelled like honey and soap. Something came floating through the room, a stinky smell. It was not ok and Serena could tell it was mean. She heard another heart beat and it was wrong. It thumped too quickly in her ears, it irritated the Mean Puppy. Serena felt something that seemed scary to her. A bad person was in their home and she could sense he wanted to hurt them, but aunty didn't know he was there.

There was a noise behind Maddie, she couldn't process it all. Her little niece was now a tiny werewolf, sniffing the air ten feet from her and from somewhere in her kitchen it sounded as if all hell broke loose. The shocked aunt couldn't take her eyes off the girl who just morphed from a toddler to a creature of nightmares. Then it started, the next few moments were both horrifying and clear. Serena was different forever, but Madeline

318

found out that though Serena was some kind of monster, she was still *her* monster.

As the monster known as Jason entered the living room, he met with the monster that Serena had become, the Mean Puppy. He thought at first she was some kind of medium sized dog. He grabbed Madeline by her hair and began yelling into her face for cash or valuables. He punched the homeowner in the jaw, thinking surely he could kick a mutt from his heels if he needed. He knew from past experience most dogs hid once the shit went down. The tweeker barely noticed Serena crouching on the floor. Jason was coming in for some shock and awe. He figured that he would rough the lady of the house up a little more and get what he wanted in no time. He was horribly wrong. A tiny mass of fur and claws pounced. Tender flesh, though weathered from the streets, was still only flesh. He soon learned that the shield the chemicals in his veins made him believe was there was completely false. Arteries burst beneath the assault of claws and teeth, spraying their content across Madeline and most of the room. Wolf Serena enjoyed the ripping of his skin, it sounded like tearing pieces of paper.

My aunty mine! The animal in her brain repeated.

This man thought to take from her the most precious thing in her existence, her Maddie mommy. He made a grave error when he thought he would steal from or hurt a wolf, and far worse… a human toddler mixed with wolf, both selfish, both ready to strike out when something of theirs was being taken. Neck flesh hung out of place at the snapping of tiny jaws. Jason's mind and soon his body were in shock.

What the fuck? That was no dog!

He was bitten severely on the back of the neck but he felt hands, something held him with fucking clawed hands! Horror replaced his feelings of invincibility, the cold fear of knowing that death was coming for him and no amount of meth could stop it…pure, sobering terror.

"That's no dog."

He stammered and looked into Madeline's eyes as she crawled away into a corner. In a blur of movement, he was released momentarily as his attacker retreated to the shadows beyond his eyesight.

Maddie laughed bitterly in the moment. "No, you fuck, it ain't no house pet."

He looked betrayed for some reason. Was she supposed to just die? The little were-baby wouldn't allow it, not on her life.

"He's all yours, Serena. Take him!" Madeline screamed.

Jason's eyes were the size of dinner plates. There was a tiny howl, a battle cry, from near the stairwell leading to the second story. The wolf emerged from a dark spot, teeth bared, displaying his own blood comingling with its drool, it ran its little pink tongue across them before growling. He was shaking and Madeline was happy to see it. If Serena wouldn't have turned, where would they be? How much mercy would they have been

319

wn? None, not a bit and she knew it. In her gut Maddie knew that his violence would have claimed her like the beast that killed her sister, leaving the fragile little girl with no one. Serena stalked the shadows of the room. This was new to her even though she felt comfortable in her new form. The wolf in her said to be cautious of the bleeding intruder, he tasted dirty and sick...unpredictable to the young hunter.

Pouncing from the darkness Serena struck, with a flash of fur and razor blade claws his stomach was laid open. Ropes of innards fell to his knees with a spray of blood and gore. Jason's eyes went wide as his body slumped to the floor. The new wolf let out a triumphant howl. The bad man was finished. He couldn't hurt them now. Madeline was kneeling on the floor, staring at the scene. Her little niece was different, forever changed, but for better or worse Maddie vowed to care for her and help her however she could. She knew that underneath the snarling creature that sat lapping blood before her was still her little Serena. Come hell or high water, she would find a way to make this work. If the new wolf needed to kill, then Maddie would have to find those people in the world who wouldn't be missed and most of all deserved this violent end.

Maddie was afraid at first to move but she knew that she had to approach the child. They would need to find balance in order for this new living situation to work, so the woman crept close to the were-baby. Maddie scooted closer to Serena as she nibbled the leg of the man who had kicked the door off its hinges. The scene was quite disturbing as she could hear her niece devouring chunks of meat from the man. She gave her a bit of space and hummed the lullaby Serena enjoyed. The little creature seemed very content with it all. Maddie kept humming and slowly put her hand out to stroke the petite fury back. She nearly jumped back when the wolf turned around; Maddie closed her eyes, waiting for mean puppy to bite. There was a soft lick on her arm and a sniff. She opened her eyes she had clenched shut as she was licked across the face. Breathing easier now, she lightly rubbed her niece's head, massaging the fur around the girl's ears.

"Love you," she said as she was nuzzled close into strong but tiny arms.

They held each other tight.

This will never change the love we have, the woman thought. *I will make sure you get what you want. No one will ever part us. Ever...*

They slept well that night, and after a morning of door repairs, strong bleach and trying to get her head straight, Madeline knew that she could find more people for Serena to wolf out on. There were scum bags all over the planet that deserved what the asshole from the night before got. Madeline had deposited his remaining fleshy pieces beneath her new tomato plants and would be adding to her new garden as time went by. As long as she was careful they could make it work. And if any complications arose they would simply leave. They could always move on to another place, another town, a new life. Madeline worked from home and made good money doing graphic design. She could make money anywhere as long as she had her lap top. That notion was comforting; as time went by she made connections that came in handy. She had an old friend with certain drug hook ups that eventually were a big help when dealing with the scum she lured home. As she originally predicted, there were a lot of people that no one missed, people who most certainly deserved what they got. The routine became familiar very quickly.

Madeline noticed that the wolf liked to eat what it killed, which made clean up easier than she expected. The months flew by and they both became used to what would be happening. Maddie found a person of low character that needed to be removed from society and lured them to the house for Serena. The little girl knew that there were special days when the wolf inside could come out and they began their lives anew with their friend the wolf, but as is always the case for parents, one can never get too comfortable with a routine. There was always a wrench waiting to be thrown into the system.

This happened one evening when Madeline invited over the wolf's gift for the night. All was right on track, the deed had been done and was over earlier than usual. Madeline did a quick initial cleaning and was planning on finishing up in the morning. At some point in the night, bordering on the wee hours of the morning, the window which was left cracked open to allow the Clorox stench to escape…Maddie had fallen asleep and didn't notice that the noxious smell of bleach wasn't the only thing that got out that night.

The little wolf sniffed the air, something smelled interesting on the other side of the wooden fence that lined the yard she had been exploring. She heard a noise, the sniffing of another animal. Smelling the air, she could tell it was a dog. Scurrying to the wooden barrier she inhaled the air again. There was another smell lingering in the breeze. The dog barked again and then again. It was beginning to annoy the wolf; she wasn't hungry but the urge to tear the yapping dog apart became too great to overcome.

Taking her clawed hands, she began digging under the fence separating her from the interesting annoyance. Dirt was flying as the tunnel lengthened and widened. Serena the wolf began to disappear into the hole. Furiously she clawed while the yapping little dog tried to warn Alice Arden of the intruder beneath the fence. The old woman always began her mornings early, before the sun even rose. She occupied herself in her home until the sky finally lightened and then she occupied herself in other folks' business. Everyone in the neighborhood had run-ins with her eventually. Even Madeline had a few arguments with her, mostly over her annoying yapping dog. Their most recent quarrel was over Madeline's mail box being four inches too close to Alice's property line. She expected to have it moved so her flowers could grow better. After screeching at Maddie in front of

321

ena, the old woman finally resorted to complaining to Maddie's
.....dlord, everyone knew it was just to be a bitch. Needless to say Madeline refused, her landlord agreed that the mailbox wouldn't be moved and the old woman still wouldn't speak to her.

Alice was washing the dishes this particular morning. Over the flowing water, she never noticed her Pomeranian Queen barking at the wolf that was tunneling between the properties. Nor did she notice the strangled howl of death Queen made as Serena popped out of the hole and slashed her guts open. If Alice only were nosier before the day light hours she would've heard her doggy door slide open behind her. Alice was quietly humming her favorite hymn and thinking of what she would yell at the neighborhood kids today...*little heathens thinking they can play on the sidewalk*. Always in her way, she enjoyed saying rude things to them and their parents, letting them have a piece of her mind. She was too caught up in her mind to see the little creature crouched a few feet behind her. The old woman didn't even turn around when she was sniffed on the leg.

"Queen," she mused "my only friend in the world."

That was her last thought ever as powerful clawed hands ripped through her spine, blood sprayed across her floral curtains as a tiny fist popped out of her chest clutching her withered heart.

Oh the fun Serena had with this one...old and mean. She recalled her human-self disliking her. Alice was always rude, always yelling at her aunt Maddie, her caring, sweet aunty who loved the little girl, and Mean Puppy so. The tiny beast was suddenly very tired and wanted her own bedroom; her interest in the tattered old corpse had run its course. Her sweet smelling sheets and comfy blankets were calling to her, even the wolf loved to snuggle there. After sniffing the old lady corpse a few minutes more and taking a few good nibbles off her legs, Serena snuck back home.

Madeline awoke with a start to find Serena nuzzled next to her, whining in baby form, wanting her bed. Maddie was ashamed that she forgot to clean the little pup so she gave her a quick bath and put her to bed. Maddie was sure the little one had been next to her the whole time, sleeping off the last moments of Mean Puppy's visit. Maddie finished a few last minute clean up tasks before laying herself down for a few more hours of rest. She had Serena's schedule down so well over the months that it didn't occur that anything amiss could have happened. In fact, she slept deep and well, assuming that they were all clear when it came to criminality. It wasn't until nearly noon when she heard a commotion on the street. Madeline peered through her curtains to see police cars and a coroner's van at Alice's house.

"The old bitch finally kicked the bucket... Good." she thought.

A nagging feeling crept into her stomach. *What if*?? There was a knock at the door and it nearly made her heart stop. Madeline slowly opened the door. A man dressed in a suit stood on the steps.

"Can I help you?" she asked, trying to not lose her composure.

"I'm sorry to tell you this ma'am but your neighbor was killed last night. Do you have any information about what happened, did you see or hear anything?"

Madeline felt like puking; she fought to maintain the appearance of being a clueless neighbor.

"No. I'm sorry; I didn't see anything out of the ordinary."

"Do you own a dog?" He asked.

"No. No pets." Maddie answered, hoping that her voice didn't give away the trembling in her body.

He stared down at a notepad in his hand, jotting things down for what seemed like forever until he finally eluded to it being an animal attack… that it appeared the animal could've even used her yard to dig into the old woman's, killing her dog and gaining access to her house. If Maddie looked shocked, it was completely real. She was kicking herself for dozing off and leaving Mean Puppy unattended.

"Yes. That's what your other neighbor said as well," The officer spoke. "The fish and game boys will be looking around a bit back there if you don't mind, but this looks like it's pretty wrapped up."

"Go ahead," She answered.

Maddie was thankful then that her neighbors on the other side of her house at least vouched that she did not own any pets. It kept the police out of her house and away from the freshly bleached bloodstains from the night before, and the shredded remains of a pedophile in her basement that she had yet to get rid of.

"Be on the look-out for any animals roaming around and it's best not leave children unsupervised and definitely lock your doggy door if you have one. There will be a neighborhood meeting in a few weeks to go over everything we find and to answer any questions you may have. Stay safe and contact me with any information. Thanks for your time."

Madeline thanked him and promised to call if she noticed anything strange. She could've laughed as she closed the door. Anything strange, that described life those last months. Madeline waited for the two men from the forestry service to leave her yard until going to inspect the scene herself. She knew as soon as she looked at the hole under the fence it was Serena and if she didn't get them somewhere safe, it was only a matter of time before they were exposed. She had considered moving from the first time Serena changed, now she knew it had to be. She needed to find a place in the country where she didn't have to worry about neighbors and have more privacy all around. Maddie couldn't keep burying leftover human pieces and throwing things in the trash, it would be a disaster if anyone found them. She lived for months in the white picket fence community where no one would even suspect such things could be taking place, the things she nessed a toddler doing, her niece, her daughter, they were all a terrible ity that couldn't stay a secret forever if she stayed.

The plans were made, Madeline's landlord just so happened to have a property outside of town and everything was falling into place nicely. She moved their belongings quickly into the new place and by night she dug up any bone fragments she had deposited in the yard, wrapping them in plastic then hiding them in a moving box that found itself in her basement. Madeline didn't want to make a big deal about them moving out of the neighborhood. She didn't want any questions as to where she was going or why.

One day, while loading some of the boxes, the bone box included, the lady she had lived next to for several years came over to ask what she was doing.

"You're not leaving us are you?" Susan asked.

"We found a bigger place, cheaper rent too."

"I don't blame you with the killer coyotes roaming the neighborhood." The woman said. "That's something you don't want around your little one!"

"Is that what got Alice?" she asked.

"Oh yes, the police confirmed it. Oh, please stop by the neighborhood meeting before you leave. The forestry service will be there to give us tips on avoiding this type of situation in the future. Even though you're going, you could still get good advice for the future."

Maddie thanked her and promised to stop by. She figured it would look better in case it were to ever be ruled anything other than an animal attack.

The date approached for the meeting to be held. Madeline was frantic that it would be the day of a full moon. She was nervous, yet everyone was to gather long before nightfall and the little one had never changed until well after dark. As she loaded the girl into her car seat she noticed something she hadn't planned on. There, hanging in the evening sky, was the making of an eclipse. They had never been through one since Serena had started to change. The child seemed fine, no indication of the Mean Puppy emerging. Madeline deduced that it must not have an effect on Serena.

"We will only go in for a few minutes and then we are leaving to go to the little puppy's new house." Maddie spoke up to her rearview mirror, watching her niece intently.

The little girl cheered happily, she loved her new house and the woods that ran along its expansive backyard.

They pulled into the parking lot and still nothing was amiss with the smiling little girl.

"Just a few minutes, we can do this. No one will notice us leave, there's so many people here." Maddie spoke in a coaxing tone though she

324

wasn't sure who she was trying to convince that it would all be ok, Serena or herself.

Entering the building, Madeline noticed a few posters hanging on the walls, all of them warning folk not to touch or feed wildlife. There on the door was another sign; one that Madeline didn't like so much: Children to be Left in Daycare Please. Serena had never been left with anyone, especially after her parents' death. Madeline considered leaving but again wanted to stay in the clear if anything were to ever come up with Alice's death. Her neighbor, Susan, came walking towards her, waving her hands.

"Come on inside. Leave the cutie pie in the daycare room. Everyone wanted to wait for you to begin since you have a little one to protect. There's lots of helpful information here today." She smiled warmly.

Maddie wanted to appear like any other citizen, concerned about wild ferocious animals though she really had no fear of ever being attacked by anyone or anything ever again as long as Mean Puppy was around.

Maddie carried Serena into the child's area, she could feel the girl tense up as she placed her on the floor in the middle of a rambunctious group of kids.

"Be a good girl. I will only be gone a few minutes." Maddie promised.

There was no way something could happen in ten minutes, right?

Serena joined a little group of kids building with Legos and Maddie stepped a few feet out the door to listen to the forest ranger who was speaking to the group of neighbors. Of course it was the usual, basically reiterating the posters: don't feed wild animals, don't touch wild animals, always report the sightings of wild animals. ...so on and so on.

A commotion from the daycare startled Madeline. She heard a child crying and Serena screaming. Madeline ran and pushed into the room. Serena came to her with tears in her eyes.

"What happened?" she yelled at a nervous looking teen in charge of watching the children.

"Thomas pulled Serena's hair, so Serena bit him pretty hard on the arm." The girl answered. "Just usual little kid stuff, no big deal."

Madeline didn't want a scene, so they left. She got Serena home and gave her dinner. Serena still seemed agitated that Thomas had hurt her. The girl had three helpings of raw hamburger and didn't touch any veggies. Madeline was happy to be home with the girl in the privacy of their home. They waited and the change never came, Maddie surmised that the eclipse was holding Mean Puppy at bay. Serena paced in frustration until she finally fell asleep, exhausted. She slept while Maddie finished packing the last few boxes. They were leaving that night. Maddie had slipped a bit of the tranquilizer she used to bring prey down on Serena's meat to be sure that even if Mean Puppy came through, the tiny wolf would sleep at least until they got out of the city. Madeline felt guilty but she wanted to slip out into

ight without having to tell anyone else where they were moving to. It
't as if she thought they were completely disappearing, just the less
nosey neighbors knowing where they went the better.

Maddie was ready for the move, she dreamed many times of Serena
having a beautiful, safe place to grow up and the house in the country was
perfect. Madeline was still thinking of the new house and picturesque
surrounding woods for them to roam. There were probably even wild
animals for Serena to eat while in wolf form which eliminated the need for
luring anymore victims to them. All of these wonderful new things were
running through her mind. This fresh start was a blessing. Madeline was
trying to decide the paint colors of bedrooms, decorative touches and all the
things a person considers when moving into a new home when she saw
something on the way out of the neighborhood. She slowed to nearly a stop
as she approached a place that she regretfully never got to let Serena enjoy,
it saddened her a bit.

The community had a really nice park and playground, surrounded
by green grassy fields to play soccer and baseball in. It was a view that went
along with the rest of the neighborhood, a picture of perfection, masking
the ugliness of the real world. Maddie felt something there in the darkness,
something frightening yet oddly familiar; eyes were watching her pass by.
Perched on the jungle gym was a silhouette, a little boy crouching above
the slide. Madeline started to come to a stop on her brakes, yet she refrained.
In the darkness she made out the profile of a muzzle, a tail… pointy ears on
top of a little head. Then it happened. He turned, eyes glowing and let out a
long howl into the night. She wondered if his parents had it in them to
protect him as she had Serena, if they too could handle a Mean Puppy.

Aaaaarrrrooooooo!!!!!

326

BIO: Michelle Garza and Melissa Lason are a twin sister writing team from Arizona. They've

been dubbed the Sisters of Slaughter by the editors of Fireside Press. They write horror, science

fiction and fantasy together. They have been published by Sinister Grin Press, JEA and Fireside Press. Their first novel, Mayan Blue was released by Sinister Grin Press in 2016. They have

much more in store for 2017.

Facebook –
https://www.facebook.com/sistersofhorror/?fref=ts

Amazon:
https://www.amazon.com/Michelle-Garza/